10TH ANNIVERSARY EDITION

SEDONA

THE LOST VORTEX

MIKEL J. WILSON

SEDONA: THE LOST VORTEX
Tenth Anniversary Revised Edition

Cover design by Damonza.com.

Author portrait by Dave Meyer at DaveMeyerDesign.com.

Mikel J. Wilson
555 W. Country Club Lane, C-222
Escondido, CA 92026

MIKELJWILSON.com

ISBN: 978-1-952112-71-3 Hardcover
ISBN: 978-1-952112-72-0 Paperback

Printed in the United States of America through Acorn Publishing at AcornPublishingLLC.com.

Dedicated to the city of Sedona.

Thank you for the magic!

"He threw Man out of the Garden of Eden and stationed angels and a revolving sword of fire east of it, guarding the path to the Tree of Life."

GENESIS 3:24

PROLOGUE

Far from its humble creation in a Pennsylvania smelter, a two-centimeter bolt had achieved the auspicious distinction of "space junk" after serving an important function in the success of a NASA mission, albeit one that received little attention from a distracted public. Now, long since loosed from its task by design, the hexagon-capped cylinder rotated above the Earth nine times a day in a decaying orbit of manmade providence.

On the other side of the world, the new Hexum Space Station sheltered a crew of six from the vacuum encasing the blue sphere below. Previous stations had been positioned within the relative security of the thermosphere, a layer of Earth's outer atmosphere where sunlight and its absence fluctuated the temperature between -100 and 1500°C. To study the effects of long-distance space travel free from atmospheric protection, however, the Hexum had become the first station constructed beyond the exosphere, the outermost atmospheric layer.

Inside the station, two astronauts exercised, two were strapped into bed, one spoke in the privacy of the control room to her Earth-bound husband and one sat in the cafeteria deciphering solar oscillations from a laptop.

The heliologist's fascination with the sun began during his childhood of religious devotion, when he first heard the story of the flaming, revolving sword God had placed at the door to Eden following the expulsion of Man. He thought if the sword spun fast enough, it could appear as a ball of fire, like the sun. Over the years that followed, he had often wondered, now that Man no longer roamed the Garden, who's behind the door? Now as he watched the sun's wonderment translated through binary code, he smiled at the cynicism of knowledge and the predictability that accompanied its possession – just before the accident occurred.

The errant bolt hit the station with tremendous force, pounding a crater into the craft's exterior. Although the projectile failed to penetrate the wall, it transferred enough kinetic energy to inflict irreversible damage to the control panels on the other side.

The space station began its descent toward Earth.

CHAPTER 1

As night aged in the valley and twisted around the unremarkable houses, a car battered from a decade of carelessness came to a rolling stop. The driver creaked open his door and withdrew a heavy canister from the trunk before scuffing up the walkway that led to a red door. After ascending the three steps to the patio, the leaning figure opened the door with a key and stepped inside. He twisted the top from the canister to release a portion of its contents into a liquid rug at the foot of the stairs. Without bothering to recap, he climbed the stairs.

The man opened a door to see a woman a year over thirty asleep in her bed, and he poured enough liquid to reach the polyester robe draped from the corner of the headboard. Proceeding down the hall he opened another door and found a boy of seven cradled in a bed of stuffed animals and downy pillows. He emptied the canister, and the liquid coursed down gaps in the slats of the hardwood floor to puddle around the foot of the nearest bedpost.

The smell of the liquid wrinkled the boy's nose and nudged him awake. Wiping his eyes, he watched the intruder in his doorway scratch a small tinderbox with the tip of a match, which dropped to the floor and ignited the accelerant with a gentle roar.

As the man disappeared into the relative darkness of the hallway, fire grabbed at the boy's quilt and pulled its way closer to him. The boy jerked his legs from under the covers. He stood on a pillow and looked at the closed window to his left and the fiery moat surrounding his bed. He took a deep breath and jumped to the floor. The edge of the moat burned the heels of his bare feet, and the boy yelped in agony. He ran to the window and tried to open it, but he couldn't reach the lock. He grabbed a thin floor lamp and swung the base at the window, creating a hole of glass shards and splintered wood. The boy slid his head and hands through the hole, but the sharp edges shaved the skin on his forearm, preventing him from moving any further. He screamed, "Help!" again and again.

A man next door turned on his bedroom light and saw the boy struggling to escape the smoking window. "Oh my god," he gasped before yelling at his wife to call for help. As he ran down the stairs for his ladder, he could hear the spiking pitch of the boy's agonizing pleas.

Gregor Buckingham shuddered awake.

Through a missing slat in the dusty blinds that drooped down the lone window, sunlight bisected the tiny bedroom. The powder-white pillow contradicted the warmth of Gregor's brown hair, as his hazel eyes focused on the water stain in the ceiling. The lips on his handsome, twenty-four-year-old face spread into a smile, and his rusty voice whispered, "Finally."

Gregor unsheathed himself from the bed, allowing the light to find the burn scars that covered most of his six-foot-two body. From the neck up and wrists down, his skin was a beautiful shade of white, but beyond that were large, mottled swatches of purplish-red keloids and smaller papules arising from drifts of fibrous dermal distortions like river islands.

Sidestepping the two packed suitcases that blocked the front door, he walked into the bathroom and flipped on the light, startling the disheveled man looking in the small window above the toilet. Gregor lowered the blinds so he wouldn't have to see the homeless man in the alley urinating on the other side of the wall.

Travis Harper never had a goal in his life that lasted more than six months – a trait that grew from indecisiveness rather than short-sightedness. He had seven declared majors in college before earning a bachelor's degree in something related to computers – even he couldn't remember the exact name of the major – but that degree did not represent a passion as much as the simplest path to graduation using the combination of credits he had accumulated.

Travis' problem, if a problem it were, was that he excelled in just about every endeavor, from athleticism to mental acumen, although he often downplayed the latter. This near omnicompetence made choosing his one purpose or happiness in life all the more difficult, which is why at twenty-four – although he had already made more than enough money through crypto-currency investing to sustain his lifestyle for several years – he was working toward another and unrelated college degree. On those rare occasions when he did not exhibit an immediate aptitude for a new enterprise, his frustration sparked an anger that prompted him to walk away, preferring to abandon the effort rather than afford himself a reasonable learning curve. He was a committed procrastinator, yet he was irked when he had to wait for others. His empathy was unbounded, particularly when directed toward the outrages of the world, but he often missed cues for that emotion in more personal interactions when not presented with clear signposts of its need. This emotional truancy was perhaps why his last girlfriend walked out on him six weeks ago, after two months together. To Travis, however, the reason remained elusive, and he consoled himself with bouts of determined drunkenness and anonymous encounters.

A handsome, six-foot-four man, he had a muscular body

with skin tanned the color of his eyes and hair so dark a shade of brown, only sunlight could distinguish it from black. His full, yet masculine lips curled below the perfect hook of his nose and the expressive, often asynchronous eyebrows that further seduced the eyes of the beholder.

Since awakening, Travis had been amusing himself on his computer, following links to newer and more interesting stories – a daily routine.

The television behind him was tuned to an all-news station, as it always was in the morning, although he didn't watch it. This morning, however, he did cock his head for a glimpse when the broadcast was interrupted with breaking news. The anchor announced, "An electrical fire broke out moments ago aboard the Hexum Space Station. The fire has reportedly damaged several primary systems and has forced the six astronauts residing onboard to evacuate using the emergency escape pods. At least one astronaut was injured..."

The alarm on his watch beeped from his nightstand, startling him. He looked at the clock on the monitor and said, "Dang." He jumped from his desk, grabbed a duffel bag from the closet and stuffed it with the items he would need.

Cadence O'Mare sat on a suitcase in the middle of her otherwise barren apartment. This place would soon not remember her, as her faint scent would fade from the walls to be replaced by the markings of new occupants. She focused her gaze to the warmer side of the curtainless window and tried not to think about the emptiness.

"I need to be outside when they come," she whispered before standing, moaning from the soreness of her muscles. Of the day before, she thought she should've exercised more control and not insisted on helping the thrift store workers load her life into a truck, but touching each item one last time was her expression of apology for abandoning them. She rolled the suitcase to the patio and locked the front door. She twirled the key from her keychain and slid it through the mail slot in the door, hearing two pings as it hit the apartment floor.

Cadence was thin for her twenty-five-year-old frame but not by intention. Her pretty face shone with determination in clearest light, but shadows exposed the fear beneath. Her brown, wavy hair was not quite long enough to conceal the spaghetti straps of the black dress she wore – a dress not in tune with the hour or the day's agenda.

She loved Southern California and never regretted quitting college to find herself. (At times she did miss her family in Baltimore, although she would have missed them more if they were close by, as they were a passionless lot.) Her pursuit had failed, but she now knew the answer was near – or rather one state over in Sedona, Arizona.

Until nine months ago, Cadence had never even heard of Sedona, but now the high-desert town called to her as if her spirit were already there waiting to be reclaimed by her body. That day, as Cadence sat in a recliner with curtains drawn around her, a gregarious woman in her early fifties entered the space with a beautiful border collie, explaining that the two were part of the hospital's pet therapy program. The woman had shoulder-length black hair with a streak of white down the right side, matching the coloring of her exuberant companion. When the dog hopped its forelegs onto Cadence's lap, the woman apologized for her forwardness, to which Cadence assured her no apology was needed. The woman never introduced herself but did her dog. "This is Sedona." Cadence had never felt such warmth radiating from another being as she did from this dog with the goofy smile and sweet brown eyes. She almost felt as if the dog belonged to her and that the woman would leave the room alone. After a few brief moments, however, the woman called Sedona's name, and the two departed.

Before stillness had an opportunity to settle back into the room, Gregor Buckingham entered wearing scrubs and a long-sleeve cotton shirt beneath the top. He checked her IV chemotherapy. "You're almost done here. How are you holding up?"

"I'm doing fine," Cadence replied. "Thank you for sending the dog in here."

With a slight laugh, as if preparing for the punch line to a joke he had not yet heard, Gregor asked, "Dog?"

"Oh, I thought maybe you sent them in. They were from the pet therapy program."

Gregor's countenance changed to puzzlement. "We don't have a pet therapy program here, and they would never allow dogs in the cancer ward."

"But they were just here."

"I'm sorry." Gregor shook his head. "You know, the chemo can sometimes play with your head." Instead of a response, Cadence diverted her eyes to the floor. "Listen, my shift is almost up. Why don't I save you the cab fare and give you a ride home?"

Over the next few months, Gregor's role in Cadence's life evolved from occasional IV tech to best friend. Also during that time, Cadence tried to find information on her mysterious visitors by Googling the only name she knew. Instead of leading her to the dog, she found multiple links to a small town in Arizona, and the online photos showcased the spectacular red rock formations that symbolized Sedona. She fell in love with the place without knowing why, but she did know that she needed to go. Plus, it was only an hour drive from the Grand Canyon.

After a rolling stop, Travis drove through the last intersection on the route to Cadence's apartment building, where she awaited on the front steps, looking lost in thought. He parked his new electric sedan curbside and tapped the horn to startle her, smiling and shrugging as if his actions had an unintended effect.

Gregor jumped from the passenger side. "Wake up."

"I'm awake." Cadence stood and rolled her bag to the car.

Gregor nodded toward her dress. "So, I guess you're definitely staying in the motel."

"Of course."

He reached for her suitcase but stopped short of grabbing the handle. "Did you lock your door?"

"Yes."

Gregor took a step up the stairs. "Let me double-check for you. You don't want to come back to an empty apartment."

Cadence grabbed his arm. "I'm sure."

"All right." He turned back to the car and opened the passenger door for her. "You can have shotgun." He loaded her suitcase into the trunk and hopped into the backseat. "Light luggage. You're certainly a frugal packer."

"We're only going for a week," she responded with a look in the rearview mirror to see his smile.

Travis entered their destination into his car's navigation system. "Okay, oh mighty navigator. We await your command."

The navigator's computerized baritone directed, "Go forward. Then turn left."

Gregor swatted him on the shoulder. "You heard the man."

"Aye-aye." Travis rammed the car into drive.

CHAPTER 2

Reverend August Briar had been chosen to see the face of God. Although this miraculous event had yet to occur, August had known of its inevitability from childhood. He perceived the words from I John 4:12, "No man hath seen God," as more of a dare than an unbreakable rule. He knew in his heart that the special attention he received as a minister's son was just the beginning of a profound life of favor, and he knew God would reveal Himself in a manner reserved for no previous purveyor of His word – not even Moses or Abraham. He lived in a manner befitting this belief, becoming the most decorated graduate of his seminary college, starting his own church with a devoted congregation in Sedona, branching into local televangelism and hitherto culminating with his self-appointment as the beacon for morality in Northern Arizona. He had driven his life down the path that would distinguish him in the eyes of God and give the Lord the confidence to come to him and, at last, anoint him His divine envoy. Any day now.

When August was a child in Texas, he delivered impromptu Biblical orations on the school playground and, although some classmates would listen, most treated his divine message with hostility or derision. Returning home with a black eye after a brutal upper classman found his words against gambling offensive, his ever-loving mother comforted him with a warm embrace on the couch and the story of his miraculous birth.

"Remember the story of Abraham and Isaac?" his mother asked her eleven-year-old son.

August answered, "Abraham almost sacrificed his son Isaac because God told him to."

"Before that. Abraham was married to Sarah, who was sterile – unable to have children."

"I know what sterile means."

His mother smiled. "All right. Anyway, one day God came to Abraham and told him that Sarah would bear a child—"

"Isaac."

"That's right. God granted her a miracle baby named Isaac, who was blessed by God and became the father of the nation of Israelites, revered by millions of Jews and Christians throughout history." She squeezed his shoulders. "Just like Isaac, you were my miracle baby."

"What do you mean?"

"I couldn't have children either, but I prayed and prayed for God to grant me a miracle. One night He came to me in a dream—"

"God?"

"Yes."

"What did He look like?" August asked.

"I couldn't see Him. I could only hear Him speaking."

"Are you not pure in heart?"

His mother asked, "What do you mean?"

"The Bible says, 'Blessed are the pure in heart, for they shall see God.' Aren't you pure?"

"That's for God to decide," she replied with some impatience. "The point is He told me He would answer my prayer, and my son too would grow up to be a great and righteous man."

From his office window, August tried staring into the sun. The severe light reflected ice blue from his eyes and ignited like white fiber optics the sparse gray strands in his otherwise black hair. When he could no longer bear the glare, he turned away and let the shadows again stream down the shallow wrinkles that Time had carved throughout his fifty-one-year-old face. His manicured hand brushed a spot of lint from his trademark two-button, non-vented black suit – the only time August would be seen in public without a suit was during his hunting trips, due to the fact that he could not find one in a camouflage pattern. In confederation with his shiny, black shoes, white shirt and navy tie, the suit gave him the appearance of someone who would be at home in a funeral parlor – in or out of the casket.

August Briar's church office was 288-square cubits of hardwood flooring that supported matching pine-paneled walls. Stretched across the length of the ceiling was a mural of the sky that captured a complete twenty-four-hour cycle – from sunshine on the western side to dusk in the middle and night in the east. Three genuine animal-skin rugs of African fauna delineated areas for study, counsel and work. The room's adornments were testaments to his love of God and to his own accomplishments since founding Christ Church of Sedona seventeen years earlier. He (of course) had bookshelves of Biblical texts and a large effigy of Jesus in tortured bronze draped from a cross, which hung as the centerpiece of the wall that his desk chair faced. Also nailed to the walls were numerous frames encasing memories that ranged from congregational outings and meetings with state politicians to close-ups of him at the pulpit and a picture with an etched base plate that read, "First Broadcast."

Mrs. Chapman, a prim and puckery graying woman on the declining side of sixty, entered August's office after a gentle knock on the door with her arthritic knuckles. "Reverend, your agent is here. Should—"

"I do not like that term," August said with no attempt to mask his contempt. "It is unseemly. Announce him as my procurator in the future." Through perseverance and harsh self-criticism, he long ago banished any twinge of the Southern drawl that, as a child, released every syllable from his tongue like a fly with one leg stuck in honey. Apart from fits of extreme anger that would devolve his speech into childhood patterns, his elocution was perfect, and he uttered every letter in a word that was not meant for silence.

Mrs. Chapman opened her mouth but skipped a beat before speaking, "Proc…"

"Procurator. Look it up, and send him in. Not in that order." He smiled at the minor joke.

Mrs. Chapman's presence in the office was exchanged for Richard Glavin's. The tall man looked like a Midwestern farmer trying on a new suit he couldn't afford. His hair was too dark to be natural, as were the off-whites of his eyes. With a jagged grin, he extended his hand and proclaimed, "August, I have some good news for you."

Shaking his hand, August said, "Do confess," allowing himself a chuckle at another minor joke. He waved to a chair in front of the desk, inviting Richard to sit.

August walked with a slight limp in his left leg to the chair behind the desk, prompting Richard to ask, "How's the hip?"

He waved off his concern. "My doctor wants to replace it, but I am not prepared to part with the original. The travails of aging. At least each day brings me closer to God."

"I almost called you, but I really wanted to tell you in person. Yesterday I had a meeting with producers from the American Christian Channel, and I showed them a clip of one of your sermons – the one where you're talking about how God punished some guy by giving him boils."

"His name was Job, and God did not punish him. He allowed Satan to test his faith."

"Tomāto, tomäto. The point is that they liked what they saw, and they're considering giving you a show."

August took a moment to dream before muttering, "A national network."

Richard pointed to him without raising his elbow. "See, that look completely paid for my airfare."

August sat back to process the possibilities. "As appreciative as I am for my congregation, my reach is so limited."

"How far does your current station reach? Cottonwood? Flagstaff?" When the reverend nodded, Richard said, "ACC has a licensing agreement with the Armed Forces Network, so you wouldn't just be national. You'd be reaching all the troops around the world."

"I have always seen myself on a global scale. Bringing God to godless lands." August's eyes lit up, and "West Canaan," burst from his lips. He walked over to a glass-enclosed architectural model displayed on a white pedestal. He was close to tears at the possibility of bringing to reality the rendering of a spectacular compound on the grounds where Christ Church of Sedona now stood. The new church retained the look of the old one but on a much grander scale, and several structures had been added to the landscape, including a massive stone fence around the perimeter. "I could raise the funds I need to build it."

Richard laughed and joined him in admiring the model. "With a national audience, I'll bet you could do that in six weeks." He pointed to the model of a building erected on the flattened summit of a red rock formation. "That mountain or hill or whatever you call it behind the church looks smaller to me than the real thing. It must be the scale."

"No, the top will be razed to flatten a space big enough for the school and youth center."

"Interesting. Listen, you don't have much time to prepare. They're sending a camera crew to record your sermon tomorrow, and they'll show that video to test audiences."

"Tomorrow? Why are they sending a crew? We already have a team."

"They liked the content of the clip I showed them, but they want one with a slicker look."

"I am not comfortable with that decision. Sam and the others have been with us since we started. They would be heartbroken if they could not continue in those roles."

"Pick your battles wisely, August. What do you really want?"

He hesitated for a breath before asking, "What would be next, after they film?"

"Phil Hedder, their V.P. of programming, will decide based on the test results."

August nodded. "Not to rush you, but I have a sermon to rewrite."

"I'll let them know we're on for tomorrow."

"Thanks, Richard. Would you send Mrs. Chapman in on your way out?"

"Sure." Richard walked toward the door, but stopped for a moment to say, "They need to see you as totally healthy and vibrant. Be sure not to limp on camera."

CHAPTER 3

While Travis drove down Highway 179 and Cadence napped in the reclined passenger seat, Gregor moved his face into the arid wind rushing through his window. Travis preferred natural air to conditioned, a choice of shunned convenience that Gregor applauded, although the heat was now causing his damaged skin to itch. "I thought the temperature would go down once we passed through Phoenix."

"At least it's a dry heat," Travis said with a chuckle. "I read somewhere that Phoenix is the sweatiest city in America. I'm not sure how they measure that." He held up an avocado sandwich missing a single bite. "This would be better with some ham. I'd even settle for turkey."

Gregor replied, "Not in my food chain."

Cadence stirred a bit to utter, "I tried being a vegetarian once."

Travis laughed. "I think you've tried everything once."

Now glaring at him, she asked, "What's that supposed to mean?"

To fight the temptation to scratch, Gregor closed his eyes and tried to meditate. Filtering out the voices of his friends, he imagined himself floating in a quiet stream.

Travis said, "You're very... What's the word I'm after? Adaptable."

"Adaptability is a good quality," responded Cadence.

"In evolution, but not when defining your personality."

Cadence straightened the back of her seat to perpendicular. "Where's this coming from?"

"I've just often wondered if who you are is driven by the people you know or by that whisper in your head that expresses your true feelings?"

"Do you want to know what that whisper is saying about you right now?"

"Okay, you said you tried vegetarianism once. What prompted it?"

"I don't know. I just wanted to try it."

"Such a selective memory. It happened when you started going out with that vegetarian from the meditation center Gregor goes to. The guy with the billy-goat beard." His description snapped Gregor from his meditation and elicited a snicker. "You're not much better, Mr. Bend-over-backwards-to-avoid-any-sort-of-fight."

Gregor opened his eyes. "What do you mean by that?"

"You're the perennial peacekeeper. Why are we in Arizona right now instead of Yosemite, which is where you have been dying to go? Because Cadence wanted to come here."

Gregor didn't want to argue, so he let Cadence do it for him. "We both wanted to come here," she said. "You're just mad because you didn't get your way."

"Actually, the real dilemma for Gregor would've been if I had pushed the issue of Yosemite, but I refused to put him in the position to have to choose sides."

Cadence crossed her arms and shook her head. "You just love to provoke."

"Nature needs provocation to adapt. Hey, just like you."

Cadence rolled her eyes and turned her attention to her open window. "Hey guys. Let's do the Grand Canyon tomorrow."

"No planning on this trip," said Travis. "We have more than a week to do everything we want to do, but let's just go where the days take us." He started rocking in his seat. "I need to find a bathroom soon."

Cadence smirked at him. "Whatever you do, don't think of cool, flowing rivers or waterfalls."

Gregor pointed at something coming up on the right. "Wow, look at that." Magnificent Bell Rock appeared as an inverted terracotta pot that had been shaped on a pottery wheel by a preschooler with all the unevenness and distortions indicative of a child's craftsmanship. Behind it was the much larger Courthouse Butte, which was paler on top as if the bottom of its pot had water stains. Glints of botanic patina on the rocks matched the surrounding landscape's hesitant flora, which stayed low to avoid obstructing the red giants. The rich, rusty pigment bled out to the earth radiating from the base of the rocks and continued as far as could be seen. Without the roads, buildings and other human intrusions, Gregor presumed an image of Sedona taken from above would have been indistinguishable from one taken by an orbiter above Mars.

"Look at that cool church," said Cadence, pointing to the group of red monoliths that comprised Cathedral Rock. On a ledge midway up another formation was an unusual church anchored between two red stone pillars, the union of which gave rise to an excessive white cross framed by a flat roof and walls that slanted outward on their way to the ground.

As they continued into town, an unusual house caught Gregor's attention. Although the structure itself was ordinary, the purple paint on the walls and the outdoor décor were definite eye diverters. Affixed to the roof was a lighted sign with the words "Land here!" next to the image of a grey alien waving, and the driveway was fashioned into a runway with colored lights on either side that lit in progression as if to flag in any passing spaceships.

"Welcome to Sedona," announced Travis. "The country's nut basket."

Moments later, they were passing shops selling crystals and other paraphernalia supporting alternative philosophies – healing through energy, astral projection and psychic journeys to the spiritual realm of Lemuria.

Cadence scoffed, "Who would believe in all this crap?"

"Unproven is not the same as disproven," rebutted Gregor. "Sedona is a harbor for people who are open to all realms of possibility."

"Disproven?" Travis asked. "Is that even a word?"

"If not, it should be," Gregor answered.

Cadence asked Gregor, "You don't really believe that crystals have special powers, do you?"

"The relationship between crystals and energy is real. Semiconductors in computers are made from silicon crystals—"

"I can't wait for the motel," said Travis, parking in the first space he found. "I have to go to the bathroom now." Without waiting for objections, he left the car and ran to the nearest shop.

Cadence shook her head. "I swear, he has the bladder of a ninety-year-old man."

Gregor looked at the shop in front of which they were parked, and the name Sedona Vortex painted in blue on the window piqued his interest. "Let's go in and look around."

On the sidewalk in front of the shop, a young man in black slacks, a white dress shirt and a maroon tie was attempting to dispense flyers to uninterested passersby. He stood by a card table that had a clipboard on top and a sign taped to the front stating, "Sign the petition to ban occult paraphernalia." The man bypassed Gregor and pushed a flyer into Cadence's hand.

She tried not to take it, but she didn't want it to fall on the ground. "No thanks."

"Do you always toss a gift before opening the box?" the man asked.

Cadence watched Gregor enter the shop before turning her attention to the brown eyes of the handsome man, whom she guessed was about her age. His stature was on the short end of average, if he stood up straight. On his left earlobe, she spotted the telltale indentation of an earring hole that had been allowed to close. "You're right. I should read it before dismissing it."

Under the header, "No Christ in Crystal," was a photo of the church they had passed on the highway. The text urged the reader not to be led astray by practitioners of divination, calling them members of the "Crystal Cult," and it provided supporting scriptural verses, along with a schedule and contact information for Christ Church of Sedona. At the bottom was an invitation for those seventeen years old and under to attend a youth conference the next weekend, with the special enticement of a free semi-automatic weapon for one lucky attendee.

"Guns for God?" asked Cadence.

"Sometimes children need an incentive to do the right thing."

"So do you think God wants more teenagers to have semi-automatic rifles?"

"We're not putting a weapon in the hands of somebody who doesn't respect it." The man released a slight, almost dismissive laugh. "Our attendees aren't killers."

"You can personally vouch for everyone who happens to show up?"

"Look, the conference isn't even about guns. It's for young people to find and strengthen their faith." The man held out his hand. "I'm Mitchell Briar."

She shook his hand and found herself titillated by the sensation of his hand cupping hers. "Cadence."

When Travis entered the shop, he was soothed by the aroma of tea tree suffusing the air and soft lights diffusing through crystals of varying hue. Much deeper than it appeared from outside, the shop carried a wide array of products for body, mind and spirit – from aromatherapy, New Age music and books on cosmic energy to archeological artifacts and every imaginable type of rock and crystallized mineral. Toward the back, a sign reading "Meditation Center" hung over a doorway obstructed by black drapes, contrasting with the fern-colored walls.

Travis approached a fiftyish woman who was ringing up a customer behind a counter stationed near the front door. "Excuse me. Do you have a restroom I could use? I swear I'll buy something."

She smiled at his offer and pointed to the covered doorway. "Right through there."

"Thank you," Travis said with relief before darting away. Waving the drapes aside, he ran into the Meditation Center, but darkness halted his progression. The room's meager lighting came from a water feature in the far corner and geodic lamps that dropped from the ceiling like stalactites. An energetic trance song played from unseen speakers, and although the volume was low, he thought it an odd choice to accompany meditation.

"May I help you?" asked a voice from the shadows.

As his pupils dilated, he saw three small boulders, weighing perhaps half a ton each, positioned within the room. His eyes focused on a tan brunette, who was no more than twenty-three – unless the dim lighting concealed lines in her face. Sporting a tan shirt tucked into blue shorts, she wore very little, if any, makeup, and her long, straight hair was bound within a ponytail. She didn't look like she spent a great amount of time preparing herself for the world, but her natural beauty made such effort needless.

"I'm sorry," Travis said. "I didn't mean to interrupt. Were you meditating?"

The woman nodded to the mop in her right hand. "Cleaning."

Referring to the darkness, he said, "At least no one can tell if you did a bad job of it."

The woman hit a switch on the wall, and an overhead black curtain retracted from a large skylight. The sun's rays parted the darkness and exposed the wet stone-tile floor of the clean room, as well as the intricate detail of the water feature, which was modeled after the red rock formations that surrounded the town and had a river snaking down one of its craggy sides.

"That's," Travis paused when he noticed the woman's illuminated face and crystal green eyes. "Better."

"Clean enough?"

"For Howard Hughes. Uh, I need the bathroom."

She pointed to a door in the wall adjacent to the room's entrance. "It's right there."

"Thanks." He was about to follow her direction when he stopped to say, "I'm Travis."

She nodded once. "Iris."

"My favorite flower," Travis lied with a smile sprouted from the self-satisfaction of his quick thinking and the thought that he would have a favorite flower. "One more question. Would you tell me the name of this song?"

"Do you like it?"

"I just want to remember the song that was playing when we first met."

She rolled her eyes. "Better hurry. I don't want to have to mop the floor again."

Gregor examined Kokopelli figurines before moving to the shop's extensive collection of natural crystals. Fascinated by the beauty and variety of the rocks, he was compelled to touch each kind, experiencing its texture to discover its feel. His attention veered to the wall a few steps away, on which were displayed a mélange of crystals tethered to braided-cotton necklaces. From the dozens of options, he was drawn to an asymmetrical amulet with an almost jagged surface that reflected just enough deep blue light to avoid a hue of perfect black. He separated the necklace from the rest and was surprised by its mass, which almost made it too heavy to wear around the neck. He put his head through the loop, and after brief contemplation, he said to himself, "I'll get used to it." He stepped over to the small selection of books on a shelf near the doorway to the Meditation Center. The cover of one a sliver thicker than a pamphlet piqued his interest. He picked up *Maps to Sedona's Vortexes* and mumbled, "Shouldn't it be vortices?"

A voice behind him answered, "You would think."

Startled, Gregor twisted around to see Iris, the black curtains behind her still swaying from her passage through them. With blushing lips, she continued, "But no one here ever says it that way. If you're interested in finding them, we offer tours – which I lead, by the way." Her ending statement added a twinkle to her eye.

Gregor returned her smile with a dash of uncertainty. He held up the book of maps and said, "You do realize you could be talking yourself out of a sale."

"I'm just trying to upgrade you. You could do both, if you're really adventurous."

"I think the true adventure would be to put myself blindly into your hands," he said as he returned the book to the shelf. "I'm Gregor Buckingham."

She laughed and extended her hand. "Iris Wickline."

Gregor noticed her necklace, which was of near-translucent opal specked with neon green. "I like your amulet."

"Thank you. I like yours. It's very masculine. It suits you." As Travis entered through the curtains behind her, she said, "I'll get you a brochure," and headed to the counter.

Travis asked, "Were you hitting on her?"

Gregor shook his head. "Why?"

"If you're interested, I'll back off, even if I did see her first." Travis smiled at his own poker-faced generosity, which held the cards of experience, physical superiority and lupine instincts close to its chest, as if Gregor didn't know the deck had been stacked.

"We're here for eight days. Why would I initiate a relationship with no possible future?"

"Those are the best kinds," said Travis.

Iris returned with a brochure and handed it to Gregor. "Here's the tour info—"

"Are we going somewhere?" Travis asked.

Gregor tried to wave him off. "I don't think you'd be interested."

"A tour of the town? I'm down."

In front of the shop, as Cadence eased her hand from Mitchell's, he picked up the clipboard and asked, "Will you sign our petition?"

Cadence responded with another question, "What are you petitioning?"

He handed her the paper to read. "We want to force a city ballot initiative that would ban selling any item of necromancy, including crystals, incense, wands, dreamcatchers…"

After the first paragraph, Cadence looked up from the clipboard. "You want first offenders to receive jail time?"

"Thirty days for the first offense, and one year for the second."

"You don't think that's a bit harsh?"

"Sometimes adults need an incentive to do the right thing," he replied with a grin. "We tried to persuade the city council to pass an ordinance to that effect, but they are all too beholden to the tourism revenue generated by the patrons of these spiritual profiteers."

Mitchell's eyes stared into hers, and no matter how she averted her gaze, when she looked back at him, they were penetrating her. She handed him the clipboard. "I don't live here."

"You can enlist in other ways. The battle for Truth is not bound by the lines on a map."

"But I am bound by Time," Cadence said. "I'm on vacation."

Mitchell tried another tactic. "Why don't you come to our church for Sunday morning service tomorrow?"

"I'm on vacation." Nodding her head toward the shop, she added, "I should really go."

"Cadence, don't go in there!"

Jolted by the change in his tone, Cadence looked into his eyes and detected signs of genuine concern. "I have to catch up with my friends." She started walking away.

Mitchell told her, "I sit in the front pew. I'll save you a seat."

Cadence muttered, "Okay," with the conviction of mediocrity.

"Cadence!" Mitchell yelled, and she turned again to him. "Find your friends, and leave that place."

In the shop, Travis told Iris, "We'll be camping a few days and likely relegated to bathing with baby wipes. Do you carry anything for odor control? I ask mainly for my friend, Gregor, here. I myself only emit what I've been told is a wondrous and irresistibly beguiling musk."

Iris laughed. "We carry a sandalwood cologne that actually fuses with that 'musk' to create a more palatable scent."

Travis placed a hand on Gregor's shoulder. "See, I have you covered, buddy." He asked Iris, "Could you show me where you keep this miracle potion?"

"Follow me," she said, and the two left Gregor alone.

Gregor frowned at their backs and removed the amulet from around his neck. He debated the merits of his potential purchase, but its allure again won him over. When he placed the amulet onto the counter, the woman at the register said, "Beautiful." She had young, chestnut eyes and a pleasant face that he thought perhaps elicited a smile from all in her presence.

With a squinch of his eyes, Gregor asked, "I'm sorry?"

The woman touched his amulet. "This is lazulite. The name means 'heaven.' Are you visiting any vortexes while you're here?"

He held up the brochure Iris had given him. "I plan on it."

"Make certain you wear the amulet when you do. Crystals absorb and store the energy from the vortex, so you can take it home and re-experience the feeling the vortex gave you."

Although he was uncertain of her statement's validity, Gregor could sense she believed it, so he left himself open to the possibility.

Cadence didn't see her friends when she first entered the shop, but she did peer through the window at Mitchell and found him packing up to abandon his post. Perhaps sensing her gaze, he looked at her and mouthed the word, "Hurry." She wasn't sure how to react, but she opted for a half-smile, wondering how someone could weird her out and turn her on at the same time.

As she walked around the shop to find Gregor, the merchandise she passed struck her as valueless but far from criminal, so she wondered why it would evoke such hostility from an otherwise delectable man. Reaching a clearing between two shelves, Cadence spotted Gregor conversing with the shopkeeper. She hurried to his side, paying little attention to the woman on the other side of the counter. "Gregor, are we ready to go?"

"Not just yet. I was talking to…"

"Lily," the woman said.

Cadence nodded to her with a glimpse in her direction, but she had no sooner turned back to Gregor when she gave the woman a double-take. Squinting and cocking her head, Cadence told her, "You look familiar. Have we met?"

"I don't believe so," Lily replied. "Have you been here before?"

Cadence stared at the woman's face. "First time." With sudden awareness, she gasped and squeezed Gregor's arm. "She's the woman who visited me in the hospital!"

Gregor pried her nails from his forearm. "What woman?"

"The one you said wasn't there."

Lily mumbled, "I don't even remember the last time I was inside a hospital."

Her impatience growing, Cadence told her, "It was in L.A." To Gregor, she explained, "She's the one with the dog."

"You met Daisy?" Lily asked.

Cadence turned up the left corner of her mouth. "Who?"

Lily answered, "My border collie."

"You told me her name was Sedona."

Iris approached the counter with Travis trailing her. "Mom, what's going on here?"

Lily told her daughter, "This young lady thinks I visited her in the hospital in L.A."

"Los Angeles?" her daughter asked. "Have you ever been there?"

"Only once, but that was before you were born."

Cadence gripped Gregor's arm and tried shaking the memory into him. "The day you asked me out."

"You two are a couple?" Iris asked.

"Oh no," responded Gregor, shaking his head more than necessary. He told Cadence, "I remember you had a dream about a woman and a dog visiting you…"

Cadence waved toward Lily with both hands. "That's the woman!"

Iris asked Travis, "What kind of hospital was this?" with air quotes around the three-syllable word.

"Not the kind you're thinking."

Lily told her, "I'm not sure what to say, but I never saw you before today."

Cadence frowned at her and insisted, "You're lying."

Iris brandished angry eyes. "Hey!"

Gregor stepped between them. "Whoa, Cadence." He looked over his shoulder and said, "Lily, I'm sorry. She didn't mean that."

Cadence snarled, "Don't apologize for me! I'm the one telling the truth!" She told Lily, "I recognize you. And your voice. And I knew about your dog."

Travis wrapped an arm around Cadence and told Iris, "We'll call you about the tour."

Cadence gave up the fight and returned with to the car with her friends. As they drove away, Gregor and Travis picked up their conversation about the passing scenery, but Cadence, arms crossed, refused further engagement.

After several minutes, Travis asked her, "Are you all right?"

"With the comforting faith of my friends, how could I not be?"

Gregor put a hand on her shoulder. "Cadence, don't be angry."

"Remind me to offer that advice the next time I don't believe you."

He responded, "Maybe something about Lily reminded you of the woman in your dream, and then you subconsciously gave that woman her face?"

"Gregor, I'm not wrong," Cadence insisted. "I've never been convinced I dreamed her to begin with, and I don't want to talk about it anymore."

In silence they traveled the remaining drive to the motel, where Cadence refused help with her luggage. Her room had nothing unexpected, with a queen-size bed, an end table, two chairs and a small bathroom. However, when she opened the drapes, she had a wonderful view of Coffee Pot Rock framed by the room's single, large window.

"Wow," she whispered. "That's high."

Perhaps Sedona's most recognizable red rock formation, it indeed looked like a coffee pot, complete with a rocky protrusion in the shape of a spout. The sun, an hour from setting on the opposing side, was turning the sky to orange and red as if to camouflage the rock's outline. She could discern silhouettes of people on the spout but saw no apparent path up the sheer sides of the rock, which rose from the ground to a height rivaling the U.S. Bank Tower in Downtown L.A. She wondered how the hikers had reached its peak. Did they walk some unseen trail or scale the side of the rock? She had never been athletic and didn't have any rock-climbing skills. Still, the large rock did afford a nearby alternative to her planned excursion. She fantasized about becoming one of the silhouettes before the week's end, to watch the sunset and welcome the darkness.

CHAPTER 4

Travis drove down Dry Creek Road and bowed to look at the sky through the windshield. "We are seriously losing the sun." He tapped on the car's navigation system, which displayed an error message regarding the lack of a clear satellite signal. "Where is Secret Canyon?"

"It really is a secret," replied Gregor.

"Should we just forget about finding the campground tonight and go back to the motel?"

"I don't want to be indoors," Gregor said, and he nodded to a small directional sign. "Boynton Canyon. Maybe we can find a campground there."

Travis turned into the setting sun. "Or an out-of-the-way place to camp for the night."

Gregor noticed a narrow dirt clearing meandering through the brushy landscape on the right, and his eyes followed it for several meters until it disappeared behind a tree with drooping branches. Further back was a canyon no more remarkable than any they had passed, but its shape and silhouette of deepening crimson cast by the fading sun enchanted him. "Go there."

Travis squinted at the path. "We'll take it as far as we can." He turned and drove with cautious speed, but the bumpy path narrowed to where he could no longer avoid the scratching branches of the junipers that lined it. "I need to stop and back out of here."

"Wait! There's a clearing up ahead."

"I see it." Travis stopped once the path opened up. "What do you think?"

Gregor looked around and shrugged. "Works for me."

Two dome tents of lime green and a rock-lined fire triangulated an impromptu campsite on an oval of sandstone amidst a forest of juniper, yucca and pine. The camp lay in the umbrage cast from the full moon hiding behind a nearby red rock formation that coupled with another a slight distance away to create a canyon. Sitting on folding canvas chairs, Travis pushed a wood-impaled marshmallow into the fire, while Gregor, positioned further back from the fire, stared at the starry night with his hands clasped behind his head.

"How could we have slept under starless skies for so long?" Gregor asked.

Travis mumbled, "Uh-huh."

When the two of them were alone without a clear topic of discussion, Gregor often sauntered into lengthy philosophical excursions, but Travis' response let him know that his friend was not in the mood, perhaps too tired from driving all day.

With eyes adrift in Orion, Gregor fantasized about worlds and life beyond. He imagined civilizations founded on the virtue of understanding, focused on achieving utter knowledge of existence. Those he envisioned were not geo-complacent and instead traveled the cosmos for true awareness of our symbiotic universe, gaining solace in the answers they found. Longing for kinship, his heart opened as if it were a beacon for rescue, and he begged the sky to embrace him. The hope of ascension turned his lips into a smile, until a loud crackle from the firewood snapped him back to Earth and his own insignificant life, marked by unimportance, self-loathing and disengagement from love's prospect. These were thoughts he tried to avoid because they invited the bitterness to which he did not want to be acquainted. He sighed, "Dreams unfulfilled asphyxiate the soul."

His mouth a gooey mess, Travis said, "I thought you didn't believe in souls."

Gregor lowered his arms and faced his friend. "I don't, but our bodies do encase an energy that could be called our souls. After we die, that energy doesn't travel to heaven or hell as determined by the type of life we've led. Our consciousness doesn't even remain attached to it. It's simply energy, and it returns to the universe to be used in some other form."

Travis responded, "Matter can be neither created nor destroyed. It just changes forms. I watch the Science Channel too."

"We're connected to every being, every rock, every star and every atom out there. We all started from the same singularity. All energy in the universe always was and ever will be, so we are as much a part of the universe now as we were in its beginning and as we will be in its end."

"So, no heaven or hell?" Travis asked.

Gregor responded, "What do you believe?"

"I'm holding out for more evidence. You know my parents made me go to church every Sunday, but somewhere along the way, God started seeming more like an interesting concept than an absolute truth. Anyway, so if there's no heaven or hell, wouldn't that rule out karma?"

Gregor nodded. "Karma presumes if you do good or bad, that's what will come back to you, but that's not always the case. Good kids, innocent kids have bad things happen to them every day, but do they deserve it? Think of Cadence with her cancer. She didn't do anything to warrant that."

"Maybe that's why she was cured."

"She's in remission. Belief in karma, or deserved consequences, germinates thoughts of entitlement and desires for retribution, neither of which promote ideal humanity."

Travis shook his head. "Sometimes bad things do seem to happen for a reason."

"Reason is a totally human invention. We feel the need to apply a reason to everything, but it doesn't necessarily factor in."

"Okay, if karma and reason don't determine the course of our lives, what does?"

"I didn't say reason is totally out the window. I just said it isn't a variable in every single event. The way I see it, our lives follow the same laws as the universe, like Newton's first law of motion – objects in motion stay in motion unless an external force is applied. We control our own inertia, our behavior, so if we were never acted on by external forces, we would totally control our own lives. However, since we don't live in a vacuum, external forces do act on us and change our trajectory, and not always in a positive way." Gregor noticed his friend was staring into the fire. "Am I rambling?"

"No more than usual," Travis answered with a smirk.

"I'm sorry," Gregor sighed and turned his eyes again to the sky. "Sometimes I just wish I had been born five-hundred years in the future, when we're out there, actually experiencing the universe."

"Do you think we ever will be?"

"Absolutely. We have to join the others," Gregor said, prompting a laugh from Travis. "I'm serious. Don't you ever feel like they're watching us and waiting for us to get our act together and get in the game?"

"What game? If civilizations out there are advanced enough to be watching us, they'd turn the channel from boredom. Why would they care about us? Unless we taste good."

"Okay then. Do you ever wonder about anything?"

"I'm not unimaginative," Travis said. "Of course, I wonder."

"About what?"

"I wonder… what the small of Iris' back feels like."

"There it is," Gregor said with mock exasperation.

"Okay, here's something I wonder about." Travis hesitated. "Do you think I'm a good person?"

"Of course, you are. Why—"

"Don't just give me the answer I want to hear. I want an honest assessment."

"Why are you asking?"

"I just want to know."

Gregor replied, "What is the definition of a good or bad person? What parameters do you use?"

"Using your personal opinion and the parameters," Travis pointed three times at Gregor's skull, "in that head of yours."

"All right. Empathy. I think that if you genuinely care about the welfare of others – all others – and don't intentionally act or fail to act in a manner that would jeopardize that welfare, you are a good person. Yes, I really believe you're a good person."

"Funny. Using that definition, I would answer that I'm not." Travis stood to stretch, and with a tone of obvious diversion, he said, "Look at the full moon. I need to take some shots." He unzipped the flap of his tent and slipped inside.

Gregor yawned and rubbed his eyes. "I'm wiped. I'm going to bed."

From inside his tent, Travis told him, "Good night."

As Gregor disappeared into his own tent, Travis reappeared with his camera in hand. Removing the lens cap, he turned the camera skyward, but he couldn't find the moon through the viewer. He moved the camera from his face and scanned the sky. "Where is it?"

He warned Gregor, "I think it might rain tonight; some clouds just rolled in." Travis returned to his tent and zipped the entrance closed.

Unseen to Gregor and Travis, a ship hovered in the sky, centered over an elevated rocky plateau five-hundred meters from their campsite. The ship was large enough to block the moon from their view, but quiet and dark enough to remain undetected. After a moment the ship ascended at an incredible speed, allowing the moonlight to once again diffuse through the nylon of the tents.

CHAPTER 5

From a Queen Anne chair in the study of his house, August Briar read with obvious impatience the staple-bound pages of a sermon, while the mountain lion mounted on the wall behind him appeared to be reading over his shoulder. On an adjacent wall hung a painting of the prophet Elijah riding a chariot of fire in the midst of a burning whirlwind as Elisha watched from the ground. A gilded Bible lay on the end table beside an upright piano, at which Mitchell Briar sat, bouncing his right leg. When his father flipped the final page, he asked, "Well, what did you think?"

August handed the document to his son. "Good."

"You really think so?" Mitchell grinned and tried not to notice his father's grimace at even the slightest inference of untruthfulness. "I'm so stoked... glad you liked it. I've had the idea for a while. I think it's totally original."

"Mitchell, I have to work on my sermon for tomorrow." August pulled a notebook from the briefcase leaning against the side of his chair.

Mitchell offered the document back to him. "Why don't you use mine? It's done."

August smirked. "Tomorrow is important for me."

"What's wrong with it?"

August sighed. "The timidity of your message. When you talk about teaching God's word to the unreceptive, you suggest a point exists at which we should abandon our mission to lead the unenlightened to Him."

"Do you mean when I reference the atrocities of the Spanish conquistadors?"

"There is nothing atrocious about fulfilling directives from God. Your you-can-lead-a-horse-to-water approach absolves God's followers from their responsibility—"

"What's responsible about torturous coercion?"

"Willing or forced, there is no wrong way to spread the word of God!"

"I disagree. I—"

"You disagree?" August cast the words from his mouth as if their very enunciation stung his tongue with bitterness. "Matthew 28:19 states, 'Go ye therefore, and teach all nations, baptizing them in the name of the Father, and of the Son, and of the Holy Ghost.' Nowhere does the Bible say that you have to be nice about it." August grabbed the Bible from the end table and held it up. "This book is in black and white. Convert or perish!"

"Forcing people might change action but not hearts, and murdering those who refuse to even go through the motions of conversion eliminates the possibility of their eventual enlightenment."

August pointed the Bible at his son. "It silences their pagan doctrine to prevent the potential conversion of others *from* God."

"Would you suggest we go kill those who don't immediately accept the word of God?"

With a lamenting downward gaze, August answered, "The world has become enemy territory for God's soldiers, where formerly rewarded acts of valor are now punished." He looked back at his son and with renewed vigor. "We must still be hyper-vigilant in shepherding people to God. Thousands or even millions of Native

Americans are Christians today because of the groundwork laid by the same people that you condemn as misguided." August returned the Bible to the end table. "If people do not want to believe, you have to make them believe. You need to have the courage to do what you know is right for them."

"Fine. I can delete that part from my sermon. It's just a few lines anyway."

"That is not the only problem."

"I thought you said it was good."

August snapped, "I do not do *good*. My congregation…" He stopped and brandished both fists. "God expects greatness from me!"

"I think this is a great sermon. I hit on several key points for relevancy today, and I backed it with solid scriptural references."

August grabbed the sermon from his son's hand. "God's words are quoted throughout this text, but I do not hear God's voice in it. This sermon is so bogged down with Biblical quotes that no one will be able to hear it over the continuous page-turning the congregation will have to do to keep up. What is original about using text comprised primarily of someone else's words?"

"The references validate the points I'm trying to make—"

"What about your references to Satan as some nebulous symbol of man's immorality? Satan is not a concept! He is very real – as real as you and I. Do you think Christ was tempted by a figment of his imagination? Even suggesting that the Deceiver is less than real grants him easier access to men's souls. How irresponsible—"

"I was going back to the origins of Satan."

"Mitchell!" August glared down at his son,

Mitchell jerked his head back as August moved his face so close, he could feel his angry breath drying his eyes. When his father smelled blood, he was incapable of stepping back to let the injured lick his wounds, so Mitchell retreated a half-step.

To his son's surprise, August laughed, lightening the gravity of his voice into a pounce. "A penguin might consider fifty degrees Fahrenheit hot, but that is not the same sensory scale I use. For you, this sermon is hot." August threw the sermon in the wastebasket and growled, "Oppose me again only if you enjoy humiliation because you will never better me. Now get out, and let me finish my work!"

For the faithful, solace lies in knowing without the intrusion of doubt. August Briar walked into the solarium of his hillside home and flicked a switch, allowing the flow of electricity into the amber light fixture on the wall. The room was a narrow protrusion from the house, with walls of paneled glass and no ceiling but a retractable awning spooled on the rod above his head.

August strode to the far end of the room and removed the lens cap from his high-powered telescope. He tipped the cylinder a degree to the left and bowed to peer at the night sky. He adjusted the focus and zoomed in on a star in his field of vision. After a few moments, August peeled his eye away from the lens and slumped onto the wood bench nearby. He looked around the sky and asked, "Why do you not come to me?"

CHAPTER 6

Iris Wickline had never been lost in time or place, but she often longed to be. She awoke at 5 a.m. every morning, regardless of the day and without the aid of a clock, and she never needed a watch to know the time within five minutes of atomic. Her GPS-like sense of direction enabled her to always find her way, although she had never strayed too far from home since her birth twenty-four years earlier. When her friends scattered to colleges in other cities and states, Iris followed for the briefest moment before opting to earn her bachelor's and master's degrees online. Fantasies of leaving crept into her thoughts every day, but she remained planted as if she were waiting for life to be revealed to her instead of finding it on her own.

With a laptop tucked under her arm and a cup of coffee in her hand, Iris opened the glass-paneled backdoor of the house she shared with her mother and stepped onto a natural stone patio. She sat at the wrought iron table three paces away and powered on her laptop with no particular notice of her surroundings, which were spectacular.

The backyard opened into a beautiful small canyon a kilometer long, carved into a red rock formation twenty meters high. Tall stone fences on both sides of the yard extended to either wall of the canyon, but no fence impeded its connection with the yard, allowing no clear distinction between where one ended and the other began, and giving the Wicklines their own private red rock canyon. An early morning mist flowed from the canyon into the yard like a timid, translucent avalanche, dispersing the sun's first scouts and salving the desert air.

Iris typed on the computer, removing her fingers from the keyboard at regular intervals only to caress the warm cup and elevate it to her rubicund lips. After a few minutes, she heard the sound of scratching glass, and with a turn of her neck, she saw a border collie staring at her from the other side of the backdoor. "Daisy," she said in a tender voice. She scooted back her chair to stand when she saw her mother appear by Daisy. As soon as Lily opened the door, the dog bolted to Iris and lifted her two front paws onto her lap to lick her chin. Iris turned her face skyward so Daisy's tongue could only reach her neck. "Okay, that's enough," she said before kissing the dog on the cheek and transferring her paws back to the ground.

"Good morning, sweetheart," Lily said while reaching for a chair at the table.

"Morning. You're up early."

Lily sighed. "My mind was racing in bed. I thought my body should try to catch up."

"What's so urgent?"

"I couldn't stop thinking about that girl yesterday. Why was she so sure she knew me?"

Iris chuckled. "She obviously wasn't the most stable block in the Jenga tower."

"I think Gregor called her Cadence." Lily looked at the dog, who was beginning her morning search for the perfect pee spot. "How did she know about Daisy?"

"She didn't. She thought you had a dog named Sedona."

"Exactly. Why Sedona, of all names?" Lily touched her daughter's hand. "I think she might've been called here."

Iris rolled her eyes. "Oh lord."

Lily lifted her hand into an off-center point. "Whether you believe it or not, my daughter, the great demythologizer, forces do exist in this world that are outside standard thinking and, fortunately, they're not reliant on belief for existence. I would appreciate you not dismissing my words without even the slightest consideration of their potential truth."

Iris dipped her head into her shoulders. "Sorry."

Lily continued her train of thought. "Why, of all images that could have easily directed her to Sedona, did her vision center around me? Maybe the universe is telling me I'm supposed to help her in some way."

"Mom, I know you don't believe our lives are predetermined."

Lily took a sip from Iris' cup. "I'm not saying they are, but maybe, every once in a while, the universe gives us little nudges toward more optimal paths."

Iris smiled. "I thought you were giving up coffee."

Lily dismissed her words with a look. "Starting Monday."

"You said that last weekend."

"I meant this Monday coming up," Lily insisted before changing the subject. "I wish I knew how to get in touch with Cadence. Did they tell you where they were staying?"

"No, but they seemed pretty certain about a tour. I'll probably hear from them."

As Daisy returned to the patio, Lily said, "Good. If they call, let me know. What are you doing today?"

"Working on my dissertation. I'll come in around one to relieve you for lunch."

Lily waved a hand in front of her. "Don't worry about me. I'll take a sandwich with me." She pointed to the laptop with a look of disdain. "Why don't you put that away and do something fun today. Go on a little daytrip somewhere. The Grand Canyon. You haven't been there in a while. Or go to Phoenix, and visit some of your friends. Doesn't Pam live there now?"

"Mom, I've barely heard from her in four years."

"She used to be your best friend. What happened to you two?"

Iris exposed her palms and answered with obviousness, "She moved away."

Lily took another sip of coffee. "What is Gia up to today?"

"Why are you trying to get rid of me?"

"I'm only trying to motivate you."

"To do what?"

"Start living your life."

"What do you think I'm doing?"

"Hibernating."

"Hibernating?"

"What I mean is that, besides helping out at the shop, you don't really socialize. You don't date. You're always home by nightfall. You even go to school online, completely skipping the social aspects of the college experience. I'm afraid you're going to waste your youth."

Iris frowned at her mother and closed her laptop. "You know, other mothers would be proud if their child were pursuing a doctorate."

"I am proud of you. Of course, I'm proud." Lily sighed. "You just never go anywhere."

"I do too! Iris stepped away from the table and tucked her computer between her arm and waist. "For instance, now I'm going to my room."

"What's wrong?"

"It's too chilly out here."

"I didn't mean..." Lily's voice trailed off as the kitchen door closed with her daughter on the other side.

From his receptionist's office, August Briar watched as the new camera crew set up their equipment in his church. He had learned this morning through a congregant that his regular crew was boycotting today's service – in deference to their silly pride and not their everlasting souls, August thought. *Their pettiness will be judged harshly by Him and me.* He turned his attention to the white-tile pulpit, on which rested a bronze podium within a crescent of two-meter gunmetal candlesticks. The distinctive giant cross, visible on the front of the church even from the highway, quadrisected a wall of paned glass that opened Sedona up as a backdrop to the pulpit. As the choir practiced in their usual spot to the pulpit's side, August had an idea. He tried with all his might to conceal his limp as he walked past the newcomers, so much so that sweat gilded his forehead by the time he arrived within speaking distance of the choir.

"Good morning, brothers and sisters."

"Good morning, Reverend," most replied.

"What is the last song you plan to sing before my sermon?"

"How Great Thou Art," the nebbish choir director answered.

"Good. I want you to do something different today. Instead of singing in front of the stage, I want you to line up on stage right in front of the podium."

"Really?" The choir director asked. "But the camera won't get your entrance if we do."

"I want to walk to the podium as the song is finishing, and then the choir can separate in the middle with the two halves exiting the stage at opposite ends."

The choir director's confusion turned to elation. "Like a curtain opening. Great idea."

"Exactly, and I also want you to come back on stage after my sermon."

"Like the curtains are closing," the director said, to which the reverend nodded.

Travis was awakened by the aroma of sizzling soy bacon, to which he snarled his nose and grumbled, "I should've learned how to hunt." He emerged from his tent to see Gregor sitting in front of a fire with a metal spatula in hand and wearing a wrinkled T-shirt. He couldn't remember the last time he had seen his friend in short sleeves, since he avoided wearing anything that would expose his burn scars.

Gregor smiled at him. "Morning."

Travis returned the greeting, and after stretching, he massaged his lower back with both hands. "Crap, my back is stiff."

"Did you sleep on it wrong?" Gregor asked.

"The ground dips right where my lower back was positioned. I need to find some leaves or something to put under my tent and soften the ground."

"Maybe the campground will have softer land."

Travis sat by the fire. "I don't want to move. Let's just stay here."

"This isn't a designated campsite. For all we know, it's private property."

"It's fine," Travis insisted without a thought for his concern. "I didn't see a fence or a 'No Trespassing' sign. Besides, didn't you say most of this area is a national forest?"

Gregor shrugged. "I hope you're hungry."

Travis looked at the off-white faux bacon cockling in the saffron oil of the aluminum skillet. "Not enough for that."

"You need to eat. We have a lot of hiking to do today."

Travis pointed to the closest red rock formation. "Let's climb to the top of that."

"That sounds like a plan. You have your gear?"

"We won't need it for that rock," he said with a dismissive laugh. "Plenty of grip."

Gregor scooped the bacon onto an aluminum plate and handed

it to Travis, who was still rubbing his lower back. "Are you sure you can climb?"

"I'll be fine once my back loosens. I'll give you a head start."

"Are we racing to the top?" asked Gregor.

Knowing he was much faster, Travis replied, "Is it a race if the outcome is predetermined?"

Cadence could hear a song of angels as she stood on the edge of a cliff overlooking much of the Verde Valley. Her white linen dress shuddering in the tepid wind, she moved her gaze along the horizon, pausing a moment at Courthouse Butte and Bell Rock. The music grew louder for a few seconds, as if someone had opened the door to enter a concert hall. She turned to face the back Christ Church of Sedona in time to see the gray metal door close behind another latecomer to the morning service. *Just go on in.* Cadence stepped back from the cliff and walked across the brick path that separated her from the church. She hesitated long enough to inhale a deep breath before pressing her palm to the door's handle.

Smaller on the inside than she thought it would be, the church housed twelve rows of benches divided by a narrow aisle. A film crew of three was positioned on one side at the back with their lens aimed at a choir of eight men and women who stood shoulder to shoulder at the front of the pulpit, leading the congregation in an honorable rendition of "How Great Thou Art."

Hoping not to be noticed, Cadence walked down the aisle at a brisk pace, but by the time she reached the halfway point, the song finished, and everyone but her and August sat. She could feel her face redden as she looked up at the reverend, who was standing behind the podium with a glare in his eyes for her and a contradictory smile for the camera. She exhaled when she spotted Mitchell on the front row next to an empty seat.

Mitchell smiled as she plopped next to him, and he whispered with a twitch of his lips, "Glad you could make it."

"Sorry I'm late," Cadence whispered back with more than his effort.

August Briar was a passionate speaker who brought his sermons to life for the audience as if he were acting them out, using vocal inflections and frequent gestures, which bordered on spasmodic during emphatic passages. He was a divine herald and the moral polestar for his devoted congregants, who directed their worship at him as if he were an immediate connection to God.

August began his time at the podium by welcoming the faithful in attendance and taking a swipe at those absent by saying, "Thank you so much for joining us on this glorious day to let God know that devotion to Him supersedes all other motivations in life." He introduced himself as he always did for the viewers who might be tuning in for the first time, "My name is August Briar, and I am a soldier of God in enemy territory." His tone became more conversational as he relayed a story that, although he told it at least once a year, was a crowd-pleaser every time. "I am originally from Texas, but I had heard about Sedona, Arizona long before coming here. I heard how the land was magical, and the red rocks were full of energy that could heal and connect you to the universe, our God!" The audience laughed at the notion of the universe being the Almighty. "You think that sounds ridiculous, but if I said the same thing outside these walls, people would nod in agreement!" More laughter. "Now I had a sister who had scoliosis, so when I heard about these magical rocks, I told my father, 'Dad, we should take Louise to Sedona so she can be healed.'"

Some members of the congregation snickered, and August joined them. "Anyone who has heard me talk about my father before can probably guess his response. His expression turned stern in a flash, and he told me in that gravelly voice that made me want to hide behind my own shadow, 'Son, go out to the hickory tree and cut me a switch.'" Several congregants moaned in recognition of the archaic punishment. "A switch? I was shocked. I saw nothing I had done to warrant getting whipped with a switch. I just wanted to help my sister. What could possibly be wrong with that? Of course, I objected and tried to reason with him. I said, 'Hold on, Dad. I do not understand. What did I do? Do you not want to help Louise?'

"My father responded with two passages of scripture. From 2 Timothy, chapter four, verse four, 'And they shall turn away their ears from the truth, and shall be turned unto fables.' Deuteronomy eighteen, verses ten and eleven, 'There shall not be found among you any one that maketh his son or his daughter to pass through the fire, or that useth divination, or an observer of times, or an enchanter, or a witch. Or a charmer, or a consulter with familiar spirits, or a wizard, or a necromancer. For all that do these things are an abomination unto the Lord.' My father then asked me, 'Do you understand.' I lowered my head and said, 'Let me get the switch.'"

The audience erupted in laughter.

"My father was right. Thy word is a lamp unto my feet – not a lava lamp." Mild laughter arose from the audience. "That is why I came here and built this church. Someone needed to fight against the rampant Crystal Cult that had arisen in Sedona, Arizona – the Gomorrah of the Southwest. By *Crystal Cult* I mean those who worship rocks and crystals, those so-called positive thinkers who believe that they can visualize their own self-determined path to salvation, and those who believe they can tap into some strange and mystical energy and manipulate it to perform miracles." August slammed his right fist on the podium and screamed, "Witches!" His eyes fixed on the woman seated by his son, who squirmed under the scrutiny. "Some of you might say, 'Reverend Briar, there is no such thing as a witch.' I want you to erase from your heads the images of witches popularized in fiction. They do not go flying around on brooms or turning people into toads. The witches we have in our midst are much more subversive. Instead of magic wands and boiling cauldrons of noxious potions, they have crystals and dreamcatchers and transcendental aromas and other iniquitous products masquerading as souvenirs that tourists to our town so readily purchase. Verily I say unto you that those who buy are equally complicit in the sins of those who sell.

"In the Bible, even Saul, the God-appointed first king of Israel, was not immune to the treacherous allure of witches. He rightfully outlawed witchcraft and aggressively persecuted its practitioners, but when the Philistines gathered in great numbers to attack his kingdom, he turned his back on God and his own edict to seek help from the Witch of Endor. How does a man favored by God fall so tragically at the feet of Satan?

"Now I do not mean to say that all purported miracles are cases of veiled witchcraft. True miracles from God are widely reported in the Bible, and although they do not receive the same publicity, I believe that he continues to express himself through miracles today. Likewise, these false prophets should not be confused with true prophets. God spoke to prophets like Isaiah, Hosea and Elisha, and they were His voice on Earth and the enforcers of His will. God granted them special abilities in His service, including second sight, command of the elements, healing and even resurrection. The most favored of these prophets not only heard God, but they saw Him as well – Abraham, Daniel, Isaac. Although they were not allowed to see His face, they did see His presence. God visited Moses several times, most notably in the form of a burning bush, but He told Moses in Exodus, chapter thirty-three, verse twenty, 'Thou canst not see my face for there shall no man see me and live.' An even more select group – a group of just two – comprised the prophets who were spared death and taken directly to God. Genesis 5:24, 'Enoch walked with God: and he was not; for God took him.'

The other was Elijah, my personal hero, who in 2 Kings 2:11 was walking with his successor Elisha when, 'Behold, there appeared a chariot of fire, and horses of fire, and parted them both asunder; and Elijah went up by a whirlwind into heaven.' All of these prophets have been revered through the ages, and thousands of years later, we remember their names. We know a special place is reserved for them in God's house.

"As with miracles, I believe that God has not completely forsaken His fondness for prophets, but how would we tell a true prophet from the false ones so pervasive in our society? In chapter thirteen of Ezekiel, the Lord warned witches and false diviners that He would remove their veils, so that His children would no longer be prey to their lies. This church, my church, is doing the work of the Lord by revealing these people for what they are, but it is not enough to simply expose them. Exodus 22:18 commands us, 'Thou shalt not suffer a witch to live!'

"Of course, the world today has changed, much to the delight of the insidious deceivers. God's law and the law of the land were once one and the same. God's commandments were enforced! When God commanded that adulterers be stoned, you searched for the heaviest rock you could throw." August focused his glare on Mitchell. "When God commanded that children who cursed their parents be put to death, you silenced their miserable tongues. And when God commanded that witches be killed, you gathered firewood for the burning!" August paused for a second to catch his breath. "What happened? God's word has been subjugated by the timid laws of man, which protect the sinner from his God-ordered fate. Unfortunately, the execution of witches is no longer an option, but here is what we can do. We can work within those laws to prevent them from practicing and promulgating their craft. We can dry up the well of filthy lucre that nourishes their prosperity by banning the vending of demonic wares and restricting access to the sites where they profess a connection to the dark arts. I urge each and every one of you to visit my website, if you have not done so already, to find out how you can help. Together we can drive a stake into Satan's charred heart and expel his disciples from this beautiful land, which God created for us – the devoted children who worship and fear him!"

As soon as the service ended, Cadence told Mitchell, "I'm so sorry I was late." Opting not to reveal that she stood outside for twenty minutes, debating whether or not to enter the church. "I had to wait for a cab."

"I'm just happy you came. Come on, I'll introduce you to my father." Without taking her hand, he led her down the aisle, past the packing film crew, to the exiting procession.

August stood outside the doorway to thank every attendee with a handshake and telling them, "Remember that next Sunday's service will be at the youth conference."

A couple with a five-year-old boy was just ahead of Mitchell and Cadence in line. August shook hands with each family member. "Welcome back. How was the vacation?"

The young woman gushed, "It was wonderful."

Her husband added, "San Diego is a beautiful city."

"To visit," August interjected. "Give no thought to moving to the Golden Calf State, where Satan walks freely among his many, many devotees. I think they have more hedonists per capita than Sodom and Gomorrah."

Laughing, the young man assured him, "We wouldn't dream of it."

The boy told the reverend, "I saw grape white sharks."

"You did?"

"At the aquarium," the boy's mother explained.

"Were they scary?" August asked, to which the boy nodded.

"Pray to God tonight, and thank him for not putting anything so scary in this state."

Mitchell waited for the family to take a single step away before bounding up to his father and announcing, "Dad, I'd like for you to meet Cadence."

Cadence shook his hand and almost bowed. "Hi Reverend Briar."

"Hello." August looked to his son as if seeking some nonverbal explanation about the woman.

Mitchell told him, "She's here on vacation."

"Enjoy your visit," August said before extending his hand to the next person in line, a man in his fifties. "Alan, how is Jason?"

Mitchell and Cadence stepped away.

Alan Hargrove answered the reverend, "He's still in the coma."

"How is Margaret holding up?"

"She hasn't left his side."

"She is a good mother. I am praying for you all."

Mitchell smiled at Cadence and started toward the parking lot. "Where are you staying? I'll give you a ride."

"I'm at a motel. Is everything okay with your father?"

"My father is a master of quick judgments, which would be terrifying if he were presiding over a court. My guess is he views you as a lost soul who will only prove to be a further detriment to mine."

Cadence stopped in her tracks. "That's pretty harsh."

Mitchell shook his head. "That's not my opinion."

"Really? How do you see me?"

With a confident smile, he answered, "As someone worth saving."

CHAPTER 7

Gregor's fingers clamped onto the edge of the red precipice, as his feet dangled more than one-hundred meters from the ground below. His scooting hands disturbed particles of eroded rock that pelleted the top of his head and, as he looked up to plot his next move, he squinted too late to keep tiny bits from entering his eyes. Through rapid blinking he could see the branches of a juniper tree protruding past the ledge but too high for him to reach. Gregor slid his left hand along the rock and toward the shadow of the branches, where he found a root anchored into the ground above him. He squeezed the root with his left hand and threw his right hand just beyond it, leapfrogging his hands along the root until he could swing his feet onto the ledge. With his face still on the ground, he sighed and panted, "Piece of cake."

Gregor pushed himself into a standing position and grabbed a branch for balance when he realized the narrowness of his current foothold, which was no more than a meter wide and two meters long. A little taller than he, the lifesaving tree was twisted and leafless with branches bent into an illogical silhouette. It was encircled by waist-high bear grass, and the trunk was no more than half a meter from the back wall, which continued upward for another fifteen to twenty meters before peaking. "I'm not even going to try that." Instead, he dusted off his long-sleeve black shirt, dropped his backpack to the bear grass and sat with his legs crossed to enjoy the view of the beautiful canyon before him. Standing about the distance of an eight-lane freeway away, the canyon's opposing wall mirrored the one he had chosen to climb – vined with sparse plants like a mangy green beard on a sunburned face. In addition to juniper, the canyon floor was carpeted with an assortment of pine trees, some sprouting from the base of each wall, as well as an occasional maple tree. The only sign of civilization he could see was a hillside two or three kilometers to his left that was pockmarked with houses worth more than he would ever make.

Gregor poked his head past the edge, looking at the treacherous path he had taken to reach his current position and scanning the rest of the rocky wall beneath him for an easier route to the ground. To the east of the taken path and ten meters below was a plateau he had not noticed from the canyon floor. Almost circular, the plateau had a radius of seven meters and no obstructions on its surface. The perimeter, however, was protected along its exposed rim by an array of flora – from juniper and yucca to bear grass and prickly pear – a natural fence that kept the plateau hidden from those below. His eyes widened as he noticed a geoglyph in the shape of a bird in flight carved into the plateau's surface. "Wow!" He pulled his phone from his pocket, aimed at the carving and snapped several pictures. *What's that?* He spotted a narrow, descending pathway leading from the plateau to an abrupt stop an estimated three meters above the ground. The pathway appeared to be a natural fissure in the canyon wall with a narrow floor two meters below the sharp edge of the outer rock. It was almost undetectable from his vantage point, and he believed it would be impossible to see from the ground. "There's my way down."

Gregor withdrew a bottle of water from his backpack and swallowed half of its contents. As he looked again at the ledge on which he rested, he noticed that a section of the wall behind the grass did not conform to the surface of the rock above it. He parted the grass with his arms and saw small slabs of stacked rocks. He pressed on the grass to flatten it, exposing a masoned wall with an opening behind the tree trunk. "A cliff dwelling!" He clicked the flashlight on his phone and aimed the beam into the dwelling, which was deeper than he imagined it would be. Anxious for a closer look, he wriggled between the tree and the masonry to crawl inside, and he was surprised that he could stand inside it because the ceiling curved upward from the manmade wall. A quick scan with the light revealed that the dwelling was a closed environment with the lone opening through which he had entered. He returned the beam to a section of the far wall on which he had glimpsed unusual colors. As the light's diameter shrunk, he realized the colors were pictographs in alignment, seven in all. At the far left was a double-peaked mountain with vertical crevices, followed by a winged serpent devouring a man. To the right of that, a group of people held hands in a circle of fire, followed by a spiral. Next was the familiar silhouette of Coffee Pot Rock, and beside that, a depiction of the bird geoglyph from the plateau outside. The final image was of a double star. Gregor stood back to take in the scope of the artwork. "This is so cool." He snapped pictures of the pictographs.

When he started to exit the dwelling, he was startled by the cooing of a mourning dove perched on a branch of the juniper tree. "Hey there," he said before contorting himself to extract his body from the dwelling. Once out and seated again on the ledge, he was surprised to see the disturbance had not driven the bird away. Gregor nodded toward the canyon. "Nice view, huh?" He returned his phone to his pocket and looped his arms into the straps of his backpack. "Don't mind me, but I'm going to have to grab that ledge just below you." Gregor crouched and grasped a root with one hand and the ledge with the other. He let his feet drop and found a foothold below. He looked up at the bird, which was still watching him. "I'll see you later."

Gregor worked his way down the wall via the route he had mapped out while on the ledge. Within a few minutes, his feet were just above the plateau, and he could see the tail of the geoglyph beneath him. He moved his foot over and stepped down, careful not to disturb the image. Still facing the wall, he saw the opening of the fissure and the path within to his right. He turned his attention to the plateau. The plants encircling it did block his view of the canyon, save for a gap between a yucca plant and the top of a tall pine tree rooted in the canyon below, which allowed him to see the homes on the hillside he had spotted earlier, as well as an elevated portion of the canyon floor that led to his campsite.

Gregor listened to Nature's breath whispering through the foliage and to his own breath entering and leaving his body. Thinking of the difficulty he had finding seclusion in Los Angeles, he whispered, "This just became my favorite meditation spot." Letting his backpack slide from his shoulders, he inserted his earbuds and played music from his phone. He stepped over the lines of the geoglyph to sit in the middle of the flying bird. Crossing his legs, he rested his hands on his knees and closed his eyes. He felt his heart pulsing to the techno beat of the music, and he focused on peaceful images, letting other thoughts drift from his mind. He imagined himself floating in the still water of a mountain lake that did not chill his skin but embraced it. As the minutes passed, he could sense a vibrating, almost rhythmic accompaniment to the beat of his heart and the tempo of his breath. The hair on his arms and legs tingled, and he lost all other sensation to the growing vibration. He felt as if he were floating and he were losing physical contact with his body. The feeling enraptured him. Never before had he been able to experience the imagery of his mind's creation to that extent.

If Gregor had opened his eyes, he would have seen a faint blue light emanating from his torso.

CHAPTER 8

Travis crouched motionless behind sagebrush, his body covered with branches and leaves in makeshift camouflage. He held his camera to his eye with the lens aimed at an approaching deer. *Perfect.* His index finger pushed down on the shutter release button just as a bubble of gas squeezed from his cheeks. The resultant toot spooked the animal, which jumped before the shutter closed. In the camera's display, he saw a blurry shot of the deer's hind legs in midair. "Stupid soy." He glanced at his watch, which read a quarter past five. "All right. Time to go."

Earlier that day, Travis had tried to join Gregor on the rock climb, after providing him a generous head start, but the twinge in his back while reaching for the first grip persuaded an agendum shift to photography. Now he regretted not working through the pain.

Travis scanned the red rock formation with the telephoto lens of his camera, but his friend was nowhere in sight. He tried calling Gregor on his cell phone, but he had no signal. Walking closer to the red rock, he yelled up the side, "Gregor!" and his voice echoed through the canyon. When he heard no other voice in return, he put his hands to the side of his mouth and tried again. "Gregor!" he shouted with the same lack of result. "Where is he?"

Travis threw up his hands and decided to return to the campsite. Once at his tent, he stuffed some clean clothes into his backpack and drove back to the road. Just short of the pavement, he noticed a tree with a sign nailed to it that read, "The U.S. Forest Service and the U.S. General Services Administration invite you to participate in this special opportunity to own property in the picturesque Verde Valley! This land sale is being conducted by the General Services Administration. Parcel A (119 acres) will be sold to the highest bidder. For more information, visit our website," which was listed at the bottom of the sign.

"I told him we're fine." He snapped a photo of the sign before driving into town.

When she heard a knock on the door, Cadence turned off the hair dryer and looked at the clock. "Crap, he's really early." Wrapped in a towel, she glanced at the clothes she had laid out on the bed and wondered if she had enough time to throw them on. Hearing another knock, she yelled, "Coming!" before answering the door with her body hidden behind it.

"I'm hungry," Travis said as he walked past her and into the room. When she closed the door, he noticed the red skin on her arms and shoulders. "How'd you get the sunburn?"

"I went for a long walk today. What are you doing here?"

Travis dropped his backpack onto the bed. "Mind if I take a shower?"

Cadence hesitated and changed the subject. "Where's Gregor?"

"Hiking." Travis kicked off his shoes and socks. "I couldn't find him. I'll bring him back something from the restaurant. Where do you want to go?"

Cadence used the closet mirror to finish styling her hair. "Listen, I don't really feel like dinner tonight."

"Since Gregor isn't here?" Travis entered the bathroom and continued the conversation through the shut door. "Are you afraid to be alone with me?"

Cadence responded, "I'm just not feeling well."

"Are you sure you're not feeling weird about the two of us. Alone."

"I thought we agreed not to discuss that anymore."

"I'm fine with that, and I haven't told anyone – not even Gregor. I just don't want it to be an unspoken issue between us."

"There's no issue. We were both drunk."

"You had a glass of Chablis."

"I don't want to talk about this anymore. Just drop it." Cadence heard the shower turn on.

Working in the solarium, Mitchell and August sat on the bench together, devising the complete agenda for the upcoming youth conference. Mitchell wrote on a legal pad while August dictated. "Move the Saturday evening devotional to before dinner."

"Are you sure? That will put dinner at eight."

"If they eat first, some of them will nod off during the devotional. I will not have it!" August insisted with a near fist to the legal pad.

Mitchell shook his head. "I just think if they're hungry, they'll lose interest in what we're trying to teach them and focus instead on watching the clock for dinner time."

"Proverbs 27:7, 'The full soul loathes a honeycomb, but to the hungry soul every bitter thing is sweet.' Feeding their souls is my primary concern and should be yours too."

"I'll move it." Mitchell drew an arrow from the dinner to the slot after the devotional. "That's it. I'll input this tomorrow and print it." He stood and walked to the door.

"Why not do it now?" August asked.

"I'm going to head into town for a little bit."

"To see that young lady you introduced me to today?"

Mitchell said, "I'm taking her to dinner."

August left the bench and stared at the canyon beyond the glass enclosure. "Who is she?"

"Someone I met when gathering signatures."

"I assume she signed the petition."

"No, she's from California."

August twisted around to face his son, who refused to look him in the eyes. "Did she enter the shop?"

Mitchell pursed his lips. "She followed her friends."

August lurched forward, warning, "Mitchell, do not be beguiled by the serpent!"

"She's not—"

"Is she a Christian?"

"She came to church today, didn't she?"

August scoffed at his argument, "Was her purpose to worship God or to inveigle you?"

"Would you not welcome either?" Mitchell turned from his father and locked his eyes on a hummingbird flying around the empty feeder that hung from the wall. "I'll get you some food tomorrow, little guy."

"You care more for those birds than you do God," August scolded, but his son entered the house without another word. "His eyes are upon the world."

August remembered a time when he cared too much for the beasts of the world. When he was nine years old, he had a white cat named Spirit, and he loved the cat – so much did he love the cat that he wanted to ensure it would be in Heaven once August arrived. He took the aluminum tub his mother used for soaking venison and filled it with water from the garden hose. With the midday sun as witness, he held Spirit in the water as he repeated the words his father had said many times before, "I now baptize you in the name of the father, the spirit and the holy ghost for the remission of your sins." Even as the cat clawed at his arms, he held it under until he was certain that every furry part of him had been immersed in the water.

"August!" his father yelled, storming toward him. "What are you doing?"

He jumped and raised his hands, but the cat remained in the tub. "I was baptizing Spirit."

His father picked up the limp cat by the nape and screamed, "All you've done is kill it. What were you thinking?"

"I love him," young August explained. "I want him to go to Heaven."

"Animals don't have souls. They're animals!" His father removed the lid from the nearby trashcan and threw the cat inside, slamming the lid down. "See what your love has done!" He pointed to the house. "Now march in there, and tell your mother what you did to her cat."

August started crying. "I don't want to tell her."

His father told him, "I will give you ten minutes to muster the courage to confess your deed to your mother. If you don't, I'll tell her, and then I'm going to take a switch to you for being too weak to own up to your actions." With that, his father walked into the house to let him ponder his course. He could think of no worse punishment than his mother's disappointment, and the thought of her love for him diminishing was unbearable.

August, who at this age did not yet agree with his father that affection for animals was misplaced, opened the lid of the trashcan and looked at the wet cat lying on top of a garbage bag. He picked up Spirit and embraced him as he looked to Heaven in prayer, "God, I don't know if you can hear me over everyone else talking, but if you can, please help me. Don't let mom hate me. I didn't mean to hurt him. Please." As August prayed harder, he squeezed Spirit tighter, expelling water from the cat's lungs. Spirit coughed twice and leapt to the ground. August's initial shock turned to elation. With a huge grin, he jumped up and down, screaming, "Yes! Yes! Yes!" At that moment he realized that God could hear him. Not only could He hear, but He also listened to him – just as He had listened to the great men of the Bible. August turned his attention back to the sky and said, "Thank you, Lord. Thank you, thank you, Lord." Scooping the cat into his arms, he entered the living room to see his mom reading a book and his dad writing in a tablet. "Dad," he called with a smile.

His father began speaking before he looked up, "What do you have to say…" He stopped when he saw the cat struggling to escape his son's arms. "How… How did you do that?"

His mother looked at him and asked, "Do what?

As his father came to touch Spirit, he said, "I asked God. He brought him back for me."

"I… I… I don't know what to say," his father responded.

"What is going on?" his mother asked.

August saw a tear drop from his father's eyes, which he wiped away to hide it from his approaching wife. She petted the cat and asked, "Why is Spirit wet?"

Henceforward, even his father believed he was special and groomed him as such.

The Red Planet Diner's extraterrestrial theme was evident throughout, including the copious flying saucer photos on the walls, grey aliens from thumb-size to two meters tall, lighted spaceships hanging from the ceiling, a UFO fountain near the parking lot, alien landscapes on many surfaces and the clever makeover of an emergency exit sign into a robot with the lights serving as its eyes.

Travis entered the diner and proceeded to the counter when he noticed the young woman from the crystal shop. Iris, her hair freed upon her shoulders, sat at the counter, sipping a purple drink in a martini glass and reading a thick paperback book with a pink highlighter at the ready. Travis approached her and said, "That's a good book."

Iris looked up and exposed the cover. "You've read *Native American Myths and Legends*?"

"Oh, my mistake. It looked like *American Gods*."

"I can see how they'd be easily mistaken, but you're right. That is a good book."

Travis gestured to the stool beside her. "Do you mind if I join you?"

"No, but so you don't get offended in a few minutes, I'm planning to leave when I finish my drink."

"Offense averted," he assured her. "What is that?"

"A vortini, the restaurant's specialty flavored martini named for Sedona's vortexes."

"I'll try one." Travis grabbed a menu from the metal clip in front of him. "What's good to eat here?"

"I like the Vulcan Veggie Burger."

Travis frowned at her. "You're a vegetarian?"

"You have something against vegetarians?"

"No, not at all. As a matter of fact, I had soy bacon this morning."

A petite waitress with ebony skin came to the counter and smiled at Travis. "Can I get you something?" The mid-twenties woman was dressed like a space vixen from a schlocky 1950s science fiction movie – black hair wrapped into an exaggerated beehive, silver knee-high boots and body-hugging, silver dress.

Travis noticed her nametag and answered, "Hi Gia. I'd like the Vulcan Veggie Burger."

"For the side, do you want Solar Fries or the Alien Autopsy Slaw?"

"Let's go with the fries, and to drink, I'll have an E. Tea."

"Beaming right up," Gia said with a pretty smile and a sly look at Iris before leaving.

Returning his attention to Iris, Travis was disappointed to see the vortini flowing past her lips like the last grains of sand in an hourglass. "Is your reading for school or pleasure?"

"Both. I'm working on my doctorate."

"What field?"

"Comparative mythology."

"Interesting. I've never heard of that."

Iris explained, "It relates to the production, purpose and promotion of mythologies in different civilizations throughout the ages, including today."

"What myths are alive today?"

Iris replied, "Name your religion."

Travis raised his eyebrows. "A field of study with an innocuous name but a highly contentious doctrine."

Iris smiled before twisting her stool around. "I need to get home."

As she stepped away from the counter, Travis noticed the shapely legs half concealed by her khaki shorts. "You really shouldn't drive after drinking. Why don't you wait and let me give you a ride home?"

Iris retrieved her purse and helmet from the stool on her other side, "I'm on my bicycle, but I appreciate your concern. Hey, does your friend still want a vortex tour?"

"Of course, we do."

While fastening the helmet to her head, she asked, "All three of you?"

"I wouldn't bank on Cadence. She's not outdoorsy."

"How's tomorrow?"

"Works for me."

"Come to the shop at ten, and we'll leave from there." Iris waved and exited the diner.

He turned back to the counter and saw the waitress. "Is it too late to change my order?"

"It's already on the grill," she answered.

"That's okay. Just throw some bacon on it when it's done. Real bacon."

Gia asked, "You want bacon on your veggie burger?"

"Actually, forget that. Just wrap it to go for my friend, and give me a real hamburger to eat here."

"You got it."

Cadence walked with Mitchell toward the diner when she noticed someone familiar exiting.

"Hi Mitchell," Iris said before giving his companion a look of surprise. "Cadence."

Cadence nodded and returned her greeting, as did Mitchell who darted to get the door before it closed. "You know Iris?" he asked.

"I met her yesterday," Cadence replied while entering the restaurant. "Is she a friend?"

"Not really. We went to the same high school." Mitchell led her to a booth and sat across from her. "Just don't tell my father we came here. He considers it an unholy pantheon to mythological demons from the sky. Although, since the idea of aliens from another planet is so outlandish and most people realize that, he views fascination with the subject as more a distraction from God's service than an imminent threat to the soul. Not like crystals and such."

Cadence smiled at him. "Are you the stereotypical preacher's son who defies his father at every chance?"

Mitchell laughed. "I don't make a habit of it, at least not anymore. In high school, I acted out to combat that uncoolness factor inherent in my ecclesiastic parentage. Now, though, I'd much rather be on the same side as my father."

"I guess it's easier."

He handed her a menu from the metal clip at the end of the

table. "That, and I honestly believe as he does on most every issue of spiritual import. What did you think of him?"

"He seems nice," Cadence answered, perusing the menu.

With a tilt of his head, Mitchell said, "You're being less than truthful."

"No, seriously," Cadence insisted before relenting. "Well from what I saw on stage and during our brief meeting, I couldn't tell what he's like in real life. What's good here?"

"In real life?"

"When he's not at work. I'm sure he's more relaxed."

"No. He's actually what you saw – every conversation a sermon, every moral question a black or white answer. I really like the Martian meatloaf."

Travis approached the booth. "Cadence, I'm so glad you're feeling better. Must've been one of those twenty-four-minute bugs."

Cadence flushed with embarrassment. "Travis, what are you doing—"

Mitchell asked, "Were you ill?"

Cadence didn't want to lie to Mitchell, but she had to cover her tracks with Travis. "I was just a little tired earlier. Too much sun."

Travis extended his hand to Mitchell. "I'm Travis Harper."

Mitchell replied with a smile and a handshake. "Mitchell Briar."

Travis squinted at him. "You look familiar."

"Have you been to my church?"

"You're a priest?"

"Reverend, actually."

Travis clapped his hands once. "You're the guy handing out flyers on the sidewalk."

"Yes, we're petitioning—"

"Politics never interested me," Travis assured him before he wasted his breath with explanation. "Cadence, we're going to tour those vortexes tomorrow. Did you want to come stare at air with us?"

"She can't," Mitchell answered, to Cadence's surprise. "I asked her to accompany me on a tour of genuine sites in the city." He looked to her as if urging her to legitimize his statement.

Adrift in Mitchell's eyes, Cadence pulled her gaze away to see his right hand resting on the table. She placed her hand in his and told Travis, "I've already made plans."

"Okay. You two have fun. Cadence, give a call when you want to hang." He offered a hybrid salute/wave with his right hand.

Once Travis stepped beyond earshot, Mitchell told Cadence, "I apologize for my presumption, but I do want to take you sightseeing tomorrow, if you'd like."

"I'd love to," Cadence answered with a wry smile. "I can't believe you lied."

Mitchell replied, "It was a chronologic misrepresentation. I had every intention of asking you during dinner, and I anticipated your answer." He nodded toward the door. "Your friend is leaving." She turned her head but was too late to see him. "What's the story with you two?"

Cadence's eyes widened at the question. "Story?"

"How do you know him?"

"Through Gregor. You saw him yesterday. They've been best friends since junior high."

"And how do you know Gregor?"

"I met him about a year ago."

"On a date?"

Cadence laughed off the notion. "Oh no. I was at the hospital he works at... visiting a friend. We started talking and just hit it off. He introduced me to Travis shortly afterwards." She diverted the conversation, saying, "We've talked enough about me. Tell me more about you."

Mitchell inhaled a deep breath. "Greatly abridged version, I'm a fourth-generation minister. I finished seminary school and received my master of divinity degree. Last year I returned to Sedona to learn from a master, my father. I'm living with him right now, but that situation will change soon. I want to start my own church, some-where away from here. Maybe Phoenix."

"What about your mom?"

"I never knew her." Mitchell looked down at his clasped hands on the table. "Have you ever heard of amniotic fluid embolism?"

"No."

"During birth, some of my amniotic fluid entered her blood stream. My father likes to say I poisoned her."

Cadence opened her mouth, but she didn't know how to respond to such a cruel revelation.

The sun clutched the sky with fatiguing fingers as Gregor awoke on the plateau with a sharp pain in his left shoulder blade. Before opening his eyes, he stretched his body and realized a strange sen-sation of exposure. He jerked up to see that he was naked within the geoglyph. Underneath him lay his clothes and his amulet, the source of the pain. "What on Earth?" He didn't remember lying down for a nap, much less disrobing.

His memory retold his last conscious thoughts of meditation and total euphoria, and even now he felt an almost drunk elation. He remembered vivid dreams of scattered images flashing before him as if seeing the world in one view – not only seeing, but know-ing it through other senses.

For years Gregor meditated at least once a day to help him relax, understand his place in the universe and push away the negative forces that threatened to drive his life. Although he preferred an outdoor venue that would allow a greater connection to the Earth's vibrancy, he often settled for a modified lotus on a rug in his apart-ment. Whenever he could, however, he hiked to the top of Runyon Canyon or drove to the ocean overlooks in Santa Monica, but no previous venue had ever aroused the overwhelming ecstasy now resonating through his being.

Turning his attention outward, Gregor noticed the lateness of the day. "I need to get down before I lose the sunlight." He dressed himself, still wondering why he had removed his clothes, and he returned the amulet to his neck before walking to the fissure. He worried the path within the fissure would narrow at some point, forcing him to find another way down, but it remained passable until it ended at an upward protrusion of the red rock that looked like a jagged canine tooth. He looked down to realize he was still at least four meters above the sloping canyon floor. He thought of jumping but doubted he could land without injury. He removed his long-sleeve shirt and tied an arm around the protruding rock. After finding a T-shirt in his backpack to put on, Gregor crouched as low as he could, clenched the body of the tied shirt and stepped off the pathway. He waited to stabilize before moving his hands down the makeshift rope, but as he started to descend, the weight of his body helped the jagged rock cut into the constricting sleeve, and he fell to the ground.

"Ooh," he exhaled, clutching the torn shirt. He looked up the wall of the canyon and grinned. Sure enough, the path and the plateau were undetectable from the canyon floor. The shape of the rocks on the outside of the path blended into the rock on the inside so that no perceptible distance existed between them, forming a natural optical illusion. Focusing on where the plateau would be, he could see only the plants.

As dusk settled in, he returned to camp and found Travis eating by lantern light. "Hey," Gregor greeted.

Travis responded, "There you are. Where have you been?"

Gregor sat on the other side of the lantern. "I was meditating, and I fell asleep."

Travis nodded to a paper bag. "I brought you food."

"Hey, I think I found a vortex."

"How could you tell?" Travis smirked. "Aren't they invisible like fern seeds?"

Gregor bit into a sandwich from the paper bag. "I could just sense it."

CHAPTER 9

Gregor kept his eyes closed while showering, as always, preferring to use his sense of touch as a guide so that he didn't have to look at his body. After arriving at the motel earlier that morning, Travis had asked Cadence out for coffee, leaving him alone to prepare for the day. The streaming droplets trilled his skin on contact, projecting faint undulations of sound to his bones. Humming in harmony, he wondered about the odd acoustics in the bathroom, but only for a moment before his mind drifted into memory.

At the age of thirteen, he moved in with a new foster family and transferred to a different junior high school – which evoked a much deeper dread in the transfigured boy than other children of his age. The classmates at his previous school were cruel to him, as all children were, but he knew them and their limitations. His introduction to the devil he didn't know began with gym class, spent learning the basics of badminton. To his relief, little attention was paid to the new kid, at first. While the other boys changed into their gym attire in the locker room, he ducked into a bathroom stall to replace his jeans and long-sleeve shirt with sweat pants and a sweatshirt. Once gym class was over, however, the coach insisted

everyone shower. Gregor tried to slip away to the bathroom undetected, but the coach – a snarling hate crime, inebriated on just two
fingers of power – called him out.

"Where are you going, twig?" Coach Gibbs inquired.

Flushed, Gregor answered, "To the bathroom."

"Pee in the shower. You got just a few minutes before next period."

Gregor looked at the showers. The boys were already starting to
stare at him. He turned back to the coach and said, "I didn't sweat."

With a face gnarled by the anger of questioned authority and
forsaking even a trace of empathy, Coach Gibbs growled, "Get your
clothes off, and hit the showers now!" The coach hooked a chunky
paw onto the hem of the boy's shirt and pulled it off in a single
determined jerk. Once he saw Gregor's skin, he dropped the shirt,
mouth agape. "What the hell happened to you?" he asked, punctuated with a snicker. "You look like a melted candle."

Gregor crossed his arms over his torso. Gasps and laughter bel-
lowing from the showers behind him, he saw a wide grin spread
across the coach's face, releasing a raspy, baying laugh of pure derision. Gregor bolted from the locker room without even stooping
to pick up his shirt. He ran across the courts and found shelter
underneath the bleachers, where he crouched on the filthy floor,
hugging his knees.

A moment later, a boy appeared at the side of the bleachers.
Catching a glimpse of him, Gregor turned away, hoping he would
leave. The boy didn't leave and instead crawled, dragging a schoolbag, to sit beside him. "You dropped this," the boy said, handing
him his shirt. Without looking at the giver, Gregor snatched it and
slipped it on. "Coach Gibbs is an ass. Don't let him get to you."

Gregor shifted his eyes to the boy with the damp hair and perfect face. "That's really easy for you to say."

The boy was silent for a moment before rummaging through
his schoolbag. He handed a comic book to Gregor. "Do you like
X-Men?"

Gregor took the comic and answered with the question, "What is it?"

The boy explained, "They're people who are different from everyone else. Outcasts. They use their uniqueness to help others. Well, the villains don't, but you get my point. Read it, and maybe you can figure out how to use your uniqueness to help yourself and others."

Gregor wiped away his last tear. "I like that."

The boy extended his hand. "What's your name?"

"Gregor," he answered, shaking his hand.

"I'm Travis," the boy said over the class bell. "What's your next class?"

"Social studies."

"Come on, I'll walk you."

Gregor smiled and followed him from the bleachers.

Gregor and Travis entered the Sedona Vortex shop to find Lily Wickline inserting the cash drawer into the register. As she turned their way, her radiant smile, like a beacon for lost travelers, welcomed them. "Good morning, boys."

While both men had backpacks slung over their shoulders and hiking boots on their feet, Travis sported a sleeveless T-shirt and short pants that displayed his muscular arms and legs, and Gregor wore a thin, long-sleeved shirt and cargo pants. "Good morning," the two men said in unison.

"Iris will be here shortly," Lily told them. "Are you two excited about the vortex tour?"

Travis answered in a sarcasm undetected by her, "I am thrilled. But I did have a difficult time convincing Gregor to come along."

Gregor frowned at him. "He's kidding about that. I definitely am looking forward to it."

"I know you'll both enjoy it. Iris is a wonderful tour guide, and contact with a vortex can be life-changing. People come back year after year – or move here like I did – to recapture the feeling." Lily cocked her head at Gregor. "You, by the way, are positively glowing."

Embarrassed, Gregor told her, "I think I had my first vortex experience yesterday."

"That's wonderful!" she exclaimed with the jubilation of a baby announcement. "I'm so happy for you, and I'm glad you're wearing the crystal. You can take that glow home with you."

Gregor touched the lazulite hanging from his neck. "I've become accustomed to the weight. I don't even notice it now."

"Well, I notice, and it brings out your eyes," joked Travis, handing Lily a credit card.

Gregor put his hand to his back pocket. "Let me pay for half," he said, but Travis waved off his offer.

As Lily rang up the sale, she asked, "How is Cadence?"

Travis smirked. "Snippy as ever."

Lily handed the card back to Travis as the front door chimed. "Could you tell her I'd like to speak to her again?"

"There's our Sherpa," said Travis, his eyes now on the front door.

Wearing a dark green tank top, khaki shorts and hiking boots, Iris held the door open, asking, "Are you guys ready to go?"

Travis hurried to the door. "Ready to lead. Ready to follow. Never quit."

Iris asked, "What?"

Gregor turned back to Lily and said, "I'll let her know," before he exited the shop.

"That's the Navy Seal motto," Travis explained.

Iris asked, "You were a Navy Seal?"

"Once a seal, always a seal. But no. However, I did an intensive two-week Navy Seal workout regimen taught by one."

She shook her head and pointed to her roofless, all-terrain vehicle. "That's my car."

"Shotgun!" Travis called, jumping into the passenger seat.

Backing out of the parking slot, Iris explained, "The tour includes stops at five vortexes."

From the backseat, Gregor asked, "How many are there?"

She looked at him in the rearview mirror. "Ten in all, but we just hit the most scenic ones." She eyed his reflection for a beat longer than needed, prompting Gregor to look away.

Leaving a trail of billowing dust behind him, Mitchell drove his car to a stable at the end of a dirt road and came to a procrastinated stop. As the dirty cloud overtook his car, he exited and jaunted to the passenger side to open the door for Cadence.

Wearing a yellow dress and a wide-rim hat, she took his hand and thanked him. "Where are we? Is that a barn?"

Mitchell laughed. "It's a horse stable."

"Seriously? I've never seen a horse before. Not up close."

"You're in for a treat then. You're going to ride one today. Well, not a horse exactly."

"A pony?"

"You'll see." Mitchell led her into the stable, and he nodded to a farrier. The older man disappeared into the first stall and returned a few seconds later holding the reins to an animal with remarkable coloring. Its face was tan with faint black stripes that deepened behind the ears and one-quarter way down the neck, where the coat became pure white. The white continued half the length of the body before changing once more to match the top of the neck, and the tail was white with black tips. "Desano here is actually a zorse."

With a radiance of wonder, Cadence muttered, "What on Earth?" She raised her hand to touch the zorse but stopped herself.

"You can touch him," Mitchell assured her, and with his hand, he pressed her palm against the animal's neck. "His father was a zebra, and mama was a horse."

"He's absolutely beautiful."

"A friend of mine breeds them. Of course, my father thinks they're an abomination – interspecies and all." Mitchell laughed at the timidity of her touch. "You're going to have to become more familiar with him than that. This one's yours to ride."

The farrier offered her the reins, but Cadence backed away, shaking her head. "I don't know how to ride."

"Desano is mellow for a zorse – perfect for the virgin equestrian." He nodded to a zorse that was tan with black stripes. "I'm riding the mean one. That's Brown Recluse."

"Here we are," Iris proclaimed, arms outstretched, once she led Gregor and Travis to the top of Bell Rock's sliding base. From their vantage point, they could see the vast, rusty valley floor, mottled with green shrubbery and occasional massive rocky obtrusions, including Cathedral Rock, Courthouse Butte and Chapel Rock.

"Cool," Travis removed the lens cap from his camera and started snapping pictures of the view.

Gregor whispered, "It's amazing."

Iris told him, "We'll stay here for fifteen minutes, if you want to meditate."

"Where's the vortex?" Gregor asked.

"Pick your spot. The vortex encompasses all of Bell Rock."

Travis watched as his friend stretched out his hands with palms facing downward. "Look over here!" Travis yelled, and when Gregor turned to face him, he took his picture. "And here's Gregor next to a vortex."

Gregor shook his head and paced around a bit more before sitting with his legs crossed and eyes shut.

"Beautiful," Travis said from behind Iris, who was now sitting near the edge overlooking Highway 179. Although he was smiling at her, he clarified, "The view," and he joined her, cradling the camera in his lap.

Iris pointed to Gregor with a tilt of her head. "Don't you want to experience the vortex?"

"I'm into actual sightseeing," he said, and while she faced forward, he scanned her body, seeing not a single unkissable spot. "Are all the women in your family named for flowers?"

With half a smile, she responded, "I know. It's embarrassing. My grandmother's name was Pussy Willow."

Travis gasped at the name. "Are you serious?"

Iris erupted in laughter. "I'm kidding. It was Rose."

Still seated, Gregor interrupted with, "Are you sure this is a vortex? I don't feel it."

Iris turned her body toward him and moved her palms up the length of her torso. "You have to relax, and let the vortex come into you."

"I didn't have to try so hard last night," Gregor muttered.

Travis asked her, "What do people do here for fun... at night?"

"Not much really. No clubs worth mentioning. How long will you be in town?"

"We're leaving on Sunday."

"You guys might want to come to a party my friend is hosting on Friday. She just started dabbling in party promotions, and she's calling this one *Rave in a Cave*."

"Sounds... damp."

"It's a cool cave – Shaman's Dome, a little south of here. She hired a bartender and DJ, and she has people distributing flyers at clubs and college campuses in Phoenix to promote it."

"Sounds like the place to be. It's a date." He was about to add that he hoped he wouldn't have to wait that long to have a date with her, when Gregor interrupted again.

Now standing above them, he said, "I'm ready to go whenever you two are."

"Any luck with the vortex?" Iris asked.

Gregor answered, "I felt a little something, but not what I expected."

Helped to her feet by Travis, Iris told him, "Maybe the next one will be better for you."

Cadence and Mitchell rode the zorses up Wilson Mountain, answering questions about their lives along the way. Although she was frightened at first, she acclimated to the ride and was beginning to develop quite an affinity for Desano. Mitchell, on the other hand, had to coax Brown Recluse from galloping spurts to a pacing gait four times during the trek. Arriving at an overlook high up the mountain, Mitchell dismounted and tied his zorse to a tree.

"This is amazing!" Cadence remarked of the Verde Valley panorama before them.

Mitchell helped her from the saddle. "That's why we're here, to see God's artistry." He tied Desano to another tree before joining Cadence at the rim of the overlook, where she sat with feet dangling a kilometer above the valley. "You're a bit close to the edge, don't you think?"

"Where's your faith?" Cadence replied with a smile, patting the ground beside her.

Mitchell hesitated before sitting an arm's length away from her and scooting to the edge. He leaned back with his hands planted behind him as he pushed the inside of his knees to the rim and let his feet drop to where he would not look.

She pointed to a feature west of downtown. "Have you ever gone to the top of that?"

"Coffee Pot Rock? No, I'm not a rock climber," Mitchell replied.

Cadence took the opportunity to put a hand atop his, caressing his large fingers. "Thank you for bringing me here. It's something I couldn't have imagined."

"Ever since the world was created," he said as if he were writing in his head, "people have marveled at the majesty of the Earth and sky. They have borne witness to God's hand – His eternal power – in the beauty of nature, and yet so many refuse Him credit."

Cadence asked, "Do you see God everywhere?"

"Don't you? Works of art are not self-created. Starry Night didn't paint itself."

A bright green hot-air balloon drifted toward them from the east, diverting Cadence's attention. "Look over there." The balloon was no more than a base-run hit from the side of the mountain and appeared to be mirroring its outline.

Mitchell asked, "Have you ever ridden in one before?"

Cadence shook her head. "I've always wanted to."

"Then that tops tomorrow's agenda," Mitchell proclaimed. "If you're up for it."

Cadence squeezed his hand. "I would love that."

As they watched the balloon pass by at their exact altitude, Mitchell asked, "Did you know that the first manned hot-air balloon was invented by a priest?"

"I didn't," she answered, exchanging waves with a little girl in the balloon.

"He was Portuguese or Brazilian. I can't remember which." He looked at her and said, "I pick the prettiest part of the sky, and I melt into the wing and then into the air, till I'm just soul on a sunbeam."

She smiled at him, looking into his eyes. "That's beautiful."

He clarified, "It's a quote from Richard Bach, author of Jonathan Livingston Seagull."

"I always meant to read that," she said with her eyes falling. "Mitchell, do you undoubtedly believe our souls continue on after our bodies die?"

The young man laughed. "I'd be a terribly directionless Christian if I didn't."

"What do you think it... feels like?"

"To die?" Mitchell took a moment before answering. "I think we're in bondage during this life, although most people don't realize it – just like an animal that's been raised in a cage doesn't perceive its confinement because it knows nothing else, and it doesn't understand the feeling of freedom that awaits beyond the bars of the cage. I believe our bodies are cages for our souls, and once the soul is released, we truly understand freedom. Of course, the damned will only replace their corporal prison for one of everlasting fire, but those who love God will experience pure joy for the first time and for eternity."

Cadence squeezed his hand. "I hope you're right."

He wrapped an arm around her shoulder, and they watched the balloon drift away.

CHAPTER 10

"I will hold briefly," August said into the phone. Seated in his church office, he tapped the eraser of a wooden pencil upon the desktop, while he locked into a stare with the bronze effigy of crucified Jesus hanging on the wall in front of him. As had happened before, he saw on Jesus' tortured body his own face, with the same skyward gaze of utter dejection at a God who ignored his pleas. He stood and walked toward the figure, his bronze countenance straining into increasing agony with each step. He reached out and touched the cold body.

"August," Richard Glavin's voice beckoned from the speakerphone.

Startled, August required a second to reacquaint with reality before he rushed to the phone. "Richard," he responded and picked up the receiver. When he turned back to the wall, Jesus' face was again staring at the ceiling. "Any word from ACC?"

"Not yet. Remember it's a big decision. Launching a new show is a huge investment."

"I understand. I just am not comfortable being in limbo."

"I'll let you know as soon as I hear anything," Richard assured him before hanging up.

August dropped the receiver from his ear. Turning from the desk, he was startled by the quiet approach of a clean-cut boy with red hair. "Who are you?"

The boy patted his chest. "It's me, Reverend. Lucas McAbel. From Colorado."

"Lucas McAbel." August squinted. "You have grown. I barely recognize you."

Lucas grinned so wide the corners of his mouth must have nicked his cheekbones. "Seven inches this year."

Mirroring Lucas' grin, but to a more reasonable degree, August put a hand on the boy's shoulder. "You are as tall as I am now. How old are you now, son?"

Lucas' obvious elation beamed from him like a full moon in January. "Fourteen."

"Why did Mrs. Chapman not announce you?"

"I think she fell asleep on the phone."

August shook his head and waved him to a chair in front of his desk. "You are a bit early for the youth conference." The reverend returned to his desk chair. "It opens on Friday."

"I know, but I was kind of hoping you'd let me help you with it, so we got here early."

August was gratified by his voluntarism, perhaps applying disproportionate credit toward his edification of the boy during the past several summers. He envisioned such selfless dedication to endeavors of morality would fashion Lucas into an exemplary soldier of God – maybe even a leader in his likeness – and he wanted to encourage that path. "Certainly, I could always use the assistance. Where is your father?"

"He's getting a hotel room. I didn't want to wait, so he dropped me off here first."

"Your eagerness is commendable. You could start by helping me compile the educational packets. Mrs. Chapman finds proper collation challenging." Concerned with the boy's motives, he warned,

"Your service will not predetermine your victory in the Bible Bowl this weekend."

Lucas laughed and assured him, "I don't need no help. What's the prize this year?"

"An FS2000 semi-automatic." August held a smile in anticipation of the boy's response.

"That's so cool!"

Releasing a grin, August bragged about his prize choice, "It will put some deer on the table. It is much nicer than that crossbow from last year."

As if transgressed, Lucas refuted with, "Hey, I really love the crossbow. I still use it. Can I see the gun?"

August raised his palm. "Patience. Besides, it has yet to arrive. Have you been studying?"

Lucas clasped his hands behind his head and stretched his legs before him. "Test me."

August began, "For God so loved—"

"John 3:16. That's not a test."

"Just providing you a warm-up. 'For there shall arise false Christs and false prophets—'"

"Mathew 24:24," Lucas responded.

August quoted another verse with the vigor of exhortation, "For we wrestle not against flesh and blood, but against principalities, against powers, against the rulers of the darkness of this world, against spiritual wickedness in high places."

"Ephesians 6:12."

"And he said unto them, I beheld Satan as lightning fall from heaven."

"Luke 9… 10. Verse… seventeen."

"Verse eighteen," he corrected, and Lucas scowled at his mistake. August gave him the smile of a proud father and said, "Those Colorado deer better start hiding now."

As Iris, Gregor and Travis trampled an upward path etched into the side of Airport Mesa, a biplane accelerated on the runway above them and exposed its belly to them when it escaped gravity just over their heads. After the engine's rumble subsided, Iris said, "This was the final destination on our tour. What did you guys think?"

Travis declared, "Best tour ever."

Gregor, however, was much more subdued. "The scenery was definitely beautiful, but I am disappointed that I didn't feel more."

Iris suggested, "Perhaps you weren't being receptive enough."

Gregor was unsure if her words were intended to be constructive or derisive, but he gave her the benefit of the doubt. "I did feel something. I just thought the energy would be stronger."

Iris tried again to quell his concern. "I think the vortex energy ebbs and flows, like a tide. Maybe it's just low tide for them right now."

"Not the time to surf," Travis remarked. "Maybe you should try boogie-boarding it."

"Very helpful, Travis," Gregor said. "Thank you."

Iris stopped walking and asked the dejected believer, "Can I be honest with you?"

"Of course," Travis answered, while Gregor nodded his head.

With the hesitation of a parent revealing the truth of Santa Claus to a young child, Iris spit out, "Sedona's biggest industry is tourism. It's known for vortexes, and people come from all over to visit them. They're lucrative tourist attractions, but they don't actually exist."

Travis exclaimed, "I knew it!"

"That's not true," Gregor disputed, garnering a surprised glance from Travis.

Iris argued, "You're being seduced into a mythology propagated solely to promote tourism, like the Loch Ness Monster."

"Hey, Nessie's real!" Travis exclaimed. "The Smithsonian website even has a page devoted to her, and when you think about the fact that the coelacanth had been considered extinct for 65 million years when one was caught off the coast of South Africa last century, a plesiosaur surviving the dinosaur extinction is not so far-fetched."

Iris redirected, "What I'm trying to say is that the land here is beautiful, and sure, you can feel connected to it if you want to, but it's a one-way connection. The red rocks aren't feeding you energy. That truly is a myth."

Gregor said, "You don't believe in the vortexes, and yet you profit from them?"

"I lead the tours to help out my mother. Besides – present company excepted – people usually walk away feeling better and more alive, so wouldn't you consider that worthwhile?"

Gregor pointed to her opal necklace. "Why do you wear that amulet?"

Frowning, she answered, "Because we sell them."

"Does your mother feel the same way about the vortexes?"

"My mom's a little nuts, if you hadn't noticed. She wholeheartedly believes in the vortexes and all matters metaphysical."

"There's nothing wrong with your mother," Gregor said in a manner implying that fault lay instead with her daughter. "I found a vortex near our campsite that's much stronger than any of these we visited today. You wouldn't doubt if you felt that one."

"You only felt something because you wanted to and believed that you would."

"I didn't imagine my experience. It was real!"

Travis seemed stunned to hear his friend raise his voice. "Whoa, Gregor, calm down."

Iris told Gregor, "Listen, I've lived here my entire life. I've been to every vortex on the map, and I have tried over and over again, year after year, to feel something. Anything. But there's nothing there."

Gregor shook his head. "You can't deny existence based on poorly executed attempts at perceiving it."

"Are you suggesting I don't know how to meditate? I teach classes!"

Travis tried again to diffuse the volatile conversation. "Can I interrupt?"

Gregor and Iris turned to him and yelled a unified, "No!"

Gregor said, "I'm not talking about meditation. Your attempts at channeling energy from the vortexes might have been based on a flawed understanding of our connection to that energy, or pure disbelief."

Iris replied, "Your arrogance is infuriating."

In like tone, Gregor responded, "So is your skepticism. And I'm not arrogant. I'm right." He calmed his voice to say, "Look, my intention is not arrogance but to open your eyes to the possibility that you're wrong."

"Well, that doesn't sound arrogant at all. What about the possibility that you're wrong?"

Gregor challenged her, "Prove it to me."

"You prove it to me."

"Done," he said as if the debate were won. "Visit my vortex and meditate with me. If you truly feel nothing, I'll concede my experience was all in my head and vortexes are total myth."

Iris stopped walking and crossed her arms. "Where is this mysterious vortex to which you're so connected?"

"Near our campsite. It's up a canyon wall, on a plateau with a geoglyph of a bird."

"There are no geoglyphs around here," she told him.

Gregor raised his index finger. "This I can prove right now." He pulled his phone from his pocket and zipped through the photos to find one of the plateau. "Take a look." He handed her the phone.

"Oh my god. It's a negative geoglyph, like the Nazca Lines in Peru."

"Negative?" asked Gregor.

"It's cut into the ground as opposed to formed by rocks placed on the ground in a pattern, which would be a positive geoglyph. Geoglyphs have been found all over the world, from North and South America to Australia and even Iceland. What's really amazing about them, though, is that nearly all of them can only be seen from high above. Why would ancient people have spent so much time working on these massive works of art that none of them would ever get to enjoy?"

"Maybe they were trying to capture someone else's attention," said Gregor.

Without entertaining the notion, Iris asked, "Where did you say you found this?"

Delighted by her curiosity, he tantalized her, "It's hidden and pretty difficult to reach."

"I need to see it," Iris insisted. Continuing to walk, she flipped through the other pictures until she saw the image of the pictographs, eliciting a gasp. "Where did you find these?"

Gregor sidled her to see the photo to which she was referring. "That's in a cliff dwelling I found higher up on the same canyon wall."

Iris zoomed in for a closer view of each pictograph. "These are amazing." Now approaching the car, she looked behind her and said, "Travis…"

Travis, who had been following, remarked, "Oh, am I suddenly part of the conversation now?"

They apologized to him, and Iris handed him the keys to her car. "Would you mind driving us back to the shop? I want to examine these pictures."

Taking the keys without answering, he unlocked her car and scooted behind the wheel, while they jumped in the backseat. "I'd like to change my answer about the tour now."

Of the double-peaked mountain pictograph, Iris said, "This looks familiar, but I can't place it." She moved the winged serpent pictograph into the frame. "That's Quetzalcoatl! He's an Aztec god... in Sedona."

Gregor said, "I didn't know the Aztec came this far north."

"They didn't – at least not that we ever knew. Very early in their civilization, however, they were more nomadic, and they are known to have traveled throughout Northern Mexico before finally settling in Central Mexico." Iris pointed to the pictograph of the people in a circle of fire holding hands. "I don't understand this image of the people in the fire."

"Human sacrifice?" Gregor asked, and as their eyes connected, so did their thighs. Puzzled by the effortless invasion of her personal space, he retracted his offending leg.

Iris smiled at his reaction. "I guess it's possible, but they usually liked to see the blood and offer the victim's heart to the sun god. They would sometimes cook and eat the bodies."

"You think they're being cooked?"

"No, because they're standing and holding hands?"

"Like they willingly entered the fire," Gregor suggested, staring at the green light in her eyes for several seconds before speaking again. "Listen, I'm sorry about earlier. Honestly, I don't know what came over me."

"That's okay," Iris whispered. "You're just passionate." She returned to the subject of interest. "I really would like to see this dwelling."

"The climb is pretty difficult," Gregor warned.

Iris beamed in his direction. "In the middle of difficulty lies opportunity."

"Albert Einstein," he said, recalling the quotation's originator. "Do you want to go now?"

With a heavy foot on the brake, Travis announced, "We're here."

Iris returned the phone to Gregor. "I have a meditation class in a few. How's tomorrow?"

"I can do that."

Travis exited, and handed her the keys. "Do you want us to meet you back here tomorrow?

"Where's your campsite? I'll come to you."

"That works for me," Travis said with a devilish grin. "We're near Boynton Canyon."

"But we went off-road," Gregor said. "I'm not sure how you would find it."

"I've an idea." Travis retrieved his camera from his backpack and showed her a picture he had taken the day before of the land sale sign. "Look for this sign."

"Perfect." With a wave to them both, Iris said, "See you boys tomorrow."

The two men watched her enter her mother's shop, waiting for the glass door to wave her inside before turning toward Travis' car. Gregor thought of a question for Iris. "Oh, hang on one second," he said and bolted toward the shop.

"What are you doing?"

"I forgot to ask her something." When Gregor entered the shop, he saw Iris talking to her mother, who was behind the counter holding up a letter. "I'm sorry to interrupt."

"Not at all," Lily said, waving her letter hand to dismiss the notion. "How was the tour?"

"It was wonderful. Thank you. Your daughter's a great guide."

Iris laughed at his revision of the day's events. "Did you forget something?"

"I wanted to ask…" His cell phone rang. "It's Travis," he said before answering it.

"What are you doing?" Travis asked from inside the car.

"Asking for the nearest hardware store. I'll be right out." Gregor disconnected the call.

Iris pointed and said, "Three blocks that way."

"Thanks. See you tomorrow."

Noticing her mother's grin once Gregor left, Iris rolled her eyes. "Erase those dirty thoughts from your mind. He's showing me a cliff dwelling he found. Now what were you saying?"

"What do you mean?"

Iris nodded to the paper in her mother's hand. "About the letter."

"Oh." Lily's demeanor turned to anger. She thrust the letter into the air and exclaimed, "Now he's mailing letters to our customers!"

Iris needed no clarification to know the pronoun stood for August Briar, her mother's most ardent harasser. She took the letter and read it. Past the personalized salutation was text condemning the addressee as unchristian for supporting an establishment "devoted to the worship of the Earth and the supplantation of God with self." The recipient was urged to repent and follow the path back to Christ or suffer an eternity of conflagrant flesh.

"I've had at least a dozen clients today tell me they received this letter. Not only that, none of them have received the newsletters that I sent out last week. If I hadn't dropped them off directly at the post office, I'd swear he switched them."

After dinner Cadence and Mitchell walked to her motel so they could enjoy the town's unique nighttime ambience. While Sedona retained an otherworldliness after the sunset, it did lose much of its visual character, as the red landscape turned to shades of silver and gray. In every distance, the waning moon brushed an argent silhouette onto the hulking earthen monuments that surrounded the town like ever-vigilant sentries at their posts.

While passing a coffee shop with patrons spilling into wrought-iron chairs on the sidewalk, Mitchell asked, "I've been avoiding this question, but how long are you staying in Sedona?"

Cadence loved walking side-by-side with Mitchell because it gave her the opportunity to stare at his profile, which was flawless. In fact, she almost preferred it to a frontal view. "Until Sunday. Why is that a difficult question?"

"Because it stamps an expiration date on our time together." Mitchell shook his head. "I just realized how desperate those words probably sound."

Cadence stopped walking and waited a second for him to look at her before she said, "Maybe from other lips, but I liked hearing them from yours."

Smiling, he took her hand and continued walking. "So as your personal tour guide, I need to know other excursions I can plan to ensure this vacation becomes a cherished memory."

"You've already done that. But I would like to see the Grand Canyon."

"A popular destination. Let's put that on the agenda for Wednesday."

"Perfect." She clutched his arm with her free hand. "I've always wanted to see it. Unbelievable what a river can create over millions of years."

Mitchell looked at her with concern. "Unbelievable because it's not true."

"What do you mean?"

"Cadence, don't be deceived by the atheistic forebears of science." Mitchell released her hand. "The Earth is only six-thousand-years old."

Uncertain if he were joking, Cadence laughed, asking, "What?"

"These supposed scientists have elevated carbon-dating to a factual technique when it's actually, at best, a greatly flawed misinterpretation and, at worst, an attempt to fully discredit the Bible and wipe God from the face of the Earth."

Cadence was stuck on his comment about the Earth's age. "What about the dinosaurs?"

Mitchell explained, "I don't dispute that dinosaurs – if you want to call them that – once roamed the Earth, but I do repudiate the belief that they didn't coexist with man. The Bible and other ancient texts spoke of dragons and sea monsters. They didn't use the word 'dinosaur' because that term wasn't invented until 1841. I also dispute that dinosaurs are somehow different creatures than the lizards that roam the Earth today. Did you know that reptiles can continue to grow their entire lives, dependent on a steady food supply?"

With the lighted sign of her motel now in view, Cadence tried to think of ways she could turn this conversation around so it would end in a long-awaited kiss. "No, I didn't."

"The climate on Earth before the Great Flood was much different than it is today," Mitchell continued. "It was unpolluted, and diseases were not at all prevalent. People lived much longer, as did animals, including reptiles like lizards. The longer life spans allowed the lizards to grow huge, and their bones are what scientists now call dinosaur fossils."

"Wow, that's really an interesting way to look at it," Cadence responded, still processing the feasibility of his viewpoint. "So do you think the flood killed off the giant lizards?"

"Many died out with the flood, but ocean dwellers survived. As for the land dwellers, either the small young or eggs were carried aboard the ark. As the world dried after the flood, diseases spread due to the exposed decaying plants and animals. People and animals stopped living so long, and eventually lizards were unable to grow to huge proportions because of disease and a limited food supply. Regardless of what scientists would have you believe, an asteroid did not kill them off." As he stepped onto the motel driveway, he frowned, adding, "I'm surprised so much of what I've said seems to be news to you. In what denomination were you raised?"

Cadence had hoped the subject would not be broached, unsure how she would address it. Resigned to end the night without feeling his lips on hers, she paused before replying, "Honestly, yesterday was the first time I had been to church since college – maybe even high school."

Mitchell kept his eyes forward in a vain attempt to hide his disappointment. "Why is that?"

"Since I moved out on my own to California, I just don't seem to get around to it anymore. None of my friends go. It's just not something we do."

Mitchell told her, "Maybe you have the wrong friends."

"No, I wouldn't say that. Gregor is a really good guy. Atheist, though, so you two probably wouldn't get along. Travis is okay too, I guess."

Reaching the motel door, he faced her and asked, "Have you at least been baptized?"

"Of course," she replied, hoping the answer would earn a kiss. "When I was a baby."

"You're Catholic?"

Seeing his slight grimace, Cadence surmised she should have kept her previous answer to two words. "I was raised Catholic, but I don't really identify myself as such now."

"Good." He nodded to the door. "I guess we'll continue this conversation tomorrow."

"What time?" asked Cadence.

"How's 10?" When she nodded, he walked away, saying, "Have a good night."

Disappointed, she searched her purse for the key until interrupted by the call of her name. She turned around and into Mitchell's arms. He did indeed kiss her, and it was spectacular.

CHAPTER 11

As Travis watched the flames of the campfire surge into darkness, he wondered why no path led to a brighter destination. Where was he headed? Every step forward had been his own, although the motive behind them had never seemed to be more than arriving at the next rest stop. His job was fine and paid him well but evoked no passion from him, and the same could be said of his dating life. He envied those who charted their life's course at an early age and never veered, in defiance of the randomness in which others drifted. He stared at the campfire as if the answer would be found in the dwindling branches. Unlike Gregor, who could never more than glimpse an open flame without retreating into panic, he was soothed by the upward fluidity of the fourth element – the randomness of its movement. Although the size and shape could be crafted, each individual flame determined its own suicidal flight into darkness, but no matter how far they pushed it back, in the end, the night always won.

Seated a body-length away, Gregor again stared at the night sky's infinite scintillating orbs, taking advantage of Sedona's inconsiderable light pollution. An electric lantern hanging from the cedar behind him illuminated his immediate surroundings and gave luster to his new aluminum ladder propped against the tree's trunk.

Travis stood and headed for his tent, mumbling, "I'm going to bed."

"Is anything wrong?" asked Gregor.

Travis scowled at him. "I usually go to bed when I'm tired."

Gregor rose from the chair. "Are you upset about something? You've barely spoken since the tour."

Travis crouched to unzip the tent's entrance and replied, "I was meditating."

"What did I do to anger you?"

After seconds of silence, Travis broke into a sighing laugh. "You can't help yourself."

"What are you talking about?"

Travis had never lost a girl to anyone, and the thought that he might lose one to his friend was disconcerting. He scooted sideways, explaining, "You have this way of sidling up to the women I like – befriending them and stopping just short of consummation. Today you even embroiled yourself in an argument – which, by the way, totally blew me away – just to get Iris interested in you."

Gregor replied, "That's not true."

"The truth is, they always like you better, and sometimes when they're with me, I feel like I'm your stand-in – like I'm there to have sex with them because they can't do it with you."

Gregor shook his head and opened his arms. "I don't understand where this is coming from. You honestly think because I knew you liked her, I purposely fought with Iris so we could make up and get her to like me instead?"

Travis pronounced his belief in the dubious strategy by saying, "You always find a way."

Gregor raised his hands in exasperation. "This argument is ridiculous."

"I saw the sparks between you two. She was mine!"

"You claimed her without any regard to her own feelings in the matter."

Travis pointed to him as if identifying a lie. "So, you think she has feelings for you?"

"I didn't say that. I do think you're jealous a girl is interested in me over you for once."

"Let's see how interested she stays when she sees you with your shirt off." Travis exclaimed with a smirk. To drive home his point, he ended with, "If she's like Cadence, she won't be able to go through with it either." Travis realized his words were damaging, but his anger chained him to them and prevented backtracking for reparation.

Gregor seemed at a loss for words. Instead, he hoisted the middle rung of the ladder onto his shoulder and walked into the canyon.

The computer's cursor had not progressed a single space during the past eleven minutes. Sitting on his bed, Mitchell had opened his laptop to work on a Bible lesson for the upcoming youth conference, but his thoughts struggled to stray from Cadence. Their kissed enlivened him, and its memory looped on constant replay in his mind.

As he lost himself deeper and deeper inside the flashback, he tried to filter out the voice of the radio newscaster, "...NASA has made several attempts, but the Hexum Space Station remains unresponsive to remote commands. Sources within the space organization are expressing fears that the station's rapidly degrading orbit will make uncontrolled reentry quote 'imminent within days.' If NASA is unable to..."

"Every Tower of Babel comes crashing back to Earth," proclaimed August.

Startled into the present, Mitchell opened his eyes to see his father standing in the doorway and wearing his familiar disappointment. "How long—"

"What are you doing?" his father asked.

He slid the laptop closer to his stomach. "I'm working on my lesson for this weekend."

"How can you work and listen to that yammering?"

"I need the noise. It helps me concentrate."

After a shake of his head and a muttered, "Ridiculous," August departed.

Seconds later Mitchell heard the door to the solarium creak open and spring shut. He looked to his mother's framed photograph hanging from the wall and fantasized about his life had she survived his introduction to the world ruled by his father. He refocused his attention on the computer document, but as soon as he had typed a single letter, he was beckoned by euphonic chimes. *Who would visit at this hour?* Putting his work aside, he headed to the front door and allowed in a most dissonant wind.

Clutching a crumpled letter, Lily stomped into the atrium and asked, "Mitchell, where is your insipid father?"

Mitchell stepped aside and pointed. "The solarium."

In the solarium, August was peering at the sky through his telescope when Lily stormed in. "August Briar!" She thrust her letter-clutching fist into the air. "How did you acquire my mailing list?"

Startled but refusing to reveal it, he told her, "True Christians are everywhere, Lily. When you send mailers to your godless brood, you dirty Christian hands along the way."

Lily sighed and shook her head. "You have someone in the post office. How can you profess to others a state of morality you yourself avoid? You abetted a felony just to get to me?"

"I have a *duty* to raise God's brilliant light into the sightline of those adrift in the filthy waters of your bewitchment, which will lead them straight into the Everlasting Fire!

"Save the eloquence for your gullible flock."

"And my contempt is saved for you!" August lurched closer to her, raising his voice with every step. "I will shut down that Babylon of a shop and ensure the exile of its whore." He now stood in front of her as if he were waiting to be slapped.

Lily tensed her arm but didn't raise it. "You will lose this battle, August, with no action from me."

"You think you will not have to answer for what you have done?"

"Is fear of retribution how you bring others to love God?"

August answered, "Love sometimes requires coercion."

"So, we're to be the battered half of an abusive relationship?"

"It is not a partnership! He is your God." He raised a hand. "When I am with Him, at His side, basking in the loving warmth of His gaze, and you are writhing in the agony of a fire that rips incessantly at your once-proud flesh, will you be content with the choices you have made? Will you beg forgiveness and for His eyes to look at you with the same loving gaze?"

Lily headed for the door, but before leaving, she held up the letter. "If you ever attempt a repeat mailing to my patrons, I will call the feds, and you will answer to a judge." She let the door slam behind her.

Inhaling deep breaths to calm his body, August reclined onto the solarium's sole chaise. He wondered how stoning had fallen out of favor, and he cursed the Constitution's authors for its omission. When he heard the door open once more, he tensed, thinking Lily had returned with a rebuttal.

"What was that all about?" asked Mitchell with a half-hearted expression of concern.

In a tone that could almost have ice crystals condensing from his very exhalation, August asked, "Why did you allow that witch into my house?"

Lying on the plateau, Gregor stared at the moon and the vast dispersal of stars pricked into the night like photonic shrapnel from an exploded beam of light. While the argument with Travis clawed at his mind, his heart drummed on his ribcage an unfamiliar techno rhythm. The rushing blood, however, did little to abate the chill of the night air. He wished he had brought a blanket.

"I need to meditate." Gregor pushed his back from the ground, sitting with his legs crossed and eyes closed, and with deep breaths, he tried to imbue his body with peaceful understanding and acceptance. He listened to the sounds of night carried on the damp breeze entering his lungs, and he relaxed. Soon his torso began circling, mirroring the counterclockwise revolutions of the vortex. He could sense it now. Its powerful energy spiraled into his body on its way to the rocky ground beneath him. Inhaling during every other revolution and exhaling in those between, he noticed through his eyelids a curious, cerulean light growing in intensity. Gregor opened his eyes, scanning the plateau and sky for the source of the light that was now shining on him, but the information filtering to his brain made no sense. The blue light was emanating from him!

The light glowed from underneath his long-sleeve gray shirt, and it was spreading. Into his thighs, the light pierced through tiny spaces in the denim's weave, giving his jeans an unrealistic blue hue as if they had been painted on by Matisse. The glow traveled down his sleeves, and seeing the blue-lighted skin of his hands, he could no longer doubt its source.

Gregor leapt to his feet in panic, attempting to jump from his body. As if unplugged, the light drained from him, leaving him in a darkness lit by the cloud-covered waning moon. "What on Earth?" He squinted to inspect the skin on the back of his hands. He clenched his fists and whispered, "The energy from the vortex."

Although nervous, he didn't believe the vortex would harm him.

He sat again to meditate – this time with his eyes open. The excitement made relaxing difficult, but as soon he was able to concentrate on his breathing, he could feel the energy from the vortex vibrating through him again. As if he were now more receptive, the blue light returned within seconds, initiating from the core of his body and flowing to his extremities until it engulfed his being. Distracted by the tingling sensation throughout his body, he didn't notice when he levitated one meter from the ground, or when his shoes fell from him as if his feet were no longer there. The vibrations grew stronger and appropriated every cell, breaking his body into particles of light that swirled in a miniature whirlwind and dispersed in all directions before leaving the visible spectrum.

Gregor was gone from the plateau, but he was not gone. His physical form converted into an energy that was unencumbered by spatial limitations. The vortex's vibrations morphed into sounds, all the sounds of the Earth – crashing waves and clashing rams, whirling electrons and splitting cells, ecstatic screams and whispered secrets. He could hear them all, but they did not deafen him. He saw every part of the Earth at once – people in cities and huts, animals in jungles and oceans, undersea vents, pyramids on three continents, Machu Picchu and Stonehenge. His vision penetrated surfaces and inside matter to the atoms, quarks and leptons. Likewise, his other senses perceived the Earth's entirety, but his perceptions were not limited to the spinning world. He could almost connect to the space beyond, but fear kept him from so doing.

Although focusing on a particular place was difficult, his current state made him much more capable of processing massive input, so with all he was experiencing, he suffered no sensory overload. Gregor was exhilarated but scared. Was his current condition permanent, or would he ever be able to return to his former state of being? He found himself thinking more and more about the plateau on which he sat earlier, though how much earlier, he didn't know as the movement of time was imperceptible.

On the plateau, blue-lighted particles manifested from every direction and swirled into a standing silhouette of Gregor, coalescing into his corporeal form. As the light drained away, he fell, disoriented, to his hands and knees, forcing his lungs to breathe. Once the dizziness subsided and his respiration stabilized, he returned to his feet. He saw that he was naked, except for boxer shorts and the amulet dangling from his neck. With his feet, he searched the ground for his clothes, and once found, slipped them on again.

Gregor spun three-hundred-sixty degrees to admire the plateau, but he saw little more than darkness in the muted moonlight. He started laughing, and with clenched fists, he screamed, "That was awesome!" He danced around with his arms extended in jubilation, and he looked to the sky to yell, "You're a beautiful universe!"

As his laughter subsided, he sighed, "I want to go again." Gregor returned to his meditative pose and, in a moment, he was gone again. He would experience several more conversions that night, unaware that he had captured someone's attention.

With his telescope, August Briar searched a narrow sector of the night sky away from the obscuring light of the moon. The affair had become a routine since he turned fifty eighteen months ago and realized that the time for his destiny's fulfillment was running short. Unhappy with the gifts he had received that day, whatever they were, the following day he shopped for one more satisfying, and when he saw the telescope on sale at the mall, he had the distinct feeling that God was urging him to take a more active role in initiating their vis-à-vis encounter. As Moses had to climb Mount Sinai just to hear the Almighty, he became convinced – whether through divine providence or hysterical desire – that he only had to look at the right place in the sky at the right time, and a window to Heaven would open to him.

He scrutinized the stars just above the horizon, until his view became blurred by a blue light from beneath his circular field of vision. "What is that?" he muttered. He leveled the line of the scope to find the origin of the light. "Is it in the canyon?" He focused the lens onto a gap in the foliage adjacent the canyon wall, and he discovered the blue light's source was a man. "What is that?" August raised his naked eyes to the canyon, but the vision was unapparent without assistance. He peered again through the telescope just to see the man disappear into flecks of light. "At last."

Fifteen minutes later, he was parking his SUV on the side of the road and limping toward the canyon with a lantern held before him. Since seeing the blue vision, August had thanked God again and again for, at last, sending the burning bush he had been seeking, but in his head whispered a nagging concern he could not drown with praise and gratitude. What if the manifestation were, instead, a serpent in the garden sent to test him?

Midway through his night-tide trek, he came upon a campsite with two tents and one snoring occupant. He shone the light onto the license plate of the car parked nearby, and a flash from his phone illuminated it further.

Continuing into the canyon, he found his destination's approximate vicinity, but he could see no way up the rocky wall. He feared he might have to abandon his quest until sunrise, but the lantern's light glimmered off an object propped against the steep slope. "Is that a ladder?" Resting the lantern's handle in the crook of his elbow, he climbed the metal rungs to the fissure in the wall and tread the narrow path within. Once he could discern the lesser darkness of the opening at the other end, he turned off the lantern, waited a moment for his eyes to adjust and walked the final few steps to the plateau. The moon had shed its cumulus cloak, casting a smoky tint that allowed him to distinguish the plateau's breadth and general features. August's foot had not yet trampled the plateau when tiny lights appeared from all around and swirled about the center. For a split-second, he thought they were a swarm of lightning bugs, but their hue and speed disproved that fleeting notion. He backed into the fissure's shrouding shadow as the lights molded the shape of a man.

Gregor returned in a seated position with his legs crossed. A quick self-inspection revealed that he was still wearing pants and the amulet, but everything else had fallen from him when he converted. "I'm getting better," he said as he stood and looked around for his shoes and shirt. Finding them a reach away, he replaced them and said, "Let's see if I can keep everything this time." Moments later, he again converted to energy and disappeared.

Once the lights dissipated, August walked on cat's paws to the plateau's center, staying clear of the exact spot Gregor had been for fear of his reappearance. "What is he?" he asked himself before directing a question skyward, "Is he yours?" If he were an angel, why did he leave before delivering God's message to him? God would know he was hiding in the shadows, so would he not have told the angel where to look? Again, he queried God, "Has he returned to you? I am here now. Send him back!"

After a moment of silence spent in utter receptiveness to any sight or sound of possible divine origin, he began rethinking his assumptions. What if he were not an angel? Who else could possess such power? He turned full circle for an answer, and whispered, "All power comes from God... or Satan." Clenching his fists, he raised his voice to Heaven, "Speak to me!" He kicked something on the ground and bent over to pick up Gregor's amulet, which had fallen from him during his last conversion. He lifted the crystal to within centimeters of his face and, with rancorous venom, spewed forth a single word – "Witch."

CHAPTER 12

Standing in the center of the plateau, August Briar saw the whiteness of his skin replaced with a glowing blue light. He felt a strange energy enter him and vibrate the very atoms of his body to the point that he didn't know how his physical being kept form. One of the plants surrounding the plateau erupted in a non-consuming flame that nonetheless produced a black smoke from its tips. The flames spread to the other plants until he was encircled by fire. The dark smoke began to twist together above him like an inverted tornado. From the swirling wind's darkness, a face took shape. "God?" August asked, to which a voice boomed imperceptible words that spit the wind into his eyes as he struggled to shut them. The Earth beneath him quaked.

August opened his eyes to find his son in boxers and a T-shirt standing over him and shaking him awake. He had fallen asleep on the chaise in the solarium, and now the morning sun was peeking over the horizon.

"What are you doing out here? Did you sleep here all night?"

Still groggy, August answered, "I was watching lights in the sky…"

Mitchell chuckled. "UFOs?"

August sat up and sneered at his mocking son. "Do not be stupid." Realizing the mistake of his waking words, he jerked his mind alert to think of a cover story. "It was a meteor shower."

"Oh, I'm sorry I missed it."

August felt something in his pocket and reached his hand inside to touch the crystal amulet he had found the night before. *It was no dream.* He saw his telescope had been exposed all night, so he walked over to replace the protective vinyl covering.

"I made breakfast," Mitchell said, and he pointed to his father's legs. "Hey, you're not limping."

August hadn't noticed before and he didn't know why, but his hip was pain-free. He moved a hand to his bad hip and instead felt the bulge in his pocket where the amulet was concealed. He didn't have an explanation for Mitchell, so he said, "I think those stretching exercises are helping."

Mitchell smiled at him. "That's wonderful. Maybe you won't need surgery after all."

"Do me a favor, and bring me a plate and orange juice. I want to eat on the bench."

Mitchell replied, "Okay," before leaving the solarium.

Once alone, August tested his hip by squatting and found he could now touch his butt to his heels and back into a standing position without pain or loss of balance. He removed the amulet from his pocket and held it dangling before him. He thought to himself, "Is this rock responsible? What manner of healing is this?" He turned his face skyward and whispered, "Are you testing me?" Frowning at the crystal, he knelt at the nearby potted Madagascar palm tree, removed some of the river rock covering the dirt and dug a hole with his free hand. He dropped the amulet inside and concealed it.

August retrieved his phone from the end table by the chaise and called a contact. After a moment, he said, "Jeff? I need you to check a license plate for me." He took the phone from his ear to find the photo he had snapped the night before. "California plate, number…"

The morning air renewed the land but did nothing to rejuvenate Travis' heavy heart. Since he had awakened – and, he thought, even in his faded dreams – he had been engaged in mental self-flagellating for the hurtful words he had hurled at his best friend the night before. He smiled in sad remembrance of high school, where Gregor and he were the classic odd couple. Gregor liked sports but would never participate, focusing instead on excelling as a student. Travis participated in athletics, often foregoing schoolwork until a test or assignment required him to catch up. To his great fortune, he could retain – at least for a day or so – as much as a semester's worth of lessons with just a few hours of study, and he had in Gregor a friend who was a virtual *CliffsNotes* in all matters of science and math.

Travis swigged from a water bottle and swished the liquid around his mouth before swallowing. Placing the bottle on the ground, he removed his toothbrush and toothpaste from his backpack and, as the gel topped the bristles, he saw Gregor approaching from the canyon. Assuming an apology carried on fresh breath would be better received, he proceeded with brushing his teeth but at a hastened pace. When he picked up the water bottle again to rinse, Gregor had already entered conversational range. Travis wanted to be the first to speak, so with his mouth still full of toothpaste, he said, "Gregor, I want to apologize…" Almost choking on the words, Travis put up his hand to signal a timeout as he took a rinsing swig of water.

He had expected anger or, at the very least, the silent treatment, but he received neither. Instead, Gregor threw his arms around him and embraced him as if a decade had separated their last encounter – a move that also squeezed air from Travis' lungs, ejecting the foamy water from his mouth. Travis reciprocated the embrace and said, "I'm sorry, man."

"Don't worry about it," Gregor told him before stepping back.

Wiping spittle from his mouth with his forearm, he saw no anger in his friend, who seemed enshrouded in an aura of peace. Confused but happy, he asked, "You forgive me? Why?"

"I know you didn't mean what you said because you've always been the one to see beneath the skin – with me anyway." Gregor laughed and added, "It helped that I wasn't a girl."

"Ah, you know me so well. What's up with you? If I didn't know better, I'd say you have afterglow. Where've you been?"

"At the vortex I found. I meditated and..." Gregor stopped when he saw the dust trail of Iris' approaching car.

"Maybe I need to try this meditation crap."

Gregor rushed to his tent. "I need to freshen up and change."

Travis ran his fingers through his hair as Iris' car came into full view and parked by his. He strode over to her door, but was too late to open it for her. "Welcome to our humble home."

"Thank you," Iris responded. Wearing a rust tank top, navy cargo shorts and brown hiking boots, she dressed with a utilitarian purpose that presented a sexiness Travis doubted was intentional.

"Gregor, we have company."

"I'll be right out," he replied from inside the tent.

Iris spoke up to ensure he heard, "I was surprised to see where exactly you were camping. There's no vortex here."

Gregor told her, "No negativity. You promised to reserve judgment."

"I'm not being negative," said Iris, her eyes drawn to the canyon. "I've just never seen a map that had a vortex anywhere near here."

Gregor emerged with a backpack and wearing a long-sleeve gray pullover and jeans. "It's well hidden." He placed water bottles from the cooler into the bag and slung it over his shoulder.

Iris watched him at the cooler, and as she did, Travis saw how the perfect morning light, her flawless profile and the red rocks not too far in the distance composed a great picture. He picked up his camera from a nearby rock and aimed the lens at her. Snapping the shutter, he also photographed Gregor, who had walked into the frame. Hearing the camera, she shielded her face with her hand. "I look awful this morning."

"You look great," Travis assured her before viewing his handiwork. The photo took his breath away – not because of her beauty but rather the captured moment in time. In the photo Iris watched Gregor as he walked toward her carrying his backpack, and the look on her face matched the serenity in Gregor's. Their eyes were engaged in the person they beheld.

Gregor asked, "Are we all ready?"

Iris nodded, but Travis waved for them to proceed. "You two go ahead."

"Travis, I really wanted you to come to the vortex," Gregor said.

Travis shook his head. "You know I'm not into meditation. I like to stay in tune to my tension. Besides, I think I'm going to visit the Grand Canyon today and take some shots."

Gregor frowned at him. "I thought we all could spend a day there later this week."

Travis told him, "My day is today."

"Okay. At least save the Meteor Crater for us to do tomorrow, as a group."

"Will do."

Gregor asked Iris, "Do you want to go with us tomorrow?"

"Let's see how today goes first."

When Mitchell stepped out of the shower, he heard voices – one his father's and one unfamiliar. As he rubbed a towel over his wet hair, his curiosity got the better of him. He wrapped the towel around his waist and followed the voices to his father's study, peeking inside with the intention of identifying the visitor before getting dressed. He saw his father, as animated as if he were standing behind a pulpit, telling a hunting story to an enthralled teenage boy.

August said, "I prefer to be active – stalking the deer, instead of hiding in wait. I went hunting with a buddy of mine, who spent a week building a nice tree stand so that it would be ready for the weekend. It had a rail, a ladder, camouflage tarp covering the sides, a tarp roof and cushioned seats, and the silly thing even had cup holders."

"Boy, I'd like to use that," the boy said. "It'd be like shooting deer from my living room."

"Exactly what he thought. That weekend he climbed into his tree stand, waiting for deer to come strolling by, while I hunted for tracks. I never did find any, but I had not been searching for more than five minutes before the good Lord led me straight to a sixteen-point buck."

The boy leaned forward in his chair. "What happened?"

Mitchell noticed his father's eyes were now upon him, although August didn't acknowledge him. Instead, he continued his story. "The buck's antlers were stuck in an old wire fence. He was struggling with all his might to break free, especially when he heard my approach. I stopped two rifle lengths from him, at which point he had exerted himself so much, all he could do was look at me with those big brown eyes. I knew all he wanted was for me to help him get free. So, I did."

"What?" the boy asked. "You did?"

"Absolutely," August assured him. "Right after I shot him."

The boy burst into laughter, as did August, who struggled to speak through it, "When he saw my kill, the first words out my friend's mouth were, 'Reverend, you have to teach me how to track.'"

Mitchell was unamused by the story at its first telling, and seeing the reaction to its retelling only aggravated him. He diverted his eyes to the stack of salmon-colored papers he had put on the desk the night before, realizing they might've gone unnoticed. He entered the room, at which point August spoke to him. "Mitchell, do you remember Lucas McAbel?"

Mitchell tightened his brow as he tried to recall the face of the boy in blue jeans and black tank top who had turned his thick neck to look at him. "Lucas—"

August reminded him, "He was the Bible Bowl champ at last year's youth conference."

Lucas stood to shake Mitchell's hand. "Good seeing you again."

Mitchell looked up at the young man with the imposing presence. He now recalled the face, in spite of the intimidating smile now splayed across it in a manner revealing extreme pleasure in his newfound physicality. He remembered him as an introverted boy who blossomed in the spotlight of competition and August's obvious admiration. At the time he was about the same height at Mitchell, but that was no longer true as he was a head taller now. Not only had he grown up, but wider and thicker as well. His shoulders were much broader than Mitchell's, and his arms were the product of years of strenuous farm work. "You've grown."

"Seven inches," Lucas said with a grin.

Mitchell pointed to the stack of papers. "Dad, I printed the agenda. Two hundred copies."

"Speaking of which, Lucas had a great idea for an activity I think the kids would enjoy. We want everyone to give an impromptu oral report on their favorite person from the Bible."

Lucas chimed in, "Only not Jesus or Moses or Adam—"

"People outside the headliners – to be terribly crass," August explained. "Any sinner can tell you about Abraham, but true Christians know the name Melchizedek."

Lucas added, "A short one to test their Christianity and show they know who it is."

"But they should also be able to tell why they identify with that person. The teachings of the Bible are lost if you do not know how to apply them to your particular circumstances." August took a breath. "I have to say, I really love this idea. We can call it the Character Test." The reverend's face cracked into a wry smile at the double meaning of the title.

Mitchell thought the idea was great for seminary school but ludicrous for children, many of whom were surely being forced by their parents to attend the event. His father, as usual, had unreachable expectations for the children in his care.

Lucas told him, "It'll help them look at Bible people like they're real people and not like they're just people from a story."

Mitchell knew he'd never dissuade his father. "Okay. We'll save that idea for next year."

Lucas cast a frown down at him. "Why next year?"

"The schedule for this weekend is already set." Mitchell nodded to the stack of papers.

"I was thinking about that." August walked to his desk, took an agenda and tossed the remainder in the wastebasket. He held the paper so his son could see and pointed to an agenda item. "If we cut the Saturday afternoon devotional to fifteen minutes, we could easily fit it in."

"The one I'm leading?" Mitchell asked, almost gasping. "I need the full hour."

"Mitchell, I am not taking any time away from you," August assured him in a manner that let him know he was appalled by his selfishness. "You can lead the new activity."

"I've already written my sermon," said Mitchell. "It's an hour long."

In a stern voice, August asked, "Which do you think would engage the children in the word of God more – listening to you quote Bible verse after verse for an hour or a dynamic exercise in which they are active participants?"

Mitchell paused before acquiescing. "I'll redo the agenda," he grumbled before leaving them to continue their conversation.

"Good seeing you again." Lucas repeated his greeting, but this time, it seemed more of a taunt.

Mitchell stormed into the solarium with fists clenched, and he told the sky, "Give me strength." A breeze reminded him of the towel he wore, now in view of the neighbors. He turned to the door but stopped when he stepped on something – a lifeless mass of green feathers.

"Oh no." He jumped back to pick up the dead hummingbird. "Why were you on the floor?" As he crouched, he saw another dead hummingbird a couple of steps away, and beyond that, two more. "What's going on here?" His eyes darted around for an explanation, but from the hummingbird feeder to the glass surrounding the solarium, nothing registered as untoward. He looked again at the feeder, which was almost full of the red sugar water that the birds loved so much. "I didn't fill that up," he whispered to himself, and his face hardened.

When Mitchell returned to the study, Lucas was standing in the same spot but with his back to the door, while August sat at the Queen Anne chair. He interrupted their discussion on matters of religion by hurling the hummingbird feeder at his father. The glass broke on the wall above his father's head and sprayed him with the sticky red liquid.

August ejected from the seat. "Are you trying to kill me?" As if panicked at the thought of poison entering his eyes or mouth, he tore off his jacket and used the lining to wipe his face.

"Why?" asked Mitchell. He lurched toward his father, but Lucas stepped into his path. With a gleam in his eyes, the boy looked down at the short man, daring him to press his luck.

"Because they are birds!" August answered. "You need to reprioritize your devotions."

"Why're you so mad?" Lucas asked. "They're not people. They don't have no souls."

August threw his jacket to the floor. "He seems not to distinguish. God gave man dominion over the animals."

"To take care of them!" Mitchell retorted, while wondering how Lucas knew what had happened. "Not to frivolously kill them as if they had no value."

Lucas laughed. "They got value. As food."

August raised his hands at the red syrup streaking down the wall and his favorite chair. "Look at this mess you made."

"I'll help you clean," Lucas told him, before yanking the towel from Mitchell's waist.

Startled and naked, Mitchell covered himself with his hands and ran from the room.

CHAPTER 13

The morning was shaping up to be the most remarkable Gregor had ever experienced. Compared to previous hikes during the past two days, the canyon looked more alive, more real – like an old film restored to former brilliance. Acute angles of sunlight bounced vibrant colors off every surface, and he felt a greater awareness of the life clinging to, scurrying over and flying above Sedona's red rocks. On top of that, he was having an enjoyable conversation with a beautiful girl, whom he would soon take on the most incredible adventure of her life.

"I'm excited to get a close-up view of those pictographs and the geoglyph," said Iris. "We need to document them. I was researching the images last night, and I didn't find them anywhere." She grinned at him. "You might be their modern discoverer."

Gregor laughed. "Does that mean I get to name the site?"

"Of course. How about the Gregor Buckingham Aztec Monument Canyon?"

"It's a little long. Iris Wickline's Secret Canyon sounds more like a place I would want to visit." He stopped when he realized the unintentional euphemism. "I didn't mean it like that."

With a smile passed down from her mother, Iris said, "I'm

flattered you would consider naming your discovery for me. However, we already have a Secret Canyon in Sedona, so we'll have to work on that last part."

"I've never met a girl, well anyone actually, who was so into Native American history."

"Not just Native American. I've devoted myself to studying world cultures through the mythology they create. Humans have an innate need to understand, and when logic fails them, they turn to mythology to fill the void. Think about fossilized fish found on mountains. Ancient civilizations didn't know about plate tectonics and that those mountains were part of the Earth's crust that was once underwater, so the only explanation that made sense to them was that a great flood must've covered the mountains. The idea of a great flood was first recorded by the Sumerians and later used in the Bible. Mythologies are a way to gain control of an uncontrolled universe and, while they might seem harmless, they have a way of supplanting natural fears with manmade fears concocted to influence behavior. Fossilized fish on mountains equals great flood equals punishment of man by an angry god equals a fear of the god who was powerful enough to flood the Earth equals doing whatever it takes to keep that god happy. And who determines what makes the gods happy? Not uncoincidentally, the morality of the gods has always reflected that of the initial espousers." Iris noticed Gregor smiling at her. "What?"

Gregor answered, "You're really cute when you're demythologizing."

"Oh whatever." Iris gave his shoulder a dismissive slap.

He laughed and stopped next to a steep canyon wall with no obvious path for ascension. "Here we are."

Iris looked up the sheer wall. "I don't see anything."

From behind the nearby shrubbery, he retrieved the ladder he had hidden. He extended it to the necessary length and leaned it against the wall. "After you."

"Are you sure you put the ladder in the right place?"

Gregor held out a hand to help her. "Trust me."

Iris accepted his hand and ascended with Gregor following a few rungs below. Nearing the top, she looked down at him. "Is this Jacob's ladder? It's not going anywhere."

"You should see an opening by now," Gregor said. "At the very top."

Iris shook her head and climbed another rung. "I don't see... Wait, I see it." She hurried up the remaining rungs and pulled herself into the mouth of the narrow crevice. "It's really dark in here."

Gregor joined her in the crevice. "You should try walking through this at night."

"You were here last night?"

"At times," he answered, and he tried not to notice her breasts against his torso as he squeezed by her to lead the way.

"Were you stargazing?"

"Not so much last night. The stars really are amazing here, but you're probably so used to them that you don't even notice the night sky anymore."

"Actually, I've studied the stars extensively. So much ancient myth is attached to them, from the zodiac to the supernova in Capricorn at the beginning of the Common Era."

"At the risk of sounding too much like a nerd, I'll confess I've always had a favorite constellation. Orion, mainly because it's one of the few I can actually see from L.A."

"I'd love to live in L.A. You're so close to the ocean. Do you go all the time?"

"Not really. I prefer the beach in winter, when no one's there. I don't swim or lay out. Sometimes in the summer, I do meditate at a park that's on a cliff overlooking the ocean."

"What about your family?"

"My parents died when I was a kid."

"I'm sorry."

Gregor said, "I wonder why 'I'm sorry' is the standard response whenever you hear of someone dying, as if the listener were to blame."

"You're right, but what else could be said?"

"I don't know. 'That sucks' maybe?"

Iris laughed. "I don't see that catching on. Where did you live after they died?"

He flashed back to the night of the fire. "I had no family left, so I was put in foster care." Emerging from the crevice, he announced, "We're here."

Iris stepped onto the sunlit ground and looked around the flora-encased plateau. "It's definitely secluded." Through the only gap in the foliage surrounding them, she saw the houses on the hill in the distance. "I think I can see August Briar's house."

"Is that your boyfriend?"

"Lord no. He's the minister who's trying to shut us down, and he's like fifty-something."

Gregor apologized and joined her in looking at the scenery through the gap. "You are so lucky you get to see this beautiful town every day."

"More stuck than lucky."

"What's keeping you here?"

Iris lowered her eyes. "My mom would be alone."

Gregor added, "And so would you." Her lack of acknowledgement made him realize his statement might have been discomforting to her. He stepped away and raised his hands in front of him with his palms down. "Do you feel it?"

Iris turned her attention back to the plateau. She mimicked Gregor's movements with tepid vigor. "Not really. Where's the geoglyph?"

"It's not easy to discern from here, but see the outline there." He pointed to a groove in the ground and followed it with his finger. "That's a wing, and there's the head and beak."

Iris exclaimed, "I see it! Oh my god. It's stunning."

Gregor rerouted his pointing to the canyon wall above them. "You can see it much better from up there. The cliff dwelling is where that juniper branch is popping out."

"Wow, that's actually steeper than I thought it would be." She walked to the edge of the plateau furthest from the wall and looked up, moving around to find the best view.

"We can climb up after we meditate."

Iris stumbled and grabbed her forehead. "Whoa."

Gregor ran to her and wrapped his arm around her waist. "Are you okay?"

"I just got a little dizzy from looking up." Iris dropped her hand and found herself looking up into Gregor's eyes. Her knees buckled.

Gregor had to wrap both arms around her to keep her from falling. "You should lie down." He helped her recline before retrieving water from his backpack.

"I don't know what's wrong with me," muttered Iris. "I've never felt faint before."

Gregor put the bottle to her lips and inclined her head. "It's the vortex. You do feel it."

"I think I just drank too much coffee this morning."

"Did you eat breakfast?"

"Never."

Gregor produced a granola bar from his backpack and opened it for her. "Here, eat this."

Iris took it and nibbled as Gregor lay down to her left. "My head hurts."

"You're getting a headache?"

Iris reached for the back of her head with her right hand. "No, this ground is really hard."

He offered the inside of his right arm as a pillow. "Is that better?"

"Much," Iris said, and she closed her eyes. "Thank you."

After a brief pause, he said, "Tell me about your family. What does your dad do?"

"He died in a car accident when I was a baby."

Gregor frowned, saying, "Oh, I'm sorry."

She waved a finger at him. "Uh-uh. You're supposed to say, 'That sucks.'"

"You're right," said Gregor. "It's not going to catch on."

"He was a research scientist at a pharmaceutical company in Chicago, where my mom used to work. She moved here right after they split and before she realized she was pregnant with me. I don't even have a picture of him. Whenever I'd ask about him, she'd find a way to change the subject. Her favorite way when I was a kid was this." Iris opened her eyes and touched the top of Gregor's head with her fingertips, which she squeezed together several times as if her hand were eating his head. "Do you know what this is?"

Gregor answered, "A head massage?"

"No, it's a brain-eater. Do you know what it's doing?"

Gregor furrowed his brow while looking sideways into her eyes. "No."

"Starving to death." Iris broke into laughter.

Gregor smiled and tickled her with his free hand, which sent Iris into a giggling fit. She rolled onto her side with her hand on his torso and face on his chest. When he stopped tickling, he looked at the beautiful face staring up at him and was surprised when she kissed him on the lips. To Gregor, who had only been kissed once before – and that elation did not last very long – the kiss felt soothing, like cold hands under warm water. He didn't know what to say, and in nervousness, his first thought was a joke. "Was this fainting spell just an elaborate ruse to get a kiss out of me?"

Iris laughed and pushed herself into a seated position. "It won't happen again."

Grinning, Gregor sat up beside her. "Are you feeling better?"

"Yes, actually." She watched the rapid expiration moving his chest and the perspiration darkening the sternum of his gray shirt. "You should've worn something cooler."

Uncomfortable with any scrutiny of his body, Gregor wanted to divert her attention, but he realized that something was amiss. He reached for his chest. "My amulet."

"I haven't seen it on you today," Iris told him.

Gregor scanned the ground. "I must've lost it last night."

"If it's not here, maybe you dropped it on the way to your campsite. We'll find it."

"I hope so." Gregor wondered if he had lost it during one of his experiences the night before. "Are you ready to meditate?"

Iris groaned, "Are you going to make me go through with this? It's a waste of time. I've meditated at every vortex in Sedona, and I've never felt the slightest twinge of energy."

"This one's different," Gregor assured her. He crossed his legs facing her and patted the ground in front of him, signaling her to do the same. After Iris joined him, their knees touching and eyes locked, Gregor spoke in the most dulcet of tones to prepare her for meditation and the journey that lay ahead of them. "Many people believe that we have a spirit inside of us that is released at our death, and in a way, we do. Flecks of energy flow within the atoms of your body, and those flecks form an energy aggregate that could be called your spirit. Your spirit connects you to the universe and gives you the presence of mind to perceive that connection. To do so, you need to open your heart and mind and understand what you truly are. What we all are."

When Gregor fell silent, Iris asked, "What are we?"

Gregor pinched the fingertips of his right hand together and separated them to simulate release. "Just energy and matter. Glints of the spark that ignited the universe. That's all anything or anyone is and forever will be." He inhaled and waited for the breath's complete exhalation before saying, "Let me introduce you to the vortex." He opened his palms to her.

"Okay. I'll try." Iris squeezed his hands and nodded.

"Close your eyes, and relax your breathing. In and out. Listen to the air enter your lungs. And leave your body. Filter out all sounds but my voice and the air that connects you to the Earth. Now focus on the part of your body that is touching the ground beneath you. Try to feel the vibration emanating through you."

Iris screamed.

Gregor opened his eyes and saw a look of terror in hers. A blue light emanated from every inch of his skin, and it was spreading from his hands to hers.

Iris jerked her hands away and scooted back. "Oh my god!"

Gregor reached out for her as he began to levitate mere centimeters from the ground. "Iris!" he called but in a distorted rasp. Seconds later every blue particle in his body separated, swirled and dispersed in all directions, even through Iris.

Iris jumped to her feet and checked her body. Her hands had returned to their normal color. She backed against the canyon wall, clinging to it. She looked around for Gregor, but a sock and a shoe were all that remained where he had been. "What has he done?"

As if to answer, blue particles sparked into existence from every direction and coalesced near the center of the plateau into Gregor's physical form. As the light faded from him, he faced Iris and asked, "Why did you let go?"

"Why did I let go?" shouted Iris with a nervous laugh. "Are you kidding?"

Gregor walked toward her, explaining, "I know the experience seems strange at first—"

"Strange?" Iris shook her head. "What I saw was so far beyond strange. It was… impossible. Where did you go?"

He extended his hands from his sides with palms upward. "Everywhere."

As Gregor came closer, Iris pointed to his foot in horror, screaming, "Look what happened to your foot!"

Any elation Gregor felt from his experience was drained by her reaction. He didn't have to glance at the burned skin on his exposed foot to know what she saw, but if he had, he would've noticed the image didn't quite match his memory. He had seen her expression before on countless other faces, and he scolded himself for being stupid enough to think her response would be any different. He turned from her, saying, "You should go."

"What?" asked Iris. "I don't get—"

"I was wrong about you. I won't bother you again." Gregor retrieved his sock and shoe.

Iris opened her mouth to speak but had no words. She complied with his wishes, leaving him alone. As Gregor slipped the sock over his foot, his eyes and attention were on Iris, watching her enter the fissure and exit his life.

CHAPTER 14

Iris left her car askew in a slot near the Sedona Vortex shop and hurried to the front door. When she saw the "Closed" sign, she assumed her mother had forgotten to flip it, but she was surprised to find the door still locked. She fumbled with her keys, and once inside, she heard Abba's "The Visitors" booming from the Meditation Center. Separating the black drapes in the doorway to the center, she saw Lily dancing by the fountain replica of Sedona. Iris grabbed the remote control from the closest boulder and turned off the music.

Startled in mid-movement, Lily said, "Don't ever stop the music so abruptly. Interrupting my pelvis mid-grind could make my hips jump track. Lower it gradually."

Iris pointed to the clock. "You're ten minutes late opening up."

Lily dabbed her forehead with a scarf from her pocket. "The time slipped away from me, but Tuesday mornings are slow anyway. Honey, you're white as a ghost. What's wrong?"

"Gregor," Iris muttered.

"Is he okay? What happened?"

"I wish I knew. He… disappeared."

"He left you?"

"And then he came back."

"Iris, I'm not following. Sit down, and start from the beginning."

Iris sat on the boulder, and Lily listened as she recounted the episode on the plateau. After which, the older woman stood in silence. When words did come, they were not of comfort to her distraught daughter. "Honey, I'm worried about your vitamin intake."

"Mom, I'm not vitamin deficient." Iris jumped to her feet. "I swear to you with every fiber of my being that every word I just told you is the absolute truth."

Lily remained quiet for several seconds as she processed the information. "How powerful is that vortex?"

Relieved her mother believed her, Iris answered, "More than any other. I actually felt this one and felt it hard. In fact, I'd say categorizing this vortex with any other is like comparing an eagle to a gnat because they both fly."

Lily asked, "You said the light was blue?"

"Yes. Why?"

"Blue light phenomenon," Lily responded, as if the words were explanation enough.

Iris waited a beat before asking, "What is that?"

"I really wish you would take more of an interest in the metaphysical. The universe is not confined within your textbooks. It refers to blue light from seemingly transdimensional sources – from floating orbs in a field to spirit-like entities to even larger objects. It's been reported for centuries. UFOs are often described as being bathed in blue light before they vanish."

Iris asked, "Are you saying that Gregor is an alien?"

"I'm saying these different phenomena could be connected by a common power source. Maybe the blue light is the energy or byproduct of the energy they use – derived from vortexes."

Iris shook her head. "Mom, you know I don't believe in that crap."

"If I had told you yesterday you would encounter a man who could glow blue and disappear, would you have believed me?"

"Touché." A light went off inside Iris. "The Blue Shaman."

"Who?"

Iris raced back into the shop and headed to the book area. "The Blue Shaman," she repeated to her trailing mother. "Hang on, and I'll show you." She found a book on the Anasazi and flipped through the pages. "The Blue Shaman is a Navajo legend about an Anasazi who guards the gates to the Underworld. Here he is." Iris handed the book to Lily to show her the photograph of a clay pot with blue figure painted on it. "He's bathed in blue light, and he periodically appears on mountain plateaus or sacred sites."

"Interesting." Lily read through the text. "I wonder why he would appear at different places if he's supposed to be specifically guarding the gates to the Underworld."

"Maybe there's more than one entrance, and he rotates. I don't know. The point is this myth could be based in reality. Maybe some indigenous peoples were able to do what Gregor did. Maybe the Blue Shaman doesn't represent one person but anyone who could use that energy."

To finish reading the passage, Lily turned the page, where she found another picture on the subject. "Look at this one." She held it so Iris could see the cave painting of the Blue Shaman in front of a double-peaked mountain, the silhouette of which looked like a pictograph in Gregor's cliff dwelling. The caption referred to the site as *Shiprock* in New Mexico.

"That's it!" Iris declared.

"What's it?"

"This same mountain is painted in a cliff dwelling Gregor found near the vortex." She tried to remember the pictograph sequence, mumbling, "After the mountain was Quetzalcoatl, then a group standing in fire, a spiral, Coffee Pot Rock, the geoglyph and the double star."

Lily closed the book. "I want to find out more about this vortex. I need to talk to Gregor."

Iris lowered her head. "He doesn't want to see me anymore."

"You really like him, don't you?"

Her daughter shrugged. "Mom, why would I want to get involved with a tourist?"

With a broad smile, Lily said, "Iris, we're all tourists."

Wearing a terrycloth robe that hid her new, conservative bikini, Cadence stopped a woman to ask, "Excuse me, but where did you get your shower cap?" After the woman informed her to ask a cabana boy for one, she thanked her. Exiting the locker room, Cadence inspected the crowd of young and old who were partaking of the day spa's various amenities. Some were covering their skin with mud from a red pool before lying on lounge chairs to let the mud bake. Others were bathing in the mineral pool or soaking in the hot tub or golfing on the lush course that lay beyond the stone-tiled area.

Cadence found Mitchell staring at a mourning dove that was nestled in the branch of a banyan tree rooted near the mineral pool. When he had picked her up from the motel earlier that morning, he apologized for not being able to reserve a hot air balloon until the next day and said that his backup plan was a spa day, which was fine with her.

Reaching the tree, she told him, "I have to say I'm surprised you brought me to a spa."

Breaking his stare, Mitchell smiled and asked, "Why? Do you not like it?"

"No, this place is beautiful. I meant that a day at the spa seems... decadent."

Mitchell laughed. "We have a responsibility to take care of the body God gave us."

Cadence looked at his abs. *And you definitely do.*

"Besides, the owner is one of our congregants. He gave me a lifetime membership, so I don't pay for anything. I do have to confess that I had an ulterior motive for bringing you here."

Assuming it was to see her in a bikini, she said, "Oh, I hope you're not disappointed."

When he said, "Me too," Cadence was insulted until he added, "I want to baptize you."

"I told you I've been baptized. I can't do it again, can I?"

"Sprinkling a baby with water is not baptism. 'Baptize' means 'submerge in water.' That's how John the Baptist baptized Christ, and it's the only correct way. I don't know where Catholics came up the sprinkling concept." He took her hands. "Will you let me baptize you?"

Cadence inhaled through her teeth. "I don't know."

"Do you not want to go to Heaven?"

"Of course, I do."

"In Acts 2:38, Peter tells us, 'Each of you must repent of your sins and turn to God, and be baptized in the name of Jesus Christ for the forgiveness of your sins. Then you receive the gift of the Holy Spirit.' No one can enter the Kingdom of Heaven without being baptized."

Cadence acquiesced with a half-smile. "Okay, but here? Don't we need holy water?"

"That's Catholic. I can submerge you in any body of water."

"I need a shower cap."

Mitchell waved to a cabana boy and pointed to Cadence's head. "Come on," he said as he led her to the pool, where she dropped her robe. As they proceeded down the steps into the water, the cabana boy came with a shower cap in hand. Mitchell asked him, "Could you stay for a moment? We need a witness." The cabana boy nodded and crouched by the edge of the pool.

Cadence noticed a few people watching them. "I don't know if I can do this here."

"Don't think about," Mitchell told her. "Just focus on me." He moved to her side so that he was facing her left profile. "Are you ready?"

Cadence glanced at his wet, chiseled torso. Moving her gaze upward, she was lulled into gentle fawning by his intense eyes. "Yes."

Mitchell raised his left hand as if taking an oath, while centering his right against her back. He maintained eye contact with her when he spoke, "Mark 16:16, 'Anyone who believes and is baptized will be saved, but anyone who refuses to believe will be condemned.' Do you believe Jesus Christ is the holy Son of God?" She stared at him but didn't answer. "Cadence?"

Realizing she had missed her cue, Cadence jerked herself into the moment. "Oh, I do."

"Do you repent of all your sins?"

"I do."

"I now baptize you in the name of Jesus Christ." Mitchell placed his left hand over her mouth and pinched her nose before forcing her backwards into the water, using his right hand to steady her. He made certain she was submerged before bringing her back to the surface. As Cadence gasped for air, startling the mourning dove from his perch, Mitchell nodded to the cabana boy, signaling him to leave. He stepped in front of her. "How do you feel?"

Still wiping water from her face, she answered, "Clean."

He placed his hands on her shoulders. "Baptism washes away your sins. At this moment you are sinless. You are reborn like a babe in the arms of Christ."

Cadence again stared into his brown eyes, entranced by the mellow intonation of his sensual voice. His touch on her shoulders titillated her breasts. She wanted another kiss from him. She could sense the air between them warming as he chipped away at the distance. She savored the anticipation of caressing his supple lips with her own.

"Cadence?" a voice called from beyond the pool. Startled, she and Mitchell both looked in the direction of the intrusive voice to see Travis walking under the banyan tree wearing a polo shirt, shorts and golf shoes. "What are you doing here?"

"Travis. I…" Cadence stammered. "Why are you here?"

He crouched at the pool's edge. "Golfing. I was on my way to the Grand Canyon this morning when this beautiful course here caught my eye. The lovely lady up front let me in as her guest." He nodded to Mitchell. "Good seeing you again."

Mitchell replied, "You as well," in a tone devoid of any welcome.

"What were you doing?" asked Travis. "It looked like you were trying to drown her."

"I was baptizing her."

Travis laughed and stopped himself when no one joined in. "Oh, you're serious. You baptized her here? Does that count?"

Mitchell insisted, "Of course, it counts."

"I have to say, I'm impressed. That's an original tactic for seduction." In a mock voice, Travis said, "Go out with me, babe, and I'll save your soul. I can literally take you to Heaven."

Horrified, Cadence began to scold him, "Travis—"

"How many times have you done this before?" Travis asked.

"I don't appreciate your inference, but for the record, Cadence was my first time."

"Your first time using that maneuver?"

"My first baptism!" roared Mitchell.

"I'm your first?" asked Cadence with a smile spreading across her face.

"Seriously?" Travis asked. "Then how do you know you did it right?"

"That's enough!" yelled Cadence. "I'm sorry, Mitchell, but my friend is a cynical jerk. Travis, don't you have to repay someone at the front desk for her lapse in judgment?"

"She doesn't get off for another hour."

"Actually, would you excuse me for a moment?" Mitchell asked Cadence.

"Sure," Travis answered.

Cadence asked, "Where are you going?"

"It's a surprise." Mitchell left them alone at the pool and entered the club.

"So, what's going on with you and the preacher's son? Are you two dating now?"

She removed her shower cap. "He's a preacher himself, and we're not dating."

"Then what are you doing?"

"I'm just…" Cadence began but couldn't answer because she didn't know herself. She had come to Sedona with a single purpose, and Mitchell had distracted her from it. He had been a wonderful distraction, though. "I don't know."

"He's short," Travis said as if it were an accusation.

"That doesn't bother me. I never wear heels. Why are you being so mean to him?"

"Don't worry about it. He'll forgive me. That's what they get paid to do. Anyway, on another subject, I know you wanted to see the Grand Canyon, so would you want to go tomorrow? Gregor wants to see the Meteor Crater, but he won't mind if we put that off."

"Actually, Mitchell and I already have plans."

Travis nodded toward the returning preacher's son. "You know they mate for life."

Mitchell squatted poolside to tell her, "I've made reservations for us to get massages."

"Wow," Travis said. "That sounds great. Thank you."

"Just for the two of us," clarified Mitchell.

130

Travis refused to let up. "Aren't you afraid Cadence will get jealous?"

"He's kidding," Cadence told Mitchell. "And he's leaving."

Travis relented. "Okay. I'm going to try the mud, but first, a drink. Want anything?"

Mitchell stood beside him, looking up at Travis to answer, "Other than privacy, no."

Mitchell slid into the pool as two security guards met up with Travis to escort him off the premises.

After Iris had left him alone on the plateau, Gregor spent the entire day connected to the vortex's energy, alternating between meditation on the plateau and travel within the realms of the Earth. He could feel his connection to the vortex growing stronger, but he remained unaware of the alterations to his being. Among them, his brainwaves were now complementary to the waves of the energy, which helped him sense the vortex without even trying.

During his experiences, Gregor was an energy without any apparent spatial bounds. Focusing on a single place remained difficult for him because his senses were bombarded with perceptions of every place, but he was also hesitant to do so for fear that he would convert back to his physical form in whatever place he happened to be thinking about at the moment. If his theory were correct, his body could end up in a lava flow or the belly of a whale. The only place on which he could concentrate without fear was the plateau.

The sun had almost dropped from the sky when he decided to stop for the day. Standing to stretch, he admired the sunset's colors stretching across the sky and imagined how much more beautiful it would be with someone beside him. He tried pushing images of Iris from his head, but he kept seeing her reaction to his exposed scars scattered with memories of their origin. "Why do I even come back?" He fell into a meditative pose, resolving not to return until morning, if then. As he converted into energy, he found that, unlike previous experiences, unsettling locales vied for his attention. He saw a man in a dark prison cell and could not draw his attention away from that place. "Oh my god," he muttered when he realized – much to his horror – he had focused on the man so much, he converted to physical within the confines of the cell.

Fifty years old and hairless, the prisoner was lying on the floor and staring at the ceiling with his hands cupped behind his head. Monochromatic tattoos adorned much of the skin covering the knotty muscles that were exposed by the short sleeves of his dirty white T-shirt.

Gregor's nose crinkled from the dank musk of showerless days pervading the cell. He hoped he could convert to energy away from the vortex, so he wasted no time in meditating to escape before being detected. However, the blue light from his entrance already alerted the occupant to his presence.

The man bounced to his feet, braying, "Who the hell are you? How'd you get in here?"

Gregor jumped up and threw his hands in front of him with palms to the man. "I don't want any trouble. If you just give me a second—"

The man clenched his fists. "Why would the guards let you in here with me? You must've really pissed them off." He laughed before swinging a fist toward Gregor's jaw.

Dodging the impact, Gregor danced around and tried to reason with him. "Look, I just need you to give me a moment to try to get out of here."

The prisoner threw a fist that connected with the side of Gregor's head, and he pushed a forearm into his neck, pinning him against the wall. "They wouldn't have put you in here if they didn't want you dead," he said with brimstone breath.

Gregor grabbed the man's forearm to stop the choking. He

pounded the man's stomach with his knee, which loosened the pressure on his throat. Gregor punched him in the face with his right hand and again with his left.

The man fell back, near the bed and reached under the mattress, pulling out a blade of twisted metal. He regained his footing and lunged forward with the blade leading the way.

Gregor jumped to the side and helped the man's momentum propel his head into the wall. The man fell to the floor, dazed.

Hoping he had at least a few seconds before the fight would resume, Gregor sat on the floor and crossed his legs. He closed his eyes and tried to reconnect to the energy. He felt the vibrations, but it was different this time. Instead of being a conduit through which the vortex energy could pass, it came from within himself.

The prisoner shook his head and pushed against the floor. He saw the stranger engulfed in blue light. He lunged for the light, which dispersed before he could make contact. Landing with a thud to the floor, the prisoner found himself once again alone in his cell.

Gregor returned to the plateau. Once he opened his eyes, he let out a sigh of relief. He sprawled himself on the ground to allow the tension to leave his body. He could still smell the dankness of the cell, and he wondered if some of the air had followed him back.

CHAPTER 15

In his church office, August edited a hardcopy of his opening sermon for the youth conference. When his cell phone rang from atop the Bible on his desk, he jumped in his seat and dropped the red pen. He saw the words "Mourning Dove Investigations" appear on his phone.

August looked to Lucas, who was busy categorizing printouts of past sermons and filing them in a thick, white binder. "Lucas, thank you for all of your help today, but I am sure your father does not want to spend his entire trip here alone."

Without looking up, Lucas replied, "I see him all the time."

August picked up his phone. "Wait outside for me, and I will take you to your hotel."

Lucas stepped away from his work, saying, "That's okay. I'll call him to pick me up."

Once Lucas left, August answered the phone. "What did you find out?"

On the other end of the call, Jeff Woodard said, "Good evening to you, too. I'm sending you a photo right now. The owner of the vehicle is Travis Harper, who currently resides in West Los Angeles. You should have the picture now."

August looked at the message coming to his phone, and watched a license photo of Travis download. Returning the phone to his ear and with marked annoyance, he said, "That is not the man. I saw two tents. Find out who accompanied him to Sedona."

Cadence was all smiles as she entered her motel room, flipped on the light and threw her purse on the bed. Mitchell followed her through the doorway and said, "I'm sorry to end so early, but I have to finish some work tonight."

"I totally understand."

"I promise to spend every non-working minute I have with you while you're here." He grinned and added, "By the time the week is over, you'll never want to leave. Oh, I almost forgot." He produced a blue velvet box from his pocket and handed it to her.

Cadence shook her head, saying, "You shouldn't have bought me anything." She opened the box to find a sterling silver crucifix necklace. "It's beautiful."

"It was my mother's. I found it in an old jewelry box in our attic when I was a kid."

Cadence looked down and ran her fingers over the gift. "I can't accept this."

"I want you to have something close to my heart as a remembrance of me." Mitchell removed it from the box and clasped the chain around her neck. His head next to hers, he looked in the mirror to admire how the crucifix adorned her sternum, but her reflection stared back in icy silence. "Are you okay?"

Cadence paused before answering, "Mitchell, we need to stop what we're doing before it goes any further." She removed the crucifix and returned it to him.

"What are we doing?"

"Pretending that we have some kind of future together when we don't."

Mitchell caressed her shoulders and looked at her eyes in the mirror, but she averted her gaze. "I told you I plan to move from here. Maybe Los Angeles is where I'm meant to be."

Turning to face him, Cadence said, "Don't plan your life around me."

"I'm not!" He calmed his demeanor, working up a smile. "I'm not. I meant that if we continue seeing each other, we might find we want to be together. If that were to happen, you should know I would be open to moving to L.A., if that's where you want to stay."

Cadence kissed him and said, "This was a mistake. Please just leave me alone."

Mitchell hardened his face and exited the room.

Staring in the mirror, Cadence watched a tear dripping from her cheek. "I did the right thing."

She took her phone from her purse and called Travis. Once he answered, she said, "Do you still want to go to the Grand Canyon tomorrow?"

Travis responded, "I'm fine. How are you?"

"I'm sorry. I've had a long day."

"Hey, I'm getting something to eat. I'll swing by and pick you up."

Cadence told him, "I've already had dinner."

"So early? What are you, sixty?"

"Just pick me up in the morning." She hung up and threw the phone on the bed. With another glance in the mirror, she reached for the front of her hairline and pulled off her wig to reveal a bald scalp.

Iris entered the Red Planet Diner and plopped herself at the counter with a deep sigh. As if awaiting her arrival, Gia approached with a blue vortini for her friend. "I want you to try my new drink," the waitress said. "I mixed a vortini with a power drink. I call it the energy vortini."

"A depressant and stimulant all in one," Iris said. "I'll probably clean house tonight in my sleep." She sipped the drink and told her, "This isn't bad."

"Good, huh?" Gia dropped her elbows to the counter. "What's wrong with you?"

Iris didn't know how to tell her, but she knew without a doubt not to tell her anything she didn't want translated into a cryptic social media post. "Nothing."

Gia rolled her eyes. "Right. Well, while you decide if you want to tell me the truth or not, let me tell you my dilemma." She pushed off the counter. "I have to cancel my rave."

"What happened?"

"August Briar had my reservation for Shaman's Dome rescinded because he won't allow a 'celebration of hedonism' anywhere near his precious youth conference."

"That doesn't make any sense," Iris said. "The two aren't anywhere near each other. Can you postpone it until next Friday?"

"I had to book DJ Revenant three months ahead of time. Plus, I have a sound system and drinks on hold. Now I have a party with nowhere to happen. Any other ideas?"

"Not off the top of my head, but," Iris nodded to her vortini, "let me see if I can find any in here."

"I thought you might be here now," Travis said from behind her. Iris asked, "What are you doing here?"

He plopped down on the barstool beside her. "I came to see you."

Iris noticed the sparkle in Gia's eyes when he arrived. "I don't think I officially introduced you two. Gia, this is Travis. Travis, Gia."

"Bacon veggie burger," Gia responded, eliciting a puzzled look from Iris. "Can I get you anything?"

Travis flashed his cocky smile. "I'll have a vortini, and let me think about the rest."

A bell signaled a ready order, prompting a curse from Gia. "Stupid work. Iris, if you think of any place—"

"I'll let you know," she assured her friend, who left to serve the fresh meal.

Travis asked, "How did it go this morning?"

Iris was surprised he had to ask. "Did Gregor not tell you?"

"I haven't seen him, which isn't that unusual these past few days. He spends every spare moment in that canyon. He even slept there last night. What could be so fascinating about it?"

"The vortex."

Travis laughed at her apparent joke. "Oh yeah, next to the unicorn stable."

"Never mind," Iris said. "Gregor... told me to leave."

"What? That doesn't sound like Gregor."

"Honestly, I don't know why he was so calm. It scarred his foot."

"What scarred his foot?"

"The vortex," Iris replied, to which he let out a great laugh. "What's so funny?"

Gaining his composure, he told her, "I'm sorry. It's not funny. The vortex didn't scar him. Gregor was burned when he was a kid."

Iris gasped and dropped her forehead into her hand. "No wonder he was upset with me."

"Yeah, he's very self-conscious about it. Haven't you noticed his long sleeves and pants in this heat? He has burn scars all over all his body, except his face and hands." Perhaps realizing he wasn't helping his friend's chances with Iris by revealing the extent of his injuries, Gregor added, "But he's really a beautiful guy underneath it."

"How did it happen?"

"Gregor's father was extremely abusive to his mother and to

him. Finally, his mom couldn't take it anymore, and she filed for divorce. When he was served, he went home and beat the crap out of her, and he probably would've killed her right then if the neighbors hadn't called the cops. He was arrested but let out of jail the next day. Then he went to the house while Gregor and his mom were asleep and poured gasoline all over."

Iris' face distorted with empathetic pain. "Oh my god."

Travis continued, "Gregor woke up in time to see his father actually light the match. He was trapped in his bedroom, and he had to break a window to escape. Unfortunately, he got stuck in the glass and couldn't squeeze through all the way." He paused as he choked up. "A neighbor heard him screaming, and he climbed up a ladder to reach him. By the time he was actually able to pull him out, the fire had already started burning his body." Travis sighed and turned away. "He spent the next year in the hospital recovering."

Iris held a napkin to her eyes to sponge away the tears. "I can't believe all he's been through. So that's how they died."

Travis corrected, "His mom died. His dad is still alive."

"Alive?"

"Serving life in prison."

When Gia returned with Travis' drink, she noticed Iris' teary eyes. "Are you okay?" she asked, and with a petulant eye to Travis, narrowed the question to, "Did he do something to you?"

Iris placed a hand on Travis' forearm. "I'm fine. I just... bit the inside of my mouth."

"On a drink?" asked Gia without a response.

Mitchell entered the diner and approached the counter. "Travis, could I speak to you?"

Travis replied, "Sure. What's up?"

Mitchell shrugged. "That's what I'd like to know. Cadence broke it off with me tonight."

"Broke it off? That makes it sound like you two were seriously dating."

"I was serious," said Mitchell. "I thought she was too, but she just ended it for no reason. Now she's not even taking my calls. Do you know why she decided to stop seeing me?"

"I'm sorry, but she doesn't really confide in me about her love life. I do have to say, however, that you are coming off a little stalkerish to me. Maybe that weighed on her decision."

Mitchell offered a resigned, "Thanks, I won't keep you," and walked away to a booth.

"Glad I could help," said Travis.

"You know what would be hot?" asked Gia before she answered herself, "Holding the rave at his place."

Iris frowned at her. "You mean the church?"

"Remember the party he threw there in high school. I wonder if August ever found out."

"I'm sure he didn't," said Iris. "Mitchell's still alive."

"Preacher boy had a moment of coolness?" asked Travis.

"More than a moment," Gia replied. "He was the total rebellious preacher's son back then."

Iris continued the story, "Before his dad sent him off to that Christian college. When he came back, his rebellion turned to obedience."

"What do you think?" asked Gia. "Would he give us a night at the church for old time's sake?" Not waiting for a response, she took Travis' vortini and went to ask.

Gia approached the booth where Mitchell sat, staring at the table. "You look down," she said as she placed a vortini in front of him and slid onto the opposing seat. She masked her face with concern. "Are you okay?"

"I'm fine," he answered, followed by a gulp of the libation.

"Anything to do with that girl who came in here with you the other day?"

Mitchell pointed toward the counter. "Did Travis tell you?"

"Who?" She glanced over her shoulder and decided to play off their obvious animosity. "That tourist? He's only spoken to me to grunt his order, the jerk. Iris keeps dropping subtle hints for him to leave her alone, but the idiot thinks they're come-ons." Noticing the slightest uptick in the corners of his mouth, she zoned back in on her opening, "So it is about that girl."

"Cadence. She's a friend of his."

"Another tourist? How could she have you so twisted up?" Gia touched his hand.

He stared at the stem of the glass. "I don't know if I can explain. I'm just drawn to her."

"Like you were drawn to me?" she asked, referring to their short-lived affair when she was a sophomore in high school and he was a grade above.

"No, this was intense," he replied, seeming not to realize he had insulted her. "Have you ever seen someone from afar and thought in that moment your souls were touching, even carrying on a little dance while you looked at each other in silence?"

Gia's expression hinted at such a memory, but she hardened it. "No."

"Well, that's how I felt the first time I saw her. Then when I actually talked to her, she was condescending and mildly bellicose, even as the dance continued. I know she felt it too."

"You know what you need?" Gia removed her hand from his. "A cool party."

"That's not the answer."

"Sure, it is. A fun dance with some cool trance. Beautiful girls. At your church."

Mitchell rolled his eyes. "No."

"Come on, Mitchell. I'm just talking about five or six hours on

Friday night, when your dad will be at the youth conference. I'll make certain the place is spotless afterward."

"Are you crazy?"

Gia caressed both his hands and asked, "What could I do to change your mind?"

"Kill my dad," Mitchell answered, with a subtle smile.

Gia tilted her head. "Are you sure?"

"I was kidding. What I meant to say is that my dad would honestly kill me."

"Funny, since he's the reason I even have to ask you. My original plan was for a rave in a cave at Shaman's Dome, but he took that location from me. The least you could do is make it up to me."

Mitchell asked, "Have I told you about my father's extensive gun collection?"

A sparkle of inspiration ignited in Gia's head, prompting the question, "Would you change your mind if I could guarantee that Cadence will be there?"

"How could you possibly promise that when you don't even know her?"

Gia had no idea how, but even if she had to pay Cadence, she would make certain to deliver on her end of the bargain. "Leave that to me. Do we have a deal?"

"If Cadence isn't there within the first half hour, I'm kicking everyone out. Understood?"

Gia grinned. "She'll be there."

"You also have to promise me the church will be spotless by morning, and every single item – down to the hymnal bookmarks – will be returned to exactly where they were before you entered. As much as I might like to stick it to my father, I want to do it stealthily."

"I promise," said Gia, and the two closed the deal with a handshake.

As the day withered into twilight, a jackrabbit scuttled toward a miniature oasis of knee-high foliage in a sparse region of the high-desert floor. Once within its umbrage, a metal trap snapped shut on one of its hind legs.

Lucas McAbel watched from beneath a brown tarp. He tossed aside his camouflage and strolled to the struggling rabbit. "Calm down," he said as he stroked its fur. He opened the trap to release the animal, and he let it limp away just far enough to welcome freedom before raising the crossbow strapped to his shoulder and shooting an arrow into its skull.

Gripping the rabbit's hind legs, the boy walked to his tent at the rear base of the red rock formation on which rested Christ Church of Sedona.

CHAPTER 16

When the morning sunlight first crept between the gap in the curtains, Cadence saw her reflection in the closet door mirror. She had difficulty sleeping, and after numerous position changes, she had left the bed in favor of the chair, where she had been sitting in darkness. The time had come for her to set aside distractions and focus her actions on the reason for her trip to Sedona. She found the motel stationery in the top drawer of the nightstand and spent the next few minutes composing a letter. Once finished she folded the paper and inserted it into an envelope, onto which she wrote Gregor's name. Leaving the envelope unsealed, she propped it against the lamp on the nightstand.

After a quick shower, she dressed and noticed that she had a voicemail. Travis' message was that the plan for the day had changed and he would explain when he picked her up. "I don't believe this!" shouted Cadence as she hung up. "I am not waiting another day. On to plan B." She draped the strap of her purse over her shoulder, opened the door and, after a slight hesitation, she threw the room key onto the bed and left.

Gregor had been in a state of energy for eleven hours. Within that time the sensory inundation became less dizzying and more relatable. His connection to life around the planet heightened at an exponential rate. He sensed every breath and every death. In fact, the Earth's vibrancy seemed indistinguishable from his own, and he felt that, if he let it, it could absorb him in entirety. Through simultaneous instants of sunsets and sunrises, midnights and noons, he felt a sudden draw to the early morning of Sedona. He could sense Travis calling to him from the canyon of the vortex with the same clarity as his awareness of two narwhals tusking in the Arctic. He concentrated on the plateau, where he converted to physical form from drops of blue light.

From the canyon below the plateau, Travis called yet again as he searched for his friend, "Gregor!"

"Coming!" he heard Gregor's voice echo, but he couldn't tell its point of origin.

Travis scanned the rocky walls. "Where are you?"

"I'll be right there!" the echoed voice told him.

Just as he spotted the ladder, he saw Gregor emerge from the crevice near the top rung – appearing from the ground as if he had stepped in from another dimension. "Now that's cool." Travis hurried to his descending friend. "So that's where you've been hiding. What's up there?"

"The vortex," answered Gregor before jumping from two rungs up.

"Why aren't they ever ground level?" Travis noticed his friend's face. "Man, you're glowing."

Gregor checked his hands. "I—"

Travis laughed. "Not literally, you dork. You have a radiance about you. Have you been using sunscreen?"

"Uh, no."

Travis wrapped an arm around his neck as they headed back to the campsite. "I'm getting worried about you."

Gregor asked, "Why?"

"I haven't seen you in almost twenty-four hours. Have you been up there the whole time? What are you eating? Do you have water? When did you last shower, and why don't you stink?"

"The vortex sustains me. Travis, I want to show you."

"Later. We have to go."

Gregor broke from him. "Listen to me. The vortex changes me. Takes me places."

"That answers the what-have-you-been-eating question. No more wild mushrooms."

"I'm serious. I can go anywhere, I think."

"I love you, man, but sometimes you get lost inside your own head. Now, speed the pace. Cadence is waiting for us."

"Where are we going?"

Travis answered, "To the best-preserved meteor crater on Earth."

Twenty minutes later, Gregor was sitting in the passenger seat as Travis drove through downtown Sedona. He had given up trying to convince his friend of the vortex's power and instead engaged in a conversation of nothing important. Gregor noticed a woman walking down a perpendicular road, and he pointed out the window. "I thought we were picking Cadence up from the motel."

Travis screeched the tires to make the turn before passing the road. He pulled up to the woman, who was indeed Cadence. "I was going to pick you up. Why are you walking?"

She hesitated before answering, "It was a nice morning, so I thought I'd walk to your campsite."

"You're going the wrong way." Travis pointed with his thumb as she slid into the backseat. "Our campsite is back that way."

"I got your voicemail," said Cadence. "Why aren't we going to the Grand Canyon?"

Travis answered, "I thought we'd save it for the end. Pull up stakes and camp there a couple of nights. I know you're adverse to camping, so I found a BNB close by."

Cadence asked, "So, where are we going today?"

"The Meteor Crater," Travis answered. "But we're taking a little detour first, and don't ask me where. It's a surprise."

A few minutes later, Travis pulled into the driveway of a Spanish-tiled, ranch-style house.

"Where are we?" Cadence asked.

"We've been offered a home-cooked meal. After days of diners and tofu by the campfire, I thought we could use it."

Gregor grabbed his arm. "Travis, whose house is this?"

Travis turned off the ignition and pocketed the keys before answering, "Lily Wickline."

Cadence asked, "Is that the lady from the crystal shop?"

Gregor crossed his arms. "Travis, no. I don't want to go in there."

"I'm with him," said Cadence.

Travis stepped from the car and looked back. "I'm staying, and since I have the keys, you guys are too." Without even closing his door, he left them for the walkway to the house.

Gregor asked Cadence, "Do you know how to hotwire a car?" He watched as Travis knocked on the front door of the house, but he couldn't see who answered. As he entered, a border collie bolted out and ran to the car.

"That's the dog I saw!" exclaimed Cadence.

Daisy bounded into the driver's seat and barked once in excitement. Her tongue hanging at the side of her mouth, she looked first at Cadence and at Gregor as if to see who would be the first to pet her. Gregor couldn't help himself. He held his hand for her to sniff and massaged her tufted cheeks with both hands. "What a beautiful girl you are." Daisy responded with a lick to his neck. "I think she wants us to go in."

"I'll wait out here."

Seeming to understand that she needed coaxing, Daisy jumped to the backseat and stretched her neck to rest her furry chin on Cadence's shoulder. Tilting her head, the young woman looked at Daisy, who responded likewise. Cadence started laughing. "Okay."

The three went to the front door, and seconds after Gregor rang the bell, Iris was standing before him. While Daisy ran into the house, she greeted, "Hi Gregor."

Gregor's heart felt cumbersome, like ballast his chest needed to dump before it could move on. "Hi," he said, and he waved toward his companion. "You remember Cadence?"

"Hello again," greeted Cadence, forcing her lips into a brief upward arc.

"Of course. Come in." Iris stepped aside to allow her guests entry and pointed to an arch. "Cadence, my mom is serving breakfast on the patio in back, if you'd like to go on out there. I want to talk to Gregor for a moment." Looking to him, she added, "If that's okay."

Gregor hesitated before answering, "Sure."

Cadence looked to Gregor, who nodded. "All right," she said, leaving them alone.

Iris took Gregor by the hand and led him to her bedroom, which had the presence of age that one would not expect for a woman as young as she. A cedar chest from decades past abutted the foot of her quilt-covered bed, which separated a dresser and end table of solid cherry, and on her wall hung a framed map of the world with Rhodesia outlined among the African countries.

Iris asked him to sit on her bed, and as soon as she closed the door, she told him, "I'm just going to spit this out, and then you can say what you want. Okay?" When Gregor nodded, she continued,

"I know you're angry at me and, although I didn't know why at the time, I do now. I freaked out, but it was because you turned neon sign on me, and I had just witnessed you evaporate and then reappear out of thin air. It wasn't because of the burns on your foot. Well, that's not entirely true. I was freaked out about the burns but only because I thought that they were the result of what you had just done. I didn't know about the fire then."

"Travis told you?"

Iris sat next to him. "Don't be angry at him, for that or bringing you here this morning. He saw I was concerned about you, and he brought you here because I asked him to."

Gregor was relieved that she knew about the burns so that he was spared from seeing her face if he had to be the one to tell her. "I appreciate your wanting to explain—"

"I didn't just want to explain." She placed her hand on his. "I wanted to see you again."

Gregor stared at her hand without saying a word. *Travis must not have told her everything. She's being nice now, but the first time she sees my body...*

Iris asked, "Now can you explain to me what on Earth happened up there?"

"It's the vortex."

"I know that."

Gregor cracked a smile. "So, I proved to you that they exist?"

Iris widened her eyes at the understatement. "More than that, but I've been around vortexes for years, and I've never seen anyone else do what you did."

Gregor was excited to explain it to someone who would listen to him. "The best way I can describe what happens is to say that the energy coming from the vortex reacts with my body, charging my atoms and vibrating them to the point that they lose cohesion. It changes my state of matter from solid and liquid to pure energy."

"Where do you go?"

"Seriously, everywhere. As energy, I'm boundless. I can feel myself everywhere on Earth and yet nowhere specifically, unless I really concentrate on an exact location." Gregor could see that Iris was having difficulty imagining the experience from his words alone. "You would understand better if you went with me." He took her hand again. "Let me show you the vortex."

With a sigh preceding a frown, she replied, "It scares me."

"I'll be right there with you, and I know I can take you with me. The more time I spend at it, the better I get. The first time, all of my clothes fell off me, but then I started taking things with me – almost *all* of my clothes when you saw me."

Iris recoiled. "I don't want to lose a leg."

Gregor locked eyes with her and refused to release them. "Please trust me. I wouldn't let anything happen to you."

"I'll think about it."

"Okay. Friends?" he asked, although feeling the urge for much more.

"Friends," answered Iris without revelation.

Gregor – and he alone – saw a faint aura arise from Iris' outline as if evoked by his stare. The light's warmth, like a siren, called to him. Before he could stop them, his lips were caressing hers in a passionate kiss unlike any in his limited romantic history. He backed away. "I'm sorry."

Iris and Gregor reclined and intertwined on the bed in a chain kiss that, after half a minute, left them both gasping for air. "All right," she said. "Not friends."

"Wait a second." Gregor pushed himself into a seated position on the edge of the bed.

"What?" she asked as she joined him.

"I don't think Travis made clear to you the extent of my scarring."

Iris told him, "Okay, you need to just rip off the bandage."

"What do you mean?"

"Your self-image is blocking you, and you're so concerned with what I'll think. Rip off the bandage now, and get it over with." After a moment of non-action, she clarified, "I want you to strip."

Appalled by the notion, he exclaimed, "No way!"

"I'm sorry, but if you don't, I'm just going to keep trying to imagine what you look like underneath those clothes, and you're going to keep wondering how I'll react. Better to just get it out of the way, and then we can move on."

Gregor turned his eyes to the floor. "I don't know." He looked at the sunlight penetrating her gossamer curtains. "It's so bright in here."

Iris took his hand and assured him, "It's okay."

Standing up, Gregor unbuttoned his shirt. "Please don't freak out."

Iris replied, "I promise," clenching the quilt as she awaited her first look at Gregor's maligned skin.

Gregor closed his eyes as he separated the front of his shirt and pushed it from his shoulders to expose his torso.

"Huh," Iris responded.

Gregor opened his eyes to see her unspectacular expression. "That's it?"

With a quick shrug, she told him, "I see a little uneven coloring, but nothing an hour in the sun wouldn't cure. I don't know why you're so self-conscious about it."

Gregor looked in the mirror above the dresser and gasped. The scars that had encased his chest, arms and back for most of his life were now gone. "That's... impossible." He dropped his pants and saw no more scarring on his legs. "What..." He kicked off his shoes and tore off his socks, at which point Iris noticed a difference from what she had seen the day before.

She pointed to them and said, "Hey, your feet are fine now."

"I don't understand. How did this happen?" Gregor peeked inside his underwear and exclaimed, "Amazing."

"Really?" asked Iris with evident curiosity.

"The vortex. It must have… healed me."

"Is that possible?" she asked before answering her own question with, "Listen to what I'm asking the disappearing man."

"I don't know how else to explain it."

"Why weren't you healed yesterday? You had already experienced the vortex."

"I've had a lot more exposure to it since then."

Grinning, Iris jumped to her feet. "Put on your pants, and let's go show your friends."

"No!" Gregor said, horrified at the thought. "I'm not ready to share this yet."

"Why not? This is wonderful."

He pulled up his pants. "I don't want anyone looking at me."

"Don't be silly." Iris grabbed his hand to lead him. "You look great."

All the faces of those who had seen him before flooded his thoughts, drowning the possibility that anyone could look at him in a positive way. "I just need some time to process this, to get comfortable with," he looked down at his torso and uttered, "this."

"Okay." She embraced him, resting her cheek on his chest. "It'll be our secret for now."

On the back patio, Lily, Travis and Cadence were seated around the table and, while the two women were engaged in a one-sided conversation, Travis listened in hungered boredom. Lily, dressed in a white linen dress with a pale floral pattern, told Cadence, "Visitors to Sedona often say they felt inexplicably compelled to come. I believe Sedona called you here."

With a dismissive gesture, Cadence said. "That's ridiculous. Places don't call people. How would that even work?"

Lily answered, "Perhaps you were looking for something

— answers — subconsciously, and the universe responded by giving you a vision that would lead you to those answers."

Seeing a nearby hammock hanging between two cottonwood trees, Travis left the table. As soon as he sat on the hammock, Daisy ran up to him. "You want on?" he asked her, and she stepped onto the hanging cloth to join him. When he lay back, the dog stretched out beside him with her chin resting on the front of his shoulder. He groaned when he realized he could still hear the patio conversation.

Cadence said, "I'm sorry, but I don't believe in that s… stuff."

Undeterred, Lily tried to explain her reasoning, "You saw Daisy and me without ever knowing us before, and you thought her name was Sedona. You were obviously gifted with a vision, one that — if my guess is correct — is directly responsible for your being here at this moment. Whether you choose to believe it or not, Sedona called you here. You need to let go of your cynicism and try to discern the reason for the message."

"I know why I'm here," Cadence insisted. "It has nothing to do with magic."

With Iris at his side, Gregor stepped onto the patio and asked, "What magic?"

Travis threw his hands in the air at the sight of Gregor and Iris. "There they are. Now we can eat." He prodded Daisy from the hammock and followed her back to the patio.

Lily stood and faced her daughter with a disquieted look. "Is everything okay?"

Iris glanced at Gregor and answered, "We're good, Mom."

A smile of relief spread across her face. "I'm so glad to hear that." She gave Gregor a warm hug. "I'll get breakfast on the table. Cadence, do you mind helping me?"

Cadence did little to conceal her surprise at the request and paused a moment before scooting her chair from the table. She entered the house behind Lily.

"Are you mad at me?" asked Travis.

"No," Gregor responded. "I can't stay angry at my best friend. Or you either."

As Gregor laughed, Travis said with mock indignation, "Whatever."

His laughter ended when he saw the canyon beyond the lawn. "Is this all your backyard?"

Iris nodded. "The property line is the top ridge of the back and side walls of the canyon."

"It's magnificent."

She clasped Gregor's hand, saying, "I'll give you a closer look."

In the kitchen, as Cadence washed her hands, Lily loaded covered dishes from the central island onto a large tray and asked, "When you're finished, would you get the pitcher of pomegranate juice from the fridge?"

Drying her hands with a dish towel, Cadence withdrew the pitcher but, as she turned to put it on the island, a tremor shuddered her hand. Lily reached for the pitcher to keep her from dropping it, and just before she could secure it, a bit of the liquid sloshed onto her dress. "I have it," Lily told her, and she brought the pitcher to a rest on the countertop. "Are you okay?"

"I'm sorry. It was heavier than I thought, and my hands are wet." She saw the small stain on Lily's dress just above the waistline. "Your dress."

Lily shrugged it off. "Don't worry about it."

"But it's ruined."

"It's old and ready to be recycled. I'm much more worried about you. You're not well, are you?" Cadence broke into a deluge of tears, and Lily opened her arms to embrace the crying girl.

The tears stopped as Cadence regained her composure and separated from Lily. "I'm fine," she responded, wiping her eyes. "Where is your bathroom?"

Gregor and Iris returned from their walk to the canyon's mouth to find a bored Travis playing with the leaves of a potted plant near the table. "What are you doing?" Gregor asked.

"Wondering if this plant is edible," he replied, but when Lily appeared with a tray full of food, he perked up. "Hallelujah! I am starving."

"I forgot to put the biscuits in," Lily said as she began unloading the tray's contents, which included muesli, fresh fruit and glasses for the juice. "They'll be ready in a few."

Pointing to a covered dish, Travis asked, "What's this?" but his chest sank at the answer.

Lily removed the cover. "Soy bacon," she replied. "Try it. You're going to love it."

Cadence emerged from the house carrying the pitcher of pomegranate juice with both hands and declaring, "Everything looks wonderful."

Fifteen minutes later the quintet had eased into a genial comfort that would have given any onlooker the impression of a routine gathering of old friends. Lily said, "When Iris was five, we went to a yard sale, and she found this large map of the world that she insisted I buy for her. I thought she just liked the different colors of the countries."

"The one that's hanging in your room now?" Gregor asked Iris.

"That's the one," Lily answered. "I guess she stared at it enough that within a month or two, I could point to anywhere on it, and she could name the country. I even covered the names with cut-up pieces of sticky pads to test her."

Travis asked Iris, "What country is bordered by Kazakhstan in the north?"

"Mom, you're embarrassing me," Iris said, but still answered the question. "Uzbekistan and Kyrgyzstan have full northern borders with Kazakhstan, while Turkmenistan has a partial."

"See what I mean," said Lily, beaming.

Cadence whispered to Travis, "Is that right?" to which he shrugged.

"She was always so eager to leave Sedona. When she left for college in Phoenix, I was afraid I'd never see her again."

"Mom, please stop there."

Lily said to Iris, "It's a cute story," and to the others, "So I was very pleasantly surprised when she quit college and returned home three weeks later with a severe case of homesickness."

Travis told Iris, "You don't seem like the homesick type."

"I wasn't homesick," insisted Iris. "That just wasn't the right college for me."

"Well, whatever the reason, she enrolled in an online college and is now about to finish her doctorate. I'm very proud of her."

Iris rolled her eyes. "Okay, let's change the subject."

Lily offered a new topic, "How about Gregor's vortex?"

Travis sighed, "Oh god."

Lily asked, "How does it allow you to disappear, and where does it take you?"

"Vortex?" Cadence asked.

Lily looked to Gregor. "Do they not know?"

Iris spoke up for him. "Mom, I don't think he wants to talk about this right now."

"I've been seeing and hearing that word a lot," Cadence said. "What exactly is a vortex?"

Lily's eyes lit up. "Vortexes are powerful spirals of energy found at hot spots throughout the world, including several special sites here in Sedona."

While the eldest woman talked, Gregor glanced at Travis, who was almost sneering in confusion as he mouthed, "Disappear?"

Cadence looked at Lily like she had just thrown a drink in her face. "You're joking."

Lily responded, "Barely more than a century ago, the idea of harnessing power from something that couldn't even be seen would've been considered lunacy, but nuclear power is commonplace today. Do you believe we're currently so advanced we've discovered every type of energy in existence? Why do you think Sedona is a UFO hot spot? A possible explanation for heightened activity is other races harness the special energy here. Their ships might even run on it."

Smirking, Travis asked, "So you think Sedona is some sort of galactic gas station?"

Cadence laughed at his comment. "Offering a free wash with every fill-up."

Travis waved his hands like he was erasing an invisible chalkboard. "Okay, rewinding just a bit. What did you mean when you asked Gregor how he disappears?"

"I'm sorry," Lily told Gregor. "I assumed your friends knew."

Gregor raised his eyes and spoke up. "Lily's right – about the vortex. The one I found is like a massive current of energy. It flows through me and permeates my body." He hesitated and looked to Iris for support before confessing, "It… converts me to energy."

Travis laughed. "Whoa bro. How many of those mushrooms did you eat? You're getting way out there, even for you."

"It's the truth!" exclaimed Iris.

Lily jumped from her seat, crying, "My biscuits!" and rushed inside to retrieve them.

Cadence took the opportunity to speak up. "Have you all gone absolutely crazy? Gregor? Converting to energy? What?"

Travis brushed it off. "What he means is that he gets so deep in a trance that he can't feel his body anymore." Eyes wide and palms exposed, he asked Gregor, "Right?"

"That's not what I mean at all," insisted Gregor. "I wanted to show you this morning."

Lily returned empty-handed. "I'm sorry, but the biscuits burned."

Travis cursed under his breath, "The one thing I could eat."

Gregor explained, "The universe is all energy and matter

interwoven in cyclical existence. Energy can be converted to matter, and matter can be converted to energy."

Travis responded, "I understand about matter and energy conversion – like a nuclear reaction converts matter to energy, and the Big Bang filled the universe with energy that eventually converted to matter. What I don't get is your giant leap to discovering some natural power source that can turn a person into energy and – I assume since you're here in the flesh – back again."

Lily chimed in. "I think I can answer that. It's too powerful to be a normal vortex." She pointed to Gregor as if naming the winner of a contest. "I believe you found the umbilical cord."

"Umbilical cord?" asked Cadence.

"The energy that sparks life doesn't originate on any planet. It's a universal energy that feeds the planet like an expectant mother nourishing a fetus. The energy fills living physical matter, and when that matter can no longer sustain it, the energy returns anew to the universe."

Gregor asked, "You think this life energy is delivered through the vortex I found?"

"How do you rectify that with your belief that there are supposed to be vortexes all over the world?" asked Travis. "You can't have more than one umbilical cord."

Lily made an imaginary circle with her hands. "The energy from the cord is veined around the world to vortexes that dispense their portion regionally, ensuring the continual regeneration of life on Earth."

Cadence threw up her hands up and kept them there until she finished speaking. "Life didn't start with some bizarre universal energy. God created life!"

"Who created God?" asked Iris.

"He just always was," replied Cadence.

Gregor could sense animus on the path of the current topic, so he interrupted with, "It's getting late. We should really head out for the Meteor Crater."

Iris touched Gregor's hand. "I forgot you're going there today"

Gregor looked at Iris and knew he didn't want to leave her. He asked Travis and Cadence, "Would the two of you mind going without me?"

"It was your idea," protested Travis. "You've been dying to see it."

"I want to spend time with Iris," Gregor explained, eliciting a wide grin from Lily.

Iris told them, "I'm up for going – if you all wouldn't mind my tagging along."

"Of course not," Travis answered, as Cadence responded with silence. "Let's go."

Lily hugged them one by one, and they thanked her for breakfast. She said to Travis, "Let me wrap up the rest of the bacon to take with you."

"No!" he responded with too much volume. "It'll just spoil in the car."

As Lily offered her final hug to Gregor, she whispered in his ear, "I need to warn you about the vortex, without the others around." When they disembraced, he nodded.

Once in the front yard, after a brief debate over whose car to take, they piled into Travis' with Gregor and Iris in the backseat. Out of the blue, Gregor announced, "Hey, I just realized that Sedona spelled backwards is 'anodes.'"

Travis cracked a smile. "You're such a nerd."

CHAPTER 17

The clatter of the keys bounced from the walls of August Briar's home office in an uninterrupted cacophony. With his eyes sealed and face toward the ceiling, the reverend rocked his upper body back and forth as he typed at his computer. As if entranced by the Holy Ghost, he had not looked at the monitor for more than half an hour when the ring of his cell phone atop the desk startled him into full consciousness, and he relaxed his shoulders in relief.

After answering the call, the man on the other end of the line identified himself as Jeff Woodard from Mourning Dove Investigations. "What news do you have for me?" August asked as he saved and closed the document on which he was working.

Jeff told him that he had found Travis Harper on a social media outlet and investigated thirty-seven of his male friends before discovering his travelling companion. He explained, "I had to find out where each one worked and then call to see who was on vacation. Then—"

"Jeff, I am not interested in the process."

Without contempt, in spite of August's candor, Jeff told him, "I'm sending you a photo now. Let me know if this is the guy."

August took the phone from his ear so he could see the image of the California driver's license loading on the screen. He smiled when he saw the headshot within, and he whispered the name as he read it, "Gregor Buckingham."

"Is that the guy?" Jeff asked.

"That is he."

"Good. I'm sending you another pic. During the background check, I found a police file on him." Jeff told him about the fire that almost killed Gregor.

August viewed the image used during the trial of Gregor's father to show the extent of the damage to his body. "Scarred by Hell fire," he muttered, and he wondered if the boy's father had attempted to destroy the evil inside his scion. Unable to stomach the image any longer, he scrolled back to the license photo, zooming in on Gregor's face.

Mitchell entered the study with a keychain dangling from his finger.

"Thanks for the information." August disconnected and placed the phone on the desk.

Mitchell asked, "Are you done with the computer?" He held up the keychain, which tethered a flash drive among the keys. "I need to transfer my files for the conference."

August pushed his chair away from the computer. "I updated the agenda once more to change the location of my Sunday sermon to Shaman's Dome."

"Shaman's Dome? But that's so far from the conference."

"It is the grand finale. People can drive to it. I will speak from the mouth of the cave, while the congregation looks up from below."

Mitchell snickered, "Your own Sermon on the Mount," earning a look of consternation from his father. "That's up too high for anyone to hear you. They'll barely see you."

"I realize that," said August as he walked toward the door. "You need to set up a sound system and a large screen for a video feed. Take care of it."

"You left your phone." Mitchell handed it to him and his thumb grazed the keypad, illuminating the last picture viewed. "Why do you have a picture of Gregor on your phone?"

August snatched the phone from him. "You know him?"

Now seated, Mitchell replied, "He's a friend of Cadence – the girl I brought to church."

"Tell me what you know."

"I only saw him once, but Cadence told me a little about him."

"Would you say he is a God-fearing man?" August still hoped the man he witnessed performing such a wondrous feat was some-how a divine messenger sent for his benefit.

Mitchell chuckled. "More like godless. Cadence told me he's an atheist."

August's heart sank. "There is my answer," he said under his breath.

"What did you say?"

"And still you question my assessment of her, when she allies herself with irreligionists?"

"Allies herself? You make it sound like we're at war."

"It is a war!" August screamed. "I have no idea what I did to produce a son with such feeble judgment that he could be so easily seduced into the company of those disdainful of God."

As his father gusted from the home office, Mitchell was left in silence to wonder how their conversation had turned into a verbal lynching. His father's criticisms seemed to be gaining in frequency since Lucas had come to town. "I'm so close to not caring anymore."

Turning his attention to the computer, he clicked on the list of recent documents to find the sermon he had written titled, "Evil in Degrees." Among them was an unrecognized document – one August in his distraction, neglected to delete from the list this time.

Mitchell clicked on "Eponym," and to his surprise, a password popup appeared on the screen.

"Password? Why would he password-protect a file?"

After a couple of failed attempts at unlocking the document, he typed "West Canaan" to open it. As the page count ran up to just over six hundred, he scrolled down the first one, and saw it was the title page of a book his father was writing. Mitchell read the title, "The Book of August," and the notation beneath it, "For insertion into the New Testament between the books of Jude and Revelation." He laughed aloud. "How... apocryphal."

In the solarium, August knelt before the Madagascar palm to sweep away a portion of the river rock covering the soil, revealing Gregor's amulet. He held the crystal up before turning his gaze to the sky. "Was it not You who healed me? Am I being tested? Did You allow the Devil to bring him here to tempt me? To see if I am truly worthy to be Your prophet?"

With all his might, August threw the amulet over the solarium's glass enclosure and into the brush along the hillside. "Tell me what You want me to do, Lord," he beckoned, but even before the words left his lips, he had an epiphany. He thought about Manasseh, the king of Judah who practiced witchcraft and later repented. "Could someone who is so beholden to the Devil that he wields his power actually be turned to Christ? Is that my test?"

CHAPTER 18

"So, you broke up with the preacher's son?" Travis asked as they waited in line to purchase tickets to the Meteor Crater's observation area. During the hour-long drive from Sedona, his eyes had shifted numerous times between the road and rearview mirror, where he observed Gregor and Iris growing closer in saltating frames. He was annoyed Cadence had slept almost the entire way, leaving him alone in his thoughts, and now he called her out in minor retribution.

Gregor released Iris' hand and turned around to ask, "You were dating a preacher's son?"

Cadence frowned at Travis and told Gregor, "We weren't dating. Mitchell and I—"

"Who's Mitchell?" asked Gregor.

Iris responded, "He's the son of the man who's trying to shut us down."

"How did I not know about the two of you?"

"There's nothing to know," Cadence insisted.

Travis told him, "You've had your head stuck in a socket, Mr. Energy," eliciting a giggle from Cadence.

"Iris!" called a man approaching from the nearby gift shop with two bottles of water. Handsome, well-built and nerdish with wavy sienna hair and brown eyes, the man wore a labcoat embroidered on the left side with NASA's insignia and the name Finn Scarbury underneath.

"Finn!" Iris responded with a corresponding hug. "What are you doing here?"

"I work here," he answered with a grin.

"Let me introduce you to my friends." Iris motioned to each as she told him their names. "This is Cadence and Travis and Gregor. This is Finn. We went to high school together."

Finn fumbled to hold both bottles as he shook hands with all. "Nice to meet you."

Iris told him, "Last I heard, you were zooming through college. Engineering at MIT?"

"Astro-mechanical engineering," Finn corrected. "I graduated, and earned my doctorate, and now I'm working for NASA."

"NASA has an office here?" asked Gregor.

"We're leasing space – no pun intended." Finn snickered alone and explained, "We're exploiting the Barringer Crater's ideal concavity to perform RTTs on our new MESH. I'm sorry. I need to speak English. We're performing real-terrain tests on our Mars Extreme Surface Hydrocar. Are you all here to see the crater? Of course, you are. There's nothing else around here until you reach the Petrified Forest."

Iris answered, "We were just about to buy tickets to the observation platform."

"That will get you a nice view from the rim, but would you like to see the crater floor?"

"Absolutely," Gregor and Travis blurted in concert.

A few minutes later, the group of five was standing outside a large aluminum building that looked like it had been erected with the forethought of quick disassembly. It stood seven meters high with walls twice that length. Finn shielded the punch-code lock from the others with his body as he entered the numeric combination and opened the door. "Welcome to my laboratory," he said with the British pronunciation that made him laugh. He nodded toward the camera hanging from Travis' neck. "No photography in here."

Inside, the laboratory appeared more permanent than the exterior had suggested. The white walls supported several shelves of tools and equipment, and four desks propped up elaborate computer systems. Besides the door they entered, the only other exit was a large garage door on a perpendicular wall. A small vacuuming robot roamed the gunmetal floor around a large, tarp-covered mass near the center of the room.

"Do you work here by yourself?" Iris asked.

"There are four of us... Well, three now. Lester went to work for SETI. Frank and Donna left for Flagstaff a few minutes ago to restock our supplies."

"What's SETI?" Cadence asked Travis in a whisper that echoed throughout the building.

Before Travis could speak, Finn responded, "Search for extraterrestrial intelligence, which would be much easier if they would just introduce themselves when they visit us." When Cadence laughed, Finn asked, "You don't believe in life on other planets?"

"Not really, but even if there were life on other planets, I don't believe they would be able to travel light years to get here. Look at us. We're probably centuries away from being able to travel to the nearest star, if we're ever capable of even doing so."

Finn shook his head, saying, "Your logic is flawed with a common misconception. Our sun is relatively young; therefore, life on our planet is young. Life on Earth began four billion years ago, but life on other planets could have started millions or billions of years earlier." He stopped speaking when he heard Cadence exhale in a scoffing manner. "What?"

Cadence pointed out, "I don't know how you rectify what you're saying with the fact that the universe is only six-thousand-years old."

Finn turned to Travis and asked, "Is she serious?"

"I'm not sure, actually."

Finn responded, "All right. Let's assume you're correct and that the other planets in the universe are all the same age as the Earth. We often think that our technology has progressed at a normal rate – that is, a rate comparable to that which any civilization in our shoes would have progressed. What if we're wrong? If you drew a graph of technological advancement from, say two-thousand years ago, the progress would not appear as a straight, steadily elevating line." Finn motioned with his hand a line moving at about ten degrees from the level of the floor. "Science has undergone centuries of dormancy, kept from sprouting by the drought of religious fervor. Consider the Dark Ages as just one example. Now consider how quickly our technology has progressed in the computer age. Pioneering technology is outdated almost as quickly as it's available, which is sending the line on our graph on a much more inclined ascension." To this last point, Finn again drew an imaginary line, but this time the incline was approximately thirty degrees. "Other civilizations that have been unimpeded by faith would have most likely reached this rate of progression far sooner than we did, so even if life on our worlds sparked at the same instant, they would most likely be technologically superior to us."

When Cadence responded with crossed arms and a roll of her eyes, Travis changed the subject by asking Finn, "So what do you think of this whole space station mess?"

"Disheartening," Finn answered. "I wish I had been there when it happened."

"Are you kidding?" asked Iris.

"Not at all. They extinguished the fire but not before it damaged the consoles that control navigation and communications, among other functions. They couldn't even call for help, but if they could, a ship with new equipment couldn't have reached them before the station reentered the atmosphere and burned. From the damage I've seen, however, it could've been repaired."

"You've seen the damage?" Gregor asked.

Finn grimaced. "Did I say that? I meant from the description of it. Let me show you my project." He hit a switch on the wall, and six cables raised the tarp that was covering the large object in the middle of the lab. He waved at the now-exposed vehicle. "Here is the MESH." With its asymmetrical frame comprised of rectangular metal plates, the black MESH looked like a stealth fighter without wings, resting on six tires that were almost two meters in diameter and lacking any discernable tread.

"Whoa." Travis' eyes widened, and he ran a hand along the frame. "This is beautiful."

"We created it for the first manned mission to Mars. We had to develop a vehicle that could seat five colonists and traverse any Martian surface."

"This is your design?" Iris asked.

"It was designed by me and my team... but, honestly, mostly me."

"I'm really impressed," Iris told him. "I knew you were going to be amazing in whatever career path you chose."

Finn revealed his extreme pleasure at her reaction with a broad grin and flushed face. "So does anybody want to go for a ride?"

"Shotgun!" Travis called before jumping into the passenger seat.

"Most definitely," Gregor answered. He helped Cadence in through the driver's side door, and she scooted into the backseat behind Travis. Iris sat in the middle of the backseat, and Gregor sat to her left with his arm around her shoulders.

When Travis shut the door, he heard a suction sound. "What's that?"

Finn pulled himself up into the driver's seat and shut the door, causing the sound to repeat. "The carriage is airtight – completely sealed."

"Good thing if it's going to Mars, right? You don't want the passengers exploding from the pressure or instantly freezing," said Travis.

Finn told him, "Those are myths."

"Oh yeah. Mars does have an atmosphere. It's not like being in the vacuum of space."

"Actually, that wouldn't happen in space either," said Finn. "You could live up to a minute or two in outer space. You wouldn't freeze instantaneously, your blood wouldn't boil, and you certainly wouldn't explode. You would eventually pass out from a lack of oxygen and then suffocate to death."

Travis responded, "Huh. I didn't know that."

"All right, everyone. Buckle up." Finn pushed the garage door opener clipped to the sun visor. "We don't want anybody tumbling around inside the vehicle." He started the engine, and the vehicle lurched forward with a sudden jerk before settling into a smooth ride.

"When you say tumbling around..." Iris began. "We're not going to roll over, are we?"

"Of course not," Finn replied. "We shouldn't anyway. We're going to be driving down a seventy-eight-degree incline."

"That's awfully steep," Gregor said.

"No need to worry," Finn assured them. "The MESH has tires made of a highly adaptable polymer that allows them to mold to the shape of the surface as additional stability is needed."

"Like Velcro?" Iris asked.

"Different principle, but in essence. The MESH has a repositioning, triple-axle system that can triangulate to climb or descend an embankment of up to eighty degrees. No more than that, though. My former colleague, Karen, found that out the hard way."

Travis asked, "Doesn't that just give us two degrees of wiggle room?"

"We won't need it," Finn said.

As they neared the rim, Cadence asked, "Aren't there stairs we could take?"

Gregor tapped the window. "Will these windows withstand the Martian winds?"

"Good question," said Finn with a grin. "The winds on Mars can reach a sustained one hundred kph – kilometers per hour. These windows are made out of a classified material that I can't really tell you about without clearance, but I can tell you it's not glass." Finn seemed to be finished talking, but he blurted out, "Think transparent alloy." After a second, he added, "By the way, don't repeat that to anyone."

Iris pointed at the rim of the crater, now five meters away. "Look!"

From the front seat, Travis could see the whole crater. As he watched the end of level ground approaching without a decrease in the speed of the vehicle, his heart began pounding against his chest. "Finn, how deep is this crater?"

"One-hundred-seventy meters."

Cadence grabbed her seat. "Stop the car!"

Without reacting to his passengers' rising concern, Finn told everyone, "Hang on!" at the same time that Cadence repeated her demand. He drove the MESH over the rim. All but the driver screamed at the sudden shift in bearing, and they clung to anything they could. Gregor tightened his embrace of Iris as she pushed her face against his chest and wrapped her fingers around swatches of his shirt. Cadence dug her nails into the seat and closed her eyes. Travis stamped his feet onto imaginary brakes and pushed his palms against the dashboard.

"Guys, calm down." Finn ordered. "We're fine."

Instead of facing straight down at the crater floor, Travis looked ahead at the crater's opposite side in the distance. "What's happening?"

Finn explained, "The front axle extends below the second so the tires can travel the steep side of the crater, while the carriage tilts forward only about thirty degrees."

Travis relaxed and caught his breath. "Hey, this isn't so bad." He looked back at the backseat passengers. "Everyone okay?"

Gregor opened his eyes, peering through the windshield and the window at his side, from which he could see they were descending. "It's like taking a glass elevator."

Iris released Gregor's shirt and lifted her head to see the side window. "You're right."

Last to open her eyes, Cadence muttered, "I'm okay," but refused to loosen her grip on the seat.

Travis turned his attention to Finn. "This is so cool."

"I told you. Nothing to worry about. The crater is approximately twelve-hundred meters in diameter and, in case you didn't hear me over the screaming, one-hundred-seventy meters deep. It was formed fifty-thousand years ago by a meteor about fifty meters in diameter and composed mainly of nickel-iron. Like other meteors, it also contained the rare element iridium. An interesting fact about iridium is that it's been found all over the Earth in a layer of sediment formed sixty-five-million years ago, called the K-T boundary, that helped prove – to most people anyway," nodding to Cadence, "the theory of a meteor impact as the causative for the demise of the dinosaurs."

When the carriage returned to a normal position, Travis said, "We're on the floor now."

Cadence sighed, "Thankfully."

Finn continued driving until they were near the crater's center, at which point everyone exited the MESH. He pointed to a chain-link fence about fifteen meters away. "Over there are the remains of a mining camp from the turn of the last century. Do you want to see it?"

Travis said, "I do. What were they mining?"

As he walked toward the camp, Finn answered, "Daniel Barringer was drilling for the meteorite, which he thought was buried in the center here. He didn't know that the bulk of the meteorite had been vaporized by the force of the impact."

Walking behind the others toward the meteor mine, Iris realized Gregor was no longer beside her. She looked over her shoulder to see him standing near the MESH and massaging his temples. She hurried back to him and asked, "Gregor, are you okay?"

Gregor replied, "I don't know. As soon as I stepped out of the MESH, I started feeling lightheaded. It's so hot."

"Really? I'm not hot." Iris took a step toward him. "Do you have a fever?"

Gregor kicked off his shoes and pulled at his socks. "Stay back!"

Iris felt an intense heat emanating from his direction. "Oh my god. Gregor, get away from there! It's overheating!"

He ripped off his shirt. "It's not the MESH." As he tried to remove his pants, he lost his balance. He took a few steps back and fell with his back against one of the tires.

"What's happening to you?"

"I'm burning up," he grunted. "I have to leave." He closed his eyes, and in a moment, he was glowing blue.

"What are you doing?"

"Trying to convert and get away."

Iris expected to see him disappear again, but instead of the energy helping him to convert, she could see it drain from him. In a lateral shower of tiny blue droplets spanning three-hundred-sixty degrees, the energy rained against the crater's wall, where it was absorbed. Like a flash storm, the rain ended seconds later, and Gregor fell to the ground unconscious.

In the dissipating heat, Iris came to his aid by slapping his face. "Gregor!" She stepped around the corner of the MESH to call the others back and saw them already returning. Gregor stirred, and she raced back to his side. "Are you okay?" He appeared groggy and weak, unable to lift his head from the ground. "Don't move. The others are coming back now."

Gregor lifted a hand to his torso. "My clothes."

"I'm more worried about you," Iris told him, brushing aside his concern.

Gregor grabbed Iris' arm and said, "Don't let them see me like this. Help me up."

Iris frowned at his lack of priorities, but she helped him to a seated position. She looked at his strewn clothing and asked, "Are you okay?" Once he nodded, she left him to retrieve his shirt, socks and shoes. As she did, Gregor struggled to pull up his pants, which were around his ankles, but he had to stop just below his underwear. "They're almost here," Iris warned as she knelt again beside him. Gregor held out his arms so that she could replace his shirt, and while he buttoned it, she slid his socks and shoes on his feet. He tried once more to pull his pants up all the way. Seeing him struggle, Iris began to help, just as the others turned the corner.

"Are we interrupting something?" asked Travis.

Gregor began to collapse, but Travis caught him. Finn rushed to his side as Iris helped lay his head on the ground, and he checked the pulse in his neck.

"What happened?" Cadence asked with an accusatory glare at Iris.

Iris answered, "He fainted."

Finn asked Gregor, "How do you feel?"

Cadence frowned at Iris. "Why were his pants down?"

"He said he was feeling hot just before he passed out."

"Thirsty," Gregor mumbled.

"I'll get water," Travis said, and he dashed to retrieve a bottle from the MESH.

"Are you okay to sit up now?" Finn asked, and when Gregor nodded, he helped him up. "I think you might have sun stroke. The bowl shape of the crater serves as a natural satellite dish, focusing the heat in the center, where we are." Finn turned to Iris. "Did you see those lights?"

"What lights?" asked Iris in her most *Gaslight* tone.

"We saw these weird blue lights," said Cadence. She guillotined her torso with the sides of her hands. "They seemed to go right through us."

Travis returned with a bottle of water for Gregor. "Here you go, buddy. I think the lights had something to do with a NASA experiment, but Finn here is being mum about it."

"It wasn't us," Finn insisted.

Travis grinned at him. "All right. I believe you."

Cadence pointed to the observation deck. "Maybe someone was using a laser pointer."

Travis told Finn, "By the way, you have a flat tire."

"Don't be ridiculous." Finn glanced at the MESH and yelled, "What happened to my tire?" He hurried to the tire Gregor had leaned on during his episode. It was now drooped over the wheel. "It looks melted, but that's impossible. The tires can withstand four-hundred Kelvin."

Cadence asked, "Could it be that satellite dish effect you were talking about?"

Finn frowned and half-rolled his eyes. "We'd all be dead now if the effect were that pronounced. I was just talking about a few degrees."

"Do you have a spare?" Travis asked.

"No, not on the vehicle. I have one in my lab."

Travis chuckled. "Not much good there, is it?"

"There's no room on the MESH for a spare."

"You might want to consider making room before you shoot it off into space." Travis pointed to where the trunk would be on a normal car. "You could bolt it onto the back there."

"Thank you for the re-design," Finn said. "Would you like it in a different color too?"

"Just a suggestion. Hope for the best, but prepare for the worst."

"Regardless, I can't drive the MESH until I get a new tire on it."

SEDONA: THE LOST VORTEX

He pointed to a wending path on a side less inclined than where they descended. "We'll hike the trail back to the rim."

"There was a path?" Cadence asked with annoyance.

Iris smiled at Gregor and felt his forehead. "Do you think you can stand now?"

"Sure. Travis, can you help me up?"

Travis wrapped Gregor's arm around his shoulders and hoisted him into a standing position. However, when given the opportunity to stand on his own strength, he again faltered. Travis caught him and held him up. "Okay you can't walk yet." He helped him back to the ground and asked Finn, "Do you have a stretcher in the MESH or something to carry him with?"

Finn smiled. "That's an emergency we prepared for."

"I don't need a stretcher," insisted Gregor.

Travis warned him, "You're doing the stretcher, or I'll fireman-carry you all the way up."

"I'll take the stretcher."

Finn entered the MESH and reemerged with a square of some exotic material the size of a briefcase.

Laughing at the sight, Travis asked, "Do you have an adult size, Boy Scout?"

Finn gave the square a quick shake, causing it to expand in an instant like a magician's cane into a two-meter-by-half-meter rectangle. "Will this do?" he asked with a superior smirk.

Travis and Finn helped Gregor onto the stretcher, and the band of five proceeded from the crater. Once they were again on the rim, Gregor spoke up, "Guys, I can walk now."

"Are you sure?" Travis asked.

"Honestly, I feel much better," he assured them. When he was lowered to the ground, all stood ready to catch him as he erected himself on his own power. "See, I'm fine."

With a snap, Finn minimized the stretcher, saying, "I need to return to my lab." He gave a nod to Gregor. "You should visit the hospital regardless, and you need to rehydrate."

Gregor shook his hand. "Thank you for your help and the ride. I'm sorry about the tire."

"You have no reason to apologize. It's obviously defective in some way, and my team will have to discern the cause." He gave Iris a warm hug. "Really nice to see you again."

"You too, Finn. Please call me the next time you're in Sedona."

Finn walked away and waved, saying, "Nice meeting you all." They replied likewise.

Travis threw his arm around Cadence. "Come on. I'll buy us all water at the gift shop." The two scurried ahead, leaving Iris and Gregor alone on the rim.

Iris asked, "What happened down there?"

"The energy stored inside me reacted with something in the crater – maybe the iridium."

"Finn said the concave shape of the crater focuses the sunlight in the center. Do you think that had anything to do with it?"

"Maybe it has the same effect with the iridium, magnifying its impact on the energy."

"Then you need to stay away from meteor craters."

CHAPTER 19

Walking alongside the road, Cadence could see a bright red, hot-air balloon coming in for a landing at the grassy launch site, where several other balloons were already being deflated. She had begun her trek an hour before, after returning from the Meteor Crater, and she was now near exhaustion. She sat on the grass to recover, waiting a few minutes longer for the gondola to touch the ground. Once the passengers had disembarked, she approached the pilot and asked, "Could I get a ride?"

Dimming the burners, he answered, "Sorry, Miss. The wind is picking up too much."

"Just a short ride?" Cadence asked with her best puppy-dog face.

Unmoved, the pilot insisted, "It's too dangerous."

"I'll double your fee."

Combing the area around the campsite for firewood, Travis said, "You know, camping is fun for two or three days, but then the chore aspects start to outweigh the escape aspects."

Arms laden with branches of pine and juniper, Gregor asked, "You prefer L.A. to this?"

"I'm just missing my bed. And girls."

Gregor unloaded near the fire pit. "That should be enough to last you through the night."

"Last me? Where are you going? Oh, let me guess."

"I need to recharge," Gregor explained, as he headed for the canyon.

"Fine, Duracell. Make me look like a wimp for complaining about my sleeping arrangements while you go off and spend the night out in the open without any accoutrements." Travis glanced at his tent and yelled to Gregor, "At least take your sleeping bag."

Gregor waved to him without looking back. "I won't need it."

As the sun leaned to the west, driving spikes of shadows into the Sedona landscape, Cadence rested her forearms on the rim of the balloon's gondola and enjoyed the view from four-hundred meters in the air. She looked at the ground below the gondola and considered giving in to her impatience, but she focused on Coffee Pot Rock, which was approaching underneath them, and she renewed her determination to fulfill the vision she had on her first day in this scenic town. Her hair whipping about her face, she pointed to the landmark and asked the pilot, "Can you land on the spout?"

"Not allowed," the pilot answered.

Cadence came back with, "I'll triple your fee."

The pilot shook his head, saying, "It's too dangerous, especially with this wind."

"You don't have to stay. Just drop me off." The pilot remained silent. "Quadruple."

The pilot eyed her with a furrowed brow. "You better not be

pulling my leg." He navigated the balloon closer to the rock. "How you gonna get down?"

Cadence nodded to her oversized purse. "I have gear with me."

The pilot maneuvered the balloon to a lower altitude. The gondola scraped across the top of the spout, but the wind swayed it back and forth, preventing a solid landing. The pilot grunted and told her, "I can't land it. I have to take us back."

"But we're here!" Cadence argued.

"I can't control the wind."

Seeing her opportunity slip away, she opened the gondola door.

"Hey, what are you doing?" the pilot yelled. He bolted to the door to close it, but Cadence jumped before he could reach it. Looking down, he saw that she had landed on top of the spout two meters below. "You're crazy!" he shouted as he closed the door.

She watched the balloon drift away before stepping onto the edge of the spout. She tried to look over the edge but was pushed back by the wind. She stooped to her hands and knees and crawled forward so that she could see if anyone were on the ground below. No one was.

Sobbing, Cadence fought her way back to her feet. Wiping away tears that were replaced before her fingers left her face, she looked up to the sky and prayed to God, "Please forgive me for what I'm about to do. I've asked you to help me, and I do understand that you can't answer everyone's request. Now I ask for your understanding." Turning her attention forward, she stepped to the edge and extended her arms like a bird. Cadence let out a nervous laugh and leapt.

When energy from the vortex began to convert Gregor, he felt as if each foot were standing on a different surface. His mind remained connected to his current environment while being flooded with dizzying sensations from the plane of existence he was entering.

He opened his eyes, and with his physical vision of the flora surrounding the plateau, he could also see his father in his prison cell. He could feel the chilled air at Machu Picchu, hear glacier fissures expanding in Antarctica and smell seaweed rising from the shallow ocean floor of Monterey. He could see all of Sedona in one glance, and he saw Cadence falling.

The sound of the wind rushing past her was a melody to the rapid percussion of Cadence's heart. She was alive and free. She squinted at the wall of rock blurring by her and tilted her head back on her shoulders. Within a shout of her destination, she could see a light turn on below her.

Shrouded in blue light, Gregor appeared where he sensed he should be – at the base of Coffee Pot Rock. He looked up at Cadence falling toward him, face down, but he had no time to act. She fell into him, as if she were water absorbed by a blue sponge. She and Gregor were one glowing mass. They could feel each other as if they were the other. Gregor concentrated on his being and with a mental push, separated from her. Cadence stumbled backward to the ground as the light faded from her body. She looked up at Gregor, whose glow was subsiding.

Once his normal countenance returned, Gregor hurried to her. "Are you okay?"

With a stunned look on her face, Cadence asked, "Are we dead?"

"No." Gregor helped her to her feet.

In a fit of anger, she pushed him. "Why were you standing there? I could've killed you."

"Why was I standing there? Why were you falling there?"

"I slipped." She looked up to see the distance she had fallen. "How am I alive?"

"I… caught you."

Cadence almost laughed. "Gregor, you're no superhero. What was that light?" She looked at her arms and asked, "Are you sure we're not dead?" She touched the side of Coffee Pot Rock as if to make certain she could.

"We're not dead, and I was able to save you with the energy from the vortex I told—"

"Don't be ridiculous."

Gregor hated that she wouldn't even consider his explanation when he had never given her a reason to doubt his word. "It's the truth!"

"Don't get angry. Prove it." Cadence dared. "Show me right now what you can do."

Gregor would have liked to display for her the power of the vortex's energy, but at the moment, he couldn't. "I was just recharging when I saw you. I don't have the energy."

With a smirk of accomplishment, she responded, "I know you don't want to hear it, but there's only one answer that makes any sense." She grabbed his forearms. "God. We've been touched by God. He saved us both."

"Cadence, out of all the people in the world dying at this moment, why save us?"

"I don't know. He must have a reason. He must have a plan for us."

Gregor slapped his head in exasperation. "How do you argue with blind faith?" He looked up at the spout of Coffee Pot Rock. "How did you get up there?"

Cadence searched and pointed to a fading red speck in the graying sky. "That balloon."

"You slipped out?" he asked, but when he spotted her tears, he knew. "You jumped?"

Cadence revealed her cancer had returned and metastasized. Within his embrace, she said, "I can't go through it again. The pain. The nausea. I couldn't even control my own bowels." She looked up at his face and broke from him. "I know you probably want to lecture me about suicide, but I... I just didn't want to fade away."

"Why didn't you tell me?"

"I knew you would give me hope," she answered through tears. "You have this remarkable ability to make me believe in a happy ending."

Gregor thought of the vortex energy and how it had healed his skin. He wondered if it could do the same for her, but he did not want to give her false hope – not that she would've believed him regardless. He needed to know for certain first. "Cadence, don't give up hope."

"See," she said as if he had just proven her point.

"I'm serious. Don't let the battle end with your sword in your sheath. Promise me." Gregor forced eye contact with her, to which she nodded. He placed an arm around her shoulders. "Now let me get you back to the motel."

As they began to walk, Cadence pointed to Gregor's feet. "What happened to your shoes?"

"We appreciate your letting us in," Gregor said while he and Cadence waited patiently for the motel manager to open the door to her room.

"Happens all the time," the elderly woman told him. "If you're staying here too, I'll have to charge for double occupancy."

"He's not staying," Cadence assured her as the door opened.

"There's your key." The manager spotted it on the bed, where Cadence had tossed it.

Entering the room behind Cadence, Gregor thanked the manager again before closing the door. Cadence saw her letter propped against the lamp and stuffed it into the drawer of the nightstand. "I need a shower," she said, kicking off her shoes.

"We need to talk about what happened tonight."

"Let's not right now. I made a bad decision, and God corrected me. Let's leave it at that."

They heard a knock on the door, and Gregor asked, "Are you expecting someone?"

"No. Would you see who it is?"

When Gregor opened the door, he found confused eyes staring at him. "What are you doing here?" Travis asked. "Is this where you've been coming at night? Is *vortex* a euphemism?" He placed air quotes around the six-letter word.

Cadence said, "Don't be gross. I was upset over Mitchell and needed to talk to someone."

Travis focused on Gregor. "So, you passed by me and my parked car, opting to walk all the way here by yourself?"

Cadence answered for him. "I was walking to your camp when I got tired, and I called Gregor to ask him to meet me halfway. Then we came back here. Why are you here?"

"My back was bothering me, and I didn't want to sleep on the ground tonight." Travis asked Gregor, "Were you planning on spending the night?"

"No," Cadence answered again.

Over her response, Gregor replied, "Yes."

"Gregor, I'll be fine. You don't have to stay."

"I'm not leaving you tonight," he insisted.

Travis hopped on the king-size bed and proclaimed, "Shotgun."

"Oh, good lord," exclaimed Cadence. "I'm taking a shower."

As Gregor made himself comfortable in the chair, Travis pointed to his dirty feet. "Did you walk here barefoot?"

With his Bible on the ground beside him, August prayed for strength to combat the evil he was destined to face. Moments earlier, he had parked his car on the shoulder of the road and proceeded past the empty campsite to the plateau, where he now awaited Gregor's imminent arrival. "If I can convert one so ingratiated to the Devil, I will prove myself God's greatest redeemer of lost souls."

As the minutes ticked away, his continuous prayers eased his subconscious into a meditative state until he passed out in a state of energy.

CHAPTER 20

As his body shivered from the chill of morning mist on his uncovered skin, the eyes of August were opened, and he knew that he was naked. The wind whistled through the surrounding foliage, and he ran to the relative protection of the nearest juniper. Still in a sleeper's daze, he squinted to see his black suit rumpled on the ground near where he had awakened. He hurried to clothe himself and, as he did, he was enlightened. August spun himself to scan the perimeter. "The evil is not just in that boy," he whispered. "It is this place."

Travis awoke with hair in his mouth. During the night, he had centered himself on the bed, forcing Cadence to the edge. The tips of her hair, however, extended to his pillow. He spit out the lock and slipped from the bed, feeling his way to the bathroom. After urinating, he washed his hands and swigged water from the tap. When he turned around, he was startled to see Gregor standing in the bathroom doorway.

"Hey," Gregor muttered.

"You scared the crap out of me!" Travis yelled in a whisper.

"Sorry."

As the two men exchanged places, Travis asked, "What's on the agenda today?"

"I told Iris I would take her to the vortex today, but I don't want to leave Cadence alone. Why don't you two come with us?"

Travis shook his head. "I had enough of those on the tour. I'll take care of Cadence."

"Do me a favor. Don't let her out of your sight, even for a moment."

Travis waved off his concern, saying, "Okay."

"I'm serious. I need you to just be with her today. Give her your full attention."

"I said I would," he assured him, after which, Gregor closed the door and turned on the shower. Travis crawled back into bed and faced the ceiling with his hands cupped behind his head. Detecting a change in the timbre of Cadence's respiration, he glanced at her lying on her side and noticed her bare shoulder shivering. He turned to his side to curl an arm around her and, to his surprise, she embraced it. Taking the cue, he scooted closer and spooned her.

In the cracked voice of early morning, Cadence told him, "I want to go home. Today."

"Why?" Travis asked the back of her head. "Are you not having a good time?"

"I'm just ready to leave."

Travis moved his mouth to her ear and whispered, "You've been cooped up in the motel room too much. Why don't we go to the Grand Canyon today? You wanted to go there, right?"

Cadence took a moment to answer, "Yes."

"Unfortunately, I don't think we'll be able to drag Gregor away from here to set up camp there, so it'll just be a daytrip."

In the shower, Gregor washed himself with his eyes closed, as was normal for him. Once he remembered that his appearance had changed, he opened them and looked down at his soapy torso.

Gregor smiled.

All the way home, August had been devising and revising theories about Gregor, Satan and the cursed plateau. He wondered how he had come to be naked and – since he didn't see Gregor last night – if he had somehow been entranced by the place. He had always assumed that Sedona's vortexes were myths created and perpetuated by members of the Crystal Cult, but now he suspected that Satan had imbued the vortex sites with dark power for his followers to use in his name. August needed answers.

Once home, he hurried to the computer to research vortexes and any legitimate references to their power. He soon found an article on vortexes as transdimensional doorways and, as he scanned the text, he paused to re-read apropos passages. "Conversion to energy could theoretically allow travel anywhere in the universe or to other dimensions." At the bottom of the article were links to additional resources, including one to information on a Peruvian scientist named Dr. León Heredia. He clicked on the link and read about the unorthodox researcher who, two decades before, had established a project called "Caminta con Dios" (Walk with God) to study a strange energy he had discovered at an undisclosed site in the American Southwest. After his last journey to the mystery site, he was never heard from again. Beside the story was a photo taken seven months later by mountain climbers on Mt. Everest of a frozen body they had discovered near the summit. The climbers left the body there because they could not carry him out, so a positive identification was not possible, but those close to Dr. Heredia insisted the photo was of him and pointed to the fact that the clothing of the dead man was identical to the panama shirt and khaki pants the doctor was wearing when last seen.

August backed from his desk. "A serpent separated from its venom is merely a pest."

Each clutching the other's hand, Gregor and Iris emerged from the crevice onto the plateau. Hearing an uneasy sigh, he asked, "Are you lightheaded again?"

"I'm fine," she said, brushing aside his concern. "I am a little nervous."

He comforted her with a pleasing grin. "You're going to love this." He led her to the center, where he saw his shoes and socks. "There they are! I lost them last night."

Iris stopped in her tracks. "Are you sure you can take me with you? You seem to frequently lose items."

"I was rushed at the time," explained Gregor, and he placed his hands on her shoulders for reassurance. "I'm not going to let anything happen to you." Once he saw the slight uptick of a smile, he dropped to the ground with his legs crossed and held his hands out to her. "Let me show you." When she joined him with her knees and palms touching his, Gregor noticed the black stones fastened to her ears. "Those are cool earrings."

Iris touched one as if to remind herself of which pair she was wearing. "They're carbonado. Black diamonds. Mom gave them to me. She always says we can't see the stars without the darkness."

"I really like your mom. Oh, I almost forgot." He retrieved earbuds from his backpack and handed one to Iris. "Since you said you need music to meditate, I have a playlist I thought might help you." He clicked the playlist on his phone.

As they inserted their earbuds, Iris frowned. "Classical?"

"That's Franz Schubert," Gregor said with mock indignation at her distaste. "Give him a chance. His music really resonates with me. Plus, he led a cool life."

Iris asked, "What's cool about a life of privilege?"

"Schubert wasn't like that. He was a bohemian artist in the early nineteenth century whose music never caught on with the mainstream, but he would play for large private parties that were kind of the raves of that time. Austrian police even raided one of the parties, and Schubert and some of his friends were arrested, one of whom was forever exiled from Vienna."

"Okay, he sounds like he might have been more fun than I imagined."

"A little too much. He died of syphilis when he was thirty-one."

"Ooh," Iris grimaced, followed by a grin. "Hey, the music switched to trance."

"The playlist is a mix of classical and trance."

"That's an extreme spectrum for a single playlist, don't you think?"

"Not really." Gregor explained, "The pattern, dynamic and tempo of a typical trance song mirrors that of a classical composition, and they each build to a dramatic crescendo that inspirits the listeners and emotionally intertwines them. The music becomes our connection to each other and to the most primitive vibrations from the very beginning of the universe."

"I don't get that last part at all."

He raised his palms to her. "Move your hands in front of mine." Iris touched her palms to his, and he shook his head. "Don't press. Don't even touch. Keep them just close enough to sense mine. Now close your eyes, and listen to your hands."

"Listen?"

"You know how you can feel the bass when you're next to a speaker?"

"Got it," Iris said with a nod. She moved her hands to allow space before them and closed her eyes to concentrate on detecting

189

sound through her skin. After half a minute, she smiled and told Gregor, "I can hear your heartbeat."

"That's good," Gregor said. "But that's just the percussion. Listen for the whole symphony."

"I can totally feel you there, like I'm touching you."

"Our bodies vibrate, but most people don't notice. Now move your hands away from mine and then back."

Iris complied. "I can feel the space between us stretch and contract."

"Our energies are commingling. Like the attraction of water molecules to each other, energy is attracted to energy." He paused before asking, "Are you ready for the vortex?"

Iris opened her eyes to see him smiling at her. "Let's do it."

Gregor nodded toward his phone. "Do you want the music?"

Iris took out her earbud. "I'll just listen to you." After Gregor did the same, she slid her hands into his, interlocking their fingers.

Excited by the clasp of familiarity, he was at a loss for words. As Iris stared in his eyes, he said, "I need to warn you that you might fall asleep."

"Seriously?"

"I did my first time. I woke up naked after having really vivid dreams, which I didn't realize until later weren't actually dreams. I think the introduction of this massive amount of energy into the body takes getting used to, and the over-stimulation initially shuts it down."

"Naked?" asked Iris, who heard nothing after he uttered the word. "If this vortex strips me and knocks me out, you better close your eyes and wake me immediately."

Gregor laughed and promised, "I will. I swear."

Iris shook her head. "I need you to explain to me exactly what's going to happen here."

"The energy vibrates every cell in my body, every atom. The vibration becomes so intense that it breaks them apart and converts the matter into pure energy, and if I concentrate, that includes the atoms with which I'm in contact, like my clothes."

"And me," she added. "All of me."

"Hopefully."

Iris recoiled from him. "Hey!"

"I'm sorry," he said through laughter. "Bad joke."

"Don't joke about that. I like my body parts where they are."

"I do too. I will keep you safe," Gregor promised, and Iris slipped her hands back into his. "Now close your eyes again, and relax. Listen to your breaths. Concentrate on the air entering and leaving you." After several seconds, he asked, "Do you feel a vibration?"

Gregor could feel Iris' body vibrate, growing into a shiver. A blue glow permeated his eyelids and, when he opened her eyes, he saw the blue light traveling from his hands to hers. Sensing apprehension in Iris, he instructed her, "Stay calm, and open your eyes."

Iris complied and saw they were now levitating. "I'm scared," she whispered.

"Trust me." Without losing contact, Gregor raised their hands so that all of their fingers pointed skyward. Excited that he had controlled the energy flux within his body, he muttered, "We're still physical." His hands pushed through Iris' glowing hands, eliciting a yelp of surprise from her, but she did not withdraw. With a grin, Gregor added, "Mostly physical." He pulled his hand back so that their palms touched once more. "If anything happens or we become separated, just concentrate on this plateau, and the energy will bring you back."

Iris almost jerked away. "Wait, what do you mean?"

"If I don't think of any particular place, I seem to go everywhere." He moved their hands from the center in a circle on a plane. "If I concentrate on a place or a person, it takes me there."

He could feel Iris relax, and she told him, "I feel... intoxicated." She merged her hands with his again and pulled them back. She smiled at the man of light before her, and her heart beat in concert with his.

Gregor reached a point where he couldn't contain himself within his body. He clenched her hands, and the two exploded into particles of light. Their photons swirled together before dispersing in every direction.

Within the maze of moments, life is lived but never unriddled. As often said, life finds a way, and indeed few requirements are necessary for its genesis. In the universe we inhabit, these integrants are found in clusters spread throughout the expanse like turtle eggs on a beach – and like the eggs, some bear life, some never hatch and some are predated from existence. The successful ones are left to determine their purpose – if one exists – or, at the very least, their place in existence. Although this moment allowed no peek over the wall, it did provide clues to the maze's end and an ultimate purpose. For now, however, Gregor and Iris – with unified energy and separate consciousness – were content to focus on their place, which could be pinpointed as Planet Earth. While he directed their journey, Gregor monitored her perceptions, which he felt as his own, to ensure her pleasure and safety. Impacted by the elemental grandeur of and deepest empathy for the world's life in all its forms, they experienced each other and the world in a brilliance of sensations, which included the smell of rain on the sands of the Kalahari Desert, the feel of still glacial waters on Severny Island and the taste of sweat beading on the hair tips of a raver in San Paolo.

When they materialized on the plateau moments later, Gregor lay on his side with Iris enfolded in his arms and legs. He was alert, but she, as expected, had passed out from the stimulation. He tilted his head and removed his right leg from atop hers so that he could scan her wholeness, and he was excited to see that he had converted their whole beings along with their entire attire – although he also scolded himself for half-wishing he had not been so successful with the clothing. "Iris," he whispered to stir her, but she did not respond. He tapped her cheek. "Iris, wake up. Iris." After two more taps, she awoke and focused on his face.

"Gregor," she whispered. "Was that real?"

"You see what I mean?"

"That was amazing," Iris said with a wide grin, and she pushed herself into a seated position with her legs curled to her side. Gregor joined her, sitting with legs spread. "I totally know what all the fuss was about now!" Throwing her legs over his, Iris scooted closer to him and embraced his neck. She kissed him and once more with duration. When their lips parted, she asked, "Did we... merge?"

Gregor brushed hair from her face. "We did."

Iris thought aloud as if she needed to verbalize the event in order to process it, and she did so at a rapid pace. "We were like a ball of energy. My thoughts were mine, but I could feel what you felt. How could I feel anything? Energy has no nervous system. I had all my senses. Totally bizarre. The experience was so... intimate. Honestly, I feel like we just slept together."

"I know," agreed Gregor, and with an impish grin, he asked, "You want to do it again?"

"Absolutely." She kissed him and kept near enough for another. "How far can you go?"

"What do you mean?"

Iris' eyes peered skyward and back at him. "How high?"

A look of concern or even mild fear ripped through his gleeful expression. "No way."

"I thought you would want to go to the stars."

He pointed to the sky. "I'm afraid I'd get lost up there."

"I can be your guide. Ooh, let's go to Orion."

"We can't do that. Interstellar travel would take years."

Iris dropped her hands behind her. "Didn't we just travel the world in an instant?"

"It might've seemed instantaneous. Light could circle Earth in barely more than one-tenth of a second. Einstein theorized nothing can travel faster than light. That's the speed limit."

"There's no getting around this limit?"

"Not unless this energy could somehow take us to another dimension, in which case we might be able to re-enter our own dimension at any point, near or far."

"How do you know that we didn't enter another dimension when we changed to energy? What would another dimension look like?"

After a moment's thought, Gregor responded, "Honestly, I don't know. Still, I wouldn't want to attempt traveling that far without a ship. Remember the Meteor Crater? The energy can obviously be depleted from my body, and I wouldn't know exactly how much energy is needed to travel that far or how to precisely gauge the amount stored in my body."

"I understand," said Iris. "You're afraid we could get halfway there and—"

"And convert back to physical form in the middle of space. However, if we had a ship that was powered by energy from the vortex, instrumentation could allow for accurate measurements of energy usage and storage. We could maybe go anywhere we wanted." This last thought prompted Gregor's mind to drift with possibilities. "We could map the planets that have vortexes and recharge as needed. Explore the universe."

Iris laughed and again embraced him. "Before you go too far, let's test Einstein's theory on a shorter trip. How long would light take to travel from here to the moon?"

"Let's see, the surface-to-surface distance is an average of roughly 384,000 kilometers. Light travels at 300,000 kilometers per second, so it would be a little over a second."

Iris gave him a kiss of thirty seconds and told him, "I can hold my breath long enough for a round trip."

Gregor moved his fingertips along the length of her arms so he could clench her hands, and by the time he did, a blue glow had already lighted within him. Moments later, the two converted and were gone. Once more, terrestrial sensations flooded through them, but Gregor soon ceded directional control to Iris, who wasted little time leading them to the pallid orb of night. The two as one explored the moon as it had never been before, examining the dusty surface and ice beneath the dust and lifeless lunar core. When Iris tried to enter the Sea of Tranquility, however, he stopped her, fearing a repeat of the incident at The Meteor Crater. Whenever she tarried a microsecond too long at one general location, he would urge her on for fear of materializing. Although they did not freeze, they could sense the impoverished heat in the negligible atmosphere, as well as the utter lack of sound. Once every space and interspace – apart from the craters – had been probed, she directed them back toward Earth, but something got in the way.

CHAPTER 21

Cadence saw the Colorado River two-hundred meters below as she walked the glass floor of the horseshoe-shaped Skywalk that jutted from the rim of the Grand Canyon. The venue afforded a remarkable, yet disorienting, view of the natural wonder. Stopping at the far end of the walkway to rest her forearms on the glass wall's railing, she smiled at the wondrous landscape, and she spoke to its architect.

"What do you want from me? Why did you save me yesterday just to kill me in a few weeks or months or however long I have? If I jump now, would you save me again?" Cadence pondered her last thought for a moment before daring, "Prove that you have some purpose for me." She put her knee up to the railing and kicked her foot to the other side.

"Cadence!" Travis caught up to her after pausing to take photos. "Are you crazy?"

Startled, she scolded him, "You scared the crap out of me."

Travis grabbed her thigh and returned her foot to the glass ground. "Out of you?"

She searched her mind for an excuse. "I wanted a cool pose so you could take my picture."

"Well, while throwing a leg in the air is a classic that I whole-heartedly endorse, it doesn't really fit the locale."

"Lord, everything is sex with you," said Cadence as she turned to leave him.

"With me? You're the one who was going out with a guy that you knew you would never see again. Our tryst to the contrary, I didn't think you were a one-night-stand kind of girl."

"I'm not, and I didn't have sex with him. We were enjoying each other's company."

"You know, when you're not angry, I enjoy your company too."

"You're killing me with flattery."

"I'm serious," said Travis. "I wouldn't mind going out with you again."

Cadence was quick to respond, "No."

"Why not?"

"You need a girl you can cheat on. You leap from bed to bed like a lemur."

"I don't think that's me anymore," responded Travis with a shake of his head.

Past the point of comfortable evasion, Cadence blurted out, "My cancer is back, and it's not going away this time."

Travis' lips parted but framed no sound. After a moment, he uttered, "Wow."

A ship of black, absorbent light hovered undetected in the cislunar space when two unexpected passengers boarded. Gregor and Iris materialized in a room of seven meters squared, walled with black metal. The room of little light was occupied by eight glass-contained, coffin-sized, erect chambers, one of which was aglow in a familiar blue light.

Bewildered, the two looked at each other, almost afraid to

breathe, but when they did, their inhalation was a potpourri of sweetness and antiseptic. "Gregor, where are we?"

Without missing a beat, he answered, "My apartment."

Iris twirled around to face him. "You live here?"

"I'm kidding," Gregor responded without a laugh. Attracted by the cyanic light, he approached the glowing chamber to see a being encased in illumination. The alien had ashen skin, high cheekbones and black, human-like hair, and with its closed eyes and absence of motion, it looked dead. When Gregor reached for the glass, Iris grabbed his forearm, but after a nod from him, she released her grip. He touched his palm to the glass, which wasn't glass at all but strung beads of white photons. "It's like solidified light," he whispered.

A breath later, the alien inside opened its almond-shaped, golden eyes. Gregor and Iris gasped and jumped back. Gregor touched the wall beside him for balance, and the blackness dissipated into a circle of transparency through which they could see the sphere of the Earth. "Wow," they both said, staring in disbelief.

Behind them another alien entered, and when the couple saw it, they screamed in a short burst that reverberated in the room. Unaffected by the noise, the alien did appear rather annoyed at their presence. Although they heard no words, they felt it ask, "Why are you here now?"

The alien placed a hand on a shoulder of each intruder. Gregor and Iris wanted to back away, but whether transfixed by fear or its golden eyes, they didn't move. Two heartbeats later they were materializing on the plateau.

Shaking, Iris was the first to speak. "Did you do that?"

Gregor replied, "I don't think so."

They both looked up at the sky.

His voice growing with each word, Gregor exclaimed, "That was intense!" He clenched his fists in jubilation. "I knew they were real.

We couldn't have been the only ones here." He turned his attention back to Iris. "Wasn't that incredible?"

Iris seemed to be in shock. "Incredible and really freaky. We just had a close encounter."

"Of the third kind," Gregor elaborated with excitement. "I don't think we were abducted, so it wouldn't really be the fourth kind."

Iris shook her head. "If anything, we were kicked out. Do you smell that?"

After a quick whiff, Gregor proclaimed, "It's from the ship. Sometimes I bring back the surrounding air." He noticed her shiver, and he caressed her shoulders. "Are you okay?"

"That scared the crap out of me, and yet I'm completely euphoric." She looked at him with a needful passion and embraced him. "You're the most amazing man."

Gregor was overwhelmed – not by the energy from the vortex but from Iris. Her whispered words eroded the barricades built from years of despondency and reinforced after her perceived rejection of him days earlier. They gave him the courage to express himself. "I'm so new to... Can I tell you..." He realized his newfound courage did little for his allocution. Instead, he kissed her, held her and spun her around once before growling with joy at the sky. He looked back at her and asked, "Where is one place that you've always dreamed of going?" He added the qualifier, "On Earth."

"Stonehenge," Iris responded, as if the answer had been given to her.

Gregor smiled in slight confusion. "Really? I thought you might say Paris or Tahiti or—"

"It's just always fascinated me. I mean, was it a place of worship, an observatory or just a giant outdoor funeral home? I always thought if I went there, I'd know for sure."

"I want to take you there. Now." Gregor sat in the plateau's center.

She joined him and asked, "Will you be able to bring us back?"

"I have enough energy in me now." Gregor opened his hands to her.

Iris placed her hands in his and said, "Let's go."

Holding a file folder, Mitchell walked by Mrs. Chapman, who was wearing earphones to watch a news broadcast on the computer, but the volume was so loud, he could hear the reporter's words. "...Now the crippled space station will most likely enter the atmosphere on Monday somewhere over the Pacific. This conflicts with European observers who had speculated a decent over the Southwestern U.S. Some are suggesting NASA is trying to minimize panic..."

Mrs. Chapman jumped in her seat when she realized Mitchell was in the room. She shook her head at the news and said, "If God had wanted us in space, he would've put air up there."

Without acknowledging her, Mitchell entered the office and found not his father but Lucas, who was seated on the unopened end of the desk with his back to the door, stapling handouts for the youth conference. The boy sang as if he were alone in the shower, but when his voice cracked, Mitchell couldn't help but snicker.

"What's so funny?" Lucas asked.

Did he really not hear that sour note? Smiling to himself, Mitchell shook his head and answered, "Nothing."

Lucas stood up and looked down at him, asking, "How short are you?"

Miffed, Mitchell stepped away from him. "I'm five-nine."

The boy grinned at his answer. "No you're not. I'm guessing you're like five-seven, maybe five-six. I was that short when I was twelve."

Mitchell's hatred of Lucas skyrocketed within seconds. He wanted to punch that smug look right off the mutant boy's ugly face.

"What is going on?" asked August, entering with a paper bag dangling from his left hand.

Lucas brandished a fresh smile for the minister. "He was complaining about my singing."

"As I remember, you had a wonderful singing voice," August said, heading for his desk chair. "Has it changed?"

"Hasn't everything?" asked Mitchell. He held the folder up and told his father, "Here are the Bible Bowl questions," before filing it in the top drawer of the desk.

August glanced at the stack of handouts and told Lucas, "I really appreciate your help, Son." He sat and scooted the paper bag across the desk. "I have something for you."

Lucas paused before reaching for it. "What is it?"

August replied, "Discover the answer for yourself."

Lucas took the bag and removed the box from inside. "Oh wow, a new cell phone! You didn't have to go do that."

Mitchell scoffed. "Are you kidding me?"

August warned, "Before you get too excited, it is only a disposable, but it has five-hundred minutes. That should be enough to get you through the weekend. Since you are helping out so much, I wanted to be able to get in touch with you if I needed."

"Thank you, Reverend," exclaimed Lucas, his thick fingers fumbling to open the box.

Disgusted, Mitchell left the room.

In the shadow of a sarsen monolith, beads of blue light collided to form two bodies. As the light faded, Gregor stood with Iris passed out in his arms. With a hasty turn of his neck, he scanned for onlookers and, although he could hear voices in the background, no eyes were upon them. "Iris," he whispered.

Iris jerked herself awake and smiled when she saw Gregor's face. "Hi handsome." Seeing the mammoth stone, she exclaimed, "We're here!"

Gregor threw a finger to his lips. He heard a tour guide speaking from a distance on the other side of the stone. "I don't think we're supposed to be this close to the monument. We should try to join the tour."

Iris shook her head. "Not if we have to view it from a distance. I want to study it."

Gregor peeked to see a group of twenty and a guide beyond the diameter of the stone circle. "We'll have to wait. They all have their cameras turned this way." His hands out to his side, palms facing the ground, he asked, "Do you feel that?"

Iris mimicked his stance and shook her head.

"You haven't had the exposure I have," Gregor said, dropping his arms into a more natural position. "I'm sure you'll become more sensitive to the energy."

"Is there a vortex here?"

"No, but it's weird. One was here."

"Was? I thought they were permanently connected to the land."

"Me too, but it's definitely gone."

"How can you tell one was even here?"

Gregor struggled to define the feeling before he thought of an apt analogy. "Like a woman leaving the room, but you can tell she was there by the smell of perfume she left behind."

"Oh." Iris pointed to the silence. "I think they're leaving." Together they peeked around the stone. The tour group was indeed heading to the bus, but as they came out of hiding, a woman from Virginia couldn't resist a final photo of the incredible landmark she would never see again.

CHAPTER 22

The chime of the opening door diverted Lily from her plan to meditate – having not seen a customer in an hour. Wearing a cobalt bodysuit and white gossamer wrap, she stopped shy of the black-curtained door to the Meditation Center to see the shop's new entrants.

Travis said, "Hi Lily," as Cadence rushed past her to the bathroom.

"Hi, you two," greeted Lily with her patented, spirit-embracing smile.

"We're supposed to meet Gregor and Iris here and go to dinner." With a nod toward the black curtains, he explained Cadence's curtness with, "She really had to use the bathroom."

Noticing a longing in his eyes, Lily asked, "Are you and Cadence—"

Without waiting for the question mark, Travis offered a pre-emptive, "No."

"But she is the one you desire?"

He shrugged, saying, "My desires are unavailing."

"Oh. You're such a good-looking man, though, I'm sure you set many hearts atwitter."

Travis grinned, returning a cocksure tone to his countenance. "I've defibrillated my share. What about you?"

Lily let loose a grand laugh. "I'm past the age of turning heads."

"You're not that old," he responded before stepping back from the statement. "I meant to say that you're not old, period."

Lily waved aside his concern over word choice. "I had a love once, but I didn't nurture it." She sighed. "Ah, but let's not delve into that. Cadence aside, what do you desire of life?"

Travis shook his head. "Every time I think I know that, I'm proven wrong. I really need to find someone who will give my life some direction."

Lily pointed to him, saying, "You're the navigator of your own life. You don't need to find a person. You need to find a purpose."

Gregor and Iris had watched the sun set and moon rise from Stonehenge, and the two now lay atop the altar stone, stargazing and recapping their lives to that point. Following a brief lull, he asked her, "Now that you've inspected it, have you determined a purpose for Stonehenge?"

Iris, her head resting on his shoulder, answered, "Art for the sake of art."

Gregor laughed. "We should probably get back to Sedona."

"Are you sure you'll be able to get us there?"

He raised his free hand before them and squeezed his fingers into a fist. "I don't know how much energy I have stored in me exactly, but I can tell it's enough to convert."

"I'm okay if you can't," she said as she rubbed his chest.

He kissed her forehead. "I think it's close to dinner time, and I promised Travis and Cadence this morning that we'd join them."

"I don't want to get up."

"You don't have to. Just close your eyes, and listen to our

breathing." He wrapped his arms around her, and moments later, they materialized in the same position on the plateau.

Iris faced him with a big grin. "I stayed awake. I'm getting better."

August Briar ignored the disdain in Gia's voice as she welcomed Lucas and him to the Red Planet Diner. He knew full well her words were empty, as would be the bill tray after he determined her tip.

As they slid into a booth near the front door, Lucas lit up at the alien theme. "This place is really cool."

August had never entered the establishment before, but they worked past the hour when most of the town's other restaurants had shut their doors for the night. To tarnish its luster, he spit out, "Idolatry celebrating mythological demons of the night sky."

With a fixed smile, Gia asked for their drink order. Lucas, his eyes glued to the lovely girl, ordered a cola, while the minister opted for sweet tea. As she walked away, August's voice broke the boy's stare. "Are you sure your father would not like to join us?"

"He said he was eating with a friend of his." Lucas took a menu to peruse. "I'm starving."

"I hoped to talk to him before the conference. I will be so busy once it starts."

Lucas dropped the menu enough for eye contact. "About what?"

"I would never want to presume the intricacies of God's intentions for me, but I believe optimism is warranted in this case. You saw the model in my office?"

"That big church you wanna build?"

"More than just a church. West Canaan will be a holy citadel with a private school and dormitories for young Christians – a twelve-year boot camp to train soldiers for God. I want you in the first class."

Lucas lowered the menu further to expose a wide grin, "I'd love that. Can I stay in the dorms?"

August chuckled. "Of course. If your father agrees."

Lucas frowned at the caveat. "When's it opening?"

"If my plans are realized, I would expedite construction with the goal of opening by the next..." August's voice trailed off as he noticed a quartet entering the diner.

Gregor, Iris and Cadence were all smiles as they entered the Red Planet Diner, but Travis shook his head, saying, "I can't believe I'm eating here again."

Iris defended the selection, "Gregor has never been here, and I want him to meet Gia."

Gia walked past them carrying drinks for August and Lucas. She told Iris, "Seat yourself. I'll be right with you."

"What's wrong?" asked Lucas. "You look like you just saw the Devil."

"Only his followers," August replied, watching them sit at a booth on the other side of the diner.

Lucas followed his stare. "Who are they?"

"The one in red is the daughter of the witch who owns a crystal shop down the street, and the other girl is my son's seducer."

"She's dating Mitchell?" Lucas asked. "Why?"

August nodded at the first question but zoned out the second as he glared at the man he had seen disappear on the plateau.

After Gia took the food order for the reverend and his young companion, she headed toward the booth where her friend was sitting.

Iris greeted her with a wave and some introductions. "Gia, I have some people I want you to meet. You already know Travis. This is Cadence."

Cadence extended her hand to Gia and said, "Nice to meet you."

Gia smiled at her good fortune, giving her an opportunity to fulfill a promise to Mitchell. "Hi Cadence. I feel like I already know you. Iris has told me so much about you."

"I have?" Iris asked.

"Really?" Cadence asked, in unison with Iris' question.

Gia continued directing her attention toward Cadence. "Listen, I'm throwing a rave tomorrow night," leaning on the table and whispering, "at August Briar's church, but he," pointing with her eyes in his direction, "doesn't know, so keep it quiet."

"Which one is August?" asked Gregor.

"The one looking right at us," Iris answered. "Gia, how did you manage that?"

"I think Mitchell's letting me use the place to get back at his dad for something. Family issues. Anyway, I'd love for you to come."

Cadence asked, "Is Mitchell going to be there?"

Gia wasn't certain if she wanted him there or not, but she figured that her appointment as a proxy inviter meant she had no desire to see him. "No, he's giving me the key. Will you come?" When Cadence looked at Gregor, Gia said, "Of course, you're all invited."

Cadence asked them, "What do you think?"

Travis smiled at Gia and answered, "Sounds like fun," while Gregor nodded.

"Great." Gia threw her fists in the air in celebration.

Iris said, "Now that that's settled, I want you to meet Gregor."

Gia nodded. "Pleasure, Gregory."

Gregor emitted an uncertain laugh. "It's Gregor. No *y*."

"Sorry," Gia responded with disinterest before a spark of excitement returned. "Let me show you my flyer." She pulled a folded paper from her pocket and handed it to Iris. "I have people giving them out at hot spots in Phoenix tonight, and I've posted the info online."

"I like the flyer," Iris said as she scanned the colorful artwork. "It's kitschy."

The header announced, "Ravers of the Lost Ark!" Gia was pictured in the ruins of a temple, wearing a fedora and a slinky black dress. She was holding a glowstick while unearthing a mirror ball hidden inside an altar.

"I'd say more retro than kitschy," Gia corrected.

"I hate to tell you, but you left out the location."

"No, I didn't. Look at the map on the ground."

On the floor of the temple was a map, on which was written, "34° 49' 57.2455" -111° 45' 57.8214"."

"That's the latitude and longitude," Gia explained.

Iris handed the flyer back to her. "Don't you think that's a little oblique?"

"A challenge piques interest. Hey, could you help me set up tomorrow? Mitchell won't let me start until eight because he wants to make sure August is completely occupied with his stupid youth conference, so I'm going to have to prep fast. I could also use a ride to Phoenix in the morning to pick up supplies."

Iris turned to Gregor, who told her, "I'll catch up with you at the rave."

"Great," Gia exclaimed. "What can I get you all to eat?"

After giving his order, Gregor asked Gia, "Where's your bathroom?"

August watched as Gregor headed for the bathroom. "Excuse me, Lucas. I'll be right back."

In the bathroom, the reverend found Gregor soaping his hands in the sink. He stood behind him and asked, "You enjoy his power, but do you honestly think he will spare your soul?"

Gregor looked in the mirror at him. "Excuse me?"

August rephrased his question. "The Devil is smiling on you

now, but do you believe your soul will be spared from his everlasting Lake of Fire?"

Gregor reached for the paper towels. "He's smiling on me?" He looked around the room. "How many people do you see in here?"

"Do not mock me. I know you serve the Adversary."

Gregor emitted a light laugh as he made his way to the door. "I'm really not sure exactly what you're talking about, but I can assure you that I don't even believe in the Devil, much less serve him."

"Your lies only put you in greater debt to the one you serve."

"Look, I don't know who you think you are or—"

"I am a prophet of God – protector of the righteous and shepherd of lost souls. I am here to pull you from the fire and guide you to His merciful light." August pointed up and extended his hand for Gregor to take. "I am your salvation, Reverend August Briar."

He shook his hand. "I know. You're trying to shut down the Wickline's shop."

"A cultic speakeasy peddling handbooks to Hell and Satanic phylactery to susceptible souls, in defiance of God's law."

"Or you could just call it a crystal shop," joked Gregor.

"Employing the Dark Lord's power is far from funny, Gregor Buckingham."

With mouth agape, Gregor asked, "How did you know my name?"

August ignored his question. "It is a seduction into unending torment."

"I'm done with this discussion." He again turned to the door.

"God wants you to repent, Gregor Buckingham."

Gregor faced the reverend. "How do you presume to speak for God regarding his wishes?"

"His wishes are explicitly expressed in His holy book."

"Did God physically write the Bible with his own hands?"

"He used devoted followers and prophets, guiding their hands as they wrote His words."

"Did any of them ever see God?"

"The words they wrote were divinely inspired by God."

"How do you know that for sure? Because the words they wrote said so?"

"Faith."

"What is the root of that faith? Have you ever met God?"

"I will meet Him. For now, I feel His presence."

"But you haven't physically seen him. How do you know for certain that he even exists?"

"Faith," August insisted.

"You believe in an unseen entity that supposedly created us for the sole purpose of worshipping him based on words written by men thousands of years ago – those who created fantastical stories to explain the world around them?"

At first infuriated, August calmed himself. Realizing his opponent's strategy, he decided to change his own from beseeching to threatening. One way or another, he would bring him to God. "You speak with the blasphemous tongue of the serpent that has coiled around your soul."

"My words are my own, just as yours are."

"What kind of name is Gregor? It sounds... devilish."

"How do you know my name?"

"How long will you be staying in my town, Gregor Buckingham?" August asked, continuing to speak his name as it unnerved him.

"That's none of your business, and you never answered my question."

"I have learned quite a bit about you."

"Okay, that's just creepy."

"My guess is you are here for a few days more, and then you will return to Los Angeles."

"Where I reside is of no concern to you."

"It should concern you. You continue on your path, and you will reside in a lake of Hell fire!" When Gregor rolled his eyes,

August said, "Your lack of spiritual concern is both troubling and liberating to me. I perform missionary work at some of the prisons here. Did you know that California's Department of Corrections has a contract with Arizona's to take on some of their overflow? Interesting fact, I thought. Just this morning I spoke via satellite at a parole hearing for someone who I recently turned to Christ."

"Do you have a point to make?" Gregor asked.

"He is being released early and very grateful for my speaking on his behalf."

"I'm happy for you. If he's truly sorry, and you think he'd never repeat his crime—"

"Now I never said that. Under my watch, I have no doubt that I can deliver his soul to the Lord, but he most definitely could be pushed back into his old ways with no more than a figurative finger." August held up his pinky.

Gregor asked, "What was his crime?"

"Murder. Via arson." August smiled at the look of horror his words brought to Gregor's face.

"You didn't... My father?"

"Oh no, not him," said August, and with a laugh. "Not for lack of trying on my part, though. No one could get that man out of prison. He is completely crazy. Did you know that your father has murdered two people in prison? That is in addition to your mother."

August could see Gregor's emotions boiling into rage. "Why have you researched my life?"

"When confronted with evil, you need to learn as much information as possible to determine a method for its defeat – or in this case, convince the evil one to repent. Getting back to my point, as you called it, the conversion of my flock's newest member will be a completely moot point if you tell me now that you will repent and accept Christ." August raised his right hand and bellowed, "Do you, Gregor Buckingham, accept Jesus Christ as your savior?"

Gregor looked him in the eyes and answered, "No," before reaching for the door handle.

"What does it feel like to have flames biting at your flesh?" asked August, who paused to savor the sudden fear he saw in Gregor's eyes. "If you continue down this unrighteous path—"

"Are you threatening me?"

"Not at all. As I said, I assume you will be gone by the time my newest congregant comes to Sedona." He paused before asking, "How serious is the situation between you and Iris Wickline?"

Gregor growled, "Listen to me. You do anything to her—"

"Her fate rests entirely in your hands. Repent! Rebuke the Devil!" August gasped in horror. "You are glowing... here." He stepped back and pointed at him. Believing the Devil was calling him, he said, "You are summoned to Hell!"

In the bathroom with August Briar, Gregor looked down at himself. Without effort or intention, he had begun to emit a blue light from his entire body. He didn't know why the energy was manifesting now, but he was trying to concentrate so that he wouldn't convert and disappear.

As he hovered between corporeal and energy, Gregor could feel his senses extending beyond himself and circling the Earth. When he heard August mention Hell, his thoughts turned to the incredible heat he experienced the day before, at the Meteor Crater. He found his senses centered on that spot, and even though his physical body stayed in the bathroom, his focused energy was now in the crater, reacting with the iridium. He could feel the heat building just as it had on the crater floor, and it followed him back to his body inside the bathroom.

August crouched by the wall as the temperature in the room jumped forty degrees within seconds.

Gregor wanted to scream, but he had no ability to vocalize in his current state. He tried to focus on the bathroom so he could pull his energy away from the Meteor Crater, but the more he reacted with the iridium, the greater difficulty he had separating from it. With a final mental thrust, Gregor was able to remove himself from the crater. His energy returned to the bathroom, and his body solidified, dimming the blue light.

August pushed from the wall. "You are unsavable," he proclaimed and left the bathroom.

Gregor looked in the mirror, waiting for the light to disappear altogether. Concentrating on his breathing, he tried to relax his shaking body. Several minutes passed before he could leave the bathroom, at which point, he saw August holding doggie bags and leaving with a young man. He wondered how the minister had explained to himself the incident he had just witnessed. Did he believe Gregor was a wielder of unholy power from the Devil?

"Are you okay?" Iris asked when Gregor returned to the table.

Gregor nodded. "I'm fine."

"Problem squeezing it off?" asked Travis.

Cadence scolded him, "That's so gross."

"What? You were thinking it, too."

Iris wiped his forehead with her hand. "You're sweating."

Gregor told her, "It's like a sauna in that bathroom."

If August Briar had any doubts of the side of righteousness Gregor represented, they were blown away by the unholy winds of Hell that were blistering through the bathroom at the younger man's behest.

As he hurried from the diner and toward his car, August tried to hide his nervousness from Lucas, but he could think of no words to fill the silence. To his relief, Lucas could. "Reverend, can I ask about something in the Bible I don't understand?"

"Of course."

"How is it decided what part of the Bible we follow and what part we don't?"

August glanced at him with puzzlement. "What do you mean? We follow it all."

"No, we don't. When you were talking tonight about witches, it got me thinking about 'Thou shalt not suffer a witch to live.'"

August scooted behind the wheel of his car and, once Lucas was seated, he explained, "That was in the Old Testament. The old laws were done away with in the New Testament."

"Does the New Testament say not to kill them?"

"Not specifically, but Jesus did reiterate, 'Thou shalt not kill,' from the Ten Commandments."

"But the Ten Commandments were from the Old Testament, and people were still ordered by God to kill after he gave us the Ten Commandments. That's what I was talking about. We're still supposed to do some things from the Old Testament, but if Jesus didn't tell us not to do something that God told us to do in the Old Testament, how do we know we're not supposed to keep doing it? That's the part I don't get."

August was silent before turning the key. "Which hotel are you staying at?"

"Could you take me back to the church? I left my backpack there."

When they returned to the campsite, Gregor made a beeline from the car to his tent, while Travis asked, "What are you doing?"

"Going to sleep," answered Gregor, unzipping the entrance.

"You're not hiking into the canyon to plug into your vortex?"

"Not tonight." Gregor zipped the door closed behind him.

"What's wrong with you?"

"I'm tired." He fell back, staring at the sky through the mesh window that topped the tent.

Travis disappeared into his own tent and within moments was snoring, which on most occasions didn't bother Gregor, but tonight he needed not to hear it. He inserted his earbuds and listened to the Benassi Bros' "Feel Alive" on his phone.

Losing himself in the trance song, Gregor entered a meditative state. When he saw the blue light erupt from his body, he concentrated on keeping corporeal but ended up in a state between matter and energy.

I have to get to the vortex.

As Gregor hurried to the plateau, he wondered why in this median state between energy and matter he seemed to get stuck without the vortex to boost him in either direction. Perhaps it was a point of stability. He was convinced he needed to learn how to better control the energy so it didn't control him. Even now, he could sense his thoughts moving away from conscious construction to drift in a plane of thought that was both his and, as strange as it seemed, the universe's.

Gregor found his ladder hidden in the shrubbery and propped it against the canyon wall. He began his ascent to the plateau, but he didn't reach his destination. Halfway up, he could no longer keep his fingers solid enough to grip the rungs. Gregor fell backwards and floated away.

August Briar honed in on the moonlight reflecting from the tents, his hunting rifle held at his side. His mind was processing the faulty logic that had led him to misinterpret God's test for him and how the innocence of youth had clarified it. Lucas helped open his eyes to his immediate destiny, which was not to convert Gregor but to remove the blight from the face of the Earth. He knew that Travis was the snorer from the last time he came, so he took a hesitant stance beside Gregor's tent and raised the rifle.

With the barrel aimed where Gregor would have to be lying, his finger tightened on the trigger. *Lord, if this is not Your will, stop me now.* He waited for any sign to appear, but the night was unbroken. He tightened his grip on the rifle and whispered, "Thy will be done."

August spotted a faint blue from inside the tent that intensified into a bright blue light within seconds. Startled and horrified, August lost his nerve. He lowered the weapon and retreated.

Awakened by rustling in the brush, Travis pounced from the tent with his fists clenched at his side. What he saw gave him the shock of his life. He watched a glowing blue figure darting into the canyon. "Holy..." His attention shifted to Gregor's tent, and he noticed the door was now unzipped. "Gregor!" Even with the moonlight, he couldn't quite make out the interior, so he jumped inside and felt the sleeping bag for his friend. Empty. As he turned to exit, he hit his head on the lantern hanging from one of the support rods. He switched it on and took it to light his way while he pursued the alien who he believed had abducted his friend.

Travis searched for his friend, scanning parallel to the ground but the vertical as well. He knew from UFO documentaries that spaceships are often silent, so he couldn't depend on hearing one if it were hovering overhead. After stepping on a protruding root, he stopped to rub the pain from his foot. He wished he had thought to put on shoes before leaving the campsite wearing only boxer shorts. Attracted by a light in the sky, his gaze shifted upward. Travis gasped. A blue figure floated by overhead as if on some invisible river in the sky.

CHAPTER 23

Iris awoke in her bed, sensing a presence. Curled on the bed at her side, Daisy raised her head and fixed her eyes on the ceiling before jumping to the floor to continue her stare.

A glowing blue hand and forearm dropped from the ceiling without causing destruction, like a ghost penetrating a wall. Startled, Iris wanted to scream but a familiarity quelled her fear. "Gregor?" she whispered. With a nervous and excited smile, she pushed aside the quilt and stood on the bed in her periwinkle nightgown to reach her hand to his. When their hands locked, the light flowed into her body and, seconds later, she ascended through the ceiling. Daisy whimpered and jumped onto the bed to await Iris' return.

Above the roof, Iris' feet rose until her body was parallel to Gregor's. In her embrace Gregor began to float again as if reclaimed by the invisible sky river's current. Their bodies rotated while they traversed Sedona from twenty meters above.

The resident of the house fashioned into a landing site for passing UFOs nodded between sleep and consciousness while seated in a lawn chair by his lighted runway. After a final droop of his head, he forced himself from the chair to end another fruitless evening. On his way to the front door, he turned off the runway lights with the switch on his porch and found that the night had a bluish tint. He tilted his face toward the sky, and his jaw dropped when he saw the glowing figures floating above. Once his mind allowed his body to move, he ran to be underneath the blue light, screaming, "Hey! Over here!"

Realizing his runway lights were off, he darted to the switch to turn them back on. He saw the figures continuing past his property line, and he ran after them, yelling and waving his arms. Almost out of breath, he saw something fall from the sky. He stopped his pursuit and reached down to pick up a periwinkle nightgown.

Friday morning, Gregor was surprised to awaken in Iris' bed with her head nestled on his chest – both of them naked atop the quilt. The last clear recollection he had was of climbing the ladder to reach the vortex. After that, his memories took on a dreamlike quality in which the world did not behave as it should. He remembered Iris coming into the scene somehow, but he couldn't recall the role she played. He wondered if the vortex took him where his subconscious wanted to go – to Iris.

Seeing his nakedness, he flipped up the side of the quilt to cover as much as he could, and in so doing, stirred Iris from sleep. She opened her eyes and saw Gregor. "Oh my god!" She jerked up and covered herself with the other side of the quilt. "What happened?"

Gregor sat up and replied, "I'm not completely sure. I remember... flying."

Iris scooted out of bed to look in vain for her nightgown. "Where are our clothes?"

"I guess—" Gregor began to conjecture before Iris put a finger to her mouth.

"Shh. I don't want my mom to hear you."

Gregor whispered, "I need to sneak out. I don't want her to be angry at me."

Iris exhaled a slight laugh. "Are you kidding? She'd be thrilled. I just don't want to give her that satisfaction." She scurried into her bathroom to retrieve a robe hanging from the door. "Gregor, this is really just too bizarre. We were... flying, weren't we?"

"We were. And—"

"And more. I remember." Iris smiled and crawled onto the bed to kiss him.

Gregor made sure the quilt was still covering his privates. "Uh, do you have anything I can wear?"

"Actually, I do have something for you." Iris went to her closet and reemerged with a paper bag from a clothier. "I did a little shopping yesterday morning."

Gregor took the bag from her, saying, "You bought me something? You shouldn't have done that." He produced a green shirt from the bag and held it up. "A short-sleeved shirt?"

"I figured you probably have never worn one before because of your... Do you like it?"

Gregor pulled the shirt over his head and shoulders and looked down at its fit. "I do, and you're right. I haven't had one since I was a kid."

"It's just a start, but I thought you could use clothing that's more summer-appropriate."

"I hate to ask, but did you possibly buy anything else." Gregor looked down at his quilt-covered area.

"No, but—"

"Iris, are you... alone?" Lily asked through the door.

Iris looked up at Gregor, signaling the need for silence. "Of course, Mom. I'm just reading aloud." Gregor frowned at her lousy excuse, and Iris shrugged.

"Okay," said Lily. "I'm going to make breakfast now."

Iris' cell phone rang from the nightstand, and, when she saw the caller, she handed the phone to him.

Gregor scooted across the bed to sit on the edge. He glanced at the ID before answering the phone. "Travis."

"Gregor?" Travis asked in a whispered yell. "What happened to you?"

"I came over to Iris' house."

From the other side of the bedroom door, Lily asked, "Is Gregor in there with you?"

Iris dropped her shoulders and opened the door to allow her mother entry.

On the phone, Travis told Gregor, "I thought you had been kidnapped. How could you leave without telling me?"

When Gregor saw Lily wearing a wonderful smile in the doorway, he waved to her and grabbed more of the quilt to ensure he was covered. He told Travis, "I didn't want to wake you. Listen, can I call you back?"

Travis' voice grew loud enough to be heard by all three in the bedroom. "Absolutely not. Wait. Are you and Iris doing it right now? Why would you answer the phone?"

Gregor and Iris both turned red, while Lily's smile broadened.

Iris told him, "Just have him come over, and get off the phone."

Still in her robe and holding a fresh cup of coffee, Iris exited the kitchen door to rejoin her mother and Gregor at the table on the back patio. Sans shoes and wearing his new shirt with Iris' white sweat pants, which left nothing unrevealed below his waist and extended only to his mid-calf region, Gregor had just finished explaining to Lily the previous night's events.

"Fascinating!" Lily exclaimed. "So did you two—"

"Mom!" snapped Iris, knowing full well the thoughts Salome-dancing within her mind. She turned to Gregor and found comfort in his lack of mortification.

Gregor smiled and said, "I need to use the facilities," before heading indoors.

Lily placed a hand atop Iris', which opened a window of vulnerability in her daughter. "I don't know what I'm going to do when he leaves," Iris confessed.

"Keep your attention on the journey and not its end," Lily told her. "Make the most of it."

"And then what?"

Lily shrugged. "That's a question you need to ask him."

"Knock-knock," interrupted Travis, appearing on the patio. "The front door was open."

"Travis sweetie," Lily greeted with a hug. "I hope you're hungry."

Iris stayed seated but offered a warm, "Morning."

With a pair of jeans, shoes and socks rolled under his arm, he told Lily, "I already ate."

Gregor reappeared behind Travis, who squeezed him in a hug of relief. "Man, I was worried sick about you. I thought you had been abducted."

Gregor asked, "Abducted?"

Travis handed him the apparel, "Here are the clothes... you asked..." He dropped the items to the floor when he noticed Gregor's smooth arms. "Your skin!" He poked his friend's shoulder with his index finger. "How, how... Did you have surgery without telling me?"

Gregor looked at Iris, who said, "Tell him."

"The vortex healed me."

Lily, who had never seen Gregor's scars, asked about the reason for Travis' bewilderment. "What do you mean, it healed you?"

Travis rolled his eyes at his friend's explanation. "What are you talking about? That's crazy." When Gregor's expression remained stoic, he asked, "Seriously?"

Gregor removed his shirt to show how his skin had been altered. "I swear."

"Your burn scars are gone," whispered Travis, circling his friend to assess his remarkable transformation. By the time he again faced him, he could no longer contain his excitement. With a huge grin, Travis exclaimed, "You look normal." He hugged him and spun him around once. "I'm so happy for you, buddy."

Iris could see Gregor fighting back tears over the joyful display. "Thanks."

"Wow!" Travis shouted after another look. "Unbelievable."

Lily asked, "You had burn scars?"

Travis waved his hands in front of Gregor's body. "All over. Really horrible."

"Thanks," said Gregor, replacing the shirt.

"I'm just trying to give her a clear picture." Travis sat next to Lily and reiterated, "Horrible." Back to Gregor, he asked, "So all this crap about Sedona and healing energy and all is true? UFOs! I almost forgot, last night I had an encounter. I woke up and saw this like glowing blue Smurf leaving our campsite. I thought he took you."

Gregor reclaimed his seat and told him, "That was me."

"What do you mean?"

"The energy from the vortex turns me a luminous blue."

Iris said, "We could take sick people to the vortex to heal."

"No! You can't do that," insisted Lily, to everyone's surprise. "Remember how we talked about the vortex being an umbilical cord, allowing the universe to nourish the Earth with life energy? It's not a one-way street. In turn some of Earth's energy can be fed back to the universe, which sets up a potentially devastating scenario. Are you familiar with Rh factor?"

Travis responded, "I know it concerns a protein found in blood. People are Rh positive if they have the protein or Rh negative if they don't. Like O-positive or O-negative."

"Exactly," Lily replied. "A potential problem arises when a pregnant woman is one type of Rh factor and her fetus is another. The blood from the fetus can enter the mother's bloodstream, and then the mother's body reacts by producing antibodies to fight the invading cells, which can take the life from the fetus. It's called erythroblastosis fetalis."

Iris explained her mother's knowledge. "Before Mom moved to Sedona, she was a VP at a pharmaceutical company in Chicago."

Lily continued, "The energy coming from the universe is pure and life-giving, but if, in turn, it happened to receive negative energy from someone with ill intent – energy that could potentially harm the universe in any way – I believe the universe would fight the invading negative energy, perhaps even sever the umbilical cord."

Gregor connected the dots. "If the vortex feeds life, wouldn't that eliminate life?"

"Without the energy necessary to create it, life would eventually die out. All life." Lily concluded, "You can only introduce people of unquestionably good character to the vortex, and its location must remain a secret."

"So, healing tours are out," said Iris.

Travis burst out with, "Heal Cadence."

"What's wrong with Cadence?" asked Iris.

"She has cancer," answered Lily. "I recognized the signs."

The men asked her in unison, "How did you know?" Travis and Gregor looked at each other, and both asked, "How did you know?"

Gregor replied first. "She told me the day before yesterday her cancer was back."

"She told me yesterday." Travis crossed his arms. "It figures she confided in you first."

"By a day," Gregor clarified.

"It's still first."

Iris touched Gregor's hand. "Do you think the vortex could heal her?"

Gregor shrugged. "I'm not positive the energy's effect is curative."

"What do you mean?" Travis asked. "It healed you."

"I'm just not even sure if *healed* is the right word. The vortex definitely fixed my skin, but the scarring was a distortion of the original cell programming, so to speak. Did it heal my damaged cells or reset them to their original programming? If it resets cell information, it could repair any damage that had been done to it, but what if the cell is inherently faulty?"

Iris frowned at him. "I'm not seeing the problem."

Lily nodded. "You mean, what if her cancer is hereditary."

"Exactly. If it's written into her DNA, there would be nothing to reset. I'm not sure it would even work on invasive diseases. The energy could feasibly reset all cells indiscriminately, which could make invading cells or cancerous cells stronger and speed their progression."

Iris asked, "So the vortex could make her condition worse?"

Gregor threw up his hands. "I don't fully understand how it works. I wouldn't want to give her false hope or put her in a possibly detrimental situation without knowing for certain."

"She's already in a detrimental situation," protested Travis. "How much worse could it be? Let's just take her to the vortex and not tell her why. We'll have a picnic or something, and you can do your thing. If it doesn't work, she never has to know."

Gregor was deep in thought as he listened to the engine humming from the backseat during a rare musicless ride with Travis at the wheel. Cadence, her hair pulled back into a ponytail and minimal makeup on her face, sat shotgun wearing a green sundress, sandals and sunglasses. "Where is this picnic area?" she asked.

Gregor answered, "It's a short walk from our campsite."

"I hope you guys didn't drag me out of bed to go hiking."

"Drag you out of bed?" Travis asked. "It's almost one."

Gregor started humming a single note, complementary to the engine's hum. Cadence looked back at him with a puzzled look on her face, while Travis emitted a laugh and asked, "What are you doing?" Gregor's only response was continued humming.

Cadence shook his arm. "Gregor?"

"Do you hear the vibrations?" he inquired.

"What do you mean?" asked Travis. "The engine?"

"If you let it in, it kind of numbs the mind."

Travis told him, "I read online somewhere about a study on the acoustics at Stonehenge. The echo within the monoliths that would have been created by the instruments of the day would have prompted a rapid, driving beat – like trance music – and would've supposedly induced a trance-like state." Without warning, he stomped on the brake pedal, sending Gregor to the floor.

"Travis, are you crazy?" asked Cadence, clutching the dashboard.

"Gregor, look!"

He pushed himself up to see Travis pointing at the dirt path to their campsite, which was now on the other side of a chain-link fence topped with razor wire. Curbside in front of the fence was all of their camping equipment in a disheveled heap. Signs warning against trespassing were affixed to the fence at every twenty meters.

"What on Earth?" Gregor muttered.

"Is that your stuff?" asked Cadence.

Travis parked near the heap, and the three loaded it into the car. "Do you think the Forest Service erected it because we were camping in an undesignated area?" Gregor asked.

Travis laughed at the thought of the extreme measure, and he pointed out the tree to which was still nailed the notice of sale he had seen on their first full day in Sedona. "I think the land was sold, and the new owners didn't want squatters."

"You guys can stay in my room," offered Cadence. "It's just two more nights."

"Maybe the fence isn't completely surrounding the place yet," said Travis. "We should drive around to see where it ends."

"Then what?" Cadence asked. "I'm not trespassing for a picnic. Let's find another place."

Once all was packed, Gregor said, "I think we should listen to Travis."

"Are you kidding?" asked Cadence with a glance to both of their faces. "You two go ahead. I'll wait in the car." She slid into the passenger seat and closed the door.

As the two men joined her inside, Gregor tried to think of way to salvage their plan. "The spot we had picked out here is really spectacular. We want to show it to you."

"It just like every other place I've seen in this town. I'm not trespassing, and that's it."

"All right," Travis said, starting the engine. "We'll find some-place else."

CHAPTER 24

"You brought a pistol?" Mitchell asked when he saw the case in back of the SUV.

August grabbed the silver case, along with a suitcase of clothes. "We are in the woods."

Mitchell loaded his arms with personal supplies for the weekend, and the two men walked from the parking lot adjacent the woods where the youth conference would begin in mere hours. After a short hike, they reached a forested section, where hired hands were erecting dozens of tan tents, each spaced at least two meters from its closest neighbor. A man on a ladder propped against a needleless pine tree lifted and tied the loose end of a banner that proclaimed, "Sedona Bible Youth Conference."

August paused to admire the setup, as he presumed God was as well. "Magnificent."

Mitchell asked, "Which tent do you want?"

Carrying a duffel bag and speaking on his new cell phone, Lucas approached the two, said goodbye to the caller and pocketed the phone. He told August, "That was my dad. He said he's on his way back home because my uncle is in the hospital with pneumonia."

Shifting his load, August put a hand on Lucas' shoulder. "We will pray for him."

"How are you getting home?" asked Mitchell, without a note of concern.

"He said he left a bus ticket in our hotel room. Reverend, where're you staying?"

August pointed to the outermost tent, and Lucas was quick to claim its neighbor, rushing to throw his duffel bag inside. His son shook his head and chose the furthest tent from them both.

A few minutes later, as the three were in the parking lot to gather the remaining items, Mitchell nodded toward a teenage congregant pulling into one of the few slots. "We have some early birds."

August realized one detail they had missed. The parking lot was too small to hold the cars for all of the older teenagers who would be driving themselves to the conference. The previous year two attendees almost came to blows, fighting over the last available space. "We need to take control of the car situation. We will have to utilize tandem parking."

"I could be the valet," Lucas offered, pronouncing the silent letter at the end.

Mitchell scoffed. "You can't do that. You're too little to drive."

With furrowed brow, August told him, "He is bigger than you are."

"I meant his age," growled Mitchell.

"I know how to drive," said Lucas. "I have to drive a tractor all the time."

Shaking off the embarrassment of his father's comment, Mitchell insisted, "That's different than driving someone's car."

Lucas fought back, "I've drove my dad's truck lots of times, too."

"Valet service might be nice," the reverend said. "Go ahead, Lucas, but be careful."

"You can't be serious," exclaimed Mitchell as Lucas ran to get the keys of the early arrival. "Think of the liability."

August opened the back of his SUV. "Do you not have more important matters over which to fret, like some much-needed rehearsal for your sermon tomorrow?"

As the blue sky retreated from the encroaching darkness, the forest perked with the sound of children. Just beyond the tents lay a triangular clearing with loudspeakers perched at various locations along the perimeter. At the center of the clearing was a wide circle of rocks at the base of a cone-shaped tent of burlap with no opening, standing more than three meters high at its apex. Facing the clearing's center were aluminum benches in arced rows with burning torches spiked into the ground at every end. On two of the innermost benches were seated twelve adults, including Mitchell Briar, while the remaining benches were filled with children up to seventeen years of age. Lucas McAbel was visible, not because he was seated front and center, but because his head protruded above the canopy of heads belonging to his peers.

With a microphone clipped to his shirt and Bible in hand, August Briar walked onto the clearing to a central location between the benches and the burlap tent. His voice boomed from the speakers as he greeted the audience, "Young ladies and gentlemen, welcome to the Sixth Annual Sedona Bible Youth Conference!" He waited for the applause to settle before continuing, "For those who do not know, my name is Reverend Briar. I am the leader of Christ Church of Sedona, which you surely saw coming into town. Are you ready for a weekend of Biblical fun?"

The crowd cheered, and August nodded to three of the elders, who each took a torch and lit the burlap cone in twelve spots before returning the torches and themselves to their original places. While the fire crawled up to the peaked center of the burlap, August continued speaking. "I started this youth conference six years ago because I was tired of seeing so many young people like yourselves growing up without really knowing what God expects from you. You all need to be soldiers for God, and I am not using that term figuratively. You need to fight sin and sinners wherever you find them and, like any good soldier, you need to be trained to fight, and you need the arsenal to win that fight." He held up his Bible. "Your arsenal is right here. Everything you need to fight sin is in this wonderful book – one that should always be near you."

As August spoke, the fire burned away the burlap closest to the rocks, revealing leaves, twigs and branches as its sustaining fuel. The only burlap remaining began to cling to an as-yet indiscernible figure in the center of the fiery pit. The flames at August's back cast haunting shadows on his face, distorting his features. "I realize some of you are here because your parents made you come. I also realize some are a little scared because this is the first time you have camped or spent the night away from your parents." He waved to the group of twelve men. "Our elders are here if you need anything, so never hesitate to ask. No child yet has become so scared that we had to call the parents to come pick him up, and I am sure none of you will be the first."

Scattered gasps and more than a couple of screams erupted in the crowd as the burlap burned away to reveal the central figure in the pit to be an effigy of Satan. The figure was constructed of wrought iron, but it had been given an artificial skin of a woven synthetic fiber that would hold flames for several minutes before being destroyed. This burning skin gave the illusion of a fire that burned without consuming. With requisite horns and tail, Satan looked down on the children with a hideous, flaming grin.

Without looking behind him, August smiled. "The reason we do not allow your parents to stay is that we want you to learn how you should conduct your lives as true Christians once you leave their homes. By the time your parents return for Sunday morning's service, you are all going to be strong soldiers of God, right?" The crowd of children shouted in the affirmative, although some remained silent, still perhaps disturbed by the burning figure that loomed behind the reverend as if it could grab him at any moment and rip away his flesh with its gnashing teeth.

"Let me see if you are ready to become soldiers with a test of your bravery." Placing the Bible on a nearby tree stump, August grabbed a burning branch from the fire and walked around with the flaming end at eye level of the children. He stopped in front of a young boy with the flame held a breath's length before his cherubic face. "Put your hand out, and touch this fire." The boy's mouth opened, but no words escaped his lips. He looked with confusion at August, whose face was stern with eyes fixed on the boy. The man asked him, "Do you not want to be a soldier of God?" to which the boy nodded. "Then put your hand out, and touch this fire."

The boy raised his right hand from his lap and moved it toward the fiery stick. At the first sensation of heat, he withdrew his hand to the safety of his chest. "I... I can't," the boy said with a pout.

August tousled the boy's hair with his free hand. "Of course not. The point is no one wants to touch fire. How many of you have ever been burned – by fire or maybe touching a hot stove or an iron? Raise your hands." More than half raised their hands. "How did it feel?"

"It hurt," one child said.

"Absolutely, it hurt. Being burned is the most horrific pain imaginable. Fire's purpose is to destroy, to consume. When you touch fire or something hot, that heat is destroying your skin, eating into you. Who can tell me what happens to people who refuse to obey God?"

"They go to Hell," a kid said, prompting snickers at his use of an otherwise curse word.

"Correct, and stop laughing. There is nothing funny about

Hell." He threw the stick into the still-roaring bonfire and pointed to the burning effigy. "Look at Satan!" He turned his pointing finger to members of the audience and, with a demonic look of his own, warned them, "That could easily be any one of you in that pit of fire. Any one of you who fails to abide by God's word. Do you hear me?" Many of the children yelled their affirmation, while some of the younger ones looked terrified.

"You will burn in the fires of Hell, but the flames will not consume you. You will burn for eternity! Do you know how long that is? Think about your earliest memory, the first thing you can remember. Now imagine at that moment, you were cast into a fiery pit like this one. Your first instinct would have been to jump out, but you cannot jump out of Hell. Fire extends as far as you can see. Fire everywhere, all around you. You have no escape. You can feel the flames biting into you, tearing away your flesh, but you look down and see that your flesh is still there. Now think about how long it has been since that first memory of yours until this very moment. Imagine being in that fiery pit this whole time. That is nothing compared to eternity. No matter how much you beg to die, to just end it all, it will never end! You. Will. Always. Suffer."

Not a child looked away. All appeared shaken, some to the point of crying. "Your only way out..." He pointed again to the fire. "Your only way to avoid the Lake of Fire is right here." He picked up the Bible. "If you do not obey God's word, you will surely burn!"

Nestled high on its red-rock perch, Christ Church of Sedona, with its large picture window, was visible from the highway almost a kilometer away, but Gregor could see no sign of the promised rave as Travis turned his car from the highway onto the narrow road leading to the church. Only when they were upon the building could he tell for certain they were in the right place – seeing a black fabric had been placed over the inside of the window to keep the ravers' presence hidden from passersby and hearing the furious bass throbbing music into his bones. The three who exited the car could not have contrasted each other more if done with purpose. Cadence wore a tight black dress that revealed how thin she had become. Travis wore a burgundy tank top and houndstooth shorts with loafers, while Gregor had on a long-sleeve black shirt and jeans.

Travis looked at his passengers. "Lady and gentleman, let's wake up this sleepy town."

A massive man of Native American descent and dressed in a sleeveless tunic stood guard at the entrance next to a table with a cashier's box tended by a woman with blue hair wearing a black vestment. Travis balked at the cover charge until the woman informed him that the drinks would be free, at which point he paid for all three. When the doorman, who the blue-haired woman called "Nickel," stamped each of their left hands, Gregor noticed he was missing the index and middle fingers on his right hand and wondered if he had lost the digits in a fight.

Once inside, they paused to take in the mystical ambiance. The church had been transfigured into a pagan temple of a civilization long lost to Time. Idolatry and masks hung from the walls, and an eerie fog of dry ice vined through the air like a mescaline mist, obscuring the eyes with transcendental awareness. Onstage, a handful of beautiful worshippers of both sexes, dressed in sarongs and bands around their chests, writhed in obedience to their timbre god's command. From two turntables resting atop a replica ark of the covenant, the DJ as high priest spun energetic, vocal trance music to deliver the message of the god. As if accepting the gift of fire, enthusiastic dance floor denizens moved to every frenetic beat with their arms outstretched to the spinning mirror ball hung from a middle rafter to reflect focused beams of colored light at every corner of the temple.

Mouth agape, Cadence said, "I can't believe Mitchell let them do this to his church."

Travis agreed. "I know. Bible Boy has got a little Gomorrah in him."

"Gregor!" a voice called, and he turned to see a beautiful vision parting the crowd to get to him. Iris greeted him with a sweet kiss. "Gia made me wear this."

In a white dress with tattered sleeves and hemline, Iris looked like a vestal virgin prepared for sacrifice. Gregor couldn't help but notice how the torn neckline accentuated her healthy bosom. "You look amazing," he said.

Travis agreed with a, "Wow."

"I'm glad you all came," Iris told them. "What do you think of the place?"

"You did a great job decorating," said Gregor.

Travis nodded to the stage dancers. "I love the show." He removed his tank top and tucked the straps into his back pocket. "I'm dancing." He disappeared in the crowd and seconds later reappeared on the stage to dance between two women, who were quick to follow his movements. They sandwiched him with their bodies and caressed his already sweaty muscles.

"Look at him," said Cadence with mock disgust. "Do you guys want anything to drink?"

Gregor responded, "I'm good."

"I'm fine, too." Once Cadence was gone, Iris asked, "So did you take her to the vortex?"

Gregor frowned at the sore subject. "The land has been sold and fenced in."

"Are you serious?"

A sudden burst of brightness and crescendo of music interrupted their conversation. The lights aimed at the mirror ball turned to focus on the large totem head that blocked the double doors to the receptionist area. The speakers blared the sound of a heavy rolling object in surround-sound so the phantom object seemed to be circling the room. Nickel moved the totem head, and the doors opened to let loose a giant black ball. The dance floor parted for the rolling plastic sphere, which stopped at the center of the floor. Two of the male dancers jumped from the stage to stand on either side, and each grabbed the center of the ball to pull it apart and expose its content – a beaming Gia, who looked like a cross between Indiana Jones and Barbarella. She wore a fedora and tan faux-leather catsuit that could have been an extra epidermal layer. A coiled, miniature bullwhip hung from the olive belt cinched around her waist. The two muscular dancers helped her out of the ball before carting the pieces off the dance floor.

"Welcome to my Temple of Boom!" Gia announced into the wireless microphone she held. "You tithed at the door, so my only commandment is that you dance!" An electrifying tempo began, and the dance floor again moved like kelp in a hurricane.

Iris smiled at Gregor. "Gia's made her grand entrance. You want to dance?"

With everyone now in bed, Mitchell unzipped his tent and emerged wearing a black, button-down shirt and dark jeans. He skulked through the woods to the parking lot, dropping his shoulders when he saw a car was parked behind him. He would need to awaken Lucas.

At the boy's tent, since he was unable to knock, he began unzipping the door so he could talk without arousing his father. Before he was halfway finished, he was greeted by the pointy end of a crossbow. He fell back on his hands and butt.

Lucas finished unzipping the door. "Why are you sneaking into my tent."

Mitchell pushed the arrow's tip from his face, shouting in a whisper, "Stop pointing that at me. I need you to move the car that's blocking me."

Kneeling on the nylon floor with the weapon aimed halfway to the ground, Lucas asked, "Where you going?"

Annoyed that the boy's position necessitated a lie, he answered, "I left my notes for the devotional at church. I need to go over them tonight." Lucas smirked at him, prompting a firm, but hollow, threat from Mitchell. "Move the car, or give me the keys. Now."

Lucas glanced at his clothes and asked, "Which car is it?" After Mitchell told him, he found the key and, with the crossbow still clutched at his side, he followed the man to the parking lot.

"Why are you carrying that?" Mitchell asked, wondering if Lucas might have plans to shoot him and hide his body somewhere in the woods.

Lucas responded, "Protection."

Once at their destination, Lucas threw the crossbow in the passenger seat of the blocking car and moved it just enough to allow Mitchell to squeeze his car out.

CHAPTER 25

The digital clock in the dashboard was less than five minutes from its maximum quantity as Lucas drove on Highway 179. He was careful to stay far enough behind Mitchell's car to avoid detection, which wasn't easy in a town that's in bed by 10 p.m. When Mitchell's car turned onto the road to the church, Lucas muttered, "I guess he was telling the truth." Regardless, he realized that he could not follow him up the empty road and expect to remain unnoticed. Instead, he passed it, found a place to turn around and began driving back to the campground. Assuming his suspicions had been unwarranted, he was about to drive past the church without another thought when he saw two more cars turn onto the narrow road. "Okay, something's going on."

Entering his church, Mitchell was appalled by its unfamiliarity. "What have I done?"

"Mitchell!" Gia called with a slosh of her drink onto an oblivious passerby. She broke through a wall of sweaty patrons, who were in line for a brew, and gave him a hug. "You're here. Thank you again for the church, although it was the least you could do to pay for your father's sin."

"Gia, I made a mistake. You need to end this now."

She waved a finger in his face. "Uh-uh. You signed over your soul for the night, naughty boy, and you'll not have it returned until morning – per our verbal contract."

"If Dad finds out, he'll kill me. I mean that in the most non-figurative possible way."

"You Bible-thumpers are always worrying about impending doom instead of enjoying the moment. He won't find out. Almost everyone here is from Phoenix." She put an arm around him and pointed to a handful of non-dancing attendees. "With a few hand-picked exceptions."

All thoughts of his surroundings blinked from his mind. "She came."

"In keeping with my reputation for always delivering the goods," Gia said with a laugh and a kiss on his cheek. "Make the most of it," she added before walking away.

Cadence's face reflected the purple light from two glow strings being twirled in a precision ballet of impossible speed by a goateed dancer, who was putting on a show for all who bothered to look. Mitchell walked behind her and stood unnoticed since she remained transfixed by the glow-string wielder. When he saw a young man sporting a spiky mohawk walking by with several glow-sticks hanging from his belt loops, he took a bill from his wallet and asked the man if he could buy a couple from him. With a glowstick in each hand, Mitchell took a deep breath and said, "I'm about to make a fool of myself." In the midst of the lurkers, Mitchell started dancing with the glowsticks – a dance free of rhythm and context. Attempting to mimic the glow-string dancer, he waved the lights around like fireflies blinded in a sandstorm.

When Cadence noticed him, she laughed and waved her hands. "Stop. What are you doing?"

Grinning, Mitchell tossed the glowsticks in the air and came up to her. "Hi Cadence."

She told him, "That was just awful."

"It worked. I got your attention."

Cadence took his hand and said, "Mitchell, I need to tell you something."

Lucas skulked around the parking lot until he found a flyer on the ground. He saw Mitchell exit the church, holding hands with Cadence, who led him behind the building to where most of the church's contents had been moved to make room for the dance floor. She sat on a bench near the podium, and motioned for him to join her.

Lucas tried calling August, but the call went to voicemail. He looked up the number for the Sedona Police and called. "Hi, there's been a break-in at Christ Church of Sedona. Yes, they're still there. My name? Bubba. Someone needs to go pick up Reverend August Briar. It's his church. He's at a youth conference at... Your son's there now? Can you get the reverend? He needs to see what they've done."

"Why didn't you just tell me at the beginning?" asked Mitchell.

Cadence rolled her eyes. "Oh yes, because nothing's a bigger turn-on than cancer."

Mitchell clasped her hands between his. "Let me help you through this."

As a giggling Gia walk by in the arms of a raver, Cadence said, "I don't need help. I need a miracle."

"All miracles come from God. We'll pray for Him to take the cancer from you."

Cadence faced the ground. "Why did he let me get it to begin with?"

"Maybe to test you or punish you for disrespecting the life He gave you with sin."

Cadence looked at him with confused anger in her eyes. "You think I deserve this?"

"No, of course not," insisted Mitchell. "You've been baptized, so all of your previous sins have been forgiven. Now you can ask God to take away your affliction."

Cadence asked, "Do you think he would listen to me?"

"I can lead you in prayer."

The DJ spun a vocal trance song about eternal love, prompting Gregor to pull Iris closer. Entangled, the two kept pace with the rapid tempo while staring into each other's eyes. Gregor had never seen anyone look at him the way she did now, and his heart wanted to melt into her.

"Don't leave," Iris said.

Her lips matched the words he heard, but he wasn't certain. "What?"

"Don't leave," she repeated.

He smiled at her, and his embrace tightened. Gregor had never been in a reciprocal love before, and he just wanted to hold on.

Iris broke from his embrace to grab the bottom hem of his shirt.

"What are you doing?" Gregor asked.

"Freeing you."

Gregor blocked her hands. "No, no, no. I don't want people looking at me."

"You've been hiding for too long," Iris told him, punctuated with a reassuring kiss.

Gregor looked at the handful of dancers who could see him

on the packed dance floor, and not one was looking at him. He relented and let her remove his shirt.

"Woooooo!" she yelled while spinning the shirt over her head.

Gregor crossed his arms in front of his torso. He could count on one hand the number of people to whom he had exposed his body since the fire. His breathing intensified as he realized some of the nearby eyes had now turned to him.

From the stage, Travis yelled, "Gregor!" With a wide grin, he pointing at his friend. "Yeah, man!" He put his arms in the air as he danced to encourage Gregor to do the same.

After tying his shirt around her waist, Iris interlocked her fingers with Gregor's, bringing their palms together. She kissed him and moved his hands upward. Her movements urged his body back to the tempo, and once it arrived, she released him. Gregor gained more confidence with every gyration, and the two returned to dancing hardcore.

Lucas watched as Gia and her companion searched for a point of seclusion, which they found at one corner of the church's plateau. Two steps forward would have sent them over the edge of a cliff, while on the other side, the massive red rock formation jutted upward, casting a shadow on the plateau. The companion hushed Gia's lascivious laughter with a deep, passionless kiss. In one sweeping motion, he had her on her back. "Ow!" Gia exclaimed.

"What's wrong?" the young man asked.

She reached behind her back and pulled out a baseball-sized rock. "There are rocks all over the ground."

When Gia sat up, the man removed his shoe and used the rubber sole to brush aside the nearby rocks. Recovering his foot, he again topped her. "Better?"

"Much," she answered with a smile. As they kissed, the man unfastened his pants and pushed them down to his knees.

"Get up," ordered Lucas, his crossbow aimed at the couple.

"What?" Gia asked.

"That wasn't me," her companion said.

Lucas insisted, "I said, 'Get up.'"

This time they both heard from where the voice originated, and they saw the boy glaring at them. The companion jumped to his feet and reached for the top of his pants.

"Leave them down," Lucas said with his aim now on the man.

"Hey, if she's yours, I'm sorry," the man said. "I didn't know."

Lucas grimaced, saying, "I'd never touch a whore."

Gia climbed to her feet. "Who the hell do you think you are?"

"The one with a weapon," answered Lucas.

"Hey, do I know you?" Gia asked with a point of her index finger. "I've seen you somewhere."

The companion wanted to run but couldn't in his current position. He reached down again for his pants, and Lucas reacted by firing a metal-tipped arrow that pierced the garment and clinked into the ground. Lucas reloaded and aimed at his crotch. "Do exactly what I say, or the next one's gonna make you squeal."

He erected himself, hands cupped over his penis. "Dude, what do you want from me?"

"I want you to follow the Bible. How does the Bible say to deal with whores?"

The man shrugged. "I don't know. Can you give me a hint?"

Lucas responded, "Deuteronomy 22, verses twenty and twenty-one."

The man shook his head and said, "I'm gonna need more than that, dude."

"If the tokens of virginity be not found for the damsel, then they shall bring out the damsel to the door of her father's house, and the men of her city shall stone her with stones that she die."

"You're crazy!" Gia yelled.

"I don't get it," the man said.

Lucas smiled and nodded at Gia. "Stone her. Stone the whore, or I'll bore your stones."

With the crossbow aimed at his crotch, the companion reached for a small rock.

Gia asked, "You're not really going to do it?"

"Not that one," Lucas told him. "The one next to it."

"Don't listen to him!" Gia screamed. "He's just a kid!"

Starting to cry, the man dropped his rock, picking up a grapefruit-sized one beside it. He was about to pitch it underhand toward Gia when Lucas instructed, "Not softball. Baseball."

The man turned to Lucas and pleaded with him, "Please don't make me do this."

"I'm not making you. It's totally up to you."

"Help!" Gia yelled.

"I will shoot you in your eye right now if you don't shut up." At his command, Gia stopped yelling, and Lucas turned back to the companion. "Throw the stone."

When the man complied, Gia closed her eyes and tried to shield herself with her hands, but she couldn't stop the rock from hitting her shoulder. She winced and grabbed at the pain.

"Again," Lucas ordered.

When Iris heard the trance remake of Gerry Rafferty's "Baker Street" start to play, her heart leapt. "I loved this song!" she yelled to Gregor. As they danced, embracing and parting to the thrilling beat, the two glistened with light reflecting off beaded drops of sweat that clung to their skin in a losing battle of attrition with gravity. Gregor closed his eyes and ran his hands from Iris' shoulders down her arms. As his fingertips grazed by, the hair on her arms stood at attention. Her breathing intensified, and she felt a growing internal spasm that sent her head back in a sensual cock. Her whole body tensed. She was no longer dancing to the music booming from the speakers but to a different tempo all together. Gregor's touch was intoxicating to her, and her wrists were now afire from his grasp like anodes connected to live wires. She gyrated in utter ecstasy and orgasmed.

When her muscles eased, Iris realized that she was moaning. Embarrassed, she turned her head right and left to see if anyone noticed her climax but saw no indication of undue attention – not even from Gregor, who had his eyes closed. She released her wrists from his grip and moved in to hug him, kissing his salty chest. She looked up to his face. "Gregor!" she called but couldn't be heard over the saxophone, so she patted him twice on the chest. He opened his eyes, and Iris jumped back. His eyes were blue with light.

"Gregor!" she called again, but he did not respond. She waved her hand in front of his face. He continued moving his body to the music, but his face was expressionless. Iris turned to the stage and waved at Travis. When he saw her, he waved back. Iris shook her head and pointed at Gregor.

Travis froze and gawked at him. He jumped off the stage and wormed his way to his friend. "Gregor!" He asked Iris, "What happened?"

"I think he's in a trance. I can't wake him up." Travis snapped his fingers several times in front of Gregor's face and called his name. Iris gasped, "Oh no. Look!"

A blue light was growing in Gregor's chest. "What is that?" Travis asked.

"He's converting."

A ring of blue light pulsed from Gregor and traveled through the dance floor before disappearing into the walls and continuing outside the church. The diameter of the ring of light increased to more than a kilometer before dissipating, and it was followed by more.

"Let me think about it," Cadence said after Mitchell asked her to stay in Sedona.

Unsatisfied with her answer, Mitchell asked, "What's waiting for you in Los Angeles?"

A pulse of blue light passed through them.

"What was that?" asked Mitchell.

"It must be a light show," she said, as pulses continued at metered intervals.

"From inside? Penetrating the walls? Is she using military-grade lasers?"

The pulse distracted Lucas, allowing Gia's companion time to change his aim and hurl the rock at the boy. Lucas was hit in the head, causing him to drop his crossbow. The man pulled up his pants and ran, leaving Gia curled on the ground with six welts on her body and blood dripping from her temple. Once Lucas reclaimed his weapon, she was alone in the crosshairs.

"Please," she begged, forcing herself to her feet. "I haven't done anything to you."

On the dance floor, Gregor continued emitting cadenced pulses of light. All eyes now focused on him. As the circular ribbons of blue light raced through the crowd, they lit everyone in its path. With each pulse, the ravers cheered approval. Some held their hands in front of their faces so they could watch the light penetrate them.

"That is so cool, man," a raver said to Travis. "How is he doing that?"

Ignoring the question, Travis asked Iris, "What should we do?" but she had no answer.

Lucas stooped to pick up a large rock and, as he moved it behind his shoulder in preparation to catapult it at her, Gia screamed, "No! No more!" She took a step back and lost her balance just as another pulse traveled through her. Still glowing blue from the energy, she screamed, plummeting ten meters to the rocky shelf below.

Lucas dropped the rock and looked over the edge but could not see her in the darkness below. He ran to the car he had borrowed and pulled out of the driveway.

Lucas drove down the road to the highway, passing two speeding patrol cars – the latter of which carried August Briar in the backseat. The boy threw a hand to the side of his face to keep his identity concealed until the cars were behind him.

As the pulses of light continued, Cadence and Mitchell could determine no method for their emanation from the wall of the church. When she realized that the color matched the light she saw when she jumped off Coffee Pot Rock, she threw her hand to her mouth. "It's God."

"What?" asked Mitchell.

"The weird light that saved me, and now the light is here again."

Mitchell, I think God wanted me to find you. He wants us to be together."

"Really? I do too. I've been..." He pulled from his pocket his mother's crucifix. "Will you accept my gift now?"

Cadence turned her back to him and lifted her hair. He wrapped the chain around her neck, and the next pulse provided the light he needed to see and lock the clasp. Another pulse was the last straw for him. "These lights have to stop. People are going to see."

From the backseat of a patrol car, August Briar saw pulses of light emanating from the church.

The officer driving asked, "What the devil is going on up there?"

"Desecrator!" August yelled, realizing Gregor must be in his church. He growled to the officer, "Get me to my church!"

CHAPTER 26

Wondering about the cause for the commotion, Nickel, the doorman, cut a swath through the crowd with his broad shoulders pushing the oblivious aside with no discernable resistance. He reached Gregor just after he ejected another pulse.

"What's going on here? Hey buddy." The doorman cupped his three-fingered hand over Gregor's shoulder. "What are you—" Another pulse surged from Gregor, and the startled doorman shivered as it traveled through him. He jerked his hand away and stumbled back until he disappeared into the crowd of excited onlookers.

Travis pointed at the next pulse from Gregor and told Iris, "Look at that! Do you see it?"

"What?" Iris asked.

Travis tapped his finger on an imaginary drum and counted. "He's pulsing to the beat. Every eight count." He smiled and added, "He's a metronome."

"I don't see anything funny about it," said Iris.

"I'm just saying." Travis yelled to the DJ, who was watching

Gregor's show, "Hey DJ!" He sliced his throat with the side of his hand. "Cut the music!" The DJ scratched the song to a halt, and Travis and Iris watched for any effect. Gregor's body stilled, and the pulses stopped. "It's working!" The blue light faded from his body and left his eyes.

The ravers moaned their disapproval.

"Gregor, are you okay?" asked Iris.

A raver interrupted with, "Dude, that was incredible. How did you do it?"

"Do what?" asked Gregor, as if he had just awakened from a deep sleep.

Travis waved the crowd back. "Let's give a round of applause to Gregor the Illusionist?"

The ravers applauded and cheered, and one asked, "Where are you performing again?"

Travis answered, "Catch him on the boardwalk in Venice."

"Cool," the raver responded.

Iris asked Gregor, "What happened to you?"

Travis explained to him, "You totally spaced out and were pulsing like a quasar."

"Seriously?" Gregor asked. "Did anyone see?"

Travis laughed. "You were really subtle about it, but yeah, I think people noticed."

"Why did you zone out like you did?" Iris asked. "I thought you were... gone."

"The music – that beat – triggered the energy in me." Gregor closed his eyes to recall the feeling. "They have similar vibrations, like complementary waves. A perfect resonance."

"Stonehenge—" Travis began to compare his words to their conversation from earlier in the day, but he was interrupted by Iris, who wanted confirmation of Gregor's health.

"Are you sure you're okay?"

"I'm fine," Gregor said and kissed her.

"What were you experiencing?" she asked.

Gregor replied, "I sensed the beginning – the birth of our universe. The energy from the vortex… is the first energy."

"You mean in ranking?" Travis asked.

"The first ever," Gregor proclaimed as if amazed at his own words. "It is genesis."

The DJ cranked the music once more, prompting renewed movement in the ravers.

Travis said, "You should get away from the music to avoid another flareup – literally."

Gregor shook his head. "I think I'm okay as long as I don't open myself up to it."

Iris suggested, "Why don't we get some air, just in case."

Outside, two patrol cars pulled right up to the door of the church, where the passengers could now hear the music. A moment later four police officers and Reverend Briar were standing in front of the lone gatekeeper. One of the officers asked the blue-haired girl at the table, "You mind telling me what's going on here, Miss?"

"This is private property!" August screamed.

Another officer held him back and said, "Reverend, we'll take care of this."

The girl explained, "My understanding is that we had permission to use this place."

"This is my church!" August yelled. "I would never allow its use as a den of perversion!"

The girl waved to the cashier box on the table. "I was just hired to take the cover charge."

Enraged, August overturned the table, sending the money into the air. He pounced through the door, and his lip trembled as he uttered, "What have they done to my church?"

Sergeant Wright told Officer Martine, "Block the door, and don't let anyone leave just yet." He instructed one of the other officers to find the lights and another to stop the DJ.

August's disbelief at the hedonism inside his sacred church morphed into unadulterated anger. He screamed, "I want these trespassers and vandals arrested! I want them persecuted!"

"Try to calm down," the sergeant said. "And I hope you mean *prosecuted*. We'll get them out, but I can't arrest them all. I don't have the facilities to hold them." The music grinded to a halt, and he announced to the grumbling crowd, "Ladies and gentlemen, I need your attention!" Once he had relative silence, he inquired, "Who's in charge of this shindig?" The silence continued for a few seconds. "No one? Okay then. The officer at the door is going to write each of you a nice little citation for trespassing, so make sure to pick one up on the way out." The ravers voiced their extreme disapproval with grunts and profanity.

Officer Martine waved for the attention of the sergeant. "Sir, I don't have my citation book. It's out in the car."

"Then go get it!" He told the officer returning from the DJ booth, "Watch the door."

Travis had been leading Gregor and Iris toward the door, but he stopped once the police entered. "Well, this completely sucks."

Iris gasped and said, "August Briar is here! He will crucify Mitchell if he knows he had anything to do with this." She started walking toward the minister.

Gregor grabbed her wrist. "What are you doing?"

"Trying to help." Iris continued with Gregor and Travis following. "Officer!" she called, garnering an I-should-have-known look of scorn from August. "I'm the one responsible."

"This is your little party?" Sergeant Wright asked.

"I knew Mr. Briar would be occupied with his youth conference, so I took the opportunity to use his church."

August's dagger-filled stare shifted to Gregor. "I knew you were here. You and your witch whore think you can defile the sanctity of my holy church?"

Gregor was not a violent person, so Travis was stunned to see him clench his right hand into a fist. Travis moved in front of his friend before he could raise it and asked August, "Do you pray to God with that dirty mouth?"

Sergeant Wright said, "That's enough all around."

Travis turned to Gregor and put a hand on his fist while whispering, "Man, are you crazy? A cop is standing right there."

Once Travis stepped aside, August gawked at Gregor's naked torso. "Your body... I saw pictures. What happened to your scars?"

Gregor took his shirt from Iris, who asked, "How'd he know about your scars?"

"I don't know," he answered before putting his shirt back on.

Unhooking cuffs from his belt, the sergeant told Iris, "Put your hands behind your back."

August pointed to Gregor, screaming, "He might have removed your shameful mark, but your physical enjoyment will be fleeting! You thought the first fire was painful? Your agony will be unending!"

The sergeant yelled, "That's enough! Reverend, you keep it up, and I'll take you in for inciting a riot or something along those lines."

August snarled at Gregor, "Your soul is damned, you defecation of Satan!"

"Reverend!" the sergeant warned a final time as he cuffed Iris' hands behind her back.

Travis asked Gregor, "Did he just call you Devil poop? I gotta remember that one."

Gregor disregarded both August and Travis. "Iris," he said, moving in front of her with his face looking down at hers. He placed his hands on her cheeks and whispered, "Are you sure you want to do this?" She kissed him in affirmation, prompting him to say, "Officer, you need to take us both in. It was our party."

"Great," the sergeant said in annoyance. "I only have one pair of cuffs." He looked around the room. "Where are my officers? And where the hell are the lights?"

Travis told Gregor, "I hope you don't expect me to turn myself in too. I'm not quite big enough to be feared, and I'm too big to be a prison bitch, so I'm not sure where I would fit in the whole penal colony hierarchy?"

As Gregor smiled and shook his head, the lights came on to expose all of the ravers inside, many of whom threw their hands to their foreheads to shield their eyes from the sudden brightness. Leaning against the wall with his arms folded and Cadence at his side, Mitchell stared forward in obvious dread of his father's impending fury. Through a thinning in the crowd, August spotted his son. "Mitchell?" He pushed ravers aside, beelining to his son.

The sergeant asked Gregor and Iris, "Listen, can I trust you two to stay here?"

Travis assured the officer, "I'll watch them."

Sergeant Wright caught up to August, who asked, "Mitchell, what are you doing here?"

The sergeant asked him, "Son, did you give permission for this party?"

Without raising his eyes, Mitchell answered, "Yes."

"Okay. Reverend, I'm sorry, but we're going to have to let everyone go."

His expression unchanged at the news, August asked, "Why?"

"They were here by invitation," Sergeant Wright replied.

"I was not talking to you," August told the sergeant before focusing on Mitchell. "Why would you do this?" The reverend fell silent when he saw the necklace around Cadence's neck. He threw an empty glance at his son and exited the building.

The sergeant told Officer Martine, who had just begun writing citations, "Stop writing. The reverend's son let them in." The ravers near the door sighed in relief. He returned his attention to Iris and uncuffed her. "You could've just told me you had permission from the son."

"Sorry," Iris responded. "I didn't realize that was important."

Once the officers exited, Travis noticed Iris scanning the room. "What are you looking for?"

"Gia," she answered.

The mohawked raver who sold Mitchell glowsticks huddled in the shadows at the corner of the plateau with another young man who wore eyeliner and four rings in each ear, waiting for the police to leave. "Dude, let's just walk away," said the raver with the abundance of earrings.

"I'm not leaving my car here."

"We can come back for it." The two heard a moan from the darkness. "What was that?"

The mohawked raver said, "It sounded like a ghost."

"Shut up."

"Dude, I'm serious."

When they heard another moan, the earring bearer said, "Wait a second." He dropped to his hands and knees and crawled to the edge before lying flat on his stomach. "Hand me a glowstick." His friend handed him one from his belt loop. "Now hold my feet."

"Dude, what are you doing?"

"Just hold my feet. I want to look over the edge."

"Okay, but if some creature grabs you, I'm letting go." The mohawked raver held his feet while he poked his head beyond the edge. He snapped the glowstick, which reflected green light from his earrings, and he dropped it. The small lamp landed on Gia's chest, lighting the prominent features of her face while casting the eyes and other depressed areas in shadows.

The eerie face freaked him out. "Ayy!" he screamed, scurrying from the edge.

The other raver also screamed. "What is it? What is it?"

"I don't know!"

After hearing another moan, the mohawked raver said, "That sounds like a chick."

"That doesn't sound like a chick to me."

"That's because you're still a virgin." He scooted himself on the ground so he could look over the edge. "It is a chick."

Exiting the church with Iris, Gregor shuddered when he felt a slight breeze blow against the back of his shirt, which was wet with sweat. "Wow, it's a little chilly."

Iris nodded toward the parking lot. "I thought Gia might be waiting by my car."

"Do you think she's hiding somewhere?"

The mohawked raver and his friend ran to Sergeant Wright, who was about to drive away with the others. Pointing toward the shadows, the raver yelled, "Hey, some girl fell off the cliff!"

Iris grabbed Gregor's arm. "Gia!"

The sergeant told Martine to call for an ambulance, and with a flashlight in hand, followed the raver to the cliff. Gregor and Iris joined them, along with several spectators. Without approaching too close to the precipice, the raver pointed. "She's down there."

Gregor walked to the cliff and looked over, while the sergeant crawled on his belly to the edge and shined the light below. As soon as the beam hit Gia, Gregor recognized the outfit.

"Is she..." Iris couldn't bring herself to say the word.

In the emptying church, Mitchell sat on the floor with Cadence. She had tried several times to get him to talk, but he refused. Travis approached Cadence and asked, "Ready to go?"

Cadence handed him the key to the motel. "You go ahead."

Mitchell said, "Cadence, go ahead and leave. I have a long night ahead of me, cleaning up this mess."

"I'll help you," she offered.

"No. I need to do it myself."

Cadence looked at the beer cans, cigarette butts and other signs of vice strewn over the floor. "You can't do this by yourself."

"Please, just go." Mitchell stood and began picking up the trash nearest him.

Leaving the church, Travis and Cadence were greeted by a blinding light from above. She latched onto his arm for balance as a powerful gust of wind almost pushed her back inside. The helicopter passed over them and to its cliffside destination. "What's going on?" she asked.

"Let's find out." The two hurried to center of the crowd of onlookers in time to see a bucket with a rescuer being lowered. They found Gregor with his arms around Iris. "Gregor!" yelled Cadence. "What's happening?"

"Gia fell," Gregor informed them, as the basket carrying her arose into view.

CHAPTER 27

"To miss the mark," August muttered as he walked to the campground after Sergeant Wright dropped him off in the parking lot. He thought about the Hebrew word het, which was translated into English as "sin." Its literal meaning was "to miss the mark," and that one, tiny word could summarize his son's entire existence. Had Mitchell not missed his delivery date by a week, he might not have poisoned his mother from the womb, and she would not have had to sacrifice her life for his. He stopped growing a little too early and just missed reaching the stature of a man. He was too weak to leave the shelter of his father's shadow, so he missed the ideal opportunity to carve out his own path after college. Most of all, his love of God would always just miss the mark of true devotion because his commitment was flawed with forgiveness.

August's thoughts were interrupted by a whispered, "Reverend." Lucas unzipped his tent door and stepped out in boxers and a T-shirt. "Why you up so late?"

August replied, "Wondering how to separate the sin from the sinner. Why are you up?"

"I had to pee."

He placed a hand on Lucas' shoulder. "I have to leave in the morning for a short while and will not be here for breakfast. Will you ask Elder Hemp to lead the morning devotional?"

"Sure. What's going on?"

"Mitchell's misdeeds have resulted in someone being seriously injured."

"Injured?" Lucas asked.

"That diner waitress fell – most likely in a state of wanton drunkenness – over the edge of the rock and had to be airlifted to the hospital."

Lucas paused before asking, "She's alive?"

"She was, but I am not aware of her prognosis."

"Which hospital was she taken to?"

"I assume Cottonwood. Why?"

Lucas shrugged. "I just didn't know where a hospital was around here."

Insulated from the morning's splendor, Gia lay unconscious in a hospital room with life-monitoring machinery arced around her head. Much of her body was bandaged, including her face, but the exposed parts, such as her nose and shoulders, were purple with bruising. A large hand reached out and cupped over her nose and mouth.

In a hospital waiting room, Gregor and Iris rested in connecting chairs, the back of her head on his chest. A nurse in green scrubs walked up to the couple and called, "Iris?" prompting Iris to raise her hand. "I'm Steve. Your sister is out of recovery and has been transferred to a private room in the trauma unit. She's still unconscious, but you can see her now."

"How is she?" Iris asked.

"Still in critical condition. The doctor will be able to give you more information."

Following Steve to Gia's room, Gregor whispered to Iris, "Sister?"

"I had to tell them that, or they wouldn't give me any information on her."

"She's in here," said Steve, approaching a door that had a wheeled bucket of water and mop parked outside, which he failed to notice until he kicked it, sloshing water onto his shoes. "Great. Who put that there?" The nurse shook his head and told Gregor, "I'm sorry, but we can only allow one visitor at a time and only family members."

"I understand." Gregor kissed Iris. "I'll be in the waiting room."

Iris entered the room without accompaniment and threw her hand to her mouth when she saw the number of monitors barnacled to Gia. She approached the bed and stroked her arm. "Your mom is flying out today," she said as she squeezed Gia's hand. Unable to bear seeing her in such a pitiable state, she closed her eyes. Seconds later, she noticed a light through her lids and, when she opened her eyes again, she gasped. "Oh my god."

From the bathroom of Gia's hospital room, Lucas watched as a blue light emerged from Iris' torso and traveled down her arm to the waitress. "Where is that coming from?" he whispered to himself. He watched as the light enveloped the unconscious woman.

At the sound of the door opening, Iris released Gia's hand, and the blue light vanished from them both.

A young doctor entered the room with a grim smile at Iris. "I need to apprise you of your sister's situation."

"Are you the surgeon?"

"No, I'm a neurologist. I'll be taking over her care. Maybe we should have a seat." The man waved to two chairs in the corner of the room. Once they were seated, he explained, "Your sister has been through two surgeries tonight to repair broken bones and to drain blood accumulating around her brain."

Lucas' gaze turned to the patient, who began to stir. Gia raised both hands to her face and felt the bandages, which she began to unravel.

A tear dripped from Iris' cheek. "Is she going to be okay?"

The doctor put his hand up and said, "There's more. Her fifth and sixth vertebrae were crushed. I'm sorry, but your sister may never walk again."

Once the bandages were off her unblemished face, Gia sat up in bed.

The doctor continued, "We're monitoring her brain function, but I need to inform you that in a typical case with so much trauma to the head, we would expect to see brain damage."

"Oh no," Iris said with tears now flowing.

Gia tossed aside the sheet covering her and scooted her legs to the side of the bed. She removed the monitor lines adhered to her head and chest, which caused the blips on her heart monitor to flat-line. She left the bed, heading toward the bathroom.

Hearing the alarm, the doctor looked to the bed, and his mouth dropped.

Iris screamed, "Gia! What are you doing?"

Gia pointed and said, "Looking for the bathroom."

As Steve and three others stormed into the room with a crash cart, the doctor hurried to his patient. "I... uh... You need to get back in bed."

Seeing the cause for the false alarm, Steve sent the others outside with the cart and told Gia, "Miss, we need to get you back in bed."

Gia frowned at them but returned to the bed as requested. She asked Iris, "Whose place is this?"

"This isn't going typically at all," the doctor said. "Miss, I need you to concentrate. Where do you think you are?"

"I figured I went home with someone," responded Gia.

Iris let out a little laugh and said, "She's fine."

The doctor dismissed Steve and told Gia, "You're in the hospital."

"What? Why?"

"You had a very bad fall," the doctor explained. "I need you to answer some questions for me. What day is it?"

"It's Friday, or no, it must be Saturday. My rave was last night."

"What year is it?"

She replied, "I know the year. I know who the president is. Get off my back."

Iris looked to the doctor to explain. "What were you saying before?"

The doctor shook his head, and his face flushed. "Obviously, someone gave me the wrong patient records." He headed for the door but, before leaving, said, "Keep her in bed."

Iris took her friend's hand and smiled. "I'm so glad you're okay."

"What happened?" Gia asked.

"That's what I'd like to know. You fell over a cliff. You're lucky to be alive. That fall should have killed you. Were you drunk?"

"I don't think so. I was with this cute guy. We went to find a private place to... He was kissing me. He was a nice kisser. I remember. Some guy – a kid – came out of the shadows... with a crossbow..." Gia trailed off on the last few words, as if questioning their validity.

Iris asked, "A crossbow?"

"I know. How medieval."

"Who was it?"

"I don't know. He was big, though." Tears started dripping from Gia's face. "He told the guy I was with to... stone me. And the little prick did."

"Seriously?"

"Yes. I think he must've hit me on the head. That's the last thing I remember."

Iris told her, "I left my phone in my purse in the waiting room. I'm calling the police to tell them what you said."

After Iris left, Gia closed her eyes, and Lucas took the opportunity to depart. Wearing an environmental services uniform, he opened the bathroom door and touched the handle of the door to the hallway, when he heard Gia ask, "Could you get a nurse? I need some water."

With his back to her, Lucas hesitated before saying, "Not my job." He left the room.

Mitchell, a mess of a man with hair matted from dried sweat and wearing the now-wrinkled clothes from the night before, shuffled backwards across the creaking wood floor as he mopped. He had tried sleeping on the counseling sofa, but the loud music still rang in his ears, while his father's look of disgust continued burning his eyes. He had returned the pulpit furniture to its proper place and planned to move the rest of the furniture once the floor dried.

"I always had the highest of hopes for you," said August, startling his son with a deep voice that boomed throughout the hollow room. Clutching a Bible, he left footprints on the wet floor as he proceeded to the pulpit. "I encouraged and nurtured you so that you would follow the path of righteousness, but I now doubt you will ever find favor in God's eyes."

"Dad—" Mitchell took a step toward his father, who was now glaring at him from the podium.

"Stay where you are!" August threw up his palm and preached to his son. "Jeremiah 2:7, 'And I brought you into a plentiful country, to eat the fruit thereof and the goodness thereof; but when ye entered, ye defiled my land, and made mine heritage an abomination.'"

"I didn't defile you."

"The way of a fool is right in his own eyes. Isaiah 59, 'Your iniquities have separated between you and your God, and your sins have hid His face from you, that He will not hear. For your hands are defiled with blood, and your fingers with iniquity; your lips have spoken lies, your tongue hath muttered perverseness.' Why did you let them in my house, in God's house?"

Mitchell shook his head. "I don't know."

"Revelation 21:8, 'The fearful, and unbelieving, and the abominable, and murderers, and whoremongers, and sorcerers, and idolaters, and all LIARS,'" he emphasized with his finger pointing at his son, "'shall have their part in the lake which burneth with fire and brimstone: which is the second death!' Speak the truth to me now, Mitchell!"

"I did it for Cadence," Mitchell answered.

"James 1:15, 'Then when lust—'"

"Stop it!" Mitchell screamed. "Speak to me like my father and not my minister!"

August again pointed. "You have forsaken me! You have forsaken God! For lust!"

"I haven't forsaken God or you. I made a mistake."

"Salome's reward for her lascivious dance was the head of John the Baptist. Will that girl's reward be your soul?" August threw his Bible at Mitchell's face, but it fell just below its target. "Recite Luke 15, verses eighteen and nineteen to me."

He didn't even look at the fallen Bible. With teary eyes fixed on his father, he recited, "I will arise and go to my father, and will say unto him, Father, I have sinned against Heaven, and before thee, and am no more worthy to be called thy son: make me as one of thy hired servants."

August stepped away from the podium and walked toward his son as if he were about to hug and forgive him. Instead, he passed by him, saying, "You can forget about speaking at the conference today. I will not have those young minds suffer your influence."

Iris stood in the hospital hallway as she waited for the police offi-cer to finish questioning Gia. When the door to her friend's room opened, the officer walked past her without saying a word. Iris stepped inside and asked, "What did he say?"

Gia didn't make eye contact with her. "He didn't believe me."

"What?" Iris said.

"They apparently took some of my blood when I was brought in, and they found," Gia deepened her voice, "high levels of a nar-cotic, possibly hallucinogenic substance."

"What did you take?" Iris asked.

"I was x-ing, but that doesn't make you see things."

Iris headed for the door. "I'll talk to him."

"Just drop it. Iris, I appreciate it, but I'm really tired. I just want to sleep for a while." Gia rolled onto her side, facing away from her friend.

Leaving Gia alone, Iris found Gregor in the waiting room, read-ing something on his phone. "There you are," she said. "I came by earlier, and you weren't here."

"I took a walk. How is she?"

Iris sat next to him and said, "Great actually," without the cheer warranted by the news.

"Seriously? That's excellent." He kissed her forehead.

"She wants to get some rest now, so we can head on out."

Gregor stood and held out his hand to help her up. "You want to grab some breakfast?"

"I am starving." Iris held his hand as they walked away. "Then maybe we could do something I had planned for today before this happened."

"What is it?"

"You'll find out."

Using a tarp underneath to slide them, Mitchell had just replaced all the pews when his cell phone rang from the floor of the pulpit. "Hello? Richard Glavin? Oh yes, I remember you. My father's agent. That's probably because he's in the woods. He can't get a signal. Of course, I can. Are you serious? Yes, I'll let him know. Thank you." He hung up and placed the phone on a nearby pew.

"Hi Mitchell," Cadence greeted from the doorway.

He faced her and said, sans enthusiasm, "Cadence."

She smiled. "This place looks amazing. You should open a cleaning business." She ended with a slight laugh that received no response from him.

"Why are you here, Cadence?"

"To make sure you're okay. And I thought we could pray together, like you suggested."

He walked by her to the back pew, which rested atop the tarp. "I think you should leave."

"Are… Are you tired?"

"No." He lifted the end of the wooden bench to scoot the tarp from beneath with his foot.

"I don't understand. Don't you remember last night?"

"I remember," he said as walked to the other end of the pew to pick it up. "I abandoned my beliefs, and I abandoned my father just for the chance to talk to you again."

"So, let's talk."

He dropped the bench to devote his full attention to the words he was about to deliver. "Actually, I am tired. Tired of being led by others. I'm taking control of my life starting now."

Cadence waited for more, but received nothing, so she turned to leave him to his work.

"Cadence," he called, sparking a hopeful smile from her. "I need the necklace back."

CHAPTER 28

A t the crack of noon, Nickel opened his eyes. A sheet of satin crumpled at his side did very little to cover the hairless torso of the stocky Native American, and his thick legs and feet were exposed to the controlled environment of his hyper-clean apartment. He lay in bed and stared at the off-white ceiling thinking about last night's job. He had never been superstitious, but the man of light reminded him of stories he had heard as a child about a tribe who could ignite blue fire from the gods. He wanted to believe that the man was in fact an illusionist, but he could not explain away the energy he felt when he touched him.

Nickel shrugged it off and crawled out of bed. Dressed in tighty-whities, he walked to the bathroom and stood in front of the commode to urinate. As the stream hit the water, a puzzled look crept over his face. Something felt strange, like someone else was touching him. He looked down and realized his penis was being held by a hand with five fingers.

He dropped his penis, letting the stream water the floor, and he raised his right hand in front of his face, wiggling his fingers. He glanced down at his left hand in case he had somehow forgotten which one was missing two fingers. He had made no mistake. Both hands now had five fingers.

August stood before the blackened effigy of Satan and spoke to the children as they ate lunch on the concentric benches. "What would you say if a friend tried to get you to blow off church so that you could watch the football game on TV?"

The children gave the response the reverend had ingrained in them, "God comes first!"

"Right! James 1:12, 'Blessed is the man that endureth temptation: for when he is tried, he shall receive the crown of life, which the Lord hath promised to them that love him.'"

A girl of fourteen raised her hand and, once August called on her, she said, "Sometimes my mom tells me that she's too tired to go to church."

August nodded at the familiar excuse for devotional avoidance. "What do you think happens to a soldier of God if he or she is too tired to serve the Lord? Just like any deserter, they are cast out of His service, and the enemy – in this case, the Devil – claims a small victory. Many of you are going to have to come to terms with the fact that one or both of your parents might be going to Hell. Do not let them take you with them. You have to be strong enough to stand alone in God's service, even against your parents. In Matthew, chapter ten, Jesus said, 'Think not that I am come to send peace on Earth: I came not to send peace, but a sword. For I am come to set a man at variance against his father, and the daughter against her mother, and the daughter-in-law against her mother-in-law. And a man's foes shall be they of his own household. He that loveth father or mother more than me is not worthy of me: and he that loveth son or daughter more than me is not worthy of me.' If your parents are not going to church and you are not old enough to drive yet, you need to call someone who is going so that they can take you with them. Then you need to tell your minister about your parents' sluggish faith so that he can confront them, adult-to-adult, and ensure they return to the righteous path from their detour to sin."

August saw Lucas enter the clearing from the woods. After telling the children to enjoy the rest of their lunch, he joined the boy and asked, "Where have you been?"

Lucas led the reverend from listening ears. "Don't be mad at me, but I borrowed a car."

With a sudden flush of anger, August asked, "You did what?"

"I wanted to check on that girl that was hurt at your church. Make sure she was okay."

"We could have called the hospital."

Lucas told him, "I saw the girl you pointed out in the restaurant, the one you called a witch—"

"Iris Wickline."

"I saw her heal the girl that was hurt. She put her hands on her, and this blue light came out of her. The next minute, the girl didn't have a scratch on her."

August would have thought the boy a liar had he not experienced the healing effect of Gregor's amulet a few days before. "She healed her with just her hands?"

"I'm not lying!" Lucas insisted.

"I believe you, Son."

"Reverend, are you sure she's a witch? Isn't healing the work of the Lord?"

"She is not a disciple of God! Do not be fooled by magic disguised as miracles." His attention diverted from the boy to his approaching son. "Mitchell, I told you to stay away."

Mitchell said, "This conference means as much to me as to you. I've worked hard on it."

"Fine," replied August. "Just stay in the background, and keep your mouth shut."

Mitchell stopped to face his father. "No! I'm not going to let you silence me. You promised I would have fifteen minutes to deliver my sermon, and I'm going to take it."

At once angry at his audacity and proud of his fortitude, he conceded. "Fifteen minutes."

With Gregor in the passenger seat, Iris steered her car off the highway and onto the small road leading to Slide Rock State Park in Oak Creek Canyon. Seeing the road sign, Gregor asked, "Are we going hiking?"

"Stop guessing. You'll find out in a minute."

Gregor stretched the front of the shirt he had been wearing all night up to his nose to sniff. "I should really take a shower before we do anything. I'm a bit odorous."

"Don't worry about it. I have something for you."

"Is it deodorant?"

Iris parked her car. "It's something I picked up for you when I was shopping with Gia yesterday." She reached for a paper bag in the backseat and handed it to him.

"Okay, I'm feeling bad now. That's two gifts for me, and I haven't given you anything."

"It's nothing. Just something else I thought you might not have."

Gregor removed a yellow bikini from the bag. "You're right. I don't have one."

Iris grabbed the bikini. "I picked up a little something for myself while I was at it."

Gregor again checked the bag and found a pair of red swimming trunks. "Shorts. Cool."

"They're trunks," she told him and waited for him to realize her motive. "We're going swimming."

After taking turns to change clothes inside the car, Iris and

Gregor headed for the water. Wearing her new bikini underneath her black top and a sarong, she found hiding her elation difficult as the two strolled past apple trees from an orchard planted when the area was private property. She slid her hand into his. "By the way, thank you for staying with me last night."

Iris noticed Gregor, now shirtless and sporting his new red trunks, seemed distracted by the numerous people passing them on the trail. He checked the eyes of every passerby and turned away whenever eye contact was made.

"What's wrong?" asked Iris.

"Everyone's looking at me."

Seeing his growing panic, she led him off-path to the shade of an apple tree.

Breathing in pants, he leaned against the trunk of the tree. "I'm sorry. I'm really uncomfortable with this. I'm exposed."

"You seemed to be okay last night – for a little while anyway."

"It's brighter now. You have to understand, I might look normal, but I don't feel it."

"We don't have to go swimming. I didn't realize how difficult it would be for you."

He watched more people traversing the trail to the water. "Are you okay if we don't go?"

Iris smiled in spite of her disappointment. "Of course, but I want you to know that you have no reason to be self-conscious about the way you look."

"You wouldn't say that if you had seen me in full a week ago."

"Gregor, I've seen you in a way that no one else ever has, and you are beautiful."

She moved her hands to his neck and drew him in for a kiss, and Gregor returned her affection with natural endeavor. Her hands found their way to his chest, and she stood on her toes to introduce her waist to his.

When their lips parted, Gregor whispered, "I hope that water's cold."

Sermon in hand, Mitchell walked in front of his audience and announced, "'The Lord your God is a devouring fire; he is a jealous God!' That's what Moses told the Israelites in Deuteronomy 4:24." He smiled at the children. "God is scary." After a few snickers from the audience and a concerned look from his father, who stood watch from beside the last bench, he continued, "We often talk about fearing God – and for good reason. He's all powerful, and he sees everything you do – like he has you on a twenty-four-hour webcam. In some ways, God is like your dad. He lays down the rules for you and, if you disobey those rules, he punishes you. God is scary because his punishment is much more severe than any your dad is capable of administering. Right?" Some children nodded, while others offered audible agreement. "From God's first punishment, kicking Adam and Eve out of the Garden of Eden, to casting sinners into Hell…" Mitchell stopped when he saw the raised hand of a pre-teen boy. "You have a question?"

"Where's the Garden of Eden now?" the boy asked.

A girl of similar age seated nearby answered, "God destroyed it."

An older boy said, "Nu-uh. You can't destroy the Tree of Life. We'd all be dead."

Mitchell told them, "The Bible makes no mention of the Garden being destroyed, and all we know for certain is that the entrance is guarded by an angel with a flaming sword. Some people think God moved the Garden where man could no longer reach it."

"How do you move a place?" the initial boy asked.

"Where could he move it that we couldn't find it?" a girl asked. "In space?"

Mitchell enjoyed their enthusiasm on the subject, and he gave them more food for thought. "Another theory suggests that it's still on Earth but in a different plane of existence."

"It's on a plane?"

"Not that kind of plane," Mitchell responded. "Think of the burning bush and how the flame didn't consume it. How is that possible? Maybe the bush and the flame occupied the same space but on different planes of existence. The Garden could be occupying the same space as something else, like a mountain, and we wouldn't be able to see it."

August stepped forth, threatening to commandeer the pulpit. "God works in mysterious ways that are not for us to understand, but we are here to learn the facts of His word." He held up his Bible for emphasis and to conceal his next words to Mitchell, "You are getting off subject."

"Right." Mitchell looked at his papers to regain his spot. "But there's another side to God. He's like your dad in other ways. He watches over you, and He loves you very much. You're His children. Like any father, God expects His children to love Him and each other. In fact, if we are without love, we are without God. In 1 Corinthians 13, the apostle Paul wrote, 'If I could speak all the languages of Earth and of angels, but didn't love others, I would only be a noisy gong or a clanging cymbal.'" He glanced at his father. "In other words, if I speak for God but not with love, my speech is nothing more than noise. The scripture continues, 'If I had the gift of prophecy, and if I understood all of God's secret plans and possessed all knowledge, and if I had such faith that I could move mountains, but didn't love others, I would be nothing.'"

Mitchell directed his next words toward his father. "Because God does love you, he is willing to forgive you when you disobey the rules. Love and forgiveness are intertwined. Proverbs 17:9 tells us, 'Love prospers when a fault is forgiven.' Forgiveness is one of God's greatest gifts to us. We all sin, so without God's capacity for forgiveness, none of these sins would be forgiven, and then none of us would enter the Kingdom of Heaven." Mitchell noticed August pointed at the watch on his wrist. "Well, my time is up. I hope you enjoy the rest of the conference." When a young girl raised her hand, Mitchell asked, "You have a question?"

"Does God love sinners?"

Mitchell answered, "God loves everyone."

Rushing to the front, August interrupted. "What my son means is if you do not obey God, you do not love Him, and He will not love you. Jesus said in John 14:15, 'If ye love me, keep my commandments.' Sin is of this world, as are sinners. In 1 John 2:15-16, Jesus said, 'Love not the world, neither the things that are in the world. If any man love the world, the love of the Father is not in him. For all that is in the world, the lust of the flesh, and the lust of the eyes, and the pride of life, is not of the Father, but is of the world.'"

A teenager raised his hand, and Mitchell asked, "You have a question too?"

"Why can't we do what we want and then ask God to forgive us right before we die?"

August walked to center stage. "I will take this one. Excellent question, and it concerns what I consider to be a problem in God's law. I call it the Forgiveness Loophole." Mitchell had heard his father's theory before and didn't care to hear it again, so he left the stage. August explained, "Take for example a mass murderer on death row who is granted absolution before they pull the switch. How can someone who has lived a completely godless life be allowed to repent of his many sins just before dying and then be granted entry into the Kingdom of Heaven? Is that for real?" He laughed while shaking his head. "The answer is yes. 'Repent ye therefore, and be converted, that your sins may be blotted out,' Acts 3:19. In fact, the Bible goes even further than just letting these sinners into Heaven. Luke 15:7 says, 'I say unto you, that likewise joy shall be in Heaven over one sinner that repenteth, more than over ninety and nine just persons, which need no repentance.' Think about that. A sinner who repents gives more joy to God than ninety-nine righteous people who have no sins to repent of.

"Now what about the man who has devoted his life in service to God and then sins right before dying suddenly in a car accident? Will he also be allowed to walk through the pearly gates? Does that one sin wipe out all the good a person did during their life? If you sin against God and do not repent of that sin, you are going to Hell, plain and simple, no matter the life you led before that sin. So, to answer your question, you better repent of any sin you commit immediately because you never know when you will die, and you do not want to take a chance on that one sin blotting out a life of devotion to God. Think about that during your recreation time. You have one hour until dinner, and then we will have our Bible Bowl!"

North of Sedona, Oak Creek Canyon provided a scenic, red-walled path for the Verde River offshoot. Over centuries, the creek had cut a smooth channel into the crimson sandstone, funneling the flow into the cascading, natural water slide for which Slide Rock State Park was named.

Gregor and Iris had hiked upcreek a short distance to where the dispersal of the crowd afforded the slight possibility of private conversation. They waded in the cool water wearing their new swimwear while maintaining sight of Iris' sarong and top, which were draped in the branches of a cottonwood tree growing from a boulder embanking the creek. Their conversation throughout the day centered on information that young lovers share to test the mettle of the other's attraction by describing the nuances of their personality. Gregor and Iris drank up the tidbits as if it gushed from a spring at the end of a long, desert road.

Come tomorrow, Gregor would be on his way back to L.A., and that fact nagged at Iris throughout the day. Finally, she worked up the courage to ask, "What happens on Monday?"

"What's Monday?"

"The day after you leave."

Sitting with his back to the water's flow, he flashed an impish grin. "Funny you should ask. While you were visiting Gia, I stopped by the hospital's human resources office to apply for a job."

"For real? What did they say?"

"The office was closed for the weekend, but I'll apply online when I get back to L.A. If they're not hiring, I'll apply at every hospital from here to Phoenix."

Iris moved against the gentle current until she could feel his exhalations on her cheeks. "Why do you even have to go back to L.A. at all?"

"I have to keep my job until I find a replacement. I don't have much money saved up."

She sat between his legs with her back to his chest. "I need to tell you something."

Gregor scooted back. "Oh no, did you just pee in the water?"

Iris laughed and splashed him with water. "No."

He returned to his previous position. "Are you sure? The water's a little warmer here."

Iris slapped his arm, and she blurted out, "I healed Gia this morning."

"What? How?"

"I guess I had energy stored in me because I saw the blue light entering her from me. One minute she was comatose with irreparable damage, and the next minute she was fine."

"That's amazing," said Gregor. "Maybe we could heal Cadence without taking her to the vortex."

Iris shook her head. "I don't think I can help. Gia seemed to drain what little energy I had in me."

"It's slipping away from me, too. I can barely feel it now. We have to get back."

"Can we climb the fence?" Iris asked.

"It's topped with razor wire, but I think I might have enough energy to convert us and get us to the plateau. The new owner will never even know we were there."

Iris looked around and nodded to a slight path in the brush above the embankment. "We'll need some privacy." She took her belongings from the cottonwood and followed him up the brushy path. Gregor spread her sarong into a makeshift blanket over the prickly ground, and after he sat, she joined him, facing him with her legs on his. They embraced with their heads on each other's shoulder and began to meditate.

"Hey, you two!" a voice boomed from a few meters away. They faced the sound and saw a ranger frowning at them. "No licentiousness in the bushes. This is a public place."

Iris removed her arms from Gregor and said, "We were just talking."

"Do you talk to everyone by straddling their lap while wearing a bikini? Then come over here and talk to me." The ranger put his hand up and curled his lips up to an even line. "I'm just kidding. Seriously, though, I need you to stick to the designated hiking paths."

"But—" Iris began to protest before Gregor interrupted her.

"Okay." He stood and held out a hand to help her up. "We'll go back to the creek."

"Thank you," the ranger said, and he refused to move until they followed through.

"Why did you agree with him?" Iris whispered as they descended to the creek.

"It wasn't working. I don't have enough energy to convert myself, much less both of us."

"How could we have traveled so far before, and now we can't even get across town?"

Once their feet were again in the water, Gregor waved to the ranger, who left perhaps in search of other rule violators. "When we're energy, that state is easier to maintain," he told Iris. "The greatest use of energy is converting from one phase to another, like a rocket trying to escape the atmosphere needs a booster, but once in space, it can continue with minimal effort."

"Too bad we don't have a booster rocket."

Her remark sparked an idea in Gregor. "Maybe we do. Sedona's full of vortexes."

"Supposedly," Iris said. "But you said they're not as strong as your vortex."

"They're not, but with the energy still left in me, maybe a weak vortex could give a needed boost for conversion. I know you didn't believe in the power of the vortexes before, but you must have heard that one or two were maybe a little stronger than the others."

Without hesitation, Iris answered, "Boynton Canyon."

CHAPTER 29

As August stood before the fiery pit in the waning glow of twilight, he was unconcerned with the beads of sweat forming on his brow from his proximity to the fire and the insulation of his signature black suit. He told the children in attendance, "All of you are familiar with the stories in the Bible, and many of you realize the moral value of them. However, since the way of life in Biblical times is so different from the way we live today, young people are disconnected from the realities of the situations and consequences people faced then. Therefore, I have amended the parameters of the questions this year to focus on the Bible's real-life applications. Instead of quoting Bible verses and telling me where the verse is found, I will give you actual problems you might face today as God's soldiers, and then you will answer how you would solve that problem and give a Bible verse to support your answer." When a girl raised her hand, the reverend pointed to her. "You have a question?"

"Can you give a for instance?"

"For instance, if you are walking down the street one wintry day minding your own business when an animal activist approaches you and admonishes you for wearing a fur or leather jacket, how would you respond as upright Christians?" Some hands went up, but August wanted to answer this question himself. He looked at Mitchell while saying, "You let them know that their beliefs directly contradict God's words. God repeatedly, not only does not mind if we wear animal skin, but He Himself used animal skins to clothe Adam and Eve. Genesis 3:21, 'Unto Adam also and to his wife did the Lord God make coats of skins, and clothed them.' Does everyone understand the rules now?" he asked, breaking his gaze with his son.

"Yes," the children chorused.

August gave a sweeping wave to the row of men in attendance, saying "Our elders will serve as judges, determining which answers are the most meritorious. The person giving the least correct or most wrong answer in each round will be eliminated." August reached out to one of the elders, who handed him a gun, and the reverend held it up to announce, "Whoever is victorious in the Bible Bowl will win this FS2000 semi-automatic rifle." Once the sounds of approval had died down, he handed the gun back to the elder. "However, because everyone should have proper instruction in the use of firearms before owning one, the gun will be given to the winner's parents after Sunday's service. They will determine when you are ready to take possession of it. All right, who is playing?" Thirteen hands were raised, including one belonging to Lucas.

"Honestly, I could kick myself for not thinking of it sooner, but you don't have to actually get her to the vortex to use its energy," said Lily.

Travis had stopped by the crystal shop to let her know about his inability to take Cadence to the vortex because of her refusal to trespass on the fenced property and to ask if any of the other vortexes would work. "What do you mean?"

"Crystals! Nature's batteries. If you can get a crystal to the vortex, you could charge it—"

"And then what? Have her hold it? I don't see her doing that either."

"Consider them wireless chargers," Lily told him. "If you could just get the charged crystal close to her for a while, the energy could reach her and, although I hate to suggest injecting subterfuge into any relationship, you could do so without her knowing."

"It's worth a shot. Can you help me pick one?"

"Of course." Lily led him to a glass case near the back of the shop and chose a black, jagged rock from the more than two dozen similar ones of various sizes and shapes.

Travis nodded to the case and said, "I'll take them all."

"All of them?"

"Better odds."

"I have more in back," Lily said with a wry grin as she took one of the white cotton bags with drawstring tops hanging on a rack nearby and loaded the crystals inside. She threw in a violet crystal from another case, saying, "If you don't mind, charge one for me too. My knees started bothering me about a year ago, and my hips began acting up on me a few months later, and now my right elbow is giving me problems. It's like all my pivot points are turning on me."

Travis laughed at her pun. "That's clever."

"You!" a voice boomed from outside the shop. "You owe me money!"

Lily and Travis turned toward the source of the disturbance to see a husky, bearded man pointing an angry finger at Cadence, who was sitting in the passenger seat of Travis' car.

"You didn't tell me Cadence was here."

"I asked her to wait in the car," said Travis, covering for the fact that his friend didn't want to see Lily again.

In petrified apprehension, Cadence moved her lips for a response inaudible from inside the shop.

"What do you mean you don't have it?" the man asked.

Bolting outside to his friend's aid, Travis yelled, "Hey, back off!" and ran between the two.

"This doesn't concern you," the man told him.

"I won't say it again," Travis warned, fists clenched.

Now outside, Lily put her hand on the man's arm. "William, what's going on here?"

William pointed at Cadence and answered, "This girl promised me quadruple payment if I'd give her a balloon ride, and she bailed without paying me."

"Well, technically, you didn't take me all the way to my destination," said Cadence.

William screamed, "You got there, didn't you?"

Lily wrapped her hand along the inside of his bicep to try pulling him away. "William, I have an idea. How would you like two months of free meditation classes to make up for the money you're owed? I think you could use it."

William looked at Travis and at Lily and decided that she would be the easier path. "You know, that actually sounds great." He let her lead him to the shop, explaining along the way, "I've been so stressed lately with the new baby and the business."

"I understand."

"Are you okay?" Travis asked Cadence.

"I'm fine. Can we go to dinner now?"

"I need to pay for some souvenirs I picked out, and then we'll go wherever you want."

In the championship round of the Bible Bowl, Lucas stood against a thirteen-year-old girl, who wore hand-me-down clothes and had hair that looked like it had never touched a shear. August raised the small stack of papers in his hand for dramatic effect as he announced, "This final question will determine the champion of this year's Bible Bowl. Will it be last year's returning champ, Lucas McAbel?" The name elicited cheers from the boys. "Or will it be newcomer Natalie Watkins?" A higher-pitched chorus of approval welcomed the girl's name. August placed the papers on his Bible, which rested atop the nearby tree stump, and he fished for a coin from his pocket. He threw it in the air, asking Lucas to call it, and the boy chose tails. After catching and slapping the coin to the back of his hand, August said, "Heads. Natalie will get to answer the question first. Are you ready?"

The girl kept her eyes on the reverend. "Yes sir."

"A new kid transfers to your school. He seems nice, and he is funny and smart, so you quickly become friends – although you barely know him. Shortly thereafter, he confides in you that he is actually a Muslim – a fact he asks you to keep secret for fear of reprisal – and then he invites you to go to his mosque one Sunday. (Natalie, as a girl, he would never ask you that, but for the sake of this question, pretend you are a boy.) What would you do?"

"I would go with him," Natalie answered – to the gasps of half who listened, including the reverend. "If he agreed to go to my church the following Sunday."

The addendum quelled the initial shock to a degree, but August was unmoved. He told her, "Remember that you need a Bible verse to support your decision."

Natalie thought for a second before replying, "In Acts 10:28, Peter said, 'You know it is against our laws for a Jewish man to enter a Gentile home like this or to associate with you. But God has shown me that I should no longer think of anyone as impure or unclean.' I shouldn't ignore the boy just because his beliefs are different. In 1 Peter 3:15, 'Instead, you must worship Christ as Lord of your life. And if someone asks about your Christian hope, always be ready to explain it.' If I could get him to my church, I could tell him about Jesus and maybe save him."

"I do wish you would cite the King James," was August's only remark to her argument. "Lucas, what would *you* do?"

Lucas smiled and answered, "Deuteronomy 13:6-10 says, 'If thy brother, the son of thy mother, or thy son, or thy daughter, or the wife of thy bosom, or thy friend, which is as thine own soul, entice thee secretly, saying, Let us go and serve other gods, which thou hast not known, thou, nor thy fathers; Namely, of the gods of the people which are round about you, nigh unto thee, or far off from thee, from the one end of the Earth even unto the other end of the Earth; Thou shalt not consent unto him, nor hearken unto him; neither shall thine eye pity him, neither shalt thou spare, neither shalt thou conceal him: But thou shalt surely kill him; thine hand shall be first upon him to put him to death, and afterwards the hand of all the people. And thou shalt stone him with stones, that he die.'" A brief pause later, he added, "*I* would not go with anyone to the house of a false god. I would tell everyone in school that he was a Muslim, so that they could all be warned that the Devil had come to our school. I would make sure that me and my Christian friends made his life a living hell until he either moved away to be with his own kind or crossed over to the real Hell."

Audience reaction was mixed, but August stood in obvious pride before his star pupil. As the elders conferred, he said, "All right. The decision now rests with the judges." A nod from the lead elder signaled an end to the brief confab, and August asked, "Have you reached a decision?"

"We have." The elder stood to render the decision. "The winner is... Natalie Watkins."

The decision was met with cheers from the girls and groans from the boys. As the elder handed her the gun, Natalie came to life with a broad smile, while Lucas looked like an oblivious deer in a scope, unaware of what had hit him.

"Is this a joke?" August roared at the elders with the fire reflecting in his eyes. He picked up his Bible and held it on high for all to see. "The word 'tolerance' does not appear even once in God's word. Religious tolerance is a convention of modern men. As far as God is concerned, there are no gray areas. Everything is black and white – either wrong or right. You either stand with Him, or you stand with the Devil. Nowhere in His book does He order us to make nice with the enemy. We are in a war, children! You follow the orders of your commander in chief, no questions asked. God is your commander in chief, and if you want to be part of His kingdom, you will follow His orders no matter what. God even made His son fight for Him and shed His blood for you. Do you think He asks less from you, His adoptive children, as He asked from His actual son?"

August looked at the elders with disgust. "I am the Supreme Court in this matter, and I am overturning the judges' ludicrous ruling. The winner of the Bible Bowl is Lucas McAbel!" Over scattered gasps, August took the gun from the girl and handed it to the elated boy. Natalie started crying, perhaps more from the embarrassment of the reverend's disproval.

Lucas pumped the gun in the air three times to welcome the decision, and while several kids cheered him, most seemed more upset for the new loser. He lowered the gun and in a show of victory, he pretended to shoot his competitor, who ran into the woods. He repeated the act with the elders and random audience members, scaring many children into screaming, crying or ducking for cover. All the while, Lucas grinned.

After dismissing the audience and the elders, August placed his hand on the gun and told Lucas, "All right, enough fun. I have to take your prize and give it to your father."

Lucas focused a look of disappointment on the reverend. "But he's already gone."

August took the gun and smiled in anticipation of the joy his next statement would bring the boy, "That is why I will be driving you home on Monday."

"What?"

"Not the reaction I was expecting," said August. "I will not let you take a bus. Too much riff-raff. Besides, I would like to tell your father how proud I am of you and discuss your participation in West Canaan."

"You can't do that."

Hiding his growing annoyance, the reverend placed a hand on his shoulder. "It really is no problem. I could use a nice drive after this is over."

Lucas burst into tears and buried his face in his hands.

"Lucas?"

Although muffled through hands and tears, August heard him say, "He's dead."

"Your... father?" When Lucas nodded, August threw his arms around him, allowing the boy to cry on his shoulder. "What on Earth happened?"

Lucas whimpered out a stuttering response, "Hun-ting ac-ci-dent. We were tracking a deer, and we were arguing about the direction it was going. He said we should each follow the path we thought it had gone and then find out who was right. When I saw the bush move, I thought I found the deer..." Crying again, Lucas couldn't finish the story.

August pushed the boy away so that he could see his face. "I know it may be difficult to feel anything but sadness right now, but his death is cause for celebration," Lucas' look of confusion was temporary as the reverend explained, "He is with God now."

Lucas, his tears subsiding, nodded. "You're right."

"Now how did you get out here from Colorado?"

"I hitchhiked."

"Son, that is so dangerous. You could have encountered a lunatic."

"I just had to see you." Lucas embraced him again. "I'm all alone now. Reverend, do you think I could stay here… with you?"

With no hesitation, August answered, "Of course you can."

Mitchell appeared behind them and shouted, "You have got to be kidding me!"

August yelled, "Mitchell! His father died."

Lucas looked at Mitchell and said, "I don't want to put anyone out."

"Push that thought out of your head," August assured him.

Mitchell said, "He's a minor. You can't just decide to keep him. You'd have to go through the state and—"

"Then that is what I will do," the reverend retorted.

"Please don't!" Lucas implored with renewed worry. "I have an aunt who wants custody of me. She's Mormon."

"I am not going to let that happen, Son. You are staying with me. End of discussion."

"You can't do that," insisted Mitchell. "It's illegal!"

"I am not going to sacrifice his soul to some godless Mormon just to satisfy the laws of man. God's law takes precedence."

"So that's it? I get no say?"

August looked at Mitchell as if he were a stranger. "Who are you?"

Mitchell answered, "I'm your son."

"How can I even look at you right now?" August shook his head. "Get out of my sight."

Mitchell appeared to be walking away when he stopped to tell his father, "I received a call from Richard Glavin."

Now interested in what Mitchell had to say, August asked, "Why would he call you?"

"He was trying to reach you, but it kept going to voicemail."

"What did he say?"

Mitchell looked him in the eyes to tell him, "They're going with someone else."

"What?" August was unable to comprehend his son's words but, when he did, he flashed to anger and screamed, "You are lying!"

"I'm not," Mitchell replied with seeming serenity. "Richard said their exact words were, 'He's not special enough to engage a national audience.' You know, I really dreaded delivering this news because I knew how much it would upset you, but I have to say, right now, I'm actually okay with it." He left his father to his misery and the devil at his side.

CHAPTER 30

August wept. As he wandered alone through the forested wilderness, its darkness incomplete from moonlight, tears dampened the breast of his black suit, which now sported rips begat by unyielding foliage. Staggering between self-pity and anger, he tried to make sense of his failure to win a national audience – the foundation of his fated plans. Not only would he never garner enough donations to build West Canaan but, with no impact beyond his local community, how could he ever be more than a small-time and very forgettable procurer of souls – one who would never gain God's undivided attention. "I thought you loved me," he told the star-freckled sky. "Your hands made me, so would You turn around and destroy me? Why are those who love You most made to suffer? Where is the logic in Your rule?" August thought for a second and screamed a follow-up question, "Where are You?"

The sound of creatures nocturne – from the shrill of late-rising cicadas to the lament of distant coyotes – seemed to him a chorus of ridicule directed by God. Behind him came a squeal and, as he turned, he saw a javelina charging at him. August darted to his right and watched as the boar-like animal raced past him. Seconds later the javelina squealed again as if it were falling. August followed the animal's trail, which ended at a brushy cliff with a drop too far for him to see in the limited light.

Stepping back from the precipice, August was greeted by a pack of six coyotes. Startled at first, his next thought was of how he had misjudged their distance from their earlier howls. Although they had lost their meal for the night, the coyotes displayed a demeanor that was not predatory but curious, as if they saw something on the man that he himself did not see. Half of the pack members cocked their heads back and forth, while the others just stared.

"Stay back!" August ordered, pulling a pistol from the concealment of his suit jacket. Three coyotes stepped closer. Without hesitation, the reverend shot the closest one. The wounded animal yelped as it hit the ground, while the members of his pack retreated into the darkness.

Carrying electric lanterns to light the narrow trail, Gregor and Iris ascended the north wall of Boynton Canyon. Halfway up, she nodded toward an ill-defined trail branching from their current path. "We need to climb up there." Clipping the lantern onto her belt loop, she proceeded on four appendages up the incline that varied from forty to seventy degrees.

Following her lead Gregor wished he had thought to come earlier in the day, when trekking the unfamiliar trail would not have relied on light from a waning moon and clunky lanterns. Along the way he noticed a lone cliff dwelling equitable to a pre-Columbian studio apartment. "Look at that," he pointed out in a tone suggesting exploration.

"There's nothing in that one," Iris replied, to his disappointment. At a tiny clearing on an overlook just below the red rock formation's apex, she stopped to declare, "This spot marks the center of the Boynton Canyon vortex. Keep in mind that this conclusion is based on the testimony of tourists, as well as some supposedly in-tune locals, so I'm not sure of its validity."

"Let's test it," Gregor said as he reached her position. "Actually, I think I should go it alone. I don't even have enough energy to convert myself. If this vortex can give me a boost, I don't believe it will be sufficient to convert two whole people. Why don't you go home, and I'll meet you there when I'm fully charged?"

"How long will you be?" asked Iris.

With a grin he answered, "I'll probably beat you home."

"Oh, while you're there..." She removed her opal amulet and gave it to him, along with a kiss. "Try charging this to see if we can use it later. Please be careful."

"I'll be fine." He sat on the ground to meditate, and within sixty seconds, he was gone.

Gregor materialized on the plateau in a seated position. He sighed in relief that he was able to make the journey, and he could already feel the energy feeding his body once more.

"You just could not stay away."

Startled, Gregor saw a man seated on the plateau with his back against the canyon wall. "August Briar?" he asked, although he could tell the answer. The reverend's forearms rested on his upward-pointing knees with his hands drooped in front of them. Glints of light revealed tears on his cheek and a pistol in his right hand with the barrel aimed at the ground. "You bought the property? You know about the vortex."

August aimed the gun at him when the younger man attempted to stand. "Stay seated."

Gregor complied, placing Iris' amulet behind him. "You can't use the vortex."

"Use it?" he asked as if it were a statement of lunacy. "I bought the land to destroy it. I am razing this entire property as flat as Kansas to drive out the evil residing here."

"It's not evil!"

August laughed without humor. "I am to believe the words of the serpent?"

His reference to Eve's temptation gave Gregor an idea. "God didn't destroy the Garden of Eden when Adam and Eve ate from the forbidden Tree of Life."

August stood and kept the gun aimed at Gregor. "I have been contemplating my life, wondering if God would send an angel like He did for Abraham as he prepared to sacrifice his only son. Instead, He sends you. Did you know that when Job was being tortured by the Devil, he twice considered suicide? I know the healing power of this place is very real, but I wonder if it could bring someone back from death. What do you think?"

"Is that a threat?"

"I think not," August answered. "Where do you go when you," he waved his hands about before finishing, "do your thing? Where do you go?"

Gregor didn't want to relay any more information than August had been able to glean on his own, so he lied, "I don't go anywhere. I'm still here but my atoms are spread so thin that I become invisible, and I enter an unconscious state. Eventually, my atoms come together again."

"How did you get here just now? You had to have traveled here from somewhere else."

Assuming the minister had not been waiting for him all day, he lied again, "No, I came from here. I snuck up earlier today to convert. You saw me when I came together again."

"Do you see your lord when you enter that other existence? Is his face revealed to you?"

"My lord?" asked Gregor.

"God is stingy with the gift of witnessing His glory. Prophets of old had to perform great tasks in His name or suffer terribly before God would even come to them. I always hoped my path would be the performance of a great task, but I am beginning to think it might be the latter. I know God is testing me with you, but – as He is wont to do with His servants – He has left the meaning of His message for us to instill. What am I supposed to do?"

"Go back to your church," said Gregor. "This place has nothing for you."

"How are you able to channel the energy when you are away from here, like you did in the diner bathroom and as Iris did in the hospital today?"

Gregor muffled a gasp. *He knows Iris healed Gia. How could he possibly know that?"*

August told him, "You have three seconds to tell me the truth, or I will surely test the resurrection capabilities of this place with your bullet-riddled body. One. Two."

Bewildered over the minister's inexplicable knowledge and nervous from the ticking clock, Gregor could not come up with a believable, non-revelatory answer. "Our bodies act like rechargeable batteries. They're able to store the vortex's energy for later use."

"Amazing." August pointed the gun skyward. "Just a second! I read of a man who used a vortex, and his body was later found on Everest with no explanation of how he arrived there."

"Did you ever think that maybe he climbed it?"

"He was found wearing a short-sleeve shirt and khaki pants, nothing to suggest preparation for a cool night in Phoenix, much less a trek up a mountain." When Gregor offered no explanation, August told him, "I want you to prove your words to me."

"You mean take you with me? I thought you were convinced that my using the vortex was a sin. Now you're encouraging me to do so with you?"

"Even Jesus walked with whores to spread the gospel. Now show me how you do it."

292

"I can't."

"Enough lies!" August screamed with the gun held at the end of his straightened arm, aligned to Gregor's head.

"I've run out of energy. I need to recharge."

"You are simply stalling." He shot him in the foot, and Gregor screamed in pain, covering the hole with his hands. "I know you can heal, and I assume it heals faster once you turn into light. Take me with you now, or I will shoot every appendage you have."

"All right, I'll do it," Gregor conceded, although he had no intention of complying. He would pretend not to have enough energy, no matter how many bullets the reverend threatened to use, and hope to convince him that he needed more time to recharge. He had to stall him long enough to plan a way out of his predicament. When August sat in front of him, gun aimed at his heart, Gregor said, "You have to close your eyes."

"I am not going to do that, and neither are you. I want to see the truth of your intentions."

With his eyes tearing from the pain, Gregor told him, "We have to touch." August grabbed his right forearm and instructed Gregor to hold his other forearm so that he could keep the gun aimed at the younger man's chest. Gregor pretended to call on the energy.

After more than a minute, August asked, "Why is it taking so long?"

"I have difficulty concentrating with a gun at my chest."

"Think of it as my magic wand. Now do it unless you want to see the spell it casts."

As Gregor tried to relax and meditate, he noticed August moving his lips. "What are you doing"

August told him, "Do not interrupt me while I am praying," before continuing his silent prayer. A moment later the emergence of the familiar blue light elicited a smile from the reverend. "You are doing it!"

Gregor was shocked to see light and, more so, its source

– August's torso. "It's not coming from me." Light engulfed the reverend and seeped into him, and the two were gone.

Although the journey was powered by August, Gregor's experience allowed him to control the direction. He needed to get the energy out of August, so he led them to the center of the Meteor Crater. Once they materialized, the reverend seemed at once angry and exhilarated. "You lied to me!" he yelled, even as a smile streaked his face. "You do travel. It was… miraculous."

Gregor knew August would be disoriented at first, so he took the opportunity to run as fast as he could with his injured foot to the abandoned mining camp – hoping he could return to the vortex before the iridium drained what little energy he had. As he ran, he felt something banging his hips and realized the lantern was still clipped to his belt loop.

He heard August say, "Lucas was right. We cannot pick and choose which parts of the Bible we follow."

Gregor unclipped the lantern and let it drop to the ground. A second later a bullet extinguished the light. August was firing at him! Gregor changed directions and hid behind a corroded piece of equipment and sat down to meditate. He could feel his temperature rise as the iridium began tugging at the energy in his body.

The energy inside him had no sooner started glowing than it began to leave in waves to the rim of the crater, and he noticed waves from another source – August.

Gregor was so close to converting but didn't know if he could do it soon enough. On top of that, he was about to pass out from the heat, and he felt a sudden piercing heat. He looked down and saw red fluid gushing from his blue torso. He had been shot!

CHAPTER 31

With Daisy at her side, Iris stood in her backyard, wearing a robe and staring at Orion.

"You're still up?" asked Lily, approaching from the house. "What are you looking for?"

"Gregor."

"I didn't know he was here." She nodded to the canyon. "He went for a hike this late?"

"He went back to the vortex."

"Then why are you looking for him here?"

"He told me he would appear once he had recharged, but that was almost four hours ago."

"I'm sure he's in bed now, which is where you should be. He'll call you in the morning."

Lily tried to lead her inside, but Iris pulled away. "I'm going to wait a little while longer."

Travis parked on a street adjacent the property surrounding his former campsite. Opening the trunk of his car, he placed the tote of crystals into his backpack, along with wire cutters from his tool-box. Arriving at the chain-link fence with razor wire spiraled on top, he moved to a spot that had sufficient foliage on the other side to conceal the damage he was about to inflict. He chose a link at eye level as the first to be cut, and he snipped each cascading link almost to the ground. He pushed apart the new portal and was halfway through when he heard approaching voices within the perimeter. As he tried to move forward, he realized his backpack was caught on the fence. He slipped it off his shoulders and dove into the bushes.

With flashlights and high-powered rifles, two guards in mid-conversation came closer. Guard one asked, "Why's this place so important he needs us to constantly walk the perimeter?"

Travis glanced at his backpack hanging from the fence. It was almost concealed by the bushes, but not in whole.

Guard two responded, "Lester thinks he might have found gold somewhere, or oil."

"There's no oil around here."

As the guards walked past his position, Travis' cell phone vibrated.

The first guard stopped and asked the other, "What's that?"

Travis reached in his pocket and felt for the button that would send the call to voicemail.

"I don't hear anything," the second guard replied.

"It was like a humming."

"All I hear is crickets chirping."

"I don't hear it anymore."

"Hey, did you know that only male crickets sing."

"Really? What do the females do?"

As they continued walking away, the second guard answered, "I don't know. Dance?"

The unique acoustics of the early morning woods, where the fog roofs sound close to the ground and silence allows its travel down longer paths, a closing zipper could be heard throughout the youth conference campground. Laden with a backpack, Mitchell left his tent and headed for his car.

Elder Jonathan Hemp intercepted him. "Mitchell! Where are you going?"

"I'm leaving," Mitchell answered without altering his pace.

"You can't do that."

"I disagree." He opened his car's trunk and threw in the backpack. "I should've left last night."

The elder said, "But your father hasn't returned."

"I don't care," Mitchell said as he climbed into the driver's seat.

"Who's going to lead Sunday service?"

"You do it." Mitchell slammed the door and drove away.

The morning mist, which had shielded Lily's backyard from a voyeuristic sun, retreated into the canyon at a defiant pace. Iris lay asleep in a lounge chair on the patio, where she had awaited an arrival that never happened. With her canine sentinel curled at her side, she had been sheathed in an afghan by her mother the night before. Daisy's ears perked up at the sound of the backdoor opening

Carrying a cup of coffee on a saucer, Lily approached her daughter. "Iris," she called in the tone of a parent reading a bedtime story.

Iris awoke with, "Gregor," on her lips.

Lily placed the coffee on the table beside her. "It's just me. He never came?"

"No. Mom, I'm really worried."

"Have you talked to Travis and Cadence?"

"I tried. Gregor has crappy cell phone service, so he had given me their numbers in case I couldn't reach him. I called them both last night and left voicemails.

"Call them again."

The motel window's thick curtains interred the room in a darkness that kept Travis sleeping in the chair past the usual urging of his internal alarm. Encircled by the charged crystals he had placed around her the night before, Cadence lay asleep in the center of the unruffled bed with her arms at her side above the bedspread. Their tandem breaths, as a delicate hymn structured in canon, were the only clues disproving the final stillness of death.

Travis stirred, awakened by the vibration of the phone in his pocket. When he saw the number, he thought Gregor might be calling from the Wickline house. He retreated to the bathroom and closed the door before answering. "Hello?"

"Travis?" Iris asked from the other end of the call.

"What's up?"

"I can barely hear you."

"Cadence is still asleep."

"Is Gregor with you?" she asked.

"With me? I thought he was with you."

"He went back to the vortex last night," she explained.

"Really? Must've been after I left." Travis' heart beat faster, as he remembered the armed guards onsite. He tried calming his voice to not worry her further. "I wouldn't be too concerned. He's spent the night up there before."

"But he told me he would come right back after he recharged. Travis, I'm worried something might have happened to him."

"I'll go look for him."

Iris said, "I'm going with you."

"I don't think that's a good idea." Travis now had no choice but the truth. "Iris, there are armed guards patrolling the land."

"What? Why?"

"I'm not sure, but if Gregor went there last night—"

"He was going to the vortex on the plateau," said Iris. "It's hidden. They wouldn't have seen him."

"Then maybe he's stuck there and can't get out. Either way, it's too dangerous."

"Travis, I said I'm going."

"Fine," said Travis. "I'll be by to pick you up in a little bit."

Travis hung up his phone and returned to the room to find Cadence stirring but not yet awake. Uncertain how she would react at the miniature Stonehenge surrounding her, he thought he should try to remove the crystals before she saw them. He found the white cotton bag on the floor and proceeded to gather the rocks one by one. He cleared the left side of the bed, as well as the foot but, as he was reaching for the first rock on her right, Cadence opened her eyes. In one motion, Travis dropped the tote and jumped on the bed, covering the remaining crystals with his body. His right hand rested on his side, and his left hand propped his head facing Cadence. He smiled as the jagged rocks dug into his left side.

"What are you doing?" a now wide-awake Cadence asked.

"Just making sure you wake up with a smile," Travis answered.

"You're dressed already?"

"Iris called and wants me to come over."

"Why?"

"She hasn't seen Gregor since last night."

Cadence sat up. "Gregor's missing?"

"He's probably gone back to where we were camping."

"Why would he go back there?"

"You know Gregor. Once he's found a meditation spot he likes, it's his – like he's lifted his chakra and psychically marked his territory."

"I can't believe he'd trespass." Cadence noticed tension in Travis' face. "Are you okay?"

The pain from the crystals digging into his flesh was excruciating. "I'm just worried about Gregor. Why don't you take a shower and, when I find him, we can all go to breakfast?"

"I want to help you look."

"Go take a shower," Travis insisted. "Now."

Cadence smelled herself without lifting her arms. "Do I stink or something?"

"No, I just want you to hurry up and get ready so we can go."

"I swear, you're always rushing me. Fine. I'm going." Cadence left for the bathroom.

Once she closed the door behind her, Travis rolled off the bed, grimacing and grunting and releasing a great sigh in relief. After lifting his shirt to see the large indentations in his skin caused by the jagged rocks, he filled the tote with the remaining crystals and shoved it under the bed.

At Christ Church of Sedona, Mitchell opened the door to his father's office. With great intent he walked to the bookshelf and lifted a grail bookend for the key hidden in a small cavity underneath. He hurried to the wooden file cabinet against the adjacent wall and unlocked it to search for the file folder containing the permission slips from the youth conference's participants. He would call Lucas' aunt to tell her of August's plans to keep the boy. At the very least, Lucas would be out of his hair, and best, his father would be arrested.

Mitchell's shoulders slumped when he realized that Lucas McAbel had no such slip on file. He knew he had not been diligent in checking that small detail for everyone, but he wondered if Lucas had removed it during his time alone in the office.

"What about last year?" he muttered to himself. Near the back of the drawer, he found the folder he sought, and inside was Lucas' slip from the previous year. Mitchell sat at the desk and phoned the number listed on the paper.

Iris busied herself with cleaning her room as she awaited Travis' arrival. Realigning the picture frames on her dresser, she found the black diamond earrings she was wearing Thursday, when she had her vortex experience with Gregor. Wondering if perhaps they were able to hold any charge from that day, she inserted them in place of the loop earrings she had on.

A few moments later, Lily approached Iris' bedroom, carrying a red toolbox. "I think we need to go to that property and look for Gregor..." Lily froze as she saw her daughter sitting on the bed converting into energy and disappearing before her eyes. "Oh... my..." She dropped the toolbox.

At the plateau, Iris was relieved that her journey was successful. A quick glance around revealed that Gregor was not there, but she did find her amulet on the ground. "He made it this far," she whispered. She slipped the chain over her neck and sat down to recharge.

The cave at Shaman's Dome was empty, save for a microphone on a stand and a running video camera. On the plain several meters below, the youth conference attendees were gathered with their parents and other congregants from Christ Church of Sedona. A huge stadium monitor had been erected with large speakers on either side. Elder Jonathan Hemp undulated through the restless crowd, which kept watching the cave's interior being broadcast on the monitor for any signs of Reverend August Briar. He heaved a very audible sigh when he spotted a welcome face near the front.

"Mitchell!" he called. "I'm so glad you're here. Where is your father?"

Mitchell shrugged. "I haven't seen him."

"Can you go on for him?"

The young minister knew that his father would not take the news of losing a national show well, but he had no idea of the impact it would have on his behavior. No matter the illness or circumstance that had arisen as far back as he could remember, his father never missed a sermon, and now he had walked away from the biggest one of the year. Mitchell found sweet solace in the opportunity to correct one of his father's mistakes – and an epic one at that. Although he had nothing prepared, the sermon he penned days earlier was still fresh in his memory. "I'll do it."

Elder Hemp dropped his shoulders. "Thank you. Let's get you up to the mic." As the elder led him to the beginning of the trail to Shaman's Dome, however, they were halted by a voice booming from the speakers.

"Children!"

Mitchell turned to the monitor and saw that his father was now in the cave. His suit jacket and tie were missing, and his white shirt was dirty and tattered, as were his pants. No two strands of his hair seemed to follow the same path, his lips were chapped and his skin was as red as the Devil's. "Oh my…" Mitchell stopped his tongue just short of taking the Lord's name in vain.

August continued his greeting, "Parents! Congregation! Welcome." He looked to the sun. "A beautiful day. A beautiful day can hide the ugliness surrounding us. Forgive me. I had a truly uplifting sermon planned for today, but I have not the heart to deliver it.

"I want to address the youngest members of the flock gathered here today. As you prepare for adulthood, many of you will leave the succor of your parents' homes and venture into this world. I would like to tell you that a life equitable in glory to your faith in God awaits you. However, that world is not the one you will find. The world you enter will be one where sinners will be your betters. Where those who outright worship at the feet of the Dark Angel will have dominion over you. Where evil is allowed to flourish and trample decency into near non-existence. Where too many good people die young, while too many evil ones become centenarians. A world in which God will be unwilling to answer your prayers or end your suffering or reward your devotion to Him. Where righteous deeds are ignored, and blasphemy is celebrated." August laughed. "Celebrity. You will find that God is the Supreme Celebrity – too aloof to attend His own party, to acknowledge His fans or even to look at those in His employ.

"Knowing this, the prophet Habakkuk asked, 'How long, O Lord, must I call for help? But you do not listen. Violence is every-where. I cry, but you do not come to save. Must I forever see these evil deeds? Why must I watch all this misery? Wherever I look, I see destruction and violence. I am surrounded by people who love to argue and fight. The law has become paralyzed, and there is no justice in the courts. The wicked far outnumber the righteous, so that justice has become perverted.'"

Mitchell was shocked, not at his father's words, but at the fact that they were not in King James text – as if he were rebelling against God. Movement above him caught his attention, and he saw Lucas ascending the trail to Shaman's Dome. "Perfect," he muttered and began pursuit.

"Have we not all seen Habakkuk's words as reality?" August asked to a muted response. "Answer me! I want this mountain to shake like the walls of Jericho! Have we not all seen the truth in Habakkuk's words?"

"Yes!" the audience responded.

"Again!" August ordered. "Of course, we have. However, if I were God, you would be blessed." Speaking with tonal stress on each word and palms outstretched over his audience, "Nations would live in harmony under one God, one absolute rule. Other religions, like the Crystal Cult, would be smashed at the instant of their genesis – aborted at conception! You would inherit a world where devotion would be rewarded to the degree it was given to me, and sinners would suffer for their sins. Absolute devotees would walk with me and see my face, while absolute sin would be met with absolute death!

"You, my true followers, would be as Jesus said in Matthew 5, the light of the world – a city set on a hill that cannot be hid. While sinners would wallow in the misery of infirmity, you would be free of affliction, and any sickness would be driven from you by my... healing... hand. My healing hand," he repeated before concluding, "But I am not God. The world is a damnable place."

Mitchell entered the cave a moment later to find Lucas but not his father. The boy turned off the camera and unplugged the microphone, as if he could undo the embarrassment the reverend had inflicted on himself. "He's not here," Lucas said, walking by Mitchell to leave the cave.

"Did you see where he went? I have some interesting news for him."

The tone of his voice seemed to pique Lucas' interest. "What is it?"

Mitchell smiled and delivered the news with glee, "Your father is alive and well." He waited for a reaction from Lucas, whose face fell expressionless. "Interesting, huh?"

Lucas shrugged and said, "So what? It doesn't matter. I don't want anything to do with him." He grinned and added, "I want your father."

"Sorry, but I'm an only child."

"It's not your decision."

"You're right," Mitchell said. "When I spoke to your dad—"

"You talked to him?" Lucas' face reddened, and his body tensed.

Mitchell savored the fact that he, at last, had the upper hand on the bullying usurper. "Yes, and he said that he had sent you to a juvenile boot camp in New Mexico, but you ran away a week ago. Why did he send you there? My guess is something like animal cruelty."

Lucas looked at him with boiling rage in his eyes and a wide grin. "I hit him."

"You hit your father?"

"And I kept hitting him until he was whimpering for me to stop."

Mitchell swallowed to push the lump from his throat. He looked to the side of Lucas' sinewy, tensing arm for the cave's opening but his view was blocked by the large boy in front of him. He talked to mask his growing fear. "Maybe that's why he mentioned bringing his brother."

"What do you mean by that?" Lucas asked, clenching his fists.

"He's coming to get you."

Lucas' composure catapulted to menacing, and he growled at the short man, "You should run."

Mitchell's uncertainty at the warning didn't stop him from taking a step back. "Why?"

Lucas lunged at him, landing on top of him, slamming his back against the cave floor. Mitchell tried to fight off the attack, but he was no match for Lucas' powerful punches, which connected with his face again and again. He could do nothing but take the beating.

Following at least a dozen punched, Lucas stopped, as if he had grown bored. He pushed himself off the ground and stood, affording Mitchell a very brief repose. Lucas leaned over him and grabbed his neck with both hands. Mitchell tried to pry away the fleshy vise but failed.

Keeping his hands clutched around his neck, Lucas straightened up, bringing Mitchell to his feet in the process. He continued lifting until Mitchell's feet were off the ground.

Mitchell's feet dangled and kicked as the powerful teenager held him high. He tried again to pry the fingers from his neck, but Lucas shook him until he stopped. He stretched his legs and feet as much as he could, trying to reach the floor for some leverage, but he was being held too high. Mitchell hit Lucas' swollen forearms with his closed hands, but the tactic had no effect.

Sweat dripping from his crimson face, Lucas looked over his shoulder at the cave entrance at the sound of approaching voices. He released Mitchell, letting his body thud to the ground, and he ran from the cave.

CHAPTER 32

Travis rang the doorbell to the Wickline house, while Cadence fidgeted beside him and said, "Maybe I should've stayed at the motel."

"Aren't you concerned about Gregor?"

"I would be if I believed he were really missing," she replied with air quotes around the last word. "You know he likes to go hiking on his own, and these two are probably driving him nuts." Lily opened the door, cuing Cadence to plant on a smile and greet her with, "Hi."

Pale and distracted, Lily responded, "Morning."

"Good morning," said Travis. "Iris said that Gregor is missing."

"Iris isn't here."

"Where did she go?" he asked.

"I'm not sure."

He specified his question. "Did she go to the vortex?"

"I'm not sure."

Cadence asked, "Do you know where you are?"

"Cadence!" Travis scolded.

His friend shrugged. "Well, she might be in one of those meditative trances and not know where she is."

Travis turned his attention back to Lily. "May we come in?"

"Sure." Lily stood aside for them to enter before she closed the door.

"Are you okay?" Travis asked with a touch to her shoulder.

"It's one thing to hear about it. It's quite another altogether to actually see it."

Growing exasperated, Travis told her, "I don't understand."

"Iris disappeared."

"You don't know where she went?" he asked.

"No, I mean she disappeared – as in, right before my eyes."

Lucas hurried to his tent to pack his belongings before his father's arrival, but when he opened the flap, he was surprised to find August sitting inside. "Reverend."

"Lucas, I was waiting for you."

The boy climbed inside and zipped the door. "Where were you this morning?"

"Hitching a ride back from the mouth of Hell. I have been a fool, Lucas. A blind fool."

Thinking Mitchell might have already revealed his secret to August, Lucas offered a preemptive apology. "I'm sorry."

"You have no reason to apologize," August said, to the boy's relief. "The fault is mine. I misinterpreted God's message to me."

"What message?"

"Remember the Parable of the Talents?"

"Of course," Lucas answered. "Matthew 25. A man gave three of his servants money. Two of them used it to earn more, and the third buried his."

"The master blessed the two who used what they had been given, and he cursed the one who did nothing with it. Lucas, I am the cursed servant."

"You think God's cursed you? Why?"

"He tried to show me what he wanted me to do, but I did not see it, so he punished me."

"What did he want you—"

Eyes gleaming, August grabbed both of the boy's arms. "He wants me to heal the righteous."

"Heal? You mean like that girl did in the hospital?"

"No!" August spewed. "That witch and her Mephistophelian suitor are defilers of God's love! Love meant for me! They are like pharaoh's magicians who turned their staffs into snakes."

"Moses' staff swallowed theirs."

"His power was greater because it came from God, whereas theirs came from the Devil. Lucas, I need your help. I want you to be my first apostle."

Lucas hung his head and said, "I gotta tell you something first."

August asked, "What?"

"Do you remember my first youth conference, when I met you?"

"I remember your eagerness. You followed me around almost to the point of annoyance."

"I'm sorry about that. When I first heard you talk, everything made sense. I don't mean the words. I mean that they applied to me. I understood why we were here. I was feeling lost, and you pointed out the way for me. Like a really great tracker. After that, I saw how weak my father was. I prayed God would make him more like you, but he didn't ever change."

"I appreciate your feelings, but do you have anything that needs saying right now?"

Lucas debated the revelation of his lie. He opted for, "I'd follow you anywhere."

August beamed with jubilance. "Pack up. We have work to do."

Iris materialized on the plateau once more and wondered, "What am I doing wrong?" After recharging, she began looking for Gregor using the method he had explained about concentrating on a person or place and the energy taking the converter there. "Why do I keep ending up where I started?" She looked all around and asked the wind, "Gregor, where are you?" She shook her head. "Okay, let's try this again." She told the ground, "Vortex, take me to Gregor," and as she meditated, she repeated his name as a chant, "Gregor, Gregor..."

Iris converted to energy and disappeared from the plateau, but no sooner had her light dispersed than it re-coalesced. She sunk into herself, about to lose hope, when a mourning dove flew to her side. She looked at the beautiful bird and smiled before she noticed the blood on his feet. "Oh no, you're hurt." As she reached for it, the bird flew above her and perched on the ledge to the cliff dwelling that Gregor had pointed out to her. The bird cooed as it looked down at her. Iris was about to look away when she saw a still hand protruding over the rim.

"Gregor!" she called but heard no response. She wanted to try materializing on the ledge, but without knowing its width, thought it too risky, so she started climbing the steep wall.

Lying on his back with a hand extended over the ledge and the other covering the gunshot wound in his torso, Gregor heard the vibrations of movement through the rock. He opened his eyes for the first time since daybreak and squinted at the light. Someone was approaching. He lifted the hand on his torso, but the dried blood stuck his palm to his shirt. Peeling it away, he tried to inspect his wound, which he couldn't see, but the fact that he saw no more blood flowing led him to believe it had clotted. However tenuous the bloody veil over the wound might be, he had to move. He rolled over so he could peek at his impending visitor, wincing at the resulting exacerbation of pain. He noticed a mourning dove perched nearby, and he tried to smile. After a few deep breaths, he poked his face beyond the edge. To his relief, he saw Iris scaling the wall a meter below the ledge. "Iris," he said in a muted rasp. He hadn't realized how dry his throat was. He tried again to gain her attention. "Iris."

Iris responded to the sound of Gregor's voice and looked up. "Gregor!" she exclaimed, releasing the tension in her face. "I'm so glad that's you. I was worried sick. What happened to you? Why are you up there?"

"I'll tell you when you get here. You need to concentrate on the climb."

Iris pushed her brows together and said, "Gregor, I'm not a child. Tell me what's wrong."

In a calming tone, he told her, "I've been shot."

Iris lost her balance for a split-second. One of her feet slipped, chipping a piece of the wall, which fell to the plateau below. She regained her footing, embracing the wall.

"Are you okay?" Gregor asked.

"Am I okay?" Tears swelled her eyes. "How did you get shot?"

"It's only a flesh wound. I'm fine. I need you to keep climbing. Can you do that for me?"

"I can't move."

Gregor tried to coax her past her nerves. "Iris, you're almost here. Two more movements, and you're done." When she didn't respond, he said, "Iris, look at me." She gazed up into his eyes. "I need you. Just focus on climbing. You're almost here."

Iris nodded, took a deep breath and continued. As soon as she moved, Gregor could see August Briar staring up at him from the plateau! "Iris, you've got to hurry!"

"I'm coming." With another step, she was able to grab the ledge with both hands, prompting the mourning dove to fly to the juniper tree. She pulled herself up, but the ledge was so small, she found herself on all fours and facing Gregor's back. When she saw the blood-drenched stain on his back, she screamed, "Oh my god! You're really hurt!"

"I know."

Through uncontrollable tears, Iris said, "There's so much blood."

Gregor scooted from the edge to escape August's stare. "Can you get us out of here?"

"I need to try healing you first."

"No! August is here. We need to leave now."

"Is he the one who shot you?"

"Yes. Are you charged?"

"I think so." She looked for a way to position herself for meditation without resting her weight on him but to no avail. She placed a hand on his shoulder and closed her eyes. "I'm sorry. I can't relax. There's not enough room here."

"Behind the tree. Relax in the cliff dwelling, and hold my hand when you're ready."

She held a branch for leverage to help her stand and parted the bear grass to find the opening of the dwelling. After entering, she announced, "It's dark in here. Okay, I'm sitting. Give me your hand."

Gregor forced himself onto his back and scooted closer to the opening of the cliff dwelling. He slid his left hand through the doorway, and she clasped it with both hands.

Holding his prized new rifle, Lucas McAbel walked around the vortex plateau, taking in the scenery. "This place is cool." He turned his attention back to his tour guide, Reverend Briar, whose eyes were focused upward. "What're you looking at?"

August answered, "That young witch and her paramour."

Lucas followed his gaze. "Where? I don't see anything." He saw a blue light burst forth from somewhere up the canyon wall. "There's that blue light!"

August did not react, except to say, "I am seriously going to have to do something about them."

"Reverend, is that why we're here?" Lucas adjusted his hold on the gun into a firing position. "To get them?"

August returned his attention to the boy. "We came here to speak to God."

"Wouldn't church be better for that?"

"God chose this place. Moses had Mt. Sinai. Now I have this plateau."

Uncertain of his true state of mind, Lucas asked, "Is one of the bushes gonna catch fire?"

"I need to pray." August knelt, and Lucas tried to join him but was waved away. "No, he will not come to you." He pointed to the mouth of the crevice at the edge of the plateau. "I want you to stand guard there. Let no one enter this plateau while I am away."

"Away?" Lucas surveyed the enclosed plateau and asked, "Where you going?"

August smiled and told him, "Witness the glory." The reverend clasped his hands, closed his eyes and prayed aloud. "God, I come before you completely humbled. I always thought I knew what you wanted from me, and I have faithfully stayed the course without veer. I have done all that you asked, everything you commanded, and I am sure any truthful tongue could not dispute that fact. God, I come to you now with expectations of my own.

"If you will not reveal yourself to me, at least touch me in blindness. The Fallen One has bestowed great power upon his disciples, but surely you would not allow such a display of dominance over you to go unanswered. Do the same for me. Through me, you can show your people you command power greater than the ruler of this Earth. I beg of you, give me the power."

As the minutes passed, Lucas wondered if the reverend might be slipping off the mental ledge. He wanted to say something to break the silence but waited for the kneeling one to tire.

August shifted position to sit on the ground with his legs crossed. He clasped his hands again, holding them closer to his mouth, and he rocked back and forth as he prayed in silence while moving his lips.

Lucas dropped his jaw and gun, causing a bullet to shoot into the crevice. The gunshot startled him, but he didn't remove his gaze from August, who emitted a blue light from his torso.

August opened his eyes and watched the light spread to his limbs. "Yes! Yes. Yes." Now levitating, he looked upward. "Thank you, God. You are with me. Thank you." As tears streamed down his face, he disappeared in a whirling flash of blue.

Lucas ran to the spot where August had been and looked up in the sky.

CHAPTER 33

In the living room of the Wickline house, Travis placed a saucer and cup of tea on an end table next to a rose slipper chair, where Lily sat, staring at the hands on her lap. He joined Cadence on the couch and asked, "Lily, are you ready to talk about what happened?"

The older woman, with shaky hand, wrapped her fingers around the cup and sipped the tea. "I walked into Iris' room, and I saw this blue light. By the time I realized the light was actually coming from her, she vanished into teeny, tiny specks."

Cadence whispered to Travis, "Are you sure that's tea?"

"I was just stunned," Lily said. "I had never seen anything like it before."

"Do you think…" Travis lost his train of thought as he witnessed blue lights swirling behind Lily's chair. Seconds later, Iris was sitting by Gregor, who was lying on the floor clutching his bleeding torso.

Cadence screamed.

Mouth agape, Travis focused on the blood. "What happened?"

"He's been shot!" Iris shouted, holding Gregor's left hand with both of hers.

Cadence said, "I'll call 9-1-1."

Now lucid, Lily ordered, "Travis, keep pressure on the wound! I'll get the first-aid kit."

Travis knelt and placed his hands over Gregor's wound. "How are you doing, buddy?"

Chilled and sweating, Gregor answered, "Not so hot." He looked to Iris, who couldn't stop crying. "Iris, I need you to try now."

She nodded, placed her hands on his chest and closed her eyes. A moment later, she opened her eyes again and shook her head. "It's not working."

Gregor squeezed her hand. "That's okay. You need to relax." He noticed the crystal dangling from her neck. "Give me your amulet." Iris removed it, and he clutched it close to his wound, telling Travis, "Move your hands." Gregor pushed the crystal lower and meditated. Within seconds, the crystal glowed blue, and the light drained into him as he lost consciousness. Gregor's hand dropped to his side, sending the empty crystal clinking to the floor.

Iris asked, "Did it work?"

Travis inspected the wound, which was smaller but still lethal, and he shot Iris a grim look.

Returning with a towel, pitcher of water and first-aid kit, Lily gasped, "Is he—"

Iris closed her eyes, held Gregor's hand in her lap and meditated. The blue light soon appeared, engulfing her and pouring into his body. She continued until she had nothing left.

Cadence returned from the kitchen, announcing, "The ambulance is on its way."

Travis took the supplies from Lily, and after wetting the towel, he pulled up Gregor's shirt enough to wipe away the blood surrounding the exit wound, which was centered in his left external oblique. He smiled when he saw that it was almost healed except for an eraser-sized open sore that looked like an injury sustained at least two weeks prior.

"Amazing," Lily said with pride in her daughter's feat.

"That's a gunshot wound?" Cadence asked. "I thought it would be bigger."

Travis looked at Iris and said, "It really works." He noticed Gregor stirring awake. "Hey buddy. Welcome back. How do you feel?"

"I feel… alive." Gregor sat up and pulled his shirt up to see the remaining wound.

"I'm sorry," said Iris. "I don't have enough to finish the job."

"It'll scab," he told her with a loving smile.

Iris kissed him and pulled away to say, "You scared the crap out of me."

"I'm sorry."

Lily clapped her hands twice. "Let's get that bloody shirt off and clean you up."

Gregor stood to comply and asked Travis, "Do you have a shirt I could borrow?"

"I think I have a dirty one in the car."

Cadence screamed again. "Gregor! What happened to your burns?"

Lily answered, "The vortex healed him." Washing his back, she said, "You have a hole here, smaller than the one in front. The bullet must've gone clean through."

Hugging herself and shaking her head, Cadence said, "I don't understand."

Travis asked, "Who shot you?"

Iris answered for him. "August Briar."

"The minister?" asked Travis.

Lily was about to apply the last piece of tape to the bandage on Gregor's back when she heard the name. She stood erect, and with shocked expression, questioned the name, "August?"

"I'll kill him," Travis declared, but as he stomped to the door, Iris grabbed his arm.

"We need to call the police."

"Does August know about the vortex?" Lily asked.

"Yes," Gregor answered, drawing a moan from Lily. He told Iris and Travis, "We can't call the police. We have no proof that he shot me, other than a wound that looks like it's weeks old – long before I ever stepped foot in Sedona. Besides, if someone actually did believe us, I couldn't explain my healing without exposing the vortex."

Lily moved to the front with her bandages. "Gregor's right. We can't tell anyone. There are bigger stakes at play here. The vortex must be protected. We're just lucky that August thinks vortexes and the ilk are satanic, so he'd never attempt to use it."

Gregor frown at her. "Lily, he said he's going to raze the land until it's flat. What will that do to the vortex?"

A look of horror gripped Lily's face. "I'm not sure. Is it dependent on the rock or inherent to the land? I really don't know the answer, but I can't imagine it would help."

On the plateau, Lucas began to wonder if August Briar had been called up to the Lord, like Elijah in the chariot of fire. During the two hours that had passed since the reverend's disappearance, he circled the plateau numerous times before sitting in the shade of the crevice. He was hot from the undiluted midday sun, and he was thirsty, and now he debated how much longer he could or should hold out.

When he saw a spiral of blue light appear, he sighed, "Finally." Once August was whole, Lucas approached and exclaimed, "That was way cooler than a burning bush."

August returned with his face skyward. Bearing a countenance of utter rapture, the reverend declared, "I have been touched by God."

"I was getting worried," said Lucas. "You were gone for so long."

"I didn't know how to return until the Lord gave me the knowledge."

"Where'd he take you?"

August stood and looked around with his hands like a blind man searching for words. "How do I describe light to one who has never seen? God showed me all of his creation at once."

"Did you see God?"

Grimacing, he admitted, "He refused to show Himself to me. Perhaps I had to close my eyes to touch His skin, and I did touch Him. Trembling, but a tiny portion of His magnificence flowed into me. The sensation was… overwhelming. I found myself wanting to return, not out of fear, but because the exhilaration was consuming me." He looked at his hands. "I can feel it. The power courses through my veins."

Lucas touched his hand, hoping to feel the described power. August jerked his hand away and said, "Come on. We have work to do."

Lily answered the door to see two young EMTs standing before her, behind them an ambulance with red lights rotating on top. "Oh good, you're here. I think he's doing okay now." She invited the two men into the living room, where Travis was lying on the couch with his head in Cadence's lap and a wet rag on his forehead.

The EMTs rushed to his side, and after a quick glance at his body, the first one removed the rag. "Excuse me, where's the shooting victim?"

"Shooting victim?" asked Travis.

The second EMT told them, "We received a call that someone had been shot."

Lily gasped and corrected him. "No, not shot. Shocked."

Travis explained, "I was trying to change a broken light bulb, and I got a jolt from it."

Lily added, "I told him he should use a cut potato to get it out of the socket, but he thought it too much trouble." She pointed a finger at him. "Maybe you'll listen to me next time."

Travis smiled. "I guess I'm just too stubborn for my own good."

Cadence told both EMTs, "I'm sorry for the call. I panicked."

The first EMT glanced at the second one, saying, "Cancel the police," sending him from the house to make the call. He told Travis, "While we're here, I should at least check you out."

Mitchell lay curled on his bed half asleep, an empty water bottle clutched in his flaccid hand. Blood from cuts on his swollen right cheek and his busted lip left uneven patterns on the white pillow-case. Voices from the other side of his closed door popped up the lid of the eye not blackened from bruising. He pushed himself up and put his ear to the wood above the doorknob. Once he had distinguished the speakers, he stormed into the living room.

August told Lucas, who plopped on the couch, "After I shower, we can go."

Mitchell had not spoken since his near strangulation that morning, so he was surprised to hear the faint voice that rasped from his mouth when he tried yelling, "Why is he here? He should be in jail!" The exhaled air scratched his throat into a brief fit of coughing.

August asked, "What are you rambling about now, and what happened to your face?"

Controlling his cough, he pointed at Lucas and screeched, "He tried to kill me!"

Lucas had remained nonreactive until August's eyes moved to him, at which point, he started laughing. "I wasn't trying to kill you. I thought we was just wrestling around. Playing."

"That's a lie! Look at me." Mitchell insisted before another fit of coughing overtook him. He pulled down the collar of his shirt to expose the bruising around his neck.

Lucas continued explaining, "Reverend, I didn't mean to hurt him. I really thought we were finally getting along. I didn't realize he was seriously trying to fight." He let out another shortened laugh. "I wouldn't have been so rough if I knew how fragile he was."

August watched his coughing son try to regain his breath, and he shook his head. "Mitchell has always been… deficient of testosterone."

Mitchell's throat again calmed. "If you're not going to call the police, I will."

"You will not," August commanded. "Do you honestly want someone else to hear that you were beaten up by a fourteen-year-old boy? I have had enough embarrassment from you."

Mitchell crossed his arms and shook his head. "What does it matter now? Actually, I'm glad you're both here now. Lester McAbel should be arriving any minute."

August snarled at him, "Mitchell! How heartless can—"

"Heartless? Ah, that's right. You don't know." Mitchell smiled at a glowering Lucas, who seemed prepared to once more pounce on him. "Daddy's alive." Mitchell took a moment to let the words penetrate the room before he added, "Praise God."

August turned to Lucas, whose complexion had paled. "Lucas?"

The boy dropped his head and said, "I've been trying to tell you—"

Mitchell sat on an ottoman. "I can't wait to hear this."

Without the slightest aversion of his eyes, August said, "Mitchell, go to your room."

"Go to my room? I'm twenty-six."

"The Devil will claim you before I repeat myself!" August warned.

Mitchell exited the living room but remained just beyond the doorway to witness how the boy would attempt to explain his lie.

"You deceived me, Lucas?"

"I didn't mean to. I just didn't know if you'd let me stay with you if I didn't."

"I opened my home to you – allowed you to share in the glory of my sacred commission – and you repay me with Satan's tongue?"

"I had a good reason. Let me…" Lucas' voice trailed off when the doorbell rang. He looked to the door and ran in front of August with palms opened in spiritual surrender. "Please, Reverend, don't let him take me back! I really can explain." The doorbell rang again. "Trust me when I say my soul is in your hands."

August stepped around him and uttered a simple, "Hide."

CHAPTER 34

When he heard the doorbell, Mitchell retreated into his room and leaned his back against the closed door. As he looked around the room, he mumbled to himself, "Why am I still here? Am I so masochistic that I can't live without my father's disapproval? His bullying? And now he has an apprentice. At least he'll be gone soon. But then what? I have nothing here, and I could have nothing anywhere. What's to keep me from packing everything I can into my car and just driving until the Lord tells me to stop?" A second later, he answered, "I'd be alone." He smiled when he heard the doorbell ring a second time. "Now, so will my father." His mind drifted to Cadence. "What if she were right and God crossed our paths with divine purpose? Maybe she's a sign I'm to follow." The doorbell rang again. "What's taking so long? I'd love to see the look on that brat's—"

Mitchell heard the turning of his doorknob. Lucas pushed his way into the room, closing and locking the door behind him. Mitchell asked, "What are you doing here?"

Lucas signaled with an index finger to his lips before pressing his ear against the door to try hearing the conversation in the other room.

"I asked you a question," said Mitchell. "Oh no, he is not covering for you, is he?" He reached for the doorknob, but Lucas pushed him back.

"Shut up!" Lucas warned through clenched teeth. "I'm trying to hear."

"He's in here!" Mitchell yelled, but his bruised throat lacked the power to project his voice to the other room.

Lucas threw the back of his hand to Mitchell's face, which knocked the smaller man onto the bed. The boy jumped onto the bed beside him and covered his mouth with the palm of his hand. "If he walks through that door, I promise you I'll finish what I started."

At this point, Mitchell knew he could not match the boy physically, so he stopped trying. He could only wait for what would happen next. The wait was brief, for within thirteen panicked breaths, came a knock on his bedroom door.

Once Lucas left the living room, August answered the front door. Standing on his porch was a tall, brutish man caged in a white button-down shirt and black slacks. Beside him stood an average man who, although much thinner than August remembered, was recognizable as Lucas' father. "Lester McAbel?"

"Hi Reverend," he greeted with a handshake. "Been a while. This is my brother, Evan."

The taller man likewise shook August's hand. "Nice to meet you, Reverend."

"You are a bit late," August told Lester.

"I'm sorry about that, Reverend. We got a little turned around."

"I meant for the youth conference," said August. "I was quite surprised you neglected to bring Lucas this year."

"The past year's been rough, to say the least, but Lucas obviously wanted to come to your youth council no matter what."

"Conference," August corrected. "How is Lucas?"

Lester snickered and said, "You tell me."

Evan told August, "I don't mean to be rude, but I have to work tomorrow, so I need to get back home. Where's Lucas?"

"Is he not with you?" August asked.

Lester tightened his eyes and said, "Your son called to tell me Lucas was here."

"I have not seen Lucas since last year. I am afraid you have been the victim of a prank."

"This is just great," Evan growled. He told Lester, "More likely, Lucas had someone call you to send us on a wild-goose chase. I'll wring that boy's neck! We drove all this way."

Lucas released Mitchell just before August opened the bedroom door. "They have left," he announced.

Lucas responded, "Reverend, thank you for—"

August raised a hand for silence and said, "I am taking a shower," before leaving the room.

Mitchell headed for the door, but Lucas crossed his arms and blocked his way. "You're not going anywhere yet – not until my dad is good and gone away. Now sit down!"

Mitchell clenched his jaw and returned to the bed. He wanted to die. He wanted to be anywhere but in his current conscious state.

Lucas turned his sneer toward the dresser, on which lay Mitchell's cell phone. He grabbed it and dropped it to the floor between them. He stomped the phone over and over, while Mitchell pretended not to care.

August entered his SUV and inserted the key into the ignition but did not turn it. Lucas came through the passenger door and glanced at him for reference to his current emotional state, but the man's forward stare offered little information. Lucas closed the door and was reaching for the seatbelt when August smacked the back of his head. Hard. Lucas raised his hands to cover, but the reverend slapped his head twice more before his hands could offer any protection from the blows. "Explain to me why I just sinned for you!" he screamed during his final swat.

Lucas cowered a few seconds before lowering his hands. "It was just a lie."

Fury over Lucas' blithe exculpation impelled August to strike the boy's head several times more. "It was a sin just as surely as if I had murdered your father where he stood."

Lucas shielded his head and screamed, "It was to save my soul!" The strikes ceased, and the boy explained, "He wants to send me away to live with his brother. He's a Mormon." Lucas lowered his hands and faced August with tears in his eyes. "Ever since mom died, dad says that he can't take care of me. He was gonna send me to live with Uncle Evan and his wife. She converted him, and I know they'll try to convert me too. If I'm living with them, I won't have a choice. When I refused to go, dad and me got into a fight. He called the cops on me and had me sent to this stupid juvenile delinquent camp. My uncle was going to check me out of it when he was ready, but I didn't wait. I came to you."

August raised his hand to Lucas' head, prompting the boy to cower again. Instead of striking him, he rubbed his head and said, "I forgive you." With that, he started the car.

Margaret Hargrove was reading a book in the hospital room's lone chair when August and Lucas entered. "Reverend Briar?" She stood to greet him, dropping the book to the chair.

August took her hand. "Margaret, how are you holding up?"

"I'm managing. It's all I can do. I just want him to wake up." She nodded to Lucas. "Who's this young man?"

"I'm Lucas, ma'am."

"Lucas is staying with me. I believe he will make a fine minister one day."

Margaret said, "Thank you both for coming to see Jason."

"Any change at all?" August asked.

Through teary eyes, she replied, "Nothing."

August placed a hand on her shoulder. "You should take a break."

"I couldn't leave Jason alone. What if he woke up?"

"I am here now. Go get something to eat."

"The nurse brought me a sandwich a while ago."

August removed any measure of assuagement from his voice, saying, "Margaret, I want to pray over Jason. In private."

Margaret seemed uncertain how to respond. "Well, I could use some tea."

"Good idea," said August. Once she left the room, he told Lucas, "Close the door."

Lucas did as instructed. "What are you gonna do, Reverend?"

"Pray." August placed hands on Jason's forehead and chest, and he prayed. "Lord, please release your power through me. I am your humble vessel. Use me. Please."

Lucas noticed a blue light in August's torso. "Reverend, you're doing it!"

August opened his eyes and saw the light traveling down his arms into Jason's body. "Yes! Heal!" He concentrated and pushed the energy into the unconscious young man with all his might, until Jason was enveloped in the brilliant blue light. A moment later,

August's hands fell to the mattress as the patient's body disappeared into particles of light.

"Where did he go?" Lucas asked.

Alarms sounded from the monitors, which were no longer receiving signs of life.

August looked in horror at the empty bed. He turned to Lucas and replied, "I have no idea."

Lucas looked under the bed. The next second a nurse bolted into the room, followed by a physician and another nurse, who was pushing a crash cart.

"Where's the patient?" the physician asked.

The first nurse said, "He was just here." She asked August and Lucas, "Who are you?"

"Jason's minister."

"Was he here when you arrived?"

Margaret returned with a cup of tea. "What's wrong?" she screamed. "Where's Jason?"

All eyes fixed on August, who for the first time, couldn't formulate a sentence. "I—"

Lucas answered for him, "God took him."

CHAPTER 35

August's speechlessness continued as the physician asked, "What do you mean, God took him?"

From inside her purse, Margaret's cell phone rang. Looking at the ID, she said, "It's my husband. What am I going to tell him?" She answered the call. "Hello? Alan, I have something to tell you. What do you mean?"

August asked, "What is it, Margaret?"

She answered, "Alan said that Jason is home. How could that be? He was just here." She returned her attention to the call. "Jason! You're talking—"

August caught Margaret just before she fainted to the floor.

August drove at a furious pace from the hospital with Lucas in the backseat and an anxious Margaret in the passenger seat.

"Reverend, help me understand," she said. "What happened?"

"I was praying for him. I prayed to God to heal Jason, and I beseeched Him. I could feel His presence – like I was talking to someone who was in the room with me. I felt His Holy Spirit enter me, and He told me that I have the power. He granted me the gift to heal."

"Oh Reverend," Margaret said with tears running down her face.

"I chose not to tell you in front of that doctor. So many of them are godless dissenters."

"I still don't understand how Jason got home," Margaret said.

"Lucas told you. After I healed him, God took him."

Margaret saw her house. "We're here!" She waited less than a heartbeat for him to put the car in park before she opened the door and ran inside. By the time August and Lucas entered the house, the family was embraced in a three-way hug. "It's a miracle," proclaimed Margaret.

Alan Hargrove greeted August with a vigorous handshake. "Look at our miracle!"

Margaret broke her embrace and caressed her son's face. "Are you okay?"

"I feel fine," Jason answered. "I feel great actually."

"Jason, what do you remember?" August asked.

"I remember the accident, and then I felt like I was asleep, dreaming. I had a vivid dream. I traveled the world, seeing everything you could imagine, and I remember thinking the only place I wanted to see was home. When I woke up, that's where I was."

"I see," said August. *Even in unconsciousness, it takes you where you most want to go.*

Margaret broke from her son just long enough to say, "Reverend, please thank God for me."

August left the room with Lucas at his side. He stared at his hands, prompting Lucas to ask, "What's wrong?"

August answered, "I feel weak. I need to touch him again."

"Jason?"

"God. We have to return to the plateau."

Gregor and Iris had moved two lawn chairs to the outskirts of the Wickline's backyard, side by side, facing the canyon's mouth to watch the rays of the descending sun baptize the landscape in a painted surrealism. Iris told him, "Mom isn't going to step away from the computer until she has researched every possibility and come up with a way to reverse the sale of that property."

"If a way exists," said Gregor.

"She's over-dramatizing the dire consequences of it all. She can't know for certain what will happen. How much of an impact could one person possibly have on the fate of the world?" Without averting her eyes from the canyon, Iris took Gregor's hand. "I can't believe you're leaving."

"I'm coming back as soon as I can," he promised.

"Gregor!" Cadence yelled from the patio.

He looked over the back of his chair to see her summoning him with her hand. "Oh no."

"What is it?" asked Iris.

"I think they want to get on the road." Far from ready to oblige, he waved off her call. "They can wait a little while longer."

To the sound of approaching footsteps, Iris said, "I don't think she wants to wait. She still has to check out of the motel, right? Let them check out and come back for you."

"Give us a little extra time? That's a great idea."

Once she arrived, Cadence said, "Gregor, I need to talk to you. Privately." After an understanding nod from Iris, the two friends trekked into the canyon. "Explain what's going on here."

"What do you want to know?" Gregor asked.

"For starters, what happened to your scars?"

"The vortex I found is incredibly powerful."

Cadence shook her head. "You know I don't believe in all that."

"Then you explain how my body healed. How did Iris and I

suddenly appear in the living room? How did I save your life when you jumped?"

A glimmer of hope lit in her eyes as she couldn't dispute them all. "Can it heal me?"

"If we could get to the vortex, I think so."

"Then take me there."

"I just promised Iris I wouldn't go back there until we find a way around August."

"You promised her? My life is at stake here. That's got to trump a promise you made to some girl you just met." When Gregor didn't respond, Cadence began crying. "You know, I haven't always been so angry. You know that! I've had this unending string of bad luck, failing health and horrible relationships, that has just wrapped around any bit of hope I had inside me and strangled it to death. I have nothing left but anger. I keep thinking, surely to God, Life has got to throw me a bone sometime, but when? Time is running out." Cadence stormed off to the house without even a glance at Iris.

As Gregor neared, Iris asked, "What's going on with you two?"

Gregor wondered if he should say that he needed to break his earlier promise, but he wasn't sure she'd agree a chance to save Cadence's life was worth risking his own, and he didn't want to position the two women against each other. "She's just ready to go."

Moments later Gregor and Iris entered the kitchen to find Cadence telling Travis, "I already missed the deadline for checkout today, so I'll end up paying for a day I don't need."

Travis told Gregor, "We were supposed to be on the road by now."

Iris asked, "Can you guys check out of the motel and come back for Gregor?"

"It's actually out of the way to come back," said Cadence. "I'll be in the car."

"She's right," Gregor told Iris. "I should just go now."

"I thought you weren't ready to leave."

"I'm not, but I'm not really being fair to them."

"Hey, don't worry about us," said Travis. "We can wait a little longer. No big deal."

Gregor said, "I need to pack my bag."

Travis dismissed the concern. "You have one duffle bag. I think I can handle it."

"I left clothes on the floor, and I know you don't want to pick up my dirty underwear." Gregor never left clothes on the floor, so he was hoping Travis would understand he wanted to leave with them.

"You're right. You should do it yourself."

Lily entered from the living room, "Cadence said you're leaving now?"

Iris looked Gregor in the eyes. "You're going back to the vortex, aren't you?"

Gregor sighed, "I have to."

"Are you crazy? This morning you were on the brink of death from a gunshot wound. Now you want to go back? How are you going to get through the fence?"

"We have wire cutters in the car."

Travis interjected, "Actually, I know where there's a hole in the fence."

Iris shot Travis a dirty look and asked Gregor, "What if August shoots you in the head this time? Do you think the vortex could heal that?"

Gregor insisted, "It's worth the risk! I need to do this."

"I think you're addicted to it, and I see now that's the only reason you want to move here. Don't bother looking me up when you do." Iris stormed off to her bedroom, slamming the door shut. Gregor started to follow, but Lily put her hand up to stop him.

"Iris won't talk to you right now. You should let her cool down. Come back to see her before you leave. Would you do that?"

Gregor looked back at Travis and said, "We will."

Leaving the house, Gregor said, "Drop me off at the vortex before you go to the motel."

Travis asked, "Are you aware there are armed guards patrolling that property now?"

"Really? How do you know?"

Arriving at the car, they found Cadence lying in the backseat and listening to music through earbuds. Travis grabbed the door handle but didn't pull it. "I went there last night," he whispered. "I charged up a bagful of crystals – at least I think I did – and I put them near Cadence as she slept last night, trying to heal her."

"Did it work?" asked Gregor.

Travis shrugged. "How would I know? I guess we'll have to wait for her next doctor's visit to know for sure. Until then, there's no need for you to risk your life going back there. Let's just go home." He opened the door and slipped behind the wheel.

Gregor rounded the car and entered the passenger side. He glanced back at Cadence, who seemed to be zoned in only to the music. "I need to go back to the vortex."

"Why do you need to go back now? Just wait." Travis started the car and pulled out of the driveway.

"I haven't reached my full potential," replied Gregor.

"What do you mean?"

"I know I can store more energy in my body than I've had in me so far, and also I think I've been doing it wrong."

"If you've been doing it wrong, I'd hate to see what you could do if you got it right."

"The energy has manifested in several ways, including ways I couldn't control like at the rave. They're all connected, and I just need to put it together. Also, I think I can recharge faster. I've always been passive before, allowing the energy to flow into me and charging me in the process. If I actively summon the energy, I think I can absorb a greater amount and faster."

Travis said, "Like sucking water up with a straw compared to drinking it by tipping a glass and letting it flow into your mouth powered by the weak gravitational pull?

"Exactly. You can drink more of it faster with a straw."

"All right. Maybe I can help you figure it out when we get there."

Gregor shook his head. "You're not joining me."

"Did you hear what I said about the armed guards? I'm not letting you go in there alone."

"You have to take care of Cadence. I don't want either of you in harm's way."

A few minutes later, Travis parked near the property, and he gave Gregor directions to the cut opening.

From the backseat, Cadence asked, "Why are we here?"

"I'm going in," answered Gregor.

Cadence unbuckled her seatbelt. "I'm coming with you."

Travis said, "You're not going in there."

"Don't tell me what to do! Gregor, can you heal me?"

"I don't need you with me," he replied. "I'll store enough energy inside me to help you afterwards."

"How long do you need?" asked Travis.

"Can you give me an hour?"

"We'll meet you right back here," Travis assured him.

On the way to the motel, Travis thought about confessing his use of crystals on Cadence the previous night, but he figured she couldn't be over-healed. If Gregor could do to her what he saw Iris do to him, it would increase her chance of full recovery. When they entered the motel room, Travis threw his belongings into his duffel bag without regard to organization. Cadence, on the other hand, placed items into her suitcase according to folded size and material. He told her as she was finishing, "I bet you'll be happy to get out of this little room and back to your own place."

"Actually, I can't say that I will." She grabbed her valise from inside the suitcase and said, "I'm going to pack up the bathroom."

When she left the room, Travis retrieved the bag of crystals from under the bed and stuffed it into his duffel bag. Making sure nothing was left behind, he checked the closet and opened each drawer. In the nightstand, he found an open envelope addressed to Gregor. He recognized the handwriting as Cadence's, and he was about to put it into her suitcase when his curiosity got the better of him. She was still in the bathroom and out of his line of sight, so he pulled the letter from the envelope.

Dear Gregor,

If you're reading this letter, then you already know I have taken my own life. My cancer returned and metastasized to the surrounding organs, so I didn't have much time left, and I didn't want to spend it in pain. I apologize for doing this so far from home, but I didn't want to die in a hospital in the city. It's ugly and depressing.

I don't want any kind of fuss over my body. Just cremate me, and release my ashes at the top of Wilson Mountain. I've bookmarked a crematorium in the phone book in the nightstand, and I listed you as the benefactor of my life insurance. It's not much, but it should be enough to cover the cost.

Finally, I want you to know how very much you have meant to me. You've been a dear friend to me – a gift – and I treasure the time we spent together. Don't forget to enjoy your life, and try not to be upset when others don't see how beautiful you really are. Please forgive me, and don't forget me.

Love, Cadence

p.s. I love you, and I'll be watching over you always.

When Cadence opened the bathroom door, Travis held up the letter. "You're planning to kill yourself?"

"You read my letter?"

"My question first."

Cadence stormed over to him and snatched the letter from his hand. "This letter is old."

"How old could it be? It's on the motel stationery."

"Gregor talked me out of it."

Travis snapped his fingers. "That's why he was so insistent on my watching you."

"Watch me?"

"And I took you to the Grand Canyon. I practically loaded the gun for you."

"What are you talking about?"

"At the Skywalk. You were going to pull a *Thelma and Louise*? How original."

"Oh, I'm so sorry my suicide plans lacked originality. Next time I'll be more creative."

"Next time?"

"You know what I mean. Just drop it."

Travis crossed his arms and asked, "So, where's my letter?"

"That's why you're upset?" asked Cadence. "I write a suicide note, and your biggest problem with it is that you weren't the addressee?"

"Not the biggest – just *a* problem."

"I wrote to Gregor because he's my best friend. He's like a brother to me. You're—"

"What?" Travis asked in the tone of a dare.

"I don't know."

"Let me tell you who I am," said Travis. "I'm the one who won't be waiting for you." He gathered all the bags but one and left the room.

CHAPTER 36

Chaco Canyon, 1182 CE

The screams seemed to come from all around, as if the night itself were in pain. The Anasazi scout looked down to the gnarling in his stomach and noticed the moonlight flared the sweat on his bare torso into a telltale beacon for the immolators below. He flew from his cliff perch overlooking the burning village and retraced his steps home. In understanding compliance, the desert kept obstacles from his path, and his heart drummed a purposeful beat for his feet to follow. The chilled air ignited in his lungs and fueled his blood, accelerating his body to a speed he had never known.

The progression of the moon's trek was imperceptible in the moments needed for the scout to spot twinkling torchlight from the village of his birth. Staggered wooden ladders reached to the stone dwellings that scaled five stories up the canyon wall. The scout slowed his pace only when impeded by the gathering of tribesmen and stopped outside a kiva.

A man of revered countenance exited the kiva, accompanied by senior members of the tribe. "Speak," the man told the scout.

"Chief, Aztec attack the South Village!" the scout said, eliciting gasps from the crowd.

"How much time?" the chief asked.

"Their footsteps echo my own."

The scout and onlookers waited for a response from the chief, whose expression refused to alter to the news. The scout was about to repeat his words, when the chief responded, "The wind is calling us."

Shielded by shadows, a scout from the Aztec watched as the Anasazi gathered on the canyon floor in concentric circles. He wondered if they were praying to their gods to deliver them, which made the scout smile at the futility of their actions. When the circles were complete, the Anasazi held hands and chanted. A moment later, every Anasazi torso glowed a pale blue. In disbelief, the Aztec scout watched as the light crept to their appendages, growing brighter and brighter. Each lighted circle dispersed into a wind blowing in every direction, and the Anasazi were gone.

Adrenalized from his latest conquest, the Aztec chief stalked his next quarry with his warriors at his side. Under the full moon, his macuahuitl sparkled with the blood of his enemies. His people had wandered many lands in search of a home, and he knew this land was their destiny. His shaman had heard the voice of Huitzilopochtli, the god with the ravenous thirst for the blood of man, and he said that the land was divinely promised to them. The chief found his scout standing above a canyon. "What do you have to report?"

The scout pointed at the deserted canyon floor.

The chief saw nothing and asked, "Where are they?"

"Gone," the scout answered. "The gods have taken them."

The chief growled, "The gods are with us!" He ordered all the dwellings searched.

The scout led the chief to where the Anasazi had last stood. When the Aztec shaman emerged from behind the chief, the scout told him, "I saw them walk into a blue fire."

The shaman knelt to rake the ground with his fingers. "The gods have touched this place, but their touch has grown cold," he said. With fear in his eyes, he warned, "We must leave."

The chief kicked the shaman and screamed, "This land is ours! It was promised!"

The Anasazi rematerialized on the plateau of Gregor's vortex in Sedona. Night gave way to day, and when they saw the barrenness of the land, they huddled together encircled and entranced by chanting drummers, and they ejected massive pulses of energy that brought life to the empty ground. As time passed, the Anasazi numbers grew. They built cliff dwellings and painted their history on the walls. They also tracked the night skies and debated the paths of the celestial objects.

They thrived in peace until the appearance of new invaders threatened their way of life. The Anasazi community divided into two factions – one that chose to stand their ground this time and fight the invaders, and one that chose to seek enlightenment among the stars. While those who stayed watched, the others crowded onto the plateau and disappeared into a blue light that shot into the stars.

The remaining Anasazi fought for their home, and they used the energy to their advantage. They sent pulses from their bodies to stun the approaching marauders. With enough warning, they were able to use the energy to disappear from the aim of weapons, and they sent away some invaders with a touch of their blue hands. However, the sheer number of the invaders eroded any advantage. Soon the Anasazi were surrounded and, separated from the vortex, they were unable to recharge their depleting energy. All who had remained in Sedona were annihilated.

In the stars, the Anasazi who had left Sedona evolved. The face of one Anasazi morphed into another face that was familiar to Iris. It was the face of the alien she had seen on a ship near the moon. The alien glowed bright blue.

Iris awoke in her bed, where she had cried herself to sleep. "The pictographs aren't Aztec. They're Anasazi. They brought the vortex with them." As she blinked, she thought her eyes had not adjusted from her dream because she could still see the blue light of the alien. She smiled when she realized the light was real and emanating from a masculine figure standing in her room. Although the bright glow prevented an accurate discerning of facial features, she knew who it was. Iris put out her hand and said, "Gregor, you're back."

Following the passage of a tithe of night, Gregor returned to the Wickline house. He left Travis and Cadence sitting in the car and walked to the front door alone. Earlier they had picked him up at the rendezvous point, at which time he had told them of his failed mission – news that earned the silent treatment from Cadence and unusual pensiveness from Travis. Gregor rang the doorbell and waited not a quarter-minute for Lily to answer.

"Gregor! I'm so glad you came back. What happened to you?"

Gregor knew she was referring to his appearance, which was that of a man who had received a sizeable jolt of electricity that sent him flying to the ground. "I tried to go back to the vortex, but the hole Travis cut in the fence has been patched, and now the fence is electrified. I couldn't get in."

Lily stepped aside to allow him entry. "Are you okay?"

"Besides a ringing in my ears, I think so. How is Iris?"

"She hasn't come out of her room since you left."

"Any chance that she would talk to me now? I can't leave things the way we did."

"Come on," Lily said as she took Gregor's hand. "We'll both talk to her." She led him to the closed bedroom door and knocked once. "Iris. Iris, Gregor's back."

When they heard no response, Gregor said, "Maybe I should go."

"Don't you dare." Lily tried the locked doorknob. "She always locks herself in her room when she's upset, although I don't know why." She reached above the door jamb for a wire key. "The key's right here." Opening the door, she hit the lights, but Iris was nowhere to be seen.

"Where is she?" asked Gregor.

"I don't know. Check the closet." As Gregor looked in the closet, Lily lifted the edge of the quilt to see under the bed. Iris was not hiding in her room.

"Are you sure she didn't leave?"

Lily told him, "I've been working on the computer in the living room the entire time. If she had come out, I would've seen her." She thought for a second and added, "I did make tea."

After searching the house, Gregor scanned the backyard while Lily looked in the garage. She met him on the back patio and said, "Her car is still here."

The two retreated to the kitchen, where Gregor held up his cell phone. "I'll call her."

"Let me. In case she's still upset with you." Lily dialed from the landline. "It's ringing."

Gregor told her, "I hear it too." He ran from the kitchen toward the sound and returned with Iris' ringing cell phone. "It was on her dresser."

Lily hung up. "Maybe she disappeared on her own and went back to the vortex."

"She couldn't."

"I saw her do it before. Disappeared right in front of me."

Gregor explained, "She didn't have any energy left to do that."

As soon as Lily arose in the morning, she checked Iris' room to see if her daughter had returned in the night, but only disappointment greeted her. She walked by the closed door to the guest room, where Cadence still slept, and the living room couch, where Travis kept a tenuous grip on his dream state. Once in the kitchen, she set the coffee to brew. As the heated water released the aroma from the ground beans, Lily wondered, "Why would she leave without a word to me?" She felt guilty for not continuing her search last night, but she knew if Iris didn't want to be found, she wouldn't be. "Still, I should have kept looking."

After a yawn she thought about Gregor's refusal to suspend his search, and she wondered where he had slept, if at all. She walked outside and found him and Daisy sleeping in the hammock. Her head resting on Gregor's chest, Daisy opened her eyes when Lily approached, but moved nothing else. Lily debated whether she should awaken him, wondering how long he had searched the back-yard canyon for her daughter before fatigue won him over. When she noticed the thick layer of mud on his shoes was still moist, she muttered, "I'll get him a blanket." As she backed away, she kicked the flashlight that had fallen from his hand.

The slight noise jarred Gregor awake, speaking the words, "He took her."

CHAPTER 37

The man who emerged from the parked car at the church was the mirror image of the one who had given the Sermon on the Mount just twenty-four hours earlier. Self-doubt and pity had been replaced by absolute assuredness and reinvigorated ego. Utter defeat had given way to visions of unprecedented victory, and suicidal thoughts had been crushed by delusions of grandeur. As Lucas followed him into the church, August continued his one-sided conversation as if every word – like a Bible passage – were to be committed to memory. "My name will rise from every tongue as the Giver of Miracles, and the world's wretched will journey from every land to be blessed by the touch of God's Divine Emissary. My ministry will be boundless."

When August cleared his throat, Lucas took the opportunity to say, "You'll have all the networks fighting to carry you then."

"West Canaan will rise..." August looked at the red rock towering above the other side of the church and envisioned the architecture it would soon hold. He tilted his head when he noticed the rock had become dotted with the greenery of new plants, some of which were sprouting delicate cerulean flowers.

"Let's announce it right now," said Lucas with a grin. "Show them what you can do."

"Before going public," August muttered as his eyes followed the new growth to the pavement at his feet, "I need to practice on someone."

Lucas shrugged, saying, "Why? You healed Jason just fine yesterday."

"His disappearance was unintentional. I need to make sure I can heal someone without losing them, and I have the perfect guinea pig." Exasperated, he threw his hands out and asked, "What is going on with all of these plants?" Past his parked car, he saw a large man kneeling on the pavement to inspect one of the flowers. "You there! What are you doing?"

Nickel answered, "Admiring the ma-esh achetl."

The reverend hurried to him, intent on confrontation. "Do you work for Luis?"

"I don't know a Luis."

"The gardener. Are you responsible for planting these weeds?"

"They're not weeds. Ma-esh achetl means the 'flower of life.' It was a sustenance plant for the people in this area centuries ago."

"You had no right to cultivate it on my property."

Nickel rose to his feet, keeping his eyes on the new growth. "I didn't plant them."

Weary of the directionless conversation, August turned his back on the man and continued walking to the front door. He told Lucas, "Luis comes on Wednesdays. Can you get his number from Mrs. Chapman and have him come today with some weed killer?"

"You can't do that!" protested Nickel. "This plant has been extinct for at least four centuries. The fact that they're here now is… miraculous."

While contemplating Nickel's words and his own next steps, August scanned the parking lot at the new life sprouting from every available crack. He said not another word to the large flower-lover and instead told Lucas, "We have to repave the parking lot as well."

A moment later the two entered the reception area to find Mrs. Chapman typing on the computer with her back to them. "Mrs. Chapman," August called, but without eliciting a response. "Mrs. Chapman!" he yelled with more volume than necessary.

The startled woman spun her chair around. "Reverend. I didn't hear you come in. How are you feeling?" she asked in the tone of a mother with a sick child.

"Fine." August looked down at his perfect black suit and wondered if his face showed some infirmity. "Why do you ask?"

"Yesterday's sermon. You seemed—"

Realizing her query regarded his mental health, August interrupted her with, "We scheduled the demolition crew for the new property today. I need you to cancel them."

"Yes, Sir." She waited for more, as the reverend seemed on the verge of speaking for several seconds. "Is there something else?"

"Mrs. Chapman, do you trust me?"

"Of course, Reverend," she answered, although the trust in her eyes was questionable.

"What would you say if I told you I could heal your ears?"

Mrs. Chapman felt her ears and asked, "What's wrong with my ears?"

"Your hearing. I meant I could fix your hearing."

"Oh. I suppose I'd say, 'Prove it,'" she answered with a slight chuckle.

"Very well." August walked behind her chair.

Mrs. Chapman looked over her shoulder. "What are you doing?"

"You said to prove it. Now give me the opportunity. Face forward and close your eyes," August demanded, and she complied. He cupped her ears with his hands, closed his eyes and prayed aloud. "God, come to me again. Let Your strength, Your power pervade me." The blue light shone through his black suit and seeped into his hands.

"It tingles," Mrs. Chapman cooed, uncertain what he was doing to provoke the feeling.

August opened his eyes and watched the light's movement, trying to ensure enough exposure for healing without crossing the threshold to full conversion. When it had traveled below her knees, he removed his hands.

"Where's that light coming from?" Mrs. Chapman asked as she opened her eyes. "Are you done..." She noticed her skin glowing blue and screamed, "Ahhhhhhhh!"

"Calm down," August ordered as the light faded from them both. "Mrs. Chapman, calm down." When she whimpered to attention, he whispered, "How do you feel?"

Mrs. Chapman felt her body and uttered an unsure, "Okay."

August whispered again, "You can you hear me?"

"Of course," she answered.

From further away, Lucas whispered, "What about me?"

She turned to him and answered, "Yes." She grinned and exclaimed, "I can hear." Her eyes welled with tears.

August was elated that he now knew how to control the energy. Walking to his office, he told her, "Call Sam to come here with his camera, and do not forget to cancel the demolition."

"Yes, Sir."

August was about to turn the doorknob to enter his office, when he heard a noise from the other side. He looked to Mrs. Chapman and asked, "Is someone in my office?"

Mrs. Chapman had pulled a bobby pin from her hair and let it drop to the desk to test her hearing. "Oh, I almost forgot. You have someone waiting for you in your office."

Entering his office, he whispered to Lucas, "Did not do a thing for her memory."

"I heard that!" Mrs. Chapman yelled.

August and Lucas found a man huddled over a small pile of books that had fallen from the bookshelf in front of him. He was wearing a gray, long-sleeved shirt of inappreciable expense with sweat-darkened patches at the armpits and lower back.

"Looking for something?" August asked.

With books loaded in his arms, the man stood and faced the door. "Something to read."

August recognized the ersatz librarian as the arsonist he had been mentoring in prison. "You made it here."

"I got out a couple of days ago and hitched here. Sorry about the books, Reverend." The man unburdened his arms by returning the volumes to the shelf in no particular order.

"Lucas, this is Frederick Jennings, my new bodyguard."

"Hi," Lucas said without extending his hand.

Frederick nodded to the boy and asked August, "Did you say bodyguard?"

"I was thinking this morning that my impending celebrity might merit creating such a position. Given your unique experience, I believe you are qualified for the post, if you want it."

Frederick grinned and said, "Of course. I'll do anything for you."

Pleased by his words, August handed him his keys, "Take my car, and go to my house. Clean yourself up, and take a suit from my closet. I believe we are about the same size."

"Thank you, Reverend. Oh, I don't know where you live."

"Use the navigator in the car to go home."

Travis leaned against the kitchen counter with his arms crossed, and Gregor tapped his foot while they waited for Lily to finish the phone conversation with the only employee who didn't share her surname. "I understand if you can't cover me. Don't worry about it. We'll just keep the shop closed today."

"Why would the preacher kidnap her?" Travis asked. "What purpose does it serve?"

"I don't know," Gregor answered. "To hurt me? He thinks I'm cavorting with the Devil."

"Stop apologizing," Lily said before hanging up the phone.

"Do you think he can do what you do, you know, the blue man thing?" asked Travis.

Gregor shrugged. "He's probably figured it out by now."

"I just can't believe he would use the vortex," Lily said with a serious scowl. "He's been a thorn in my side for years over such practices. Hypocrite!" She took a deep breath and grabbed her purse from the table. "That's it. I'm going to see him."

"Wait," Travis said. "Don't you think we should be sure before we accuse him?"

"That's why I'm going," Lily replied. "I want to look him in the eye when I ask if he's done something with my daughter."

Gregor said, "No, don't do that. If I can get to the vortex, I can find Iris and bring her back here. If you confront him now, he'll probably camp out there."

Lily asked, "How are you going to get there?"

"I'll get you in," Travis vowed. "I don't know how, but we'll figure it out."

Lily told them, "Please be careful."

August emerged from the hospital elevator with Lucas, Frederick and cameraman Sam in his wake.

Seeing a sign painted on the wall, Lucas asked, "Why are we in the pediatric ward?"

Without missing a beat, August answered, "Kids get better coverage."

With great purpose the reverend headed to the nearest patient room, but he was intercepted by a middle-age nurse named Wanda. "Excuse me. What are you doing?"

"God's work," August answered without a adjusting his gait.

"You can't come in here with a camera. We have patient privacy laws."

"I answer to God's laws, as do you, and today I remind everyone of that forgotten fact."

The nurse darted in front of him to stop his progression. "You can't film patients without a signed consent form."

"Then get the forms," August demanded, sidestepping her. "Believe me, they will sign."

"I'm calling security," the nurse warned before rushing to use the nursing unit's phone.

Undaunted, the reverend reached for a doorknob and turned to Sam. "Are you rolling?"

After apologizing for missing his cue somewhere along the way, Sam lifted the camera from his hip to his shoulder and pointed forward to signal that recording had begun.

August entered a room with two beds and a young patient for each. The boy closer to the door had bandages over his eyes, while the other had no obvious ailment. August touched the arm of the bandaged boy and said, "Hello, Son. My name is Reverend Briar."

"Hi," the boy responded. "Do I know you, Reverend?"

"Not yet. Tell me your name."

"Kyle Thompson."

August shook the boy's hands and asked, "What church do you attend?"

"Christ Protestant."

"Then I am here to help you," August assured him. "What happened to you?"

"We had some fireworks, and…" the boy started sobbing, although no tears were evident. "I can't see no more."

"God is here for you, Son." He placed hands on the boy's head and chest.

"What are you doing?" the boy asked.

"Kyle, no talking while I pray." August closed his eyes and prayed aloud, "Lord, work your healing power through me. Let me heal this boy and make him whole again."

Nurse Wanda barreled into the room with a hefty security officer at her side. She pointed at August and said, "There he…" Her mouth agape, the nurse watched as blue light, originating from within the minister, forced its way into her patient. "Jesus!"

When he was done and the light subsided, August asked Kyle, "How do you feel?"

"Weird. Tingly."

"Remove your bandages," ordered the reverend.

As the boy reached for his bandaged eyes, Wanda told him "Don't do that!" and she ran to his bedside to grab his arms.

"Take off the bandages," August insisted to the nurse. His tone was such that left no wiggle room for interpretation or action, so after a second's hesitation, the nurse unwrapped the bandages. August urged Kyle, "By God's power, open your eyes and see!"

Kyle blinked several times and focused on the reverend. "I… can see you."

"Impossible," Wanda said. She held up her hand. "How many fingers am I holding up?"

"Three," Kyle answered.

The nurse looked at August and said, "I'll get you those consent forms."

"Mister," called the boy in the next bed. "Can you help me?"

"Follow me," August told Sam, approaching the second bed. "What is your name, Son?"

"Jonas Metzger," the boy with the sad brown eyes answered.

August cocked his head. "Metzger? What church do you attend?"

"I go to temple."

"Ask your rabbi to help you," August said and turned away. He told Sam, "Cut that part."

With his entourage increased by a security officer, August entered the next patient room, which held two beds but only one patient – a girl whose father sat bedside. The man stood and smiled when he saw August. "Reverend, how did you know Amy had been admitted?"

August shook the hand of Tim Adamly, one of his congregants, and tried to act as if he knew that his daughter had taken ill. "I did not hear the details."

"What's with the camera?" Tim asked.

"Documentary," August answered. "What exactly happened with Amy?"

"Early this morning, she started having breathing problems, and then I noticed the lesions on her shoulders. The doctor thinks she might have relapsed with the sarcoidosis."

August placed a hand on the man's shoulder. "I am sorry. Amy, how are you feeling?"

"Not great," the teenager answered with a mordant touch to her raspy voice.

"Will you please pray for her, Reverend?" Tim asked.

"Dad, you're embarrassing me," the girl said.

"Amy, he's here to help you."

"You don't ask someone to pray for you. They should only do it if they want to."

"I do want to, Amy," August said. "I will not only pray for you, but I will heal you."

"Reverend!" Tim interjected as he moved between August and his daughter. "I'm sorry, but could I speak to you privately for a sec?" When August nodded, Tim led him to the far corner of the room, and the cameraman followed. "Privacy please," Tim insisted, and after Sam lowered the camera, he told August, "I appreciate your prayers, Reverend, but we've always been completely upfront with our children. I don't like to stretch the truth or give false hope."

The nurse entered the room, holding consent forms, just as an angered August responded, "Tim, although I agree that children should learn the world's harsh realities quickly so they have more time to forge an effective armor against its temptations, I assure you that my words are free of prevarication, and the hope I offer is not false."

The nurse nodded and said, "He really can heal your daughter, Mr. Adamly."

Tim asked, "How's that possible?"

August responded with another question, "Have you lost your faith?"

"Of course not. I just—"

"Do you not believe God has the power to heal your daughter?"

"I don't doubt the power," Tim said, "just the inclination."

"I have both," August said with a single clenched fist. "I am telling you now that God wields His healing power through me, and I most definitely am inclined to heal Amy."

"I've seen him do it," offered the nurse with an encouraging dip of her head and sincere eyes. "He just healed a blind patient in the next room – right in front of me."

Wanting to believe, Tim looked to August for signs of truth, and the hopeful father nodded once. He walked back to his daughter and said, "Amy, Reverend Briar is going to try—"

August nodded to Sam to start filming and interrupted Tim, "I AM going to heal you."

"You're going to what?" asked Amy, who started a laugh that morphed into a cough.

"Don't be disrespectful," Tim said.

"Do not mock the Lord and His power," August told her.

Amy shrugged and dared him, "Go for it. What do you need me to do?"

"Be quiet. You can close your eyes if you want, while I pray. I need to put my hands on your shoulder and arm. Okay?"

"Sure," Amy said, closing her eyes.

August touched her and prayed as he had for the previous patient. This time, however, the light that emerged from his torso was too dim to penetrate his clothing or to travel to any portion of exposed skin. As the others watched with mounting anticipation, August prayed harder.

Amy opened her eyes and asked, "How long is it supposed to take?"

August looked into the camera and told Sam, "Turn that off." He removed his touch from Amy and said, "I am truly sorry, but I seem to be too weak from healing the little blind boy."

"Right," Amy said with a skeptic's contempt.

Tim again moved to separate August from his daughter. "How could you do this?"

August explained, "I just need to speak to the Lord in private. I will return to heal her."

"No, you won't!" Tim said. "I can't believe I let myself believe your ridiculous claim."

"He's telling the truth!" Lucas insisted.

August showed his palm to the boy. "Lucas, we are going." The reverend and his entourage left the room. Without directing his words to a particular person, he said, "One at a time is unacceptable. I need more." The reverend regained his composure and told Sam, "Take the first clip alone to the station immediately and post it online."

When Sam left, Lucas asked, "Reverend, what happened?"

"God is testing me again," he spit out as if in the face of the one he served. "He is teaching me humility. I need more power."

CHAPTER 38

Travis leaned against the side of his car holding binoculars, through which he saw guards patrolling the property around his former campsite. Travis lowered the lenses. "Have you given any serious consideration to the possibility that Iris left on her own accord?"

Keeping his eyes on the property, Gregor replied, "No. And she wouldn't have left without telling her mother."

"Okay, are you certain that this preacher is capable of kidnapping?"

Gregor lifted his shirt and pointed with his other hand to his bandage. "Remember this?"

"All right. What's on the other side of that mountain, or whatever you call it, where your vortex is?"

"I don't know. I never explored it."

Raising the binoculars once more, Travis said, "Maybe we could climb up the other side and then rappel down to your plateau."

Gregor looked at his friend. "Let's do it."

The two men jumped into the car and searched for a drivable passage on the other side of the property. Travis turned off the main road at a clearing that looked like it might extend to the back of the red rock, and after a few meters, the car began bouncing from the rugged terrain. He warned Gregor, "If I break an axle…" without committing to a consequence. Their body-jarring trek, which felt much longer than the dashboard clock suggested, ended at a botanical roadblock that forced Travis to stomp on the brake pedal. "We'll have to walk from here."

The area before them was overrun with wild flora, including bushes, succulents and trees, but above that, they could see the top of a red rock. After cramming the rock-climbing gear from the trunk into their backpacks, the two hiked forward. Within five-hundred meters of the rock, they came upon the chain-link fence crowned with razor wire.

Gregor surveyed the land beyond. "Hopefully, the overgrowth in this area keeps the guards away." After Travis, heeding his warning about the electrified fence, used rubber gloves and wire cutters to create a sizable hole, Gregor told him, "I'll go the rest of the way myself."

"Okay, I'm not listening to you this time. I'm a better climber than you. You need me, and I'm not abandoning you. What kind of friend do you think I am?"

Gregor looked at him with affection and answered, "I know what kind of friend you are." He waved at the new opening and followed him through it.

A few moments later, Travis touched the red rock and looked up its steep face. "I'll go first." After they had harnessed up, he began the ascent, determining the best path and hammering in anchors like a trail of breadcrumbs for Gregor to follow. Fifty meters up, Travis reached for a bantam outthrust, which chipped away before his eyes. Startled, he retracted his hand to his chest. "What was that?" He looked behind him, and found the answer. On the ground a guard brandished the high-powered rifle that had seconds earlier propelled a bullet into his planned path.

"Gregor!" he called to his friend below. Travis pointed with his head. "Look over there!"

Gregor looked down at the guard, who was now motioning for them to descend. "Hurry up!"

"To do what?" asked Travis.

"We're closer to the top than the bottom."

"He doesn't want us to go higher, and we're easy targets right here."

"He's just trying to scare us."

"And doing a good job of it! Gregor, our dead bodies won't be any help to Iris."

Gregor conceded, and they rappelled to the ground, where the guard was standing in wait.

"What do you guys think you were doing?" he asked.

"Rock climbing," answered Gregor.

"I could see that." The guard pointed to the perimeter. "What I meant was why did you cut the fence to do so?"

Travis recognized him from his last trespass. "Actually, we heard there's gold here."

Caught off guard at the second mention of the same rumor, the guard said, "I could've shot you for trespassing."

Annoyed at the common misconception, Travis told him, "If you're referring to the Castle Doctrine, that only applies to unlawful entry to an edifice, such as a home or business, and sometimes a car. It does not apply to unimproved property, or land, which this is."

Squinting his eyes in anger, the guard asked, "What?"

Travis nutshelled it for him, "Shooting us would be murder."

"Really?" the guard asked before ramming the butt of his gun to Travis' mouth. "Is there a doctrine for hitting trespassers?"

With Lucas in the passenger seat and Frederick in back, August drove to the gated property as two pickup trucks were leaving with three men each. He rolled down his window to ask the guard at the gate, "Who were those men that just left?"

The gate guard answered, "They're the earthmovers you said were coming today."

"What?" screamed August, furious at Mrs. Chapman for neglecting his orders yet again and at the guard for not perceiving his wishes. "I canceled them. Do not let them back in here."

"But they left their equipment," the guard said, pointing to the canyon. Deep tracks extending from the gate, down a trail of flattened and twisted foliage, into the canyon.

August told Lucas, "Remind me to fire Mrs. Chapman." The boy's attention, however, was on the approaching guard and captives. Following his gaze, the minister jammed the car into park and stormed from the vehicle. "What are they doing here?"

The escorting guard came from behind the intruders and asked, "You know them?"

With Lucas and Frederick now sidling him, August pointed to Gregor and told both guards, "He is the reason you are here. Where were they? Did he make it inside the canyon?" When the guard explained where they had been discovered, the reverend sighed in relief that they had not reached the plateau. He sneered at Gregor and asked, "Are you out?" From the look on the younger man's face, he could tell he was indeed out of energy. "You are."

Gregor had a question of his own. "What have you done with Iris?" He lunged forward, but Frederick put himself in front of the reverend. Both guards fixed their guns on Gregor, prompting Travis to pull him back to his side.

August asked, "How would I know the whereabouts of your beloved?"

"Because you took her!" yelled Gregor.

"Took her?" August repeated with a forced chuckle. "I am twice her age. That accusation compliments neither my judgment nor your appeal." His demeanor devolved to taunting pleasure. "You love her, do you not? That is a major difference between us – one of many. My love, like the love I have for God, strengthens me because of its purity. Your love, grown from carnality, weakens you. Perhaps the one you think you love flew on her broom to be with the one she truly loves, the master you both serve." He stepped closer to Gregor and, with whispered venom, threatened, "I should have you shot."

The escorting guard, who was close enough to hear, told August, "You can't do that, Reverend, because of the cattle doctrine."

"What are you rambling about?" August asked.

"I don't want to go back to prison," the guard explained.

"Then shut up!" August looked at all the witnesses and raced through possible scenarios to determine his most beneficial course of action. He knew Gregor was now only a threat if he could reach the plateau. "Let them go."

Gregor objected. "I'm not leaving until you tell me what you did with Iris!"

August responded, "If Iris is gone, you are most surely to blame. Perhaps if you left Sedona for good, she would return safe from any harm she might otherwise face."

"If you hurt her—"

Travis grabbed Gregor's arm. "Come on. Let's just go."

August told the guards, "Expel them, and feel no need to do so gently."

Once the guards had the intruders moving toward the gate, August told Frederick and Lucas, "When we are finished here, I have a feeling I will need to ask… more from you both. Just understand that the work you do is in service to the Lord."

Lucas told the reverend, "We're with you no matter what."

Inside the closed Sedona Vortex shop, a blue light flashed in front of the shelved crystals. Two minutes later another flash appeared and faded before the barren shelves.

While Lily paced in the kitchen and called everyone she knew to ask if they had seen Iris, Cadence sat on the couch in the living room half-listening to the female reporter on the TV news relay the latest information on the falling Hexum Space Station. "NASA is still trying to gain control of the crippled station to force reentry over the ocean. If unsuccessful, within the next two to four hours, the station will reenter the atmosphere possibly over a populated area, sending large pieces hurtling to the Earth with potentially devastating consequences."

Following the report, the news anchor announced, "Coming up, a local minister claims to have the power to heal, and he's got the amazing video to prove it."

Now attentive, Cadence watched the teaser clip of August Briar glowing blue with his hands on a hospitalized boy. She gasped and whispered, "He can do it too."

Lily came out of the kitchen to answer the front door even before the doorbell rang. "Boys, what happened?" she asked as Gregor and Travis plodded inside.

"The guard caught us before we could reach the vortex," answered Gregor.

"Was August there?" Lily asked, to which Travis nodded. "Did you get any sense of whether he had anything to do with Iris' disappearance?"

Travis answered, "Oh yeah, he took her."

Cadence stirred from the couch to join them. She saw Travis' bloody lip and asked, "What happened to you?"

"I tried biting my tongue and missed," he answered.

Lily clipped her keys from a wall hook near the front door. "I'll confront August myself."

Cadence, who was unconvinced of his guilt, suggested, "You should talk to Mitchell."

"Do you think he's involved?" Gregor asked.

"Of course not, but he'd have a better chance of learning what his father might know."

"That's not a bad idea," said Lily. "Mitchell is much more level-headed, but my relationship with him is not much better than mine with August."

Cadence told them, "Mine is."

In his church office, August inspected himself in the mirror. Over his white shirt he now wore a fishing vest that had each of its fifteen pockets filled with charged crystals. He slipped his arms into his black suit jacket and buttoned it to conceal the sartorial addendum, patting down the most protrusive of the bulges. He called for Mrs. Chapman, but she did not answer and, when he walked to her desk, he discovered a note stating that she had gone to lunch. As he crumpled the note and tossed it, he heard the door open behind him. "That was a quick trip." August stopped talking when he saw that Lucas had not entered his office.

"Expecting someone else, Reverend Briar?" Lester McAbel asked.

"My bodyguard."

"Bodyguard?" asked Lucas' father with a bit of a sneer. "Who would want to harm a man of God?"

"I thought you had returned home."

"I sent my brother on a train yesterday, but I decided to stay."

"For what purpose?"

Lester sat in the nearest chair, an indication he would not be leaving anytime soon. "I have to tell you that I found your behavior yesterday strange."

"In what way?" asked August, refusing to join him in sitting to converse.

"You never invited us into your house."

August laughed. "The only mystery is why my housekeeper decided to call in sick last week. My house was not kempt for company."

"Is it kempt enough for a visit from the police?" When August failed to respond, Lester added, "I want you to tell me where Lucas is, or I will involve the police in this family matter."

August thought for a second before relenting. "I will take you to him."

A moment later, as the two men walked to Lester's car, August said, "I remember when you first brought Lucas to our youth conference. You gave the impression of a devout Christian."

"So did you," Lester replied, opening the driver-side door of his car. "I do consider myself Christian, but I don't religiously go to church to prove it. My crops don't stop growing on Sunday." When August reached for the back door, he asked, "Don't you want to sit up front?"

"Only to drive," August responded taking the seat behind Lester.

"A housekeeper and a chauffeur now," Lester said. "Must be nice." He turned the ignition. "Lucas' mother was the churchgoer, and she's the one who insisted I bring him to your conference that first time. Last year I brought him because I felt guilty about her leaving, and I thought it would get his mind off her." He proceeded to drive from the parking lot.

"Is your brother truly a Mormon?"

"Evan converted to Mormonism for his wife when they married. Where am I going?"

"Turn right at the highway. Why would you want to hand your son over to that heretic? Do you not care for his everlasting soul?"

Lester frowned into the rearview mirror. "Evan's not a heretic. I know you're sold on your religion, and so is Lucas, but they all lead to the same place. Same God. Same Bible. Same Heaven. To answer your question, though, Lucas has become unmanageable, at least by me. My brother is better equipped to handle him; he was a green beret, and he can put him in his place."

August responded, "If that place is Hell, he is, in fact, correct."

The two men continued their discussion as the reverend gave the visitor directions that led to a mountain road overlooking Verde Valley. "Look at that view," August told him. "What a testament to God's glory."

"It is beautiful," Lester said with a sigh. "I can see why Lucas loves this town. You know, ever since that first conference of yours he came to, he's tried to get me to move here. I've never seen a kid get so attached to a place that wasn't home. I should've known this would be the place he would run to." Noticing a strange light in his rearview mirror, he glanced over his shoulder. A look of disbelief fell upon him when he saw a blue-lighted August.

The reverend grabbed Lester's shoulders, and the light flooded into him. "I will not allow you to corrupt his soul." The two figures of light dispersed and disappeared. The car continued forward, crashing through a metal barrier and to the ground far below.

August thought of a place described to him by one of his young congregants more than a week earlier. At the aquarium in San Diego, he materialized on the air side of the great white shark exhibit with his still-blue hands and forearms protruding through the glass into the water. Before the light could leave him, he retracted his hands to his side, leaving Lester McAbel gasping for air in the massive tank of water.

Only a child saw the sudden appearance of the two men, and he tugged on his mother's shirt to point out the man in the water. As people did notice, they thought he was part of a show.

Facing August, Lester began pounding on the glass. He looked up and swam one stroke before he was jerked away by the jaws of the aquarium's largest great white shark. As blood fogged the water, the onlookers screamed, many covering the eyes of their children.

With his hands touching the glass, August muttered, "Convert or die."

CHAPTER 39

Cadence took a deep breath as Lily drove into the driveway to August Briar's house and parked. The older woman squeezed her hand and thanked her, and Lily smiled at her before exiting the car. She rang the doorbell, and Mitchell soon answered. "Hi Mitchell. I tried to call…" She stopped when she noticed the bruising on his face. "Were you in a fight?"

He turned from her, leaving the door open for her. "My phone's broken. You'll have to talk fast. I'm getting ready to leave."

Cadence was surprised at his abrupt invitation – if one could call it that – to enter, but she followed him, asking, "What happened to your voice?"

"I'm coming down with a cold."

"That explains the turtleneck," she said in reference to the odd summer apparel he now sported. "Are you okay otherwise?"

"I've never been more clearheaded in my life." He entered his bedroom, where two suitcases lay open on the bed, and he returned to the task of packing. "Why are you here?"

"Where are you going?"

"I'm just going. Maybe L.A." He looked to her for a response, and she pretended not to see. "Or a place I've never heard of. Wherever the Lord decides to lead me. Why are you here?"

"I need information from your father, and I thought if the request came from you—"

"Believe me, you stand a much better chance if you speak to my father without me. Maybe if I asked for the opposite, you'd get what you want." He chuckled and looked at her. "Why don't you come with me?"

"What? You don't even know where you're going?"

"So what? I'm telling you, letting go of all that weighs you down is absolutely liberating. God will let us know when we've arrived at our destination, and that's where I'll start my church. We'll pray together every day, asking God to heal you, and if He wills it, we will have a beautiful life."

"Actually, that's one of the reasons I'm here. I wanted you to ask your father to heal me."

Mitchell looked at her as if she were speaking in tongues. "My father can't heal."

"I saw him on the news. He healed a blind boy."

"I don't know what he's up to, but I can assure you it's nothing more than propaganda to drum up business. My father only thinks he's a new Jesus."

"But—"

"Enough about him." Mitchell slid his hands around hers and pleaded, "Come with me."

Cadence thought of her options and before the pause became too uncomfortable. "I think I'm one of the weights you need to let go of." With that, she left him alone.

An inverted image of Earth appeared in a symmetrical drop of water suspended far above the blue planet. The salty sphere fell forward from Iris' right eye and floated in front of a window of the Hexum Space Station. Watching the planet, she muttered, "It's definitely getting bigger," comparing it to when she first arrived aboard the doomed station.

"Give it up," Iris told herself as she pushed away from the window. "If Gregor were coming for you, he would've been here already. I have to save myself." The words offered little comfort since she had been trying to formulate an escape plan from the moment she had arrived almost twenty-four hours earlier. She no longer had any of the vortex's energy stored in her, and her attempts at using the charred communications console had been fruitless. Regardless, she decided to look again for any missed options.

The microgravity allowed her to corkscrew through the station, being careful to avoid entanglement in the network of cables that strung together numerous consoles mounted on the walls. Each module of the station had its own purpose, much like the rooms of a house, including: a kitchen, which was little more than a pantry since no actual cooking occurred there; sleeping quarters with eight modified Murphy beds, complete with asylum restraints to keep occupants from sleep-floating; an exercise room with a treadmill and stationary bike; a storage room with supplies in white cloth boxes; and a control room that served as the central brain – in the way a room in a house would if the power to control all light switches, electrical outlets and electronic devices were centralized instead of in the room of their actual locations.

Iris made her way yet again to the control room, which bore the blackened scars from the incident that had rendered the station a shooting star in waiting. She tried again to bring the charred communications console back to life through sheer force of will and by touching every button in varying sequence. When the results repeated that of previous attempts, she became angry and kicked it in frustration, which sent her flying backwards to bang her head on the opposing arc of the cylindrical room. Rubbing her head, she was startled to hear static.

Iris kicked her way back to the console. "Hello?" she called and waited for an answer. She repeated herself and pushed buttons one-by-one while saying the word.

She heard a female voice from the console's speaker order, "Identify yourself."

Iris' eyes began to tear as a sad grin broke across her face. "Hello? Can you hear me?"

The voice responded, "This is NASA Ground Control in Houston. Identify yourself."

She let loose a relieved laugh and said, "This is Iris Wickline. I'm trapped—"

The voice interrupted, "This is a restricted S-band frequency. Cease communications."

"You're joking, right?"

The voice threatened, "Civilian intrusion on this frequency is a federal violation. Cease communications, or I will have your position traced."

"Do it!" Iris yelled, slamming her fists on the console. The static stopped. "Hello?"

From San Diego, August materialized in his church office, where Lucas sat playing on his phone and waiting for him to come through the door. When he saw the lights, the boy popped up from his seat and said, "I didn't know you could do that away from that place."

The startled reverend paused to think before explaining, "God has given His prophet more than the power to heal."

"Amazing. What can't you do now? Do you think God would give me some power?"

Without hesitation, August answered, "No," to squelch any

thoughts he might have of following in his footsteps in that regard. "What are you doing?"

"We picked up a cell phone for Frederick, like you asked. He's sitting at Mrs. Chapman's desk trying to figure it out. I tried to show him, but he frustrates me."

August motioned for him to sit at his counseling sofa, where he joined him. "Lucas, I need to talk to you about your father." He wanted to tell the young man about Lester's death so that the unwarranted guilt now weighing on his heart could be lifted. He wanted to assure Lucas that he was killed in defense of his soul, to clear his path to Heaven, but he was not sure the boy was old enough to understand. "Would you be upset if you never saw him again?"

Lucas shrugged. "I'm glad he's gone. I know he's glad I'm gone too. The only reason he came to get me was to punish me, not because he wanted me back. Why do you ask, Reverend?"

With his guilt somewhat abated, August told him, "If you intend to live with me, you need to stop calling me 'Reverend.'"

Lucas laughed and asked, "What should I call you?"

"I will leave that to you. What do you want to call me?"

Lucas thought for a moment before answering, "Uncle August?" The new title was not what August anticipated, and perhaps sensing his disappointment, the boy explained, "I would call you 'Dad,' but that'd be confusing with my real dad."

"Uncle August is fine for now."

As the reverend was pushing himself out of his seat, Lucas locked him inside a hug. Disembracing, the boy looked at his torso and asked, "What do you have on? You feel bumpy." August pulled away from him to stand, and in so doing, a crystal was released from one of his fishing vest pockets. When the purple rock hit the ground, confusion took over Lucas' face. "Is that a crystal?" August swooped it up, but Lucas had not forgotten what he saw. "Why do you have a crystal? Was I feeling crystals on you?"

August opened his jacket to expose the crystal-laden vest he wore underneath, and he tried to explain the reason why their possession was not hypocritical. "To defeat an opponent, you both need to be playing the same game. You do not go to a chess match with checkers."

"I don't understand the connection to the crystals you have on."

"I have to use the tools of the Devil to defeat the Devil. I cannot go into the details right now. I just need you to trust me."

"I do trust you, Rev… Uncle August."

August's phone rang and, seeing the caller was Richard Glavin, he told Lucas, "I have to take this. Can you give me some privacy?" The boy nodded and stepped out of the room, closing the door behind him. August answered, "Richard, did you have them check out the clip on the news station's website? It is not a hoax! I can give them a demonstration in person, if they would like. Just do what you can." After hanging up, he yelled, "Damn!" He threw a hand to his mouth in shock that he uttered a curse word – something he had not done since college.

The challenged man fell into his desk chair and tried to think of a way to convince the TV executives that he was legitimate and they were fools for not recognizing his significance. "I should materialize right in their offices," he snickered while he fiddled with the stapler on the desk. His thoughts shifted to God's energy. "People can direct where they materialize. What happens to inanimate objects?" He clutched the stapler and prayed, and a moment later he was sending blue light into it until it disappeared. A second later it reappeared half buried in the wall beside him. August went to retrieve it, and instead of being able to pull it out of the wall, the visible portion broke off. The remainder had fused with the wall. From the experiment, he surmised, "Inanimate objects cannot hold the energy, so they can only travel a short distance." August heard a commotion outside his office, but was unable to make out the voices until the door blew open and Lily stormed in, followed by Cadence, Frederick and Lucas.

"August Briar, you pious wretch, give me back my daughter!"

"I will not have that tone used in the house of the Lord," he responded.

Frederick grabbed Lily's arm. "Let go of me!" she screamed, trying to pull free.

Maintaining his demeanor, August said, "Now, Lily, if you wish to speak to me, I will need your word, such as it is, that you will be more respectful in your manner of address."

"I always knew you to be hateful, but I didn't know your capacity for cruelty!"

Still unhappy with her tone, the reverend told her, "You will have to do better than that."

Cadence spoke up, "Reverend Briar, please, we just want to talk."

The reverend could sense sincerity in the younger woman. "You can go," he said to Frederick, dismissing him. He told the straggling boy, "You too, Lucas."

Once he was alone with the women, August said, "I apologize for the manhandling, but my security team has quickly become a necessary evil. You would be surprised how many people would love to harm God's prophet."

"No, I don't think I would," said Lily. "A security team, new property – God must be quite the revenue stream."

"Getting back to the reason for your visit, why do you think I would know the whereabouts of your wayward daughter?"

"She disappeared from her room last night, and I think you know exactly how I mean."

"No, I think not. Enlighten me." August paused to enjoy his pun, but when it elicited no response, he stopped smiling and said, "Lily, the last I saw of Iris, she was vandalizing my church on Friday night with her lascivious friend and some tourist boy, who I believe is an associate of this young lady here. Perhaps you should ask him."

"You mean the man you shot?" asked Lily.

"If you choose to trespass, you must accept the penalties exacted for that action. Besides, he seemed miraculously healthy the last I saw of him."

Frustrated, Lily threatened, "Look, either you tell me where she is, or I'll call the police."

"And tell them what?" August asked. "Do you have any witnesses who have seen me anywhere near your daughter since Friday? Are my fingerprints in her room? Do you have any evidence whatsoever? Do you even have a motive?"

Lily offered as a motive, "You want the vortex all to yourself."

August laughed. "Now that is a hoot, and I would love to be there when you make your case to the police. Who do you think they would believe – a kooky witch who sells cultic paraphernalia or a respected minister who heals the sick?"

"Heals the sick?" asked Lily.

"Perhaps you should occupy your time with newscasts instead of spell casts. If you did, you would know that God has touched me so that I may help His children."

"If you ever help anyone other than yourself, it's simply an accidental byproduct to your acts of self-glorification."

"As much as I enjoy lectures on morality from godless Wiccans with one toe already dipped in the Lake of Fire, I do have to work."

"August, listen to me," Lily implored. "You have to stay away from the vortex. You could be irreparably damaging our connection to the universe."

"Make sure you tell that to the police too. They will certainly have to believe you then. Leave me now. This is private property, and you know how I hate trespassers."

Lily stomped her way to the door, telling Cadence, "We're wasting our breath. Let's go."

"Give me a minute," said Cadence, and Lily left alone. "Reverend Briar, I saw the news. Can you really heal?"

August's curiosity was piqued by hers. "What is your infirmity?"

"Cancer," answered Cadence. "It's incurable."

"I tell you what. You convince your friend Gregor to leave town, and I will heal you."

Cadence lit up at the prospect, but asked, "Why are you so angry at Gregor?"

"I cannot abide people without love for God," August replied. "His presence pollutes the air of the righteous, and his very existence mocks the Creator. I want him gone!"

"I don't know how I can do that. Gregor is a protector, and he won't leave until he knows that Iris is safe. I wish she would just come back, so we could go."

August raised his hand to signal an end to their conversation. "You know my terms. Return when he is gone." As soon as Cadence left, Lucas and Frederick came back to the office. August told them, "I have a task to discuss with you both. Shut the door."

"Goodbye, Sedona!" Mitchell said as he drove out of town. He felt the weight of his history blow from his shoulders like a bug clinging to the hood of his speeding car and, at last, he could breathe.

On his way, he noticed a new sign in front of the house with the UFO runway. It read, "I have your underwear. Come see me to get it back."

"I'm never coming back here," Mitchell affirmed, and he tilted the rearview mirror down.

CHAPTER 40

"I've got to get to the vortex," Gregor said, once Lily and Cadence returned from their fruitless venture.

"You want to try again?" Travis asked. "What approach haven't we tried?"

"We have to keep trying!" Gregor told him. "There's no other way."

"I have another way," Cadence said, and all eyes turned to her. "Leave town."

Gregor was confused and disappointed at her idea. "I'm not leaving until she's back."

"Even if your leaving would bring her home?"

Travis asked, "What do you know?"

After some slight hesitation, Cadence answered, "I saw Iris."

Gregor jumped toward her. "What?"

Lily asked, "Where is she?"

"She was with Mitchell when I went to see him."

Gregor saw anger in Lily's face. "Why didn't you tell me she was there?"

"She told me not to. She thought you would try to stop her from leaving, and she really wanted to go clear her head."

Gregor backhanded Travis' arm and said, "Let's go," as he headed for the door.

"You're too late," Cadence warned.

Gregor turned to her. "What do you mean?"

"I caught them just as they were about to leave."

Travis asked, "Leave for where?"

"They didn't say. Iris wanted to get out of town for a few days… until you leave. I'm sorry, but she doesn't want to see you anymore."

Gregor was devastated. "I don't understand."

"It's my fault," suggested Lily. "I shielded her from problems when she was growing up, and I guess I stunted her ability to cope with stress. It's college all over again."

Gregor leaned against the wall. "One argument. I didn't think it was terminal."

Placing a hand on his shoulder, Travis asked Cadence, "Why go to Mitchell?"

"They were high school friends. In spite of their differences of opinion, she trusts him."

Gregor headed to the door and told his companions, "Let's go."

"What?" Travis asked. "You're giving up?"

"She's made her choice, and I… I have to honor it."

"Man, that's just wrong," Travis told him. "You should fight for her." He looked to Lily and asked, "Right?" but she shrugged with uncertainty.

Gregor told Lily, "Please let me know that she's home safely."

"I will," she promised.

Travis shook his head and told Cadence, "Well, let's go."

Cadence said to Lily, "If you don't mind, I'd like to stay with you until Iris comes back, to keep you company and make sure you're both okay. It might put Gregor's mind at ease."

Lily smiled and said, "You don't have to do that, but, of course, you're welcome to stay."

"We can't leave you," said Travis. "How will you get back?"

"I'll take a train."

Resigned, Travis spit out, "Fine."

With her feet in stirrups and a seatbelt around her waist, Iris sat at the zero-gravity commode. She reached between her legs for the tube topped with a cup, which she held to her body, and she turned on the suction that would remove her urination. She congratulated herself on learning the apparatus. When she felt she was done, she turned off the suction without realizing she had stopped it a second or two too soon. A few drops of liquid didn't make it into the tube, and after she unbuckled herself, they floated from the seat. When Iris saw the yellow drops, she screamed and tried to push away to avoid touching them. "Floaters!" She escaped the bathroom sans external moisture and closed the hatch. "Now how am I going to use it again? Maybe there's another bathroom."

On the off chance and to keep her mind occupied while she waited for the inevitable end of her journey, Iris explored the station again for anything she might've missed. She passed an exterior door in the docking compartment, which was at the opposite end of the station from the control room. "Ladies and gentlemen, we've reached the end of our tour. Please remember to check that you have all of your belongings." She took a deep breath and screamed in frustration.

"Iris?" a faint voice called.

"Gregor?" she asked with sudden hope, but she saw no one. She pulled her way to the exterior door, but through its window saw only stars, the sun and the blue light of the Earth.

"Iris!" she heard again, but in place of one faint voice was a small chorus of voices.

She looked over her shoulder at the direction from which the voices emanated. On the wall hung six space suits. Was someone inside them? She moved closer to one but could see nothing through the tinted visor. She took a deep breath, squinted from fear and opened the visor, wondering if she would find a face staring back. The suit was empty. She heard the loudest voice call her from inside the suit, "Iris move closer to the spacesuits! I can barely hear you."

She realized the same voice was coming from the radio headphones built into the helmets of the suits surrounding her. Iris removed the helmet of the suit closest to her and held it against her chest with the bottom facing her. "Who are you?" she asked.

"It's me, Finn."

"Finn!" She cried in relief. "I'm so glad to hear you. How did you know I was here?"

Finn told her, "Go back to the control room, where the fire was. I'll explain on the way."

As Iris made her way back to the damaged area, she told him, "I was trying to get the radio in the control room to work, and when it did—"

"The suit radios are on a UHF frequency that NASA typically doesn't monitor unless someone is on a spacewalk. Do you want to tell me how exactly you came to be where you are?"

Iris laughed. "I don't think you would believe me."

"Why? Are you going to tell me that an alien ship picked you up and dropped you off at the station on their way home?"

"You're in the ballpark."

"Okay, now I'm super-intrigued. Explain."

"I promise I will when I see you again." Iris floated to the burned console. "I'm here."

"I see you," said Finn.

"You do?"

"Look behind you at the environmental console," he said, and Iris turned around to face the only undamaged board. "I don't know if you can discern it, but the camera is in the middle."

Iris squinted at a tiny black dome on the panel. "I see it! Is NASA watching me now?"

"No. Can you keep a secret?"

Iris looked around and asked, "Who am I going to tell?"

"I worked on the console you're facing, and I placed the hidden camera in it. It's transmitting to my computer on an encrypted signal."

She smiled in the camera. "You nanny-cammed the space station?"

"I've always dreamed of going into space. I just wanted to watch them at work. I can't believe you beat me up there."

"I'm willing to trade places," she joked. A sudden jolt accompanied by a loud creaking noise sent Iris to the ceiling and knocked the helmet from her grasp. As she floated back down, she regained the helmet. "Finn, what was that?"

His tone was much more somber as he told her, "You've reached the mesopause."

"What does that mean?"

"You're skipping along the mesospheric layer of the atmosphere. The station is traveling too fast and coming in at too shallow an angle to immediately penetrate it."

Iris sighed and said, "Well that's good."

"It buys you a little time, but each interaction slows the station's speed. Eventually, when it slows enough, the station will enter the mesosphere."

"And then what?" When she heard no answer, she asked, "Finn?"

"The mesosphere is much more densely populated than the thermosphere, where you are now, meaning there are a greater number of particles with which to interact. The station will experience a surge in frictional heat and then... burn up."

Gregor stared out the window as they drove from Highway 179 to Interstate 17. "Travis, what did you do with those crystals you used on Cadence?"

Travis pointed with his thumb. "They're in back."

"If they still have a charge, I could use them to get to Iris."

"I thought you didn't want to fight for her."

Gregor said, "You've had much more experience with women than I have. Do you think the argument we had was justification to break up?"

"She obviously did. Women have different motivators and stressors than we do. You can't expect the same results from the same stimuli."

A news break came over the car radio. "In a video that has already gone viral, the preacher from Sedona appears to be healing a young boy…"

"Not this again," said Travis, turning the station.

"Turn it back!" Gregor ordered.

Travis jumped at his friend's raised voice, and he returned the radio to the news. "…statement released by the church, Briar claims God gave him the gift so he could heal the righteous. I'm guessing by that, if you have an STD, you're on your own…"

Gregor looked at Travis with disbelief and said, "She lied."

CHAPTER 41

Refresh. Refresh. Refresh. August hit the Refresh button on his web browser to track the ever-increasing hits on his video clip. Cadence walked into August's office. "Reverend Briar?"

Annoyed, August looked past the monitor at the intruder. "What news do you bring me?"

"Gregor left town with Travis. I told him Iris would come back once he was gone."

"Then you have done well."

Candence asked, "How does it work?"

He walked to stand before her. "As with any treatment, it starts with an assessment. My son believes you to be a God-fearing woman, but his judgment is a shaky barometer. Convince me."

"Convince you?"

"Do you fear me?"

"You or God?" she asked. "Yes, to both. I know I haven't always been a good Christian, but I'm trying, and Mitchell was helping me—"

August's phone rang, and he saw that Lucas was the caller. He had the boy and Frederick Jennings staked out across from Lily Wickline's house, and they had already reported Travis and Gregor's departure to him. Without bothering to dismiss Cadence, he sat at his desk and answered the call.

August heard Lucas say, "Travis came back. Gregor's not with him."

Fearing Travis had dropped Gregor off at the vortex, August told him, "Meet at the burning bush." He hung up and turned his attention back to Cadence. "Well, I am convinced. Shall we get you healed?"

"Where are we going?" she asked as he led her from the office.

"I need a quieter place to pray for you."

As the space station entered the Earth's shadow, Iris came to grips with Finn's grim prognosis. She knew she wouldn't survive if Gregor didn't find her. She asked Finn, "Would you call Gregor to tell him where I am?"

"Of course. Give me his num—" Finn began to ask before she interrupted him.

"Wait! It's too dangerous. Besides, if he were able to reach me, he would've by now."

"I don't understand. How?"

Avoiding an explanation of the vortex, Iris changed the subject. "Finn, you said that you could've repaired the damage and saved the station. Tell me how."

"Maybe I could have—"

"Maybe? You didn't say 'maybe' before."

Finn hemmed a little. "I might have expressed too much certainty before. I should have said that I believe I could, but I can't tell for certain without actually being there."

"Tell me how."

"I can't possibly explain everything."

"Try," she insisted.

"Iris, even if I were there right now and I could fix everything perfectly, we're too late."

Iris lowered her head. "I understand."

"I'm sorry."

Again facing the camera, she asked, "Could you talk to me?"

"About what?"

"I don't care. Just... talk."

Finn nodded. "You know, I always wanted to be an astronaut, and I've tried twice now to get into the program, but I failed the physical stress tests both times. What's it like to actually be up there?"

"Apart from the frightening aspects?" Iris replied with a nervous laugh. "It's surprisingly peaceful. Almost familiar. Like this is where we belong."

"Iris, I hate to ask again, but could you please tell me how you got there?"

She wanted to tell him about the vortex, but she also now believed her mother was right to promote its secrecy. "I need you to deliver a message to my mother." Iris turned away from the monitor when a blue light appeared to her right.

A smile spread across Iris' face. "You're here!" she said before dropping the helmet and pushing away from the camera.

"You're here?" Finn asked. "Who's there? Iris, stay out of the light! Iris!" He put his ear to the speaker and looked again at the monitor. "I can't hear you! Come back to the camera."

On the Hexum Space Station, Gregor had materialized in the control room, parallel to and facing the ceiling. "Iris?" he asked when he heard her voice.

Floating above his head at the other end of the room, Iris answered, "I'm here!"

Disoriented, Gregor looked up to see her grabbing a bar grip on the wall and pushing her way toward him. When Iris reached him, she tucked her legs to spin herself into a position that mirrored his. The two embraced and kissed with relief and passion.

"I'm so happy to see you," she said between kisses. "How did you get to the vortex?"

"I didn't." Gregor showed her the cotton bag of crystals clutched in his right hand. "Travis had some charged crystals."

"Thank goodness for Travis." Iris kissed him again. "I can't believe you're here."

"Where exactly is here?" Gregor looked around the compartment and answered before Iris had a chance. "Oh sh... We're on the space station? The one that's going down?" Still adjusting to the lack of gravity, he tried to right his position, bumping his head on a console.

"Be careful," Iris warned after the fact. "You get used to the weightlessness after a while. Just avoid the sleeping quarters. There's some floating vomit from when I first arrived."

Gregor ran his fingers through Iris' hair, which haloed her like a kelp forest submitting to coaxing waves. "I thought I wouldn't see you again. How did you get here?"

"August kidnapped me and brought me here last night."

"I knew it!" Gregor took a brief moment to celebrate his intuition and curse the minister.

"Let's talk when we're home. We need to leave. Now." She wrapped herself around him.

Gregor smiled at her and was just closing his eyes to meditate when he saw a blue flash from the adjoining kitchen compartment. After the light subsided, August floated before them.

As he stabilized himself parallel to the floor, the reverend tilted his head to see the young couple. "You are a slippery serpent," he told Gregor. "No matter the barriers I build, you keep finding a way around. How did you find her?"

"I have a better question," said Gregor, clutching the nearest bar grip while keeping one arm on Iris. "How could you bring her up here to die?" He glanced below and saw the control room ended under his feet with no connecting module. To his side, he saw a door with a latch wheel and circular window, through which he could see white boxes. *Storeroom.* He looked up at August and realized he was blocking the only way out of the control room. "Does the Bible condone killing?"

"Repeatedly," August answered.

With his arm around Iris, Gregor applied subtle pressure to pull her further away from August.

Iris asked the minister, "What did we do to you?"

"Not just me. Any shepherd would kill a wolf that could attack his flock. I have a divine duty to protect all those you would take from God. 'For false Christs and false prophets shall rise, and shall show signs and wonder, to seduce, if it were possible, even the elect.'"

"We're not prophets, false or otherwise," exclaimed Iris.

"You could be perceived as such! Both of you know how to heal. Where does that leave me? If others wield the same power, no one will understand that I am God's chosen prophet! I will not allow it. I have waited too long."

Gregor saw a blue light in August's torso, so he forced the bag of crystals into Iris' hands and pushed her back. "Storeroom!"

As the energy engulfed him, August asked, "How cold do you think it is outside?"

Iris struggled with the latch wheel on the storeroom door but couldn't budge it. "It's stuck!" Gregor tried pushing himself to Iris to help her open the door, but before he could, the space station bumped the atmosphere, bouncing all three off the floor and the ceiling.

Once stabilized, August held the edge of a food cabinet and

propelled himself into the control room, his blue hand reaching for them.

Gregor kicked off the wall to reach a bar grip on the ceiling and drew his knees to his chest to avoid August's touch. The reverend's momentum carried him under Gregor's feet, toward Iris. Gregor stomped his feet onto August's back to force him to the floor. With one hand pushing from the ceiling to keep the reverend stationary, Gregor reached for Iris' hand with the other and threw her into the kitchen compartment.

August felt behind his back for Gregor's ankle, but the younger man stomped him again, propelling himself into the kitchen. Iris shut the hatch between the kitchen and the control room and locked the handle. She looked through the window in the hatch. "I don't see him."

Gregor told her, "We need to go now!"

"I'm ready." Iris held up the bag.

The two embraced with the bag between them and closed their eyes to meditate. Through his eyelids he soon saw the blue light, although he could not yet feel the energy. Gregor peeked to check the energy's progression and was surprised to find the light beside them. "Iris!"

Startled, she saw the cause for Gregor's alarm. The hatch separating them from August was aglow. Seconds later it was gone, and August was before them with his palm facing their direction. A blue flash on the other side of the exterior window caught Gregor's attention, and he glanced to see the hatch materializing a few meters outside the station.

Gregor took the bag from Iris and swung it to August's head, knocking him backwards. He returned it to her and nodded toward the adjoining gym compartment.

In the control room, August placed his hands on the burned navigator console and forced energy into it and tried directing its destination.

While Iris headed for the gym, Gregor stayed behind to give her time to leave. "What are you doing?" he asked August.

"Getting rid of you one way or another," August answered as the console disappeared, leaving exposed and sparking wires.

Iris screamed when the console reappeared in her path.

Gregor looked over his shoulder at Iris and realized August's intent. "Oh crap. Iris, go!"

"I'm not leaving without you!"

"He's trying to materialize objects inside us. Go!" Gregor looked back at August, who was pulling on a bar grip, propelling himself into the kitchen.

Iris made her way around the floating console and entered the gym compartment.

Gregor tried to back away from August, who was floating toward him, but he was too slow to avoid the minister's grasping of each wrist. With August now above him, he struggled to gain the leverage he needed to break away.

August sent the blue light into Gregor.

"Move down!" Iris yelled before pushing the loose console hurtling toward the two men.

Gregor looked at the floor behind him and saw a bar grip. Twisting his right wrist free from August's left hand, he reached for the bar grip and pulled himself down.

Seeing the approaching console, August released Gregor's other wrist and put his hands up to defend against the impact. As the console connected, pushing him backwards, the energy from his hands drained into it, causing it to convert. It reappeared embedded in one of the oxygen tanks in the control room behind him. August's reverse motion continued until his back slammed into the rogue console, which broke away from the tank, resulting in the release of a fine stream of ejecta. A spark from the exposed wires ignited the stream into a mini flame thrower. The flame's cusp touched the left sleeve of August's jacket. The reverend screamed in pain, as he pushed himself away from the fire. He removed the jacket but not before the flames had burned the now exposed skin of his arm and the left side of his face. He cried in agony for only a moment before the crystals in his vest began healing him.

When Gregor saw August's skin repairing, his only thought was to head to the gym.

August sighed once the healing completed and pain was gone. He hurried toward Gregor, but stopped at the kitchen table to convert it. When Gregor entered the gym, part of the table materialized in front of him, and he bumped his head on the corner protruding through the roof – the remainder extending outside the station. "I am getting better at this," August growled.

Dazed, Gregor saw Iris near the stationary bike. "Iris, I can't keep holding him off. You've got to leave now!"

"I'm not going alone!"

"If you don't, we both die. Please."

August zoomed into the gym just when the station again bumped the atmosphere. He fell on top of Gregor as the younger man's back hit the floor, knocking the wind out of him. When they returned to weightlessness, August held him and tried again to convert him.

"Gregor!"

"Iris! Leave!"

Perhaps wondering how Gregor intended for Iris to leave, August looked at her clutching a bumpy, cotton bag – the same bag Gregor had hit him with. "Crystals," he muttered. He released Gregor and pushed off his shoulders to get to Iris.

Realizing August had a new target, Gregor grabbed the minister's ankles and kicked his toes up to the table protruding from the ceiling. Gregor used his new footing to pull August underneath him and hurl him back into the kitchen. "Iris, go now!" Gregor ordered as he kicked off the table corner – causing it to break from the ceiling – and propelled himself into the kitchen. He grabbed

August's shoulders from behind and kicked off the food cabinet to keep them moving forward into the control room.

With her feet inserted into the stationary bike's pedals for stability and tears floating from her eyes, Iris squeezed the bag of crystals and meditated.

From the control room near the flaming jet of oxygen, Gregor could see the blue light emanating from the gym, and he knew Iris would now be safe. Still holding August from behind, he wondered about the numerous protrusions from the fishing vest that he could feel all along his torso. *What does he have in his pockets?* He had little time to ponder as August's elbow found his right cheek.

"Get off me!" August screamed. The two were now drifting close to the fire.

Gregor struggled to maintain his hold. He reached for the vest, ripping one of the pockets. A lazulite crystal floated away toward the hatch to the storeroom. Shocked, Gregor said, "A crystal." He realized the other pockets contained them as well. "You hypocrite!"

August took advantage of Gregor's loosened grasp and turned to face him. He wrapped his fingers around a bar grip and punched the younger man in the face.

Gregor flew backwards with drops of blood from his nose floating in his wake. He focused on August's attire. *I've got to get that vest.*

The station bumped the atmosphere, and both men bounced off the floor. Gregor used the upward momentum to reach the bar grip above him, and he pushed himself feet first toward August, his soles connecting with the minister's face. Gregor grabbed at the buttons of the vest.

August sent his knees to the other man's head. The two wrestled for dominance until Gregor was again behind August. He wrapped his arms around the minister's neck and tried to lock him into a sleeper hold. August held Gregor's forearm, forcing energy into him. Gregor continued with his hold, even as he saw the blue light entering his arms. He didn't know if he could put August to sleep before the minister would gain control of him through conversion, but he was out of options. The light traveled through Gregor's body, and he could feel the familiar tingle that preceded the change from physicality. His time was out. He released August to sever the conduit.

As August, still blue with energy, gasped for air, Gregor pushed himself to the floating crystal. Once he had it, he jerked the wheel latch to the storeroom, and it began turning. He entered the small room and locked the hatch behind him. Afraid to close his eyes, he meditated while looking at the white-cloth covered packages Velcroed to the walls of the tiny room. He held the crystal in cupped hands and said, "I hope you're enough." He concentrated until, to his great relief, a blue light emerged from his torso.

Two blue hands penetrated the hatch – without damaging its integrity – and snatched the crystal from him. The crystal almost phased with the hands that held it and slipped through the hatch. Startled, Gregor paused before reaching for the handle to unlock the hatch, but the hands reappeared and held the handle until it converted and disappeared. Gregor was now trapped in the store-room. He looked through the window in the hatch to see what August would do next.

In the control room, a blue August threw aside the hatch handle he had just taken and made his way to the flaming jet of oxygen. He placed his blue right hand inside the fire, and in a few seconds, the flame disappeared.

Back in the storeroom, the converted flame appeared on one of the packages, which began to burn. Panicked, Gregor pounded on the hatch. Smoke filled the room, choking him. He backed away from the hatch to the furthest point from the fire. His only hope now was that the smoke would take him from consciousness before the flames touched his skin.

CHAPTER 42

In the control room of the Hexum Space Station, August was no longer blue as he looked through the hatch window at the smoky storeroom. A noise from behind prompted him to turn around.

Iris stood in the control room with her feet locked in a nearby bar grip and both hands hurling the now-free stationary bike to his face. The force sent the back of August's head to the hatch, knocking him out. Iris took the bag of crystals she had released and pushed the unconscious minister out of her way. She touched the hatch and converted it.

Once the hatch was gone and drifting in space, smoke pillared into the control room. "Gregor!" Iris called. Unable to see into the storeroom, she let go of the bag of crystals so she could feel her way through the smoky room but, as she was about to enter, Gregor emerged from the gray cloud. She took his hand and led him into the more breathable air of the gym.

In between raspy coughs, Gregor sputtered, "I thought... you... left."

"I told you I wouldn't leave without you. I hid until August had his back to me."

Gregor coughed, saying, "I could've used you sooner."

"I really thought you had him," she said with a smile.

Out of the gray smoke that now engulfed most of the control room and kitchen, August came forth. He touched the largest object available, the food cabinet, and forced energy into it.

From the next compartment over, Gregor pointed at August and yelled, "Look!"

Iris noticed the blue light from August was extending beyond the cabinet and into the surrounding wall. "August, stop! You'll kill us all!"

Gregor told Iris, "Hang on to something." She locked her arms into a bar grip, and Gregor pushed himself forward to the hatch that would close off the gym from the kitchen, where August was. As he tried to shut it, the food cabinet and part of the wall converted to energy, creating a hole to the void outside.

The smoke and all loose items, including August, were sucked through the large aperture. Gregor had grabbed the treadmill just before the vacuum began its tremendous pull on his body. Iris was clinging to the bar grip for dear life. With his foot, Gregor kicked at the hatch. On his third attempt, the hatch slammed shut.

"Are you okay?" Gregor asked.

"I'm fine. Is he... gone?"

Gregor nodded and sighed. Exhausted, he clung to Iris and rested his head on her shoulder until he realized her hands were empty. "Where are the crystals?"

Iris gasped and looked toward the hatch window.

The station again skirted the atmosphere, and the jolt was too much for the broken kitchen module, which cracked from the top and bottom of the hole August had created. When the two cracks met, the portion of the space station comprised of the kitchen, storeroom and control room separated from the remainder. They looked out the window to see the broken section rotating nearby, along with the debris from inside. They could now see the large solar panels attached to that section's exterior like the wings of a

Phoenix. Beyond that, the wall that once separated the kitchen from the control room entered the atmosphere and ignited from the friction.

Realizing a similar fate awaited them, Iris looked at him with tears flowing. "I'm sorry."

Gregor held her face and asked, "Why?"

"I should've held onto the bag."

"You're not at fault." Gregor kissed and embraced her, and the two rotated parallel to the floor like a rotisserie. "You know, I once danced naked in the rain outside my college dorm."

Iris laughed at the context and timing of his odd segue.

Gregor explained, "Everyone was gone for the Christmas holiday except me and a few foreign students. After years of hiding my scars behind long-sleeve shirts and long pants, I had an overwhelming urge to free myself. I put my speakers to the window, took off my clothes and went outside to dance."

Grinning at the image in her head, Iris asked, "Did anyone see you?"

"Not that I know of. I tell you, I had never felt so free. Until I met you."

Iris held him tighter, resting her cheek on his chest. "What brought that up?"

"I just wanted to tell you something I had never told anyone else."

Iris knew he was trying to keep her mind off their impending descent, and she offered her own secret. "I didn't leave college because I was homesick."

"Really?" he asked with mock accusation. "What's the story?"

"This is embarrassing, but my roommate talked me into going to a soothsayer with her."

"You? I thought you didn't believe—"

"I don't, and don't ever tell my mother I went. I'll deny it. Anyway, my roommate didn't want to go alone, and I was trying to be a friend."

"Did she tell you your lucky numbers and that you would meet a handsome stranger?"

"Nothing so cliché, and forty-four." Gregor tilted his head, and she explained, "My lucky number. That was her only revelation of levity. Apart from that, she was really quite foreboding. She told me a darkness would emerge from la tierra de las rocas rojas."

"Tierra de?"

"Land of the red rocks. I'm sorry. I remember it in her words. She said a darkness would emerge from Sedona unless I returned to guide the guarda de la luz – guardian of the light."

"That sounds like a religious prophecy. I'm surprised you believed her."

"I didn't, but then to prove herself, she brought up past events in my life that she couldn't possibly have known. Private events. She scared the crap out of me. As time passed, I convinced myself that my roommate must have fed her the information so she could get rid of me. But then you showed up."

"You think that prediction was about me?"

"She also said I would fall in love with the guardian and we would be one."

Gregor had not heard another woman connect love to him since his mother died and, even though he felt it, the word caught him by surprise. "Are you in love?"

"That depends," Iris answered. "Are you?"

In answer, Gregor kissed her.

The space station skirted against the atmosphere again. Iris clenched her face, and once it was over, she opened her eyes and said, "You shouldn't have come for me."

Gregor assured her, "I'm where I want to be."

Another tear floated from Iris' eyes. "I do love you."

Gregor placed his hands on her face and said, "I love you too, my beautiful Iris." They kissed and rotated in their embrace, preparing to die in each other's arms.

They floated closer to the hatch that once led to the kitchen, and Iris noticed something on the other side of the circular window. Hanging in the night sky like a pearl mounted in onyx was the white cotton bag of crystals. "Gregor, look!"

"The crystals!" Gregor moved to the hatch window for a closer look, and Iris joined him. The bag floated apart from the other debris, above the detached section of the space station. "We have to get that bag."

"How?" Iris asked before an idea struck her. "We can use the spacesuits!"

"Where are they?"

"At the end of the station. I think it's the docking area." The station experienced a tremendous bump against the atmosphere. "They're becoming much more frequent."

Gregor floated back to the window. "We're lucky. The bag's closer now."

"Let's get the suits."

"Iris, how long do you think we'll need to get there and suit up?"

"I don't know. Ten minutes maybe."

"I don't think we have time for that."

"We have to," Iris argued. "It's the only way."

"No, it's not. Remember what your friend said? Finn?"

She shook her head. "Gregor, I don't like what you're thinking."

"Freeze or burn. Either way, we only have a moment. At least one way we have a shot."

"You saw what happened with August. If we open the door, we'll shoot out like a bullet."

Gregor put his hands on her shoulders. "I can grab it. I know I can."

Iris thought for a moment as she saw another piece of debris light up. "Let's do it."

Gregor positioned himself with the hatch above his head. "Get on my back, and hold on tight." Iris locked her arms under his, holding onto his shoulders. "Are you ready?"

Iris pressed as hard as she could against his back and answered, "Yes."

Gregor placed both hands on the handle to the hatch and squeezed. "Here goes." He was about to pull it when the space station again bounced off the atmosphere, jerking his hands free.

Iris screamed, and Gregor tried to calm her, "It's okay. It's okay." He looked through the window. "I don't see the bag." The solar panels of the other section rotated like a windmill in a light breeze. When one panel moved upward, they spotted the bag on the other side. He sighed, "It's still there. Just a little further away. Are you okay?"

"Can we reach it now?"

"We have no other options."

The station jerked and moaned, sending them to the floor.

"Hurry!" Iris exclaimed as she latched onto his back again.

"All right," Gregor said, squeezing the handle. "Iris, whatever happens—" He turned the handle sooner than anticipated, and the two lovers ejected from the space station.

CHAPTER 43

The cold vacuum of space sheathed Iris and Gregor's skin in excruciating pain and an almost paralytic numbness. With her face buried between his shoulder blades, Iris knew she was screaming, but she heard nothing, and the lack of sound chilled her further.

As momentum carried them to the side of the detached modules, Gregor reached for the white bag of crystals. Still meters away, their forward motion slowed. The bag was almost within reach when they came to a stop. Gregor, his eyes frosting over, tried to corkscrew for the few needed centimeters. His fingers caught the corner of the bag.

He brought the bag to his chest, embraced it and meditated. He could no longer close his eyes, and his vision was almost gone, but he could see the edge of the solar panels rotating upward right below them. Gregor concentrated with all the mental strength he could muster as his mind began to shut down. The solar panel turned closer, but a blue light enveloped the young couple, and they disappeared.

Gregor and Iris materialized atop the plateau of his vortex, both lying on their sides. Shivering, he released the bag and, since the ice crystals in his eyes blinded him, he felt for Iris' hand on his chest. He wanted to call her name but couldn't. He thought he heard far-away voices but couldn't distinguish the words. He placed the palm of his other hand on the ground and tried to siphon enough energy from the vortex to heal them both. He was weak, but he could feel the tingle. The energy turned them blue, but they remained physical as they healed.

When Gregor was strong enough, he decided he could no longer wait to check on Iris' condition. He moved his hand and let the energy ebb away. Warmth entered his body. He blinked, and he could see. He saw four legs, and one of them was coming at him.

A shirtless Lucas kicked Gregor in the torso as August yelled, "I will send you to Hell!"

"August, stop it!" Lily screamed from behind Gregor.

Iris' arms slipped away from him, and Gregor pushed himself up to a seated position to survey his surroundings. August had what he presumed to be the boy's shirt draped over his shoulders, and Gregor knew that the minister had endured a similar journey since he last saw him on the space station. To the side, he saw Travis and Cadence standing with a gun aimed at them by a large man. Gregor looked over his shoulder and saw Lily kneeling to help her shivering daughter sit. "Iris!" He reached out to her. "Are you okay?"

Her teeth chattering, Iris nodded and touched his hand.

"He tried to kill me!" August told Lily with a hard kick to the side of Gregor's head.

"Gregor!" Iris called as he fell backwards and into unconsciousness.

As August stood over Gregor, admiring his handiwork, Lily asked, "What are you going to do, August? Kill us all? Have you completely lost your mind?"

"Your souls are dead anyway," August spewed at her. "What does your flesh matter?"

Lucas sidled the minister. "Reverend, could I ask you something in private?"

"Now?"

"It's important."

August told Iris, "Stand up." When Iris remained huddled over Gregor, trying to awaken him, he nodded to Frederick Jennings, who forced her to her feet.

"No!" screamed Iris, wobbly-legged from her time without gravity.

August ordered, "Keep him unconscious and the rest of them standing. Do not let them close their eyes, and if anyone starts turning blue, shoot them all!"

As Frederick herded Iris and Lily with Cadence and Travis, August huddled with Lucas. "What is it?" August pointed to Gregor. "The longer he stays here, the more dangerous he becomes."

"You want them killed?" asked Lucas

"You have seen what he can do. Mix that with the guile of the Devil, and the stupid people of this world will elevate him above God! Think of the lost souls blinded by the wonder of his deeds and entrapped by the murk of his words."

"I know him and the witches are lost causes, but do you know for sure about the other two?" Lucas nodded toward Travis and Cadence. "Isn't she a Christian?"

August knew why the boy spoke up for her. "You are just like Mitchell."

With obvious offense, Lucas asked, "What do you mean by that?"

"First John 2:16." He waited for Lucas to recite the passage, but when he hesitated, he began it for him, "For all that is in the world—"

Lucas finished the verse. "The lust of the flesh, and the lust of the eyes, and the pride of life, is not of the Father, but is of the world."

"Lucas, these are the moments that determine the kind of man you are to be. Will you be a soldier for God, or will you be a disappointment that He casts from His house? Those two are purveyors of Gregor's message. Left alive, they will spread his gospel. We must douse every demonic spark with the waters of righteousness."

Lucas raised his new gun and said, "Let's put out the fire."

While August and Lucas confabbed, their conscious captives stood at the lethal end of Frederick's gun and watched blood trickle from Gregor's forehead to a crimson puddle on the ground a meter from the gunman's boot. "Why doesn't he heal?" asked Travis.

Iris answered, "He's out of energy. We both are."

Unable to bear the pang in his chest, Travis averted his eyes to the blue sky, which was tinting orange from the dipping sun. He didn't see a scenario in which the minister would let them walk away for he had to know they would report the kidnapping. Left to his own devices, August would ensure none of them saw the sun return to the sky. Travis needed to think.

Iris told Frederick, "I need to see if he's okay. Please, let me check on him."

"He's just sleeping." Frederick grinned and added, "But you could check on me."

Lily wrapped an arm around Iris and said, "You're freezing."

"I'm fine," she replied. "By the way, what are you all doing here?"

Lily answered, "Those two hooligans brought Travis and me here at gunpoint. Cadence was already here with a guard down in the canyon. August showed up out of nowhere a few minutes before you and Gregor." Lily turned to Cadence. "Why were you here?"

Cadence dropped her chin and muttered, "I need to confess something to you all."

Lily told her, "A confession has little value to those who already know the truth."

"You know?"

Travis nodded. "Gregor figured it out before he left to get Iris. I told Lily everything."

"Know what?" asked Iris.

Her mother answered, "She led us to believe that you had left town with Mitchell."

Iris looked at the prevaricator with shaming disbelief. "Why would you do that?"

Through tears, she replied, "Reverend Briar promised to heal me if I convinced Gregor to leave town without you."

Shaking now from anger, Iris pointed toward Gregor and told her, "This is all your fault!"

Cadence looked to Travis. "I'm sorry."

Travis responded, "I forgive you."

"What?" Cadence asked. "Just like that? I don't deserve your forgiveness."

"You came here to kill yourself," he explained. "Somewhere along the way, you found the will to live." He wrapped her in a consoling embrace.

August returned to the group with the boy, who looked as if he were about to win a prize at a carnival stand. The reverend zeroed in on Iris. "How did Gregor find you?"

Iris glanced at the others. "Let them leave, and I'll tell you whatever you want to know."

Without hesitation, August said, "A bargain with the Devil is no bargain at all."

"Then I forgot."

"By choice or coercion, you will tell me. I will not barter with you, but I can state with certainty that your refusal to cooperate will not aid your associates." August looked at Frederick and Lucas, prompting both to raise their weapons to the captives. "How did he find you?"

Iris replied, "He thought about me, and the energy took him to where I was."

"It is not just locations?" August asked. "The energy can find people as well. All I have to do is think of someone, and I can see them. Face to face." He walked to the center of the plateau and pointed to the hostages, telling the gunmen, "Watch them until I come back. Same rules, Frederick."

"August, no!" shouted Lily. "The vortex isn't a toy. You don't realize the consequences."

August ignored her warning and prayed until he was gone, and once the light dissipated, Lucas asked, "Is this place one of those vortexes?"

"What did you think it was?" asked Iris.

Lily frowned at the boy. "Where are your parents?"

Seconds later, August rematerialized on the plateau, looking surprised to be there. He stormed back over to Iris. "You lied to me!"

"I did not! Who were you trying to find?"

August nodded to Frederick and ordered, "Shoot her mother."

"No!" Iris screamed. "It's the truth! I swear it."

Lily guessed, "You looked for God, didn't you?" The reverend pivoted at her question. "What does that tell you?"

Maintaining his silence, August walked over to Gregor, where Lucas now stood guard.

"He's hiding from you!" shouted Cadence. "Why would He let you see Him? You're an evil man, and you will never see God."

"Shut up!" August growled.

Travis grabbed Cadence's arm as she stepped from the captives. "What are you doing?"

Cadence broke from his grip and continued toward August, under two watchful guns. "You think you serve God? Where is, 'Thou shalt kidnap?' written in the Bible?"

"I said shut up!"

"I know 'Thou shalt not murder' is in there somewhere."

"Killing you all would not be murder," said August "It would be punishment for disobeying God."

She pointed to her friends. "You need to let us go and beg for God's forgiveness."

"I need no forgiveness from God." August growled, "He should ask my forgiveness! This situation is His doing. His will. Not mine."

"You've turned your back on God for your own glory," Cadence continued.

Seeing August's anger seething like magma under thin crust, Travis called, "Cadence!"

Undeterred, she continued past Frederick, who looked at August for direction, but the reverend only had eyes for her. Travis realized she wanted to die, either to complete her mission or to give them an opportunity to escape, so he ran for her as she goaded the minister further, "That story sounds familiar. You're not following God. You're emulating the Devil!"

August screamed in anger. He grabbed the rifle from Lucas and aimed it at Cadence.

"No!" Travis yelled, and he jumped on Cadence, knocking her to the ground.

August couldn't adjust his aim before pulling the trigger. The bullet missed Cadence and struck the upper left torso of the person behind her.

Iris fell backwards. Lily tried to catch her but was only able to soften her fall to the ground with her forearm.

Cadence, now lying underneath Travis, asked him, "Why did you do that?"

Travis pushed off Cadence and ran to Iris to apply pressure to the wound.

With Iris' head cradled in her lap, Lily lied to comfort her, "You're going to be okay. The vortex will heal you." Unable to speak, Iris nodded. "We'll just stay here until you're healed."

Cadence sat up and screamed at August, "Heal her!"

August handed the rifle to Lucas. He told the gunmen, "You two do the rest."

Travis yelled, "Wait!" and told Cadence, "Keep applying pressure." Once his hands were replaced with hers, he stood to tell August. "Gregor can take you to God, but I guarantee you if we're all dead when he wakes, he'll die before he tells you anything."

August argued, "If I cannot find him, the Devil's servant certainly would not know how."

"You're wrong." Travis pointed skyward. "The Devil was cast out of Heaven, but he lived there once. Do you remember the location of your childhood home?" He could see his argument was being considered by the reverend. "Gregor said that the Devil told him where Heaven is."

"Why would the Devil tell him?"

"He tells all his disciples. Do you really think there won't be another war for Heaven? You can't fight a war if you don't know where the battlefield is."

Cadence asked, "Travis, what are you saying?"

"You know as well as I do Gregor has changed since we've been here. He's not the same person we knew before he found this vortex. Why do you think that is? I didn't tell you before, but he's been coming here to walk with the Devil." She was about to retort, but Lily grabbed her hand to shut her up. Travis asked August, "This energy makes you powerful, doesn't it?"

"Yes," August answered.

"You feel more powerful than any normal man because it gives you God's powers – healing, the ability to travel anywhere in an instant. This vortex was put here by the Devil to give his army the power of God and to give them a route to Heaven when the time is right to attack."

"The Devil?" asked Lucas. "Uncle August, if this place is evil—"

"We must use the tools of the Devil to fight the Devil!" screamed August. "Behold, there appeared a chariot of fire, and horses of fire, and parted them both asunder; and Elijah went up by a whirlwind into Heaven." He turned to Travis and said, "If Gregor did take me to God, He would surely punish me for bringing a follower of the one He cast out."

Travis pointed out, "You're forgetting that you're the one with the power. Gregor is out." August looked at the bag of crystals near the unconscious man. "Once you're almost there, you could... let go of him."

Cautious, August asked, "Are you offering up your friend's life to save your own?"

Travis released a heavy breath and waved his arm back at the others. "Our lives."

August cast a smile to Lucas and Frederick, saying, "The son of Satan has his own Judas Iscariot," eliciting chuckles from both. He kicked Gregor in the stomach. "Wake up!"

Coughing awake, Gregor grabbed at the new pain as August forced him to his feet. "Iris," he called although he had not yet seen her. His eyes moved from Travis to the three huddled women, and an anguished look befell him.

Iris looked at Gregor through half-closed eyes, her hands resting on the ground.

"Iris!" Gregor started toward her but was stopped by Lucas' rifle aimed at his forehead. Gregor looked at the eldest man, who was now holding tight to his arm. "You shot her?"

August told him, "And I will heal her once you take me on a final journey."

When Lily relayed the situation's direness through her eyes, he screamed, "She's dying!"

"Then I will bring her back," August assured him.

Tears pouring from his eyes, Gregor said, "I'm not taking you anywhere until you let me help her." Unconcerned with Lucas' line of fire, he grabbed the nearby bag of crystals and started toward Iris.

"Stop him!" August ordered, and Frederick moved into his path. The reverend took the bag and hurled it to the canyon below. "Your time with this power is over."

Eyes down, Gregor reminded him, "I couldn't take you if I wanted. I'm out of energy."

"I will provide the power. You provide the direction."

"Where?"

"You are taking me to God."

Gregor sneered at the minister, asking, "Are you insane?"

"Gregor, he knows," said Travis. "Just tell him what you told me. About God."

"That he's a myth?" he asked with a slight shrug.

The question prompted a swift punch in the gut from August. "Blasphemer!"

Travis announced, "God is in the sun!"

Clutching his abdomen, Gregor eyed his friend in complete confusion, while August dismissed the statement outright, saying, "Do you find me stupid?"

"It's the truth! Gregor told me in confidence. There's a portal in the sun that will lead you directly to Heaven. The only way to get there is to convert to pure energy, which is what the vortex does." Travis hammered the point home. "The Devil put his vortex here, in Sedona, the heart of cultic worship, where his followers congregate in droves." He pointed to the ground. "This vortex is the key to Heaven."

"Exodus 24:17," muttered Lucas.

"What?" asked August.

Lucas recited, "And the sight of the glory of the LORD was like devouring fire." His voice growing louder, he referenced another scripture, "Psalms 89:36, 'His seed shall endure—'"

August finished for him, "...forever and his throne as the sun before me. He threw Man out of the Garden of Eden and stationed angels and a revolving sword of fire east of it, guarding the path to the Tree of Life."

"Travis, what are you saying?" Gregor asked.

Travis appeared to get angry. "Gregor, he's not playing around. He'll kill us all unless you help him. Forget your loyalty to the Devil, and think about your loyalty to your friends."

Gregor told August, "Don't listen to him. He's not telling you the truth."

"Your protestations only add veracity to your betrayer's words," said August. "I will settle the matter with a test." The reverend positioned himself for prayer and told Lucas and Frederick, "Kill them all."

Gregor screamed, "No!" and ran between the gunmen and the others.

"Wait!" yelled Travis, raising his bloodied hands. "The sun is three-hundred-thirty-three-thousand times the mass of the Earth. Do you really think you can find the portal without knowing exactly where it is? You need Gregor."

August hesitated. "What if I am never able to find it on my own?" he whispered.

"Why should I help you?" Gregor asked in a tone without the slightest lilt. "You've already said you're going to kill us all."

August turned to Lucas and Frederick and said, "Once we have gone, just let them go," but with the sincerity of a cardsharp.

Gregor scoffed. "I'm to believe you? I need more from you—"

Travis scolded him, "Gregor, stop being so selfish!"

"Selfish?" asked Gregor, further confused. "What are you talking about?"

Travis responded, "He's just given you the opportunity to save us, and you need more? Who are you? I swear, since we've come to Sedona... I don't know why I'm surprised. From the first day I met you, I had a feeling you were going to turn out to be a rogue, and today I realize that's exactly who you are. For our sakes, go with him."

Gregor didn't know what to think anymore. He didn't understand why Travis was lying about the sun or the reason for his apparent animosity. Was it some mad diversion? He looked to Iris, Lily and Cadence. Perhaps Travis was right that if he didn't go with August now, they would all never leave the plateau alive. At least if he did go, a chance existed that the reverend would be truthful to his word, letting the others survive. Without saying another word, he walked to the minister and sat before him. He resolved to try occupying him at the sun as long as possible, hoping that August would run out of energy and they would both incinerate. If August tired of the fruitless search beforehand, however, he would drop Gregor into the fire and return to kill the rest. Either way, Gregor knew his life would be forfeited once August converted him.

The reverend grabbed Gregor's forearms with no thought to the younger man's comfort. He prayed with both pairs of eyes locked in a stare. The blue light came from his torso and soon enveloped them both. They converted to particles of light that swirled together and disappeared, but something was different about this experience.

Unable to remove his thoughts from Iris, Gregor stayed connected, in part, to the plateau.

A wind swirled around the plateau, picking up dust from the ground and giving a nebulous but physical substance to the vortex.

"I thought the vortex was invisible," said Travis. "Are we supposed to be able to see it like this?"

Lily replied, "I've never heard of a vortex inciting winds within the path of its energy, but I have no other explanation."

Cadence shivered. "I'm getting cold."

"It's Gregor," Iris mumbled. "His thoughts are here. Connected."

"Oh no," said Travis. "He needs to stop!"

Lily said, "I don't think he realizes what he's doing."

Cadence asked, "What happens when they reach the sun if he's still connected?"

Travis looked at them with renewed worry. "We need to get off this plateau. Now!"

As the air had thinned and chilled, Travis wondered if he had done the right thing. After all, it was the only plan he could think of under the stress of imminent death. Would Gregor understand? He could only hope the seed he had planted would not go untended. At present, he had more immediate concerns. *Light from the sun reaches the Earth in just over eight minutes, so assuming they travel at light speed, we have about sixteen minutes for them to reach the sun and the sun to reach us. If I can't get us away – far enough away – from here...* He didn't want to finish his thought. Travis left his friends and approached the gunmen, who stood between them and the crevice that led to the ladder and escape. Although he knew the answer, he had to ask Lucas, "So what are the chances of your letting us go like the minister promised?"

Lucas, his hair blowing from the strange wind, smiled and answered, "You have to use the tools of the Devil to fight the Devil. That includes lying."

"That's what I figured."

408

As one entity of energy, Gregor and August reached the midpoint of the astronomical unit that measured their journey. Although he did not realize the physical impact his connection was having on the plateau, Gregor could sense the growing fear in his friends, as well as Iris' tenuous hold to life. Since leaving the Earth, he had been trying to separate himself from August, but the energy stored in the man and the crystals he possessed was too great.

Gregor's thoughts expanded from the plateau to the greater concern of life on Earth. He could sense tumult within the vortex, and he feared their current action was weakening it. He communicated to August, "We have to stop. The Earth will die!"

August ignored Gregor's ridiculous warning, and he was aware of Gregor's attempts at escape, and they only satisfied him more, knowing his power was greater than the pharaoh's magician. Soon he would realize his destiny. God could no longer ignore him once he showed up on His doorstep. He would see the face that had eluded all prophets before him. His would be the greatest story in the Bible because he would be the Man Who Saw God.

Above the plateau, the blue color of the sky began to rotate to the dusty swirl below it and, like a tornado dropping from a funnel cloud, it descended until they combined as one. The sky's azure circled the top of the vortex like water round an emptying tub. The sky's color drained into the vortex, disappearing into the ground once it reached the plateau, and in defiance of the still-present sun, night overtook the sky.

With the blue encircling them, those on the plateau could

no longer see anything outside the vortex, save for the dark sky overhead.

Looking around and up, Lily announced, "Something's wrong."

Over the growing whooshing of the wind, Cadence asked, "What?"

Lily raised her voice to answer, "I don't think this is all Gregor anymore!"

"What do you mean?" asked Travis.

Lily pointed to the sky. "Our connection is being severed!"

From the town of Sedona, tourists and denizens alike looked up in awe and fear at the Stygian sky. As the remaining azure drained into the strange whirlwind in the distance, they could see the orange sun shining in the same sky as the surrounding stars and the waning moon.

On the plateau, Lucas was now growing concerned. He knew Uncle August would not allow any harm to come to him, but what if God was now angry with them? He looked toward the crevice, which was now blocked by the circling wind, and he saw Frederick doing likewise.

Travis again came to his captors. "See what's happening? We have to get out of here!"

"Get back over there!" Lucas ordered.

Frederick, on the other hand, headed to where the crevice would be. Leading with his pistol, he poked the barrel into the blue whirlwind to judge its strength. The gun disappeared from his hands.

Travis reached for Lucas' rifle, but the boy kept control and aimed it at Travis, who backed away and joined the others.

Approaching the sun, August began asking Gregor for direction, but the young man had no idea what message to relay back. To appease him, he responded, "I'll know it when I see it."

Although he did not have a true sense of touch in his present state, Gregor could almost feel the heat from the sun. The panic within him grew as he recalled the fire that had touched his skin as a boy. He had to think of something else. His thoughts drifted to his lifelong friend. *Why did he betray me? Purely self-preservation?* That answer didn't sit well with him because he knew that was not in Travis' character. He flashed back to their first meeting – how Travis had stood up for him when no one else would. Travis had even soothed his tormented psyche with a gift from his heart. The gift! At last, he understood.

Gregor tried to focus all his attention on August, but it was diverted for a second when he spotted a solar flare extending far beyond the sun's surface on an erratic path threatening to intersect their own. He wouldn't have much time now before August realized that he didn't have the knowledge Travis had professed. A moment later, Gregor was able to shift their direction.

"Where are you going?" August asked. "I thought you were out of energy."

"I was."

"Then where are you getting it?"

Gregor answered, "From you." At last, he had realized the meaning of Travis' departing words to him. When he called him a rogue, he was telling him to *be* Rogue. Travis had been listening when Gregor told him that he felt he could actively draw energy from the vortex, and by referencing the X-Men character who could siphon power from others, Travis was trying to tell him to drain August's energy. Once he made the connection, Gregor succeeded in usurping all of the vortex energy from August and the crystals he possessed.

Now powerless and dependent on Gregor's energy, August fought to regain control, but Gregor blocked his attempts by continuing to feed on him.

As Gregor directed them away from the sun, the reverend tried to break free. "What are you doing?" Gregor asked. "You can't survive without me."

"I am not leaving without seeing God!" August prayed to God to take him, and he struggled even harder until he and Gregor became a hybrid of corporeal matter and energy. The single blob of blue light twitched and twisted for duality like a mitotic amoeba.

Gregor saw the solar flare shattering the spatial vacuum between them. If he couldn't return them to a state of pure energy, he knew it would burn them both. He tried changing their state, but August was now feeding enough energy to keep them stabilized in a semi-solid state. "Are you crazy?" Gregor asked. "We'll die!"

"You will not keep me from Him!" August insisted. With all his might, he was able to push himself from Gregor, and as soon as they were separated, August converted to a physical state. Within the microsecond that followed, August could feel God's presence upon him. Although blinded by radiation, he saw the face he expected to see gaze at him with fiery eyes. An overwhelming peace invaded and engulfed his soul as a chariot of fire carried him home.

To the sole witness, August's body vaporized at the instant of separation, and all that he was returned to the universe. A microsecond later, like The Creation of Adam, the sun's finger reached just far enough to touch Gregor in his semi-corporeal state. With his connection to the plateau serving as a weak conduit, a portion of the solar flare's energy now raced to the Earth.

CHAPTER 44

With every trace of blue now drained from the sky, the whirl-wind outlining the vortex shifted to black. Inside its eye, with chaos around her and losing cognition, Iris tried again to meditate. She grabbed at the ground with both hands and concentrated with all her remaining acuity. "Please," she begged of the vortex.

Iris felt the energy coming into her, and she was going to need it all to transport everyone. "Hold on," she said as the blue light traveled through her body and into Cadence and Lily. Travis touched Iris' arm, and he too became a body of light.

Succumbing to the thinning air, Lucas and Frederick were now seated. Blinking his eyes closed at increasing intervals, the boy kept his hand on the rifle on the ground at his side, but he remained ready to lift it at the slightest move by the captives, who were all huddled together about three meters away.

Lucas opened his eyes, and when he saw the blue-lighted tetrad, he jumped to his feet clutching his gun and dove to the ground to touch Iris' leg.

The five materialized in the canyon, near the earthmoving equipment. "Whoa." exclaimed Lucas, and the others mirrored his amazement at the experience.

Travis broke up the awe-fest, saying, "We have to move!"

Lucas stood and trained his gun on him, "Where do you think you're going?"

"Look, cowboy, do you see what's going on up there?" Travis pointed to spinning black vortex halfway up the canyon wall. "I estimate we have about a minute before it brings a little piece of the sun right here, and this whole canyon is going to get very, very hot."

Lucas lowered his gun.

Travis looked around for a place to hide, and he spotted the large front loader. He picked up Iris, who was now unconscious after expending all of her energy in their escape from the plateau. "Follow me!" He ran a few meters and placed Iris before the front loader's bucket. "Everyone huddle together!"

Lily and Cadence sat next to Iris, but Lucas started to sprint from the canyon. Travis yelled to him, "You can run if you want, but you won't get far enough!" The boy stopped and turned around. "Get over there with them and huddle as small as you can."

Clutching his gun, Lucas gathered with the rest, and Travis jumped into the cab. "Hallelujah," he sighed when he saw the key in the ignition. "Don't anybody move!" he yelled before turning the key and lowering the concave shovel on top of them.

Travis jumped out of the cab and crawled into the back of the nearby dump truck, which was full of dirt and rocks. He covered himself as much as he could.

Still stuck on the plateau, Frederick looked up at the yellow light that had appeared at the top of the vortex. Panicking, he ran to the mouth of the crevice to take his chances with the swirling wind, but he was too late.

Flames spiraled down the vortex and poured into the canyon below. Seconds later, the fire stopped flowing from the sky, but not until much of the land within half a kilometer had been set ablaze.

The next instant Gregor returned to physical form on top of the plateau in the center of a ring of fire formed by the botanic perimeter, where every bush was now burning. The vortex kept its forceful wind but lost its black color, supplanted by smoke spiraling upward in a twisted chimney. The sky above remained dark, although the sun was only now setting – sans the brilliant hues typical of the event.

Gregor emerged from a fetal position in a panic at the surrounding hell. As he stood, his damaged shirt fell away to reveal a body that was different now, altered by the touch of the sun. The lines and shapes were the same, but the lighted matter within appeared to be in flux. Crystal tears flowed down his cheeks as his thoughts turned to his friends. Had they survived?

Gregor closed his eyes to block the fire from his vision as he extended his arms at his side and felt for energy. A mini spiral, like a little blue tornado, funneled into his right hand from the wall of the fearsome cyclone surrounding him. Another spiral entered his left hand, and others entered his chest, back and head. Soon he was drawing energy from no less than twenty spirals from various points in the circling vortex. He became no longer physical, but neither was he energy. He had evolved into a stable hybrid, with physical outlines and features but a core of pure energy in his torso.

Gregor dropped his hands, and the spirals returned to the vortex, which stopped spinning until it was no longer visible. He could now see the fire raging in the canyon below, and he saw himself again as the little boy burning. He was paralyzed with fear. In place of the flames around him, he saw the flames in his bedroom. It was going to happen again.

Gregor heard a voice. He jerked his head around, but no one was there. "Gregor," the voice said, and he realized it belonged to Iris. She was calling to him, but from where? "Concentrate. You're not the little boy. You're strong. Push the flames aside."

Down in the canyon, the others were surrounded by fire. Travis emerged from the dirt and gasped for air. He jumped from the truck and had only taken a few steps from it when the gas tank exploded. He ran for the front loader to release the others, but he was too late. To his horror, the front loader's gas tank exploded, sending the cab jumping two meters in the air. When Travis lowered his shielding forearm, he saw a ray of hope. The front loader's bucket remained in place.

He ran to the bucket and touched it, burning his hand. He called to those inside, but he heard no response. The smoke was becoming unbearable, and he was coughing with every other breath. He saw no way to move the huge hunk of metal, so he knelt beside it and began digging at the ground with his hands.

He noticed a disturbance in the fire to his left. Gregor was now walking toward him with the flames stepping aside like the Red Sea parting for Moses, allowing him clear passage. Travis was shocked at the metamorphic sight before him. "Gregor?"

Without saying a word, Gregor placed his right hand on Travis' left shoulder. He touched the bucket with his other hand, and it disappeared in a blue flash. He pointed to a spot several meters away, and that's where it reappeared.

Gasping for air, both Cadence and Lucas stood, but Lily remained by Iris. Lucas aimed his rifle at Gregor.

Unfazed by the weapon, Gregor emitted a huge pulse from his body that extinguished all the fire in the canyon. As the remaining smoke lifted from the ground, Gregor looked at Lucas and told him, "You should run." Lucas thought for less than a second before bolting away over the charred ground.

Gregor turned his attention to Iris and was horrified by the sight he beheld. Not only did her body appear lifeless, but her energy was rising from it. "No!" he screamed and dove to her side. "Iris, no!" he grabbed at the blue light hovering above her, but since the others could not see the light, they had no idea what he was attempting to do. Gregor pushed the energy back into her body. "Come on, Iris. Wake up. Come on, baby." The light again rose from her body. Crying, Gregor reached for the light again.

Travis placed a consoling hand on his friend's shoulder and, as soon as he did, he could see the blue light hovering above her body. "Oh my god!" He grabbed Cadence's hand, and once she too saw, she took Lily's hand. The three watched as Gregor tried again to replace Iris' energy, and they all cried when it rose again. He was too late to save her.

"No, no, no!" Gregor screamed. He watched as the light began to swirl. He knew any second now the light would disperse, and that all Iris was — all her energy — would be reclaimed by the universe to be reused in another form. The light spun faster and faster. Just before the particles could spin away, Gregor grabbed at them a final time, and with both hands, he re-cohered the mass of energy. He drew the light closer and absorbed it into himself.

The light shining from him grew even brighter. Travis, Cadence and Lily hugged Gregor to comfort him and themselves. Gregor looked up at Iris' favorite constellation, and without hesitation, he announced, "I'm going to Orion."

"Orion? The constellation, Orion?" asked Travis.

"It's where she wanted to go."

Cadence protested, "Gregor, no! I know you're hurting—"

Lily caressed Gregor's face, her tears mirroring his, and nodded in agreement with his plan. She said, "Take my girl home," and embraced him a final time.

Encircled by his friends, Gregor converted in an instant, and he was gone.

Lily fell into Travis' arms weeping.

"What happened to Iris' body?" asked Cadence. Lily broke from Travis to see that her daughter's body was no longer on the ground.

Travis said, "He must've taken it with him." They all three looked up to Orion.

From his laboratory by the Meteor Crater, Finn watched his monitor for the final moments of the Hexum Space Station as broadcast from his hidden camera. He saw a bright orange glow as the burning station entered the Earth's atmosphere, and then only static.

As he walked the crispy ground to leave the canyon, Travis noticed a streak of light in the sky, and he pointed it out to the women walking next to him. "Look at that."

"Wow, is it a shooting star?" asked Cadence.

The white light broke into five smaller pieces, each hurtling toward the Earth. Travis figured out the source of the light. "The space station!"

They watched as the streaks spread across the sky, but one lost momentum before the others. "That one's going to land nearby," said Lily.

"Not nearby," Travis said as he gauged the trajectory. "Here. Run!"

The three ran as fast as they could from the canyon, while the space station's gym module flew overhead and crashed into the red rock formation that held the vortex plateau.

EPILOGUE

At Christ Church of Sedona, Mitchell Briar was nearing the end of his Sunday sermon, when he saw a familiar face sitting in one of the pews. There before him was his father, his face awash with consternation. He was listening to his son's words as if he were waiting for a mistake so he could jump up and ridicule him in front of his congregation. Mitchell's voice fell silent as he stared. Someone in back coughed, prompting him to turn his eyes to the sound's source. When he looked back, August was gone.

"I want to close today with some wonderful news in which we can all rejoice. Thanks to your heroic efforts in the war for the souls of this city, and now the state, we have crossed the threshold on our petition signature drive." Members of the congregation started applauding and as the applause gained momentum into a jubilant crescendo, he raised his voice, saying, "Come November, the voters in the great state of Arizona will vote on Proposition 44, which will outlaw the sale of items of necromancy once and for all. We cannot yet claim victory, but we're on our way. We have Satan and his Crystal Cult on the run. Amen!"

Afterwards, as Mitchell shook hands with his exiting congregants, Richard Glavin introduced him to two network producers who had attended the service. Richard told him, "They were very impressed with you today, and they want to offer you a national show."

Emotionless, Mitchell told them that he would think about it, and sent them on their way. Once everyone had departed, he retired to his office and sat at the computer. Closing the document of the sermon he had just delivered, he saw the secret file containing his father's addition to the Bible and, after some hesitation, he opened it. Mitchell stared at the first page for a moment and at the title, "The Book of August." He moved the cursor to the end of the title and deleted the word "August," typing "Briar" in its place.

Six weeks after Iris Wickline's funeral, Travis was at home working at his computer and listening to the radio. His career had been moving forward on its own momentum, leading him away anytime he neared his own trail of thoughts. While researching his current work project, the browser window was interrupted by a popup ad for a travel adventure in Arizona. Travis dropped his hands from the keyboard, and he wondered if should call Lily to find out if she were all right. He felt guilty about the lack of communication between them since leaving Sedona, and he figured he had waited too long to call her now.

His thoughts drifted to Gregor. "God, I miss you," Travis said to the ceiling as if he could somehow hear him across the light years that perhaps separated them. At the sound of the front door to his apartment opening, he stepped away from his desk so he could see who was entering. "You're home early."

"I didn't get the job," Cadence said, closing the door behind her. "However, I did find an apartment. The person who interviewed me has a place to sublet."

"I'm sorry about the job, and I've told you that you don't have to move out. You can stay here as long as you want – rent-free."

"Travis, I need to get my life back. I've spent so much time preparing to die. Now I need to plan my future, and part of that is regaining my independence."

"How are you going to pay for this new place without a job?"

"I have a little money in my account, enough to get through two or three months."

On the radio, Gerry Rafferty's "Baker Street" began to play. When he heard the familiar saxophone lead-in, Travis' mind was carried back to the night of the Sedona rave. He smiled.

"What is it?" Cadence asked.

"I was just thinking of Gregor."

"I have been too, especially lately. Everything seems to remind me of him, of Sedona."

Travis nodded in agreement. "Last night I dreamt I was lying in the hammock in Lily's backyard with Daisy by my side, and we were just staring at the stars."

"I can top that. I could've sworn I saw Gregor outside the window to my interviewer's fifth-floor office. I actually stood up and called to him, and when she turned to see who I was talking to, he was gone. She looked at me like I was crazy for the rest of my very brief interview."

Travis laughed. "Yet she's willing to house you?"

Cadence chorused his laughter. "I guess she's not particular about who *gives* her money."

"Do you think it was... actually him?" Travis asked.

"To be honest, I did wonder. If so, he couldn't have picked a worse time to appear. He totally sabotaged my chances of landing that job."

Travis told her, "Maybe the timing wasn't inadvertent."

423

Lily was sitting on the gliding chair of her front porch gluing a newspaper article on the declining bee population to one of the back pages of a scrapbook. Once done, she closed the book, pausing for a moment before reopening it to the first page. The headline of the first article on the page read, "Strange Early Night Blamed on Solar Flare." Below that was an article on the tragic falling of the Hexum Space Station and the two deaths attributed to it – August Briar and Iris Wickline. The body of August's bodyguard was confirmed male but otherwise unidentifiable, so when August's pistol was found in the canyon below and the minister was nowhere to be found, the body was presumed to be his. As for Iris, Lily had told the police that her daughter was hiking at the site of the space station impact in Sedona, after which, she was presumed dead without any remains being found.

The sound of a car door shutting wrested her attention away from the book, and she saw a man with sienna hair approaching from a hybrid parked at the edge of her front yard. As he traversed the walkway to the porch, he waved at her. "Hello." He ascended the steps and extended his hand. "Ms. Wickline, I'm Finn Scarbury."

"Hello," Lily greeted as she shook his hand.

"I went to high school with your daughter. I believe we met once, but you probably don't remember me."

"No." She motioned to the space beside her on the gliding chair.

Finn sat and he told her, "I've been repeatedly debating with myself over whether I should come see you or not."

"About what? You know that my daughter died a few weeks ago."

"I read she died in the impact, along with that preacher. That's what I wanted to discuss."

"I appreciate the condolences—"

"No… I mean of course I do wish to express my condolences, but why I'm here… What I wanted to say is that I saw her. I saw Iris."

"You saw her… spirit?"

"I saw her before she died. On the day she died. She wasn't in

424

Sedona. She was on the Hexum Space Station." Lily let out a little giggle, thinking he was making a strange joke, but Finn remained stoic, saying, "I'm serious."

Lily shook her head and asked, "How on Earth would she have been on the station?"

"That's my point. I work for NASA. I had a video camera on the station. I saw her. I talked to her before it burned in the atmosphere."

Lily's countenance took a sudden shift to somber as she realized that August must have imprisoned her daughter on the space station before Gregor found her. "I'm sorry, but you really must be mistaken. Iris wasn't an astronaut."

"Her body wasn't found here after the fire."

"The fire was intensely hot."

"Every piece of the space station that made it to Earth has been collected, and no human remains were found inside any of it, but I know Iris was on that station. Either she somehow was able to leave the space station the way she arrived – which I haven't yet figured out – or she died in one of the sections that burned in the atmosphere. She did not, however, die while hiking."

Lily began to tear up. "Even if your version – however impossible it is – were correct, how does that change the outcome? My daughter is still dead."

"I'm sorry Ms. Wickline. I really didn't mean to upset you. I just want to understand how." Finn stood and said, "Again, I apologize." He stepped off the porch and told her, "By the way, I have video of your daughter's last moments, if you ever want to see it."

Not waiting for her visitor to drive away, Lily retreated inside her house and closed the door. After placing the scrapbook on the coffee table, she continued into the kitchen for a cup of tea. She filled a pot with water and, as she touched it to the flame on the stove, she noticed the beauty of the canyon through the window. She thought about her daughter and the last time she saw her here before she died. She saw a reflection of her and Gregor sitting at the mouth of the canyon holding hands between their chairs. Lily smiled as a tear dripped from her cheek.

Stepping into the pantry for a teabag, Lily's eyes instead focused on the coffee maker. She had stored it away on the lower shelf so she wouldn't be tempted, but now she really wanted a cup of coffee. Her silent debate over the merits and demerits of partaking in just one cup was interrupted by the sound of the doorbell. Lily's shoulders dropped, and she muttered, "I really don't want to be rude, but if he doesn't leave me alone…" She returned to the front door and was stunned to see Travis and Cadence standing on the other side. Before a word could be spoken, she threw her arms around them and hugged them.

"Hi," Cadence greeted.

"I'm so happy to see you both," Lily said before looking at them with a huge smile and teary eyes.

"We're happy to see you too," Travis said.

"What are you doing here?"

"I…" Travis started and looked at Cadence. "We felt the need to return, so we hopped in the car and drove here."

"You must be exhausted. Come on in, and I'll fix you some dinner."

Half an hour later, Travis was seated around the table on the back-yard patio with Lily and Cadence, eating a dinner of salad, succotash and soy meatloaf. As Lily talked, Travis finished his first serving and reached for the last slice of meatloaf, prompting an amused look from Cadence.

Lily told them, "I've been out to the vortex, what's left of it, and I felt nothing."

"You went back?" Cadence asked. "Isn't that dangerous?"

Lily shook her head and said, "The guards are gone now, and the gate isn't even locked."

Travis asked, "Are you sure you would know what to do, what Gregor could do?"

"I did the feel the energy that night."

"I'm sorry, but I have to be honest," Cadence said with a scowl. "I have a hard time with this cosmic umbilical cord theory of yours."

"Do you seriously think it's been damaged?" Travis asked.

"I do think it's weaker. Less energy is being funneled to Earth. Five percent less."

Travis laughed. "You can measure it?"

"I've been tracking a five-percent increase in the number of still births in the month since you left – anecdotally of course, since no one else is actually looking for it."

"I hope you're wrong about that," Cadence said, to which Travis grunted agreement.

Lily watched him eat the last bite. "You were hungry. I've never seen you eat so much."

Travis rubbed his stomach. "I never thought I'd say this, but I think I'm developing a taste for soy." He stood and stretched. "Hey, your hammock fell."

Lily saw that the hammock was detached from one tree and said, "We had a strong wind storm here last week. It must have unhooked it."

Travis walked over to investigate, and seeing the steel ring at the fallen end of the hammock, he realized that the ring was broken. He looked at the hook in the cottonwood tree to which it was attached and saw that instead of being on the side of the tree facing the hammock, it was about a forty-five-degree arc on the side, as if the tree had twisted around.

Lily said, "I've been rambling on, and I haven't even asked how long you're staying."

"We were talking about that on the way out here," Travis said with a glance to Cadence.

Cadence added, "We have nothing holding us to L.A."

"My job is online, so I can work from anywhere."

"And I don't have a job at the moment."

Lily asked, "Are you moving here? Cadence, you could work at the shop!"

Daisy perked up, but not at Lily's heightened voice. She ran barking to the canyon.

"What is she barking—" Travis asked but stopped himself when he saw the answer.

Lily pointed, saying, "Look!"

Daisy stopped running at the mouth of the canyon. Before her, a blue-glowing figure coalesced out of miniscule drops of light from every direction.

"Gregor!" Cadence screamed.

All three bolted toward the nebulous shape that was levitating from side to side as if on shoreline waves of air. When they approached it, they could see the figure almost bisected before remerging again and again. When merged, the figure was almost featureless, but when it would separate, half was Gregor, and the other half was Iris!

"Iris!" Lily cried out. She reached out to touch her the next time the figure separated, but she stopped herself, as if uncertain of the consequences.

The blue figure began to speak, and their two distinct voices spoke in unison. "Our universe is in between."

Travis whispered to Cadence, "In between? In between what?"

The blue figure continued, "The First Energy is all. The First Energy must be cherished. Many worlds have died, while others thrive in harmony. The Dimensional Wars—"

Tired of following the moving figures, Travis threw his hands up and interrupted with marked frustration, "Excuse me! Can you stop doing that? I can't focus."

The figure complied by separating into two. The blue light faded from Gregor and Iris as they became corporeal, maintaining a slight glow.

Lily touched Iris' face and stared into her eyes. "Iris, is that really you?" Her daughter smiled. "How is this possible? You were—"

"We ran into a friend who was able to unite her with her body," Gregor explained.

Lily nodded, although she didn't comprehend. "That's why you took her body." She turned back to Iris. "So, it really is you."

Iris nodded. "It's really me, Mom."

Lily threw her arms around her daughter and squeezed tight. "I've missed you so much!"

The other three did likewise, and Cadence said, "I can't believe you're here."

Travis joined in the hug. "Great to see you again, buddy." He broke away and motioned to Gregor's physical form. "Why didn't you do this to begin with?"

Cadence smiled in agreement. "Yeah, why the light show?"

"Sorry. I haven't been physical in a while, and I'm a bit out of practice."

"And what's with the oracle speak?" Travis mimicked, "The first energy is everything."

Gregor laughed. "Again, I apologize. The others communicate in a different manner."

Travis and Cadence both asked, "Others?"

"Our other friends. The same ones who called us here to Sedona through Cadence."

"What do you mean?" Cadence asked with a frown.

"Your vision of months ago was to draw us here, the same way I called you here today."

"I knew you were behind it!" Travis exclaimed.

Lily broke her embrace and touched Iris' stomach. "Are you pregnant?"

Iris grinned and answered, "Yes."

"Wow!" Cadence exclaimed.

Travis shook Gregor's hand. "You're going to be a daddy?"

"Yes," Gregor replied with a wide grin.

Lily told Iris, "I can't believe it! You've come back to me and with a baby on the way."

The smile left Iris' face, and she explained, "Mom, we're not staying."

Cadence asked them, "What do you mean you're not staying?"

Iris looked at Gregor and at the others. "We have a debt to repay."

Gregor told them, "We were granted a brief respite to deliver a message."

"You must protect the vortex," Iris said. "Protect it against all threats."

Gregor added, "Be warned. The threats will not only come from this planet."

"Uh, what does that mean?" Travis asked.

When Iris took his hand, Gregor said, "We can't say more."

Turning blue, together they said, "Know that you don't have to worry about us."

"Don't go!" Lily cried.

Cadence said, "You just got here!"

"We love you," the glowing couple told them.

Travis turned to Cadence and asked, "How can we protect the vortex when we don't have control over that property?"

"The vortex has been moved," Gregor and Iris said as their lights merged.

Confused, Lily asked, "It can be moved?"

"Where is it?" Travis asked.

With arms outstretched, Gregor and Iris' blue light began to separate into particles. Their parting voice said, "Here."

Lily, Travis and Cadence all looked at each other and at the backyard canyon.

In the canyon where the vortex had resided, Lucas found life returning in the form of saplings and green leaves on blackened branches. He had descended from the plateau, where he tried for several hours to duplicate the feats of August Briar and Gregor Buckingham, but the blue light eluded him. As he walked from the canyon, he twisted his ankle. He looked down for the cause, and he found an unusual protuberance from the ground. He inspected it, and pulled away the melted cotton covering to discover several blackened crystals. He knew he had found the bag that Gregor was cradling when he materialized on the plateau and August had thrown away. He rubbed one of the crystals with his thumb to remove the crust, and the crystal emitted a faint blue light.

THE END

CPSIA information can be obtained
at www.ICGtesting.com
Printed in the USA
LVHW091943070921
697224LV00010B/85/J

9 781952 112713